THREE WO...
AND THE MAN THEY WANTED

Dulcie was the sensual beauty who offered Dan Castle everything he lusted for—and all the freedom he demanded in his drive to wealth and power.

Louisa was the ravishing heiress whose perfect face and flawless body fed Dan Castle's appetite for pleasure.

Mary was the tempestuous charmer whom Dan Castle desperately desired—even though she was pledged to his best friend.

One man, three women, in a time of limitless opportunity—when all things were possible for the defiant and passionate men and women whose strength and courage matched their dreams and desires. . . .

DENVER

DENVER

Sara Orwig

AN ONYX BOOK

Published by the Penguin Group
Penguin Books USA Inc., 375 Hudson Street,
New York, New York 10014, U.S.A.
Penguin Books Ltd, 27 Wrights Lane,
London W8 5TZ, England
Penguin Books Australia Ltd, Ringwood,
Victoria, Australia
Penguin Books Canada Ltd, 2801 John Street,
Markham, Ontario, Canada L3R 1B4
Penguin Books (N.Z.) Ltd, 182-190 Wairau Road,
Auckland 10, New Zealand

Penguin Books Ltd, Registered Offices:
Harmondsworth, Middlesex, England

First published by Onyx, an imprint of Penguin Books USA Inc.

First Printing, August, 1990
10 9 8 7 6 5 4 3 2 1

 REGISTERED TRADEMARK—MARCA REGISTRADA

PUBLISHER'S NOTE
This is a work of fiction. Names, characters, places, and incidents
either are the product of the author's imagination or are used
fictitiously, and any resemblance to actual persons, living or dead,
events, or locales is entirely coincidental.

To Bernadine and Lisa Rhoades
with many thanks for answering questions.

1

California, October 1866

Below a precipice on a rugged, windswept coast lay a winding trail where a coach was canted at an angle. Men worked on a broken wheel while the passengers huddled on the grass or meandered around the stage.

Above them on the bluff, Tigre Danby Castillo sat on his horse. It would be so easy to take what he wanted. The stage was loaded with trunks and boxes, and a man had been riding shotgun, an indication of something valuable on board. But Tigre could clearly recall his promise to Melissa Hatfield that he would never again take what wasn't rightfully his. While Melissa's brown eyes and rosy lips danced in his memory, he tugged the reins, turning the horse down the slope away from the coach.

He had to find work, a means of income, yet every town he stopped in, he felt as if someone would arrest him at any moment. He was out of New Mexico Territory, safe from the law, but bounty hunters didn't observe boundaries and a reward had been offered for him, dead or alive. As he rode, he pulled out his knife and cut loose his bear-claw necklace, letting it fall to the ground. He removed his broad-brimmed hat, and the wind tangled his golden hair while he extracted three long eagle feathers from his hatband and let them blow in the breeze.

He slipped his feet out of the stirrups and removed his silver spurs, giving them a toss as he rode on. His beard and mustache were gone, his hair cut short. He had sold one six-shooter a week earlier and now wore only one. He had worked in New Mexico Territory at a livery stable, but he had quit as soon as he had collected his wages.

Wages. They were skimpy compared to clearing out a bank vault, but he had given that up forever. He shifted in the saddle, coming down the winding trail to meander along the ocean's edge.

He rode into a town that night, stopping at a saloon and tying his horse to the hitching rail. Inside he had a drink, watched the action, and finally got into a game of faro. In an hour he had won enough to sustain him for a few days, so he bought one more drink and left. He mounted up with a creak of leather and ambled through town and out, feeling a forlorn longing as he left the lights and music and people. He ached for Melissa, thinking about her constantly, hoping she was happy. His thoughts were so wrapped up in Melissa that he barely heard the jingle of a harness. He listened, turning in the saddle. He couldn't spot anyone moving in the dark behind him, but he knew someone was following him.

Tigre tried to determine how many riders there were, and where they were coming from. He decided it was a lone rider, and he scanned the land ahead. He was riding uphill, away from the ocean and shoreline. It was rocky, filled with trees, and he couldn't make a run to get away.

He rode far into the night until he was satisfied he had lost the person. Weary, he finally paused beside a creek and dismounted. He splashed water on his face, wiped his hands on his trousers, then gathered up his reins as he started to mount. He heard a jingle of spurs and the click of a hammer. A man with a revolver stepped into view across the creek in front of him.

"Hold it right there, mister. You're a wanted man and I aim to get my reward." He gave a long, low whistle. "My partner's behind you. We've been closing in on you for hours now. We're going to mount up and ride back to the Territory to collect our reward, and I don't care whether we bring you in dead or alive."

Five days later Tigre and his captors rode into the wide-open expanse of the western boundary of New Mexico Territory. As the sun slanted behind them in the west, they halted close beside a sloping hogback.

"Let's make camp before we're out where we don't have any shelter," the man called Gus said.

He dismounted and looked up at Tigre, who gazed back with smoldering blue eyes. "Get down," Gus ordered.

With his hands tied behind his back, Tigre threw his leg over the horse and dropped to the ground. Gus swung his fist, dealing Tigre a swift blow that sent him sprawling.

"Stay right there, renegade. We're going to go get some grub."

By the time their fire burned low, the two bounty hunters sat eating, their roasting rabbit sending forth an aroma that made Tigre's stomach grind with hunger. While the two men talked and ate, Tigre heard hoofbeats. He tried to decide whether it would be to his advantage to keep quiet or warn Gus and Snake, Gus's shorter, wiry friend.

It could be a traveler who might come to his aid— or a renegade who would try to kill them all. Tigre decided he didn't have much to lose. "When are you going to feed me?" he yelled, to warn the approaching stranger of the situation.

Startled, both men looked up. Tigre yelled again. "Untie me and let me eat, you sons of bitches!"

"Shut up!" Gus snapped, getting to his feet and striding to Tigre to slap him. The sound was a sharp crack that sent Tigre sprawling, his yellow hair falling over his eyes.

As Gus sat back down, the sound of the approaching horse had ceased. Tense, Tigre waited. He glanced over his shoulder into the murky gloom on the fringes of light from the campfire. The hairs on the nape of his neck seemed to crawl as he looked at a ghostly apparition. High on a projecting rock stood a man, but he didn't look like any man Tigre had ever known. His skin was pale and he had light eyes and white hair, a young face, and white clothes. He turned to look at Tigre, and Tigre stared back. The man drew two glistening silver six-shooters and held them out, pulling back the hammers.

"Don't move," he ordered in a raspy voice that was as eerie as his appearance.

Both Gus and Snake leapt to their feet. They froze, seeing the muzzles of two pistols aimed at them.

"Holy hell," Gus breathed, while Snake stared with slack-jawed awe at the man standing on a rock. A chill ran down Tigre's spine.

"Mister, what the hell?" Gus asked. His voice had lost all its force. "We're law-abiding citizens," he added.

"Is that right? Who's he?" the stranger inquired, jerking his head toward Tigre.

"He's a murderer," Snake said swiftly, his quavering voice filled with fear.

"We're taking him in," Gus added. "We're lawmen."

"No, they're not," Tigre snapped. "They're bounty hunters and they plan to kill me before they turn me in."

"He's lying. He's a murderer and a thief. Here's a poster."

"Forget the poster!" the man commanded, coming down off the rock with a jingle of spurs. "Keep your hands reaching for stars." He looked at Tigre. "Stand up and come over here. I'll cut you loose."

"Mister, you're making a hell of a mistake," Gus said. "He'll slit your throat. He's wanted for crimes all over the Territory."

"That true?"

"The wanted part is," Tigre answered frankly. "The other isn't. I won't slit your throat. I killed a man long ago, but only to keep him from killing me." Tigre moved closer and turned his back.

"Drop your six-shooters," the stranger ordered. As soon as Gus and Snake obeyed him, he waved a revolver at them. "Face the other way. Get on your bellies, hands behind your necks."

"Mister, you're going to regret this," Gus said again as he stretched out on the ground. Ignoring him, the man cut Tigre's bonds. "Get your horse."

Tigre needed no urging. He snatched up his own six-shooter and mounted his horse, turning to see the other man gather up the revolvers. "Get their horses."

Tigre gathered the reins to the other two horses and took off after the stranger, galloping away from the bounty hunters, turning to the north.

When they finally slowed to a walk, the moonlight was bright. Tigre extended his hand. "Thanks, mister. I was a dead man for sure if you hadn't shown up. I'm Tigre Castillo."

"Silas Eustice. Here," he said, offering Tigre a strip of jerky.

"Thanks. I haven't eaten for two days."

"I figured they were starving you."

"Where are you headed?"

"Northern California, up into gold country. I'm looking for the mother lode. I panned in the Clear Creek strike in Colorado Territory, and I aim to get more."

"You from Texas?"

"No. Colorado Territory. I've been in Kansas City, Missouri, taking my aunt to live with other relatives. Where you headed?"

"Anywhere out of the Territory. I'm wanted here. My pa was a sheepman. Cattlemen tried to drive him off the land, and we fought them for years. I was young when one tried to kill me. I killed him instead, and a posse tried to hang me the same day without a trial. Pa and his friends got me free, and I've been on the run since. Thanks for coming to my rescue."

"Sure. I probably scared them. I'm so white, and my voice has been this raspy since I was twelve years old. Sort of sets women off."

Tigre glanced at him in the moonlight and saw that his features were pleasant, with a straight nose, a firm jaw, a broad forehead, a wide, square face. "I wouldn't think it would set them off too badly."

Silas grinned. "Most of them don't mind too much.

Kind of draws some. Besides, there's a special one in my life now. That's why I'm here. I want gold to take home to Denver. Ever been to Denver in Colorado Territory?''

"No, I haven't."

"Going to see the elephant brings droves of people."

"What elephant?"

Silas laughed. "It's a saying. People pass through, saying they're going to see the elephant, to see what all the fuss is about out west. Some enterprising men in Denver named their corral the Elephant Corral. Men parked their buggies and wagons there. It expanded to a store and saloon. Anyway, Denver draws people. The air is clear and fresh, the summers are warm, and in winter the snows come."

"That's like home," Tigre said, and couldn't keep the sound of longing out of his voice. "I lived in the Sangre de Cristo Mountains."

"You Secesh or Yankee Doodle?"

"I was too young and too far west in the mountains for either, but my half-brother and my brother-in-law were Secesh. My half-brother, Luke Danby, is a lawyer in San Antonio."

"I don't know anything about San Antonio, but I tell you, Denver's the best city in the whole country. When I make my fortune, I want to go home and settle. And then I'll marry her."

"Who?"

"Mary Katherine O'Malley, with big green eyes and hair like fire. She's beautiful and she's waiting for me to make my fortune and go home to her." Even with the rasp in Eustice's voice, Tigre heard the longing and understood how the man felt.

"You're damned fortunate," Tigre said bitterly, a tight knot in his chest, and Silas' head snapped around.

"Sorry. You must have had a loss."

"Yes, I did," Tigre admitted in milder tones. "So where are you getting this fortune?"

"I'm trying the California gold fields."

They rode in silence, each lost in thought while Ti-

gre relished his freedom. By the time two more days
had passed, Tigre felt he and Silas were close friends.
Silas rode during the day with a bandanna high on his
neck, his wide-brimmed hat pulled low, and gloves on
his hands, trying to keep sheltered from the sun. They
had passed through a small town and had left the extra
horses behind.

They halted at a creek. "I've been thinking it over,
and I'm going to turn back south," Tigre said.

"Sure you don't want to come along to Sacramento?
There are riches for the pickin', like apples off a tree."

"No, thanks. I think I'll ride to Texas. My ma's
there in San Antonio with my brother."

"You'll have to ride through Apache and Comanche
land in New Mexico Territory a long time to get to
Texas."

"I'll be careful. Thanks, Silas. I owe you my life.
I heard those buzzards talking. They were letting me
live because it was easier to travel that way. When we
got close to the first town to where they could collect
their reward, they were going to shoot me."

"Glad you're free. Good luck, Tigre."

"Same to you, Silas." They shook hands and
parted, Tigre wheeling his sorrel to the southeast, Silas continuing to the northwest.

Less than two hours later, Tigre saw a cloud of dust
on the horizon as a large number of riders approached.
He changed direction to ride back the way he had
come. Within the hour the riders drew near enough
that he could see the long, flowing black hair and
copper-colored chests of Apache warriors.

He retraced his journey, riding hard, knowing he
had to get to a town. It was another hour before he
could look over his shoulder and see the cloud of dust
diminishing. When he reached the place where he had
parted with Silas, he turned north, deciding to take
that course out of New Mexico Territory, circling down
through Indian Territory to Texas. An hour later he
spotted a riderless horse ahead. When his gaze swept
the land, he saw a body stretched on the ground. On
closer inspection, he saw it wasn't a white horse like

Silas' mount, but a gray. Tigre urged his horse forward and in minutes he had dismounted, walking to a
man who had been beaten badly. Tigre knelt beside
him, holding a flask of water to his mouth.

"Mister. Here."

The man's eyes fluttered.

"What happened?"

"Renegades." His voice was a croak.

Tigre frowned and glanced around. "Did you see a
pale man?"

Brown eyes gazed up at him and the man bobbed
his head a fraction. "Eustice. They took him. He's
probably dead now."

"How far ahead are they?" Tigre asked, glancing
into the distance. The man's head lolled on his arm.
Scowling and swearing under his breath, Tigre tried
to find a pulse. Feeling none, he took the man's horse,
mounted, and urged his own horse to a gallop.

Within a quarter of an hour he heard shouts. He rode
closer and dismounted, crawling up a bluff to gaze
below. The renegades were tormenting Silas, who
looked near death. His arms were tied to tree branches,
his weight sagging while three men inflicted wounds.

Tigre drew his six-shooter and aimed, waiting for a
moment when Silas would be in the clear. With three
quick shots he picked off the outlaws before any of
them had time to draw. He slid down the bluff, running to Silas. Tigre's heart pounded in fear, because
Silas was limp, hanging by his wrists. With a slash of
his knife, Tigre cut him down and knelt to feel his
pulse, which fluttered erratically.

"Silas! Dammit, Silas, I'm here!" Tigre shouted.
"Live, man!" He ran to his horse, yanking out the
flask of water to tend to Silas' wounds. Working
swiftly, he hacked down thin saplings to make a tra-
vois. That night Tigre killed two rabbits and boiled
them to get some broth for the still-unconscious Silas.

The next day, when he still couldn't rouse Silas,
Tigre's desperation grew. The sun was high overhead
when he spotted smoke curling into the sky, and in a
few more minutes he came over a rise to see a town.

He found a woman who would rent them a room and tend Silas' injuries. She put poultices on his wounds, telling Tigre what to feed him. During the night Tigre sat beside the bed, spooning water between Silas' swollen lips. Tigre slept lightly, and he stirred when he heard Silas whispering his name.

"You son of a bitch, get well," Tigre said with joy.

Silas tried to smile and failed, while Tigre grinned with relief.

It was two weeks before Silas had enough strength to mount a horse. His ribs were cracked, but no bones were broken.

"Tigre, come with me to look for gold," he said one morning. He lolled on a sagging iron bed, his white hair tangled, his white cotton shirt rumpled.

Tigre sat in a wooden chair at a table while he counted his money. "I did all right last night."

"You're an absolute natural at faro. I guess you don't need to hunt for gold."

"I got paid yesterday too."

"You always surprise me when you talk about that job."

"I like building houses. I used to be good with a hammer when I helped Pa. I'm learning with Enrique. I'm almost tempted to stay right here for a time and keep on building." He grinned, shoving a cheroot to the corner of his mouth, squinting as the smoke curled upward in front of his face. "I can see what I accomplished at the Oro Cantina too. *Es muy grande.*"

Silas laughed. "Where did you learn to speak the lingo?"

"I'm Tigre Castillo, remember? My father had a Spanish heritage. Two hundred years ago the Spanish explored and settled in the Sangre de Cristo Mountains."

"Come with me," Silas urged, returning to his argument. "Men are finding gold all over the West. I promised Mary I would strike a vein and come home a millionaire, rich enough to give her a life of ease."

"Mary must be the most beautiful woman on this earth. I've never seen a man so damned loyal."

"She is. She has the biggest green—"

"I know. The biggest, greenest eyes that make you feel as if you're tumbling into a lily pond. Red hair like flames dancing in the night, skin like peaches in the spring, a waist so tiny you can circle it with your fingers and have room left over," Tigre said dryly, stacking coins.

"That's right," Silas said, staring into space, his voice wistful.

"There's a stage going through tomorrow, and they'll take mail to Sacramento. You could write to her."

"No, I can't. I don't write well."

"Well, I can write. Tell me what you want to say, and I'll write it."

Silas ran his slender fingers over the covers. "No. Mary's accustomed to not hearing from me. She knows I don't write."

"She might lose interest."

"Not my Mary."

"Aw, hell, Silas, you ought to have some fun in your life. Come down to the Oro Cantina and let me show you the girls. There's Lolita and her friends Carmen and Cayena, and I'll tell you, they would make you forget all about Marvelous Mary."

"Impossible. Mary is prettier, more fun, more intelligent."

Tigre laughed. "I'll give you that one! When it comes to brains, don't count on the cantina girls."

"Mary is sweeter."

For an instant Tigre's smile vanished while he thought of Melissa Hatfield, whom he had left behind in Albuquerque. He still carried the gold ring she had returned. *Sweet.* Melissa was sweet, intelligent, and beautiful, and it hurt badly when he thought about her. "Dammit," he swore, and scooped up the money. "I'm going to the bank."

"Tigre, come with me when I go."

"Maybe I will," he answered, thinking he might cause his brother's family trouble if he went to Texas. He'd already had two bad encounters with bounty hunters, and he didn't expect them to be the last. He gazed around the small, sparsely furnished room with its crudely made wooden furniture and bare earthen floor. "What's a grubstake cost?"

"You've got more than enough," Silas said dryly. "I've got it down to where I figure twenty-five dollars is all you'll need. Rubber hip boots, a couple of woolen blankets; you have your rifle, pistol, and ammo. You have plates and eating utensils. You'll need a shovel, a miner's pick, a gold pan, and food. That'll get you started."

"You know what folks around here call us?"

Silas grinned. "I can't imagine."

"Gringos pálidos. Pale gringos."

Silas laughed. "You're a damned sight less pale than I am."

"Next to most of the locals, we're both oddities."

Silas chuckled. "Sometimes that works to my benefit."

"So I've noticed. They think that's why I'm winning at faro, that I've got supernatural powers."

"Maybe word will get out to the bounty hunters, and they'll leave you alone."

"Most bounty hunters aren't scared of anything, including the supernatural," Tigre said, scooping his winnings into a bag. He saw the curious gleam in Silas' eyes and knew his friend was too polite to ask questions. Tigre jingled the bag. "This goes to the bank. I always keep my money in the bank until I move on. I've got my cash under another name." He paused, his face flushed with embarrassment. "I've been thinking about it. I might start using another name all the time."

"Hell, that's not so bad. Lots of men have done that."

"I didn't make much of a change: Dan Castle," he said, tucking his blue chambray shirt into his faded denim pants.

Silas knotted his forehead a moment as if considering the name, and he nodded. "That's fine. Want me to call you Dan instead of Tigre?"

Tigre nodded. "I feel peculiar with it right now. I might not answer you, but I ought to start getting accustomed to it. If the wrong person hears you calling me Tigre, or word gets around about Tigre Castillo, it'll be easy for bounty hunters to pick up my trail." He knotted a bandanna around his neck, hiding the old scar.

"Okay, Dan Castle it is. I'll start gathering up supplies. Go to the bank and then to work."

"Here's money for my share of the supplies," Tigre said. Then he left, striding down the wide dusty street lined with adobe structures. Saloons were more prevalent than any other businesses.

Tigre climbed rafters, nailing boards in place, watching Enrique when he could. While it wasn't sheep ranching, his first love, he liked the work in the open, using his hands. There were moments he was tempted to stay until he knew more about building. And Enrique Cordoba had already made Tigre a good offer.

They waited three more weeks before Silas felt ready to travel. At dawn one December morning they left town, heading north, and in another week they stopped in Sacramento to get the rest of their supplies. Facing the prospect of winter in the mountains, they decided to stay in Sacramento, where Tigre went to work for another builder, discovering techniques and styles that were far more intricate than those used by Enrique Cordoba. In late February they left town with two pack burros trailing behind them. By now Tigre was accustomed to the name Dan Castle.

"We're looking for placer gold," Silas said, pronouncing the word in a rasp, "plass-er."

"What's placer gold?" Dan asked, thinking of the dance-hall girl he had left behind.

Silas ducked his head beneath a low-hanging limb. "Placers are deposits washed down from a vein. It's ore on top of the ground, covered only by a thin layer of soil or a stream. For some reason—erosion or rivers—lodes get exposed. The gangue, worthless minerals mixed with ore, will crumble, and rain or melting

snow will carry it downhill. The best placers should
be in foothills where swift-running mountain streams
level off and drop their treasure. Watch for gravel bars
or transverse ridges, rim rock protruding from streams,
anything that becomes an obstacle where specks of ore
will lodge.''

"You can see it?"

"No. In that pack your burro is carrying is a pan.
You scoop up dirt and swish it around in the water.
The dirt will wash out, and hopefully you'll find a scad
of gold remaining.''

"Sounds like hunting a diamond in a gravel pit,''
Dan said dubiously.

"Wait until you find your first nugget.''

"Bucking the tiger might be more certain,'' Dan
rejoined, thinking about his faro winnings.

When they reached Stockton, rumors of gold began
to crop up. Six weeks later they found a prospector
panning for gold in a clear stream. They headed east,
camping by a swift-running stream in the Sierra
Mountains. Both of them worked, icy water sloshing
over Dan's hands until they became numb while he
fanned out the drag, looking for color.

Once he gazed down and his breath caught as bits
of shiny rocks glittered in the sunlight.

"Silas! Silas!''

Silas dropped a pick and came running through the
middle of the creek, slipping and splashing until he
gazed down at Dan's find, and his hopeful expression
faded. He bit on the stone.

"Sorry. Pyrite. Fool's gold, my friend. Look at it.
It winks in the sunlight. Gold always looks the same
from any angle; this doesn't. Bite on it. Gold doesn't
feel the same, and gold won't break. Go back to
work.''

2

Denver, Colorado Territory, April 1866

East of the Rockies, a growing town lay nestled at the junction of Cherry Creek and the Platte River. Patches of snow dotted the roofs and streets, smoke spiraled from chimneys, and lights burned brightly in the windows. Music drifted out from the city hall, where a town celebration was under way. Inside, banners draped from the walls, festooned with red bunting, proclaimed: "Denver City and Auraria United; Denver born April 1860" and "Happy Sixth Anniversary, Denver!"

On a platform made by planks on blocks of wood, fiddlers tapped their booted toes while they spun out a song. Dancers swirled around the floor as older couples sat watching. Women congregated in clusters at the south end of the room, and men gathered beside the serving tables at the north end. Heat came from two glowing potbellied stoves.

Dressed in blue gingham, Mary Katherine O'Malley gazed over her dance partner's shoulder while his brow furrowed in concentration. He stepped on her toe.

"Sorry, Miss O'Malley. I ain't very good at dancing," Leonard Wilson said, blushing deeply, his freckled face turning crimson.

"That's all right, Mr. Wilson," she answered politely, smiling encouragement at him, grateful that he had asked her to dance. "I'm not so good either," she added softly.

Stumbling his way through the dance until the end,

he escorted her to a bench along the wall and thanked
her politely.

"Thank you," she answered. "I enjoyed it."

"I don't see how you could have, I stepped on your
toes so many times," he said, shuffling his feet and
pushing a stray lock of brown hair off his forehead.

"I did enjoy it," she answered with sincerity.

"Would you like some punch, Miss O'Malley?"

"Yes, thank you."

"You sit right here. I'll bring you some."

He left and she was alone, aware she had danced
only once the whole evening. Yet she knew that at
sixteen she was younger and plainer than most, with
her simple gingham dress and her red hair in a braid
wrapped around her head. The fact that she had a slight
limp seemed to make some men hesitate to ask her to
dance. She looked at the other girls. Her friend,
sixteen-year-old Bessie, whose golden curls shone,
wore a fancy blue faille dress, an achievement of hours
of sewing by both Bessie and her mother. Louisa Shumacher danced past. She was the belle who had men
lined up to dance with her, her blue eyes sparkling,
her black curls caught up behind her head and fastened
with a sprig of holly. Only seventeen, Louisa had been
educated back east until this year. She had a figure
and enough charm to attract any man she wanted.
Mary watched her dance past. Her coral grosgrain
dress with a cluster of silk roses at the neck was the
fanciest dress in the room.

The dance finished and Mary stood up, leaning forward to see what was keeping Leonard. He was in a
line congregated at the punch table, probably too shy
to move ahead.

Music commenced and she glanced around to see
Dewar Logan heading toward her, a gleam in his black
eyes. His bulky shoulders strained his rough woolen
coat, and he towered over her.

"Evening, Miss O'Malley," he said, the fumes of
strong whiskey assailing her, and she was surprised he
was going to ask her to dance.

"Getting lonesome?"

"I'm fine," she said quietly.

"Guess you miss Eustice."

"Yes, I do," she admitted, surprised Dewar would pay her any attention. He was darkly handsome, and usually danced with the older girls.

He stepped closer, taking hold of her wrist. "I can show a lonesome little gal like you a good time. Come outside for a buggy ride."

She stiffened, insulted by his invitation and the lusty gleam in his eye. Stepping back, she shook her head. "No, thank you, Mr. Wilson is bringing punch," she said stiffly.

Dewar glanced toward the punch table, where Leonard was still behind a crowd. "He won't be back for another three dances. C'mon, sugar. I know you're lonesome. You been sitting here all alone the whole evening."

"No, thank you," she said, moving back another step.

"Come on!"

"No!" she snapped, her patience wearing thin. He wavered, and she realized he was drunk. His dark eyes narrowed.

"You cold mick," he said in a loud voice, "you can sit here alone until that freak Eustice comes back!"

Mortified, she burned with embarrassment. People stopped and turned to stare, and Mary knew they would think she had refused to dance with him.

"Little wonder men don't ask you to dance!" he added loudly.

Her cheeks flamed, and she turned to flee as Bessie came up. "Dewar Logan, you leave Mary alone!"

"Bessie, never mind!" Mary said.

"C'mon, Bessie, you're a sport. You'll dance with me," Dewar said, sweeping Bessie onto the dance floor, laughing as her brow furrowed and she glared at him.

Mary gazed into curious and amused eyes, and humiliation engulfed her. The room seemed hot, the walls closing in. She locked her fingers together nervously, wanting to escape the curious stares. As soon as attention shifted from her, she searched for Michael and Brian, her younger brothers. Finding them in the hall with the other boys, she pulled them with her.

"We have to go home right now."

Protests arose, but she hurried them to the door, taking their coats down off hooks.

"Please, Mary." A pair of eyes as green as her own gazed beseechingly at her as Brian tugged on her arm. "Michael was going to arm-wrestle Sam Hopkins."

"We have to go now." She raced outside into the cold night. Humiliated by Dewar's outburst, she rushed down the street, the boys in tow. At the boardinghouse she sent her brothers upstairs to bed, scurrying down the darkened hall to her room at the back of the first floor. Behind a closed door she cried, vowing silently she wouldn't go to a dance again until Silas came back to town. No matter how lonesome she got, she wouldn't give Dewar or anyone else a chance to humiliate her again.

3

Montana Territory, 1867

The woody scent of Douglas firs spiced the fresh
mountain air as Dan moved in the sunlight up Rabbit
Creek. After six weeks in California with little success, Silas had heard a rumor of big gold discoveries
in Montana Territory and they had ridden north. Now
it was early fall, and the quaking aspen leaves were a
golden color, shimmering in the sunlight. Dan worked
in the icy water, patiently searching, deciding that if
they didn't have success soon, he would pull up and
go back to Last Chance Gulch.

A bird's whistle sounded, the clear melodic cry min-
gling with the whispery rustle of wind through the
leaves and the gurgling splash of water. The silence
was suddenly broken by a yell, and Dan's head snapped
up to listen.

"Dan! Dan!"

Dan dropped his pan and started running, his hand
going to the revolver on his hip, although they hadn't
seen another person since they had made camp.

Silas ran toward him, stopping to jump up and down
with eagerness, his hat tossed aside, white hair falling
over his forehead. "Dan, I've got a scad! Look!" Silas
thrust out the flat pan with drops of water clinging to
it while chunks of metal sparkled in the sunlight. "Bite
on 'em."

Dan did, rubbing his hand over the metal, looking
at it glisten in the sunlight, and both of them began to
whoop. "C'mon. I'll show you where."

Dan ran behind him, and soon both of them were

working swiftly, yelling when the gold specks would
appear, Dan's pulse jumping when he found a nugget
as big as the end of his thumb.

"Holy Mother," Silas breathed as he turned the
nugget. "We've hit a big one."

"When do we stake our claim?"

Silas' eyes narrowed. "We're working this first. We
haven't seen another man, and we've got supplies. This
is our secret."

Dan slapped Silas on the back with such a resounding whack the nugget bounced out of the pan. Instantly
they searched until they retrieved it, then went back to
work in earnest.

"We could have snow anytime now," Silas said.
"We better take time to build a cabin."

"I'll start on the cabin," Dan offered.

They commenced a race against the weather, building a sluice of six boxes twelve feet long, each box
having a fall of four inches, which made a trough to
wash placer gold.

Silas talked while they sawed lumber. "We shovel
soil into the sluice; the creek will provide a steady
stream of water. Each of these boxes will have cleats
or riffles, and the nuggets and specks will be caught
against them."

"And my hands won't freeze off," Dan remarked
dryly. "Why didn't we do this sooner?"

"We didn't know it would be worthwhile until we
found something."

Dan thought about the nuggets and specks they had
collected so far. Their find was growing with won-
drous speed, and he now knew why Silas had gold
fever. It made his pulse race to think about the money
he was scooping out of the stream.

"What are you grinning about, compadre?" Silas
asked.

"You know damned well."

"We're going home rich men. I want to give Mary
the world."

"Do you ever forget Mary? Never mind! I know the
answer."

"If we find a vein, we can name it the Mary Katherine Mine."

"I have to see this woman," Dan said as he leaned down to pick up a log, rolling it out of the way, while his muscles bulged with effort.

They found enough large nuggets to indicate a vein, but they continued working the area where they were as long as it yielded a good return. Snows came and they rode back to town, spending time in the saloon, both of them claiming to be trappers. Silas even bought traps in the general store so they could keep their discovery a secret.

In the spring, as soon as the weather permitted, they went back to work, moving upstream, taking pannings at every possible outcropping. When Silas found a blowup, the protruding end of an underground vein of cloudy quartz, his excitement was as great as it had been with his first discovery.

"We better stake our claim now. We'll dig a shaft here and pray we hit."

On their next trip to town, they registered their claim, paying two dollars. Dan watched the recorder's scrawl as he penned: "Personally appeared before me Dan Castle and Silas Eustice and recorded the undivided right, interest, and title to Claim Number Twenty-eight above Rabbit Creek of three hundred feet for mining purposes. Recorded this twenty-ninth day of March, 1868."

Silas and Dan signed the claim and received their miners' certificates. When they stepped out into the sunlight, they paused to gaze at each other.

"The whole town will know now," Dan said.

"I heard of another strike south of here three days ago. There was a rush south, so a lot of men are gone."

"I'm going to the bank and the saloon."

"Your usual routine," Silas said with a chuckle. "I'll get supplies and head home."

"I'll be there in a day or two."

"That's one reason no one thinks we're panning.

You're never in a hurry to get out of town, and you don't gamble with gold dust.''

Dan grinned and strode off, his long legs stretching out as he went up Bridge Street in a town of hastily built wooden buildings that had been thrown up by miners.

Late that night, in Montana Nola's sporting house, as Dan sat near a glowing potbellied stove, a man joined him in a game of faro. Within minutes Dan was aware he was being watched closely, and some deep instinct made him wary, his interest shifting from the game to the man. He lost, pocketed his earlier winnings, and left, sauntering across the saloon, ignoring women dressed in silk, their perfume assailing him. He stepped outside, yanking on his coat, trying to keep his steps slow and casual, moving so he could watch the door of the saloon.

Out of the corner of his eye he caught the movement of a dark shadow filling the lighted doorway.

"Hold it, mister," a deep voice said.

Dan leapt for the side of the building as a gunshot blasted the air behind him. He ran toward the back of the saloon between buildings, stretching out his legs as he fled.

Behind a bawdy house was a long line of cribs, pale in the moonlight. They were narrow structures, with a boardwalk running the length of each row. The dirt between the rows was muddy from the recent snow. Knowing the man was right behind him, Dan darted into the back door of the bordello and opened the door to the first room he found.

In the yellow glow of a kerosene lamp, two startled people looked at him. In an iron bed, a woman was astride a man, covers rumpled around them. The man started swearing. The woman, black hair tumbling over her bare shoulders, gazed at Dan with wide brown eyes.

"Hide me, please," Dan asked. "I'm dead if you don't."

"Get the hell out of here, mister!" the burly naked

man snapped, his black mustache adding to his glowering menace.

"Please!"

"Get under the covers," the woman ordered, and threw back the blankets on the far side of the bed.

While Dan ran to do as she said, a woman in a room across the hall screamed as a door banged open.

"Dulcie, what the hell! I don't want no man in bed with me!"

"Shh, Treen. Give the man a chance."

His swearing and fuming stopped when she placed her lips over his. Assailed by pungent smells of lovemaking and a sweaty body, Dan slipped beneath the covers. He had one glimpse of two naked bodies, hers pale against the man's, her knee drawn up to his waist as she straddled him.

The door was yanked open and Dan felt her move, her leg brushing his arm.

"Get the hell out!" the man shouted. The woman gave a weak scream and the door slammed.

There was a wild scramble that knocked Dan to the floor. "You get in a damned bed with me again and you're a dead man, you hear?" the man snapped, stepping out to yank on his pants, swearing steadily.

"Thanks, mister. Here's my winnings from tonight." Dan tossed a bag across the bed and it clinked as the man caught it in his big hand.

"Aw, hell, keep your money." he growled, dropping the bag on the bed and pulling on his shirt. "But don't ever breathe a word you've been in bed with me, mister, or you're buzzard meat! 'Bye, Dulcie." He yanked on his boots and snatched up his coat to stomp outside. The minute the door slammed behind him, Dan turned to look at the woman. She sat up in bed, sheet drawn to her chin, black hair tumbling over her shoulders, her eyes wide. Dan guessed her age at twenty-six, somewhat older than his eighteen.

"Thanks," he said, smiling.

Gazing at him with speculation, she smiled in return. "Sure. Hate to see anyone killed around here. What did you do?"

Dan shrugged. "Some man is after me over an old argument. You keep my winnings."

She smiled and reached for the bag. "Thank you, honey," she drawled, giving him an appraisal. "You might as well get your money's worth. Besides, it won't be safe to go out yet."

"That's true," Dan said, thinking he would have preferred the offer if he hadn't found her in another man's arms.

As if she guessed his hesitation, she wiggled toward the edge of the bed. "I think I'll wash first, and we'll discuss what we want to do."

She smiled at him again before she stepped out of bed, without any coyness, moving around the room as if she were fully clothed. He drew a sharp breath as he watched her, unable to pull his gaze away. She was slightly heavier than he preferred, but her flesh was smooth and taut, her breasts jiggling with each step, her legs long, her bottom ample and enticing. His mouth went dry and his hesitation vanished. She wrapped a long robe around her, smiled at him, and disappeared into the hall.

While he waited, he looked around at the small room. A square of red satin was hung over the one window, and the kerosene lantern shed yellow light. There were a washstand, a chair, the iron bed, a trunk with dresses spilling out of it, a table, and a cracked mirror on the wall. The plainness prevalent here was common in the small mining towns that had sprung up, different from the lavish decor of the bordellos of the cities. Dan gave little thought to the squalor, knowing it was better than the cribs, where the girls usually got paid two bits to a dollar. In minutes she returned. When the door opened, his hand flew to his revolver. He relaxed as she appeared with a steaming kettle, a large woman coming in behind her with a copper tub. Dulcie poured water from the kettle into the tub and gave the empty kettle to the woman.

"She'll be back with another kettle of water, and we can have a bath," she said, hanging the robe on a hook, giving him a view of her bare backside that set him on fire.

She smiled at him. "In the meantime, want a smoke?"

She moved to a chiffonier to pick up two cheroots, crossing the room to hand him one. He stared at her, trying to get his gaze up to her eyes and away from breasts that were full, upthrusting, and conical, with rosy-brown nipples.

"Honey," she prompted in a voice filled with amusement, "want a smoke?"

"Huh? Oh, yeah! Sure." He pulled out a match and struck it, lighting hers first, fascinated as he watched her. She was the first female he had ever seen smoke, and she seemed to enjoy it as much as any male connoisseur. Dan inhaled without knowing what he was doing. He couldn't keep his stare at her face—the pull was too great, and his gaze slid down slowly, setting him on fire.

"Maybe we should forget that bath," he whispered, and she laughed.

"You'll be glad you waited," she said, moving away from him. In seconds she had smoothed over the bed-covers, pulling up a coverlet. She answered a knock on the door. Dan forgot about danger, his pursuer, and sat on the chair openly in view as the woman returned to add two more steaming kettles of water to the cop-per tub. Dulcie closed the door after the woman left.

"Care to join me?" she asked.

He stared while Dulcie moved to the tub and stepped in. "Yeah, oh, yeah!" he said, standing up and plac-ing the cheroot in an ashtray. He crossed the room to the tub, gazing down at her body, which was slickly wet now, more appealing than ever.

"I'm Dulcie."

"I'm Dan Castle," he said, his voice husky.

"Gonna bathe in all your clothes, Dan honey?" she drawled.

Flushing, feeling young and foolish, he started yanking them off. "No. No, I'm not."

He stepped in with her, sinking down beside her,

and all his hesitation vanished as he pulled her onto his lap.

He told Silas about Dulcie, recalling every detail of her looks, until Silas leaned on a shovel, whistled, and grinned. "Dan, no woman is that marvelous—except Mary, of course."

Dan grinned and flushed. "Sorry. I have talked about her a lot, haven't I?"

"Yes. The only thing you haven't mentioned is her age."

Silas said it lightly, but his eyes narrowed and Dan felt his face flush. Silas focused more intently on him. "How old is she?"

"Well, it doesn't matter."

Silas blinked. "I guess it doesn't, at that.

"She's twenty-six."

Silas grinned. "And to someone of your young years, that's damned ancient."

"She doesn't look old," Dan said. "And I'm not so young. I'm eighteen, and out west that isn't young."

"That's a little young for twenty-six."

"You'll have to come to town with me some weekend."

Dan went to town each week, keeping a wary eye out for the man who had tried to shoot him. Late in April he arrived on a cold, blustery night and couldn't find Dulcie in the parlor. One of the girls told him she was in her room. He knocked, and when the door opened, he gazed at her in shock. Facing him in a red silk kimono, she clutched it closed over her breasts. Her eyes were puffed and black, her jaw cut. An ugly bruise darkened her cheek, and black spots were on every visible part of her. He stepped inside.

"What happened? Tell me his name," Dan said, anger surging in him.

Moving carefully, she turned away and shook her head. "Leave me alone. It wasn't a man. It was Nola."

"Why?" Nola owned the sporting house, and Dan stared at Dulcie in shock.

Dulcie's lower lip jutted out. "I wanted to quit."

"Surely you can quit!"

"No. When I came I promised I'd stay until I was thirty-five. They always make the good ones promise to stay. While we work here, Nola gets part of our earnings each week. She holds our money until the time is up on our agreement. She has several thousand dollars of my money. If I run away, she gets to keep it."

"Well, hell. Can't you go to the sheriff?"

"Dan," Dulcie said as if she were talking to a backward child, "right now this town doesn't have a sheriff, and if it did, he would uphold my agreement with her. She pays taxes to the town, so what little law there is will side with her."

"You can't leave the money behind?"

"No."

"How much is it?"

"Too much," she said, her voice softening as she crossed the room. Her hips swayed provocatively, and for an instant the fleeting thought crossed his mind that she was in the right profession. She was sensual in every way, her walk, her glances, her body, her voice, her movements.

"Do you have family anywhere?" he asked, sitting down on the creaky bed.

She gave him another pitying smile as if she found him incredibly naive. "No. My pa was a bully and a drunk who beat me. My ma worked the same way I do and didn't want me around when I was a kid. She's how I got started. She made me do this."

"Jesus!"

"I married when I was fifteen and I found out all he wanted was to keep me doing the same thing and turn the money over to him instead of my mother. I decided that if I'm going to do this, I'm keeping the money. So I ran away."

Dan stared at her, thinking how different her life was from that of anyone he had ever known. He wondered what she could do now.

"How much money is it?"

"I keep telling you, more than you'd want to give

me. You're a generous man, that's for sure, paying for whole nights with me so I can stay with you, and giving me extra that I don't have to turn over to Nola, but you can't come up with four thousand dollars.''

"Four thousand even?"

She stared at him. "You're a good man, but you can't—"

"Even?"

"No. Four thousand, three hundred and fifty-five dollars."

"I've got that much in the bank. I'll give it to you."

She crossed the room to put her arms around his neck. He eased her to the bed beside him and gazed at her battered face.

"That's the sweetest thing anyone has ever done for me. Absolutely the sweetest thing, and I won't ever forget it."

"The money's yours. Will you leave?"

"I can't take your money."

He stared at her while he decided what he would do. It was useless to argue until he had the money in hand. He grinned. "You can't make love either."

She smiled up at him. "There are some parts of me that aren't black and blue. I'll show you."

As she pushed away the red silk, he forgot about the money.

Dan rode back to town the following Friday and got in before the bank closed, withdrawing the four thousand, leaving a still-sizable account. Next he rode to Nola's and went to Dulcie's room.

Dulcie was soaking in a steamy tub of water, head back against a water-splotched pillow. A sweet perfume smelling like roses cloyed the air while she read a tattered book. She dropped the book to the floor and sat up.

"Dan! You're early."

"I needed to come to town. It's cold out, and that bath looks mighty inviting."

She grinned at him and scooted to the side. "There's room. You should know that."

He laughed as he pulled off his muddy boots.

An hour later he rolled over in bed, the iron frame creaking with each movement while he stretched out a bare muscular arm sprinkled with short golden hairs to yank up his sheepskin coat. He pulled out a wad of greenbacks and dropped them on her bare belly.

She yelped, saw what it was, and sat up. "What's this?"

"Your money. Where will you go?"

Her eyes got round and she turned to look at him. "Dan, you can't!"

"I can. I want to and I won't take it back."

"In my whole life no one has ever . . . It's the nicest—" She broke off to cling to him.

"Where will you go?"

"I thought I'd go to California or Colorado Territory and set up a little place of my own. This is all I know. I don't want to work anymore, but I can run a sporting house."

"Will Nola have you followed?"

Dulcie looked away and bit her lower lip, which was thick and full, giving her the appearance of constant pouting.

"Big Bob takes care of troublemakers for Nola. When Etta ran away, he went after her. She never did come back. I heard he beat her badly. I don't think Nola cares if a girl doesn't come back—that leaves her the money—but she wants the rest of us to see what happens to anyone who doesn't stay in line. I don't think Big Bob would actually kill someone, but I'm not sure."

"Dulcie, come with me. I have a cabin," Dan said. "I stay with another man, but there's room for you. We'll leave sometime this year or next, and you can go with us to a big town. You'll be safe."

"You might change your mind," she said softly.

"If I do, I'll tell you," he answered frankly, and she grinned.

"That's as good an offer as I've ever had." She flung her arms around his neck and he hugged her close,

breathing deeply the rose scent in her hair, wondering
what Silas would say.

Silas stared at him. "You've lost your mind."

"No. You saw her bruises. They might kill her."

The two men stood in the snow between tall spruces
that towered over them. The stream that had been such
a boon gurgled between dark brown banks, the only
sound except for their voices.

"She's accustomed to men. She won't be trouble.
Ignore her."

"Well, I can't lie around in my underwear."

Dan grinned. "Let me say this slowly and clearly:
she's accustomed to men. You can lie around jaybird
naked and she won't care. We can both sleep in the
same bed with her and she won't care."

"To hell with that!"

"She's a tolerant woman and she needs a friend."

"A friend is one thing. A lover is another. Oh, hell,
let her stay. Why not?"

Smoke curled from the chimney and the odor of fry-
ing meat reached both men at the same time. Their
heads turned in the direction of the cabin.

"Holy saints," Dan said softly, "maybe she can
cook."

Within two weeks they had settled into a comfortable routine. Dan built a wall, giving Dulcie and him
their own tiny bedroom while at the same time giving
Silas privacy. Silas didn't lie around in his underwear,
and he was politely cordial to her, becoming friendlier
as time passed. Dan was delighted, spending hours in
bed with her the first two weeks she was with them,
lost in fleshly pleasure while Silas spent the days working outside. The third week, Dan joined him, grinning
sheepishly at Silas.

"I'm surprised you can walk."

Dan blushed and grinned. "I thought I'd better get
back to work or you'll claim it all for yourself."

"I was about to do just that," Silas answered good-
naturedly.

"Silas, don't you miss a woman something fierce?"

"Of course, but all I have to do is—"

"Think of Mary," they said in unison, and Silas laughed. "She's worth waiting for, Dan," he said solemnly.

For the first time in weeks, Dan thought of Melissa Hatfield, and nodded, but he knew Silas had left Denver in 1866, and it was getting to be a hell of a long time to be without a woman.

"A woman like Mary happens once in a man's lifetime."

"I suppose you're right," Dan said, knowing if he could go home to Melissa, he would be true to her and avoid the bawdy houses as much as Silas had.

"Sorry," Silas said. "There'll be another fine woman in your life."

Dan glanced at the cabin. "There is now."

Silas gazed at their sturdy log home. "Dulcie *is* a good woman. Lord knows she's a beautiful one."

"But not like Mary!" Dan teased. "Someday I'm going to Denver to see Mary Katherine O'Malley."

"I hope you do. In the meantime, we better dig if you have the strength."

They had sunk a shaft to bedrock; the shaft was drained by a pump powered by the stream. From the bottom of the shaft, a drift ran along the bedrock, where the richest gravels were extracted. They took turns working, knowing it was dangerous as well as uncomfortable. Their excavation was shored up by timbers that could easily give way. Both of them often worked in wet gravel that could flow like quicksand, but they were bringing out sizable nuggets of gold, their money growing.

An extra boon was the fact that Dulcie could cook. Their meals went from just edible to marvelous. Game was abundant and Dulcie was an inventive cook. They worked diligently all summer, and Dulcie stayed with them. Dan no longer went into town, letting Silas take his money to the bank for him. Winter set in and all three of them put on weight from Dulcie's roast venison, baked pheasant, and roast turkey.

Dan filled out, his shoulders growing thicker, while

Dulcie grew more round and soft, which was fine with Dan. He still enjoyed the sight of her moving around naked, and on the rare occasions when they had the cabin to themselves and it was heated sufficiently to go without clothes, he could simply sit back and watch her, trying to coax her into cooking and cleaning naked—until one afternoon hot grease spattered on her belly. Thereafter she insisted on an apron.

With the spring thaw their lives changed. They mined in earnest, working long days, eating and falling into bed. Between his mining and his nights with Dulcie, Dan was exhausted. By the end of July, the lode was playing out.

Both men had a fortune, a little over thirty thousand dollars. Dan's was in the bank, while Silas stubbornly refused to part with his money, keeping it in a metal box in the cabin.

"We've got to move on," Silas said one night over roast pheasant. "But I think we can get out another few thousand dollars' worth if we stay two more months."

"Suits me. I don't mind staying all summer again," Dan said. He smiled at Dulcie, who wore a red calico dress that buttoned to her chin, but he knew there was little underneath.

"We can move on to new diggings."

"I think what I'd like to do is find a town and settle. I'm ready to use my stake and do something more fun than digging in wet gumbo like a mole." Dan glanced around the cabin that had grown more comfortable and attractive with Dulcie's arrival. Now the windows were covered in gingham curtains, and a braided rag rug covered the floor in front of the hearth. He and Silas had made furniture. "I've been thinking about Denver. You've talked about it so damned much, I think I'll go see for myself."

"Oh, you won't regret it! It's a great town," Silas proclaimed with enthusiasm, placing his fork on his plate and brushing locks of straight white hair off his forehead. "But it's a town that takes money. Come with me first. I want to go to Nevada. I know we can get much more gold there. We need a vein in hard rock, the kind that's down in the earth in quartz. When you strike there, you get ten times more gold than we've found here.''

Dan laughed. ''Silas, you're a dreamer. And you take big risks. I've had enough risk. I want to settle down. I've got a new name. My skin is darker from the sun. I've gained a little weight. I've shaved off a beard and mustache and cut my hair. If I can lead a normal life, I want to. We've got enough money.''

''No, we don't,'' Silas said, his tone sobering. ''Not nearly enough. I want to go home a millionaire. We're a long way from that.''

''We've got a fortune! I can take my thirty thousand dollars and use it to make more money. You've got enough to open a store—hell, enough to open three stores—and build a house!''

''I want to go back to Mary a millionaire.''

''Well, I want to settle somewhere,'' Dan said, washing down a succulent bite of fowl with hot black coffee.

''You can't hide who you are from anyone who knows you,'' Silas remarked. ''You haven't changed that much.''

Dan shrugged. ''I'm going to Denver.''

''Suit yourself, but I wish you'd think about it. We could go home wealthy men.''

''One-hundred-year-old wealthy men. And we're wealthy now. No, thanks. You should come back to Denver with me. How long do you expect Mary O'Malley to wait?''

Dulcie, who had remained silent, finally entered the conversation. ''He's right, Silas. Your Mary would rather have you come home. I would if it were the man I loved. You can't expect a woman to wait several years.''

''I can't go home yet.'' Silas frowned and his eyes developed a faraway look. ''We lived on the Texas frontier, and my folks were killed by Indians. I was shuffled from place to place and was finally sent to live with an aunt and uncle in St. Louis. There was never enough food, and my aunt and uncle never had it easy either. I didn't have anything. That's why I can understand a man who had a turn of bad luck like you did."

"You've never said anything about your childhood before," Dan said, having wondered occasionally why Silas was so silent about his family.

"I don't talk about it to people. But I'm not going to be poor again."

"You're not poor now. You have a fortune."

"No. I want to shower Mary with everything. Her life hasn't been easy. Her pa is nice, but he's a drunk and a dreamer. Always trying to invent something that never works or that someone else has already invented. He's been sober about three hours out of all the years I've known him."

"How does he support the family?"

"They have a boardinghouse. Mary's the one who runs it. Her mother died and left Paddy with Mary, Michael, and Brian. Mary runs the boardinghouse and Paddy drinks and whittles and invents. Mary is mother to the boys and Paddy, except she can't control Paddy." He pushed away from the table. "Good dinner, Dulcie."

"Thanks, Silas."

Dan rose at the same time. "I'll help you feed the horses as soon as I give Dulcie a hand with cleaning."

"Oh, sure, Dulcie. I'll help," Silas said instantly.

"Go on, you two. It's easier if you're not underfoot," she said, shooing them away.

"Sure?"

She nodded. "Absolutely. I can go faster alone than with you two moving around."

They pulled on caps and coats because there was a light drizzle and the night was chilly. They shut the door quickly behind them as they stepped out into the dark to walk to the shed they had built for the horses and equipment.

They carried logs to the house, then watered and fed the animals. As they worked, Silas halted. "Dan, if you're going to Denver anyway, will you do something for me?"

"Of course."

"I'd be real obliged if you would. I want you to take half my money back to Mary."

"Oh, hell, Silas, you might fall in love with another woman," Dan protested, already regretting his hasty answer.

"No, sir. There's no chance of that. My Mary is the most wonderful woman on this earth. Will you take the money to her?"

"I can't guarantee anything. There are bounty hunters, Indians—"

"I understand that, but provided you get through to Denver, will you take the money to Mary?"

"Against my good judgment, yes."

"Good. I'll always be indebted to you."

"You saved my life—you don't need to feel indebted."

"And there's one more thing."

"Sure, name it," Dan said, wondering what Dulcie was doing, wanting to get back to the cabin and be alone with her.

"You know I'm not a man to write. Actually, I'm not good at reading and writing. So I don't write, and I warned her I wouldn't, but the time is getting long. Will you take Mary out sometimes, since I can't be there, and she's had a lonely life? You know, just friendly."

Dan's head snapped around. "You want me to squire your woman? If she's what you've told me, I'd fall in love with her." Dan was teasing now, half-annoyed with the request, half-joshing Silas, who was as earnest as a new pup.

"No, you won't."

"Look, we're both young and healthy, and from what you say, she's the most beautiful woman in the whole country. I couldn't keep from falling in love. And suppose she falls in love with me?"

"She won't and you won't."

Dan's teasing changed slightly as irritation struck him at Silas' obstinate certainty.

"Silas, you always think you have everything in life laid out in neat little plans and it's all going to fall right into place."

"Well, yes, I do. I think it helps to plan and not drift through life, but I know you'd rather take life as it comes."

"Well, what makes you so sure she won't fall in love with me? I'm not that all-fired ugly!"

"You're not ugly at all," Silas said, laughing, the tenseness going out of his shoulders. "You attract the ladies like whiskey drawing miners, but my Mary is loyal. She promised to wait, and wait she will."

"She probably didn't know you meant *years*. You might put a hell of a temptation in both our ways."

"Nope. Mary's not your type of woman."

"Now, look, if you think I'm marrying Dulcie, you're only kidding yourself. She's knows I'm not."

"That wasn't what I meant," Silas said in earnest, rubbing his hands on his hips and staring down at the ground. He raised his head and looked Dan in the eye. "To me, Mary is beautiful. She won't be to you. I've seen the women you attract. They're like Dulcie, real beauties, the kind that take a man's breath away and dazzle him like the sun at high noon. I've praised Mary, but you're going to find her plain. And she has a little limp."

Astounded to learn the truth, suddenly Dan was sorry he had teased Silas. He clasped his friend on the shoulder. "I'll take her out sometimes and be on my best brotherly behavior."

"Thanks, Dan. I'd feel a lot better if I knew you'd be there in Denver. Mary's a good girl, and special, but she's not the kind that catches your eye. You'd never look twice at her."

"I'll bet she's as pretty as a speckled pup."

"Are you taking Dulcie with you?"

Dan looked at the cabin. "If she wants to go, I'll take her. She knows I won't get tied permanently. I don't want an obligation."

"I'm going to miss you."

Dan faced his friend, gazing into eyes as pale as water in the clear creek. "I'll miss you too, Silas, Hurry up and get your gold and come home."

"I will. I damned well will."

Dan smiled and turned for the cabin. "I'm going up to see Dulcie."

"I'll stay away for an hour before I come in."

"Thanks."

They worked through August, mining down to the last trickle, before deciding they had gotten all they could from the Mary Katherine Mine. When the time came, they faced each other as they said good-bye. Dan gazed into Silas' eyes a moment, and the two of them hugged. Then Silas hugged Dulcie, mounted up, and waved to them as he rode away, his burro following behind.

Dan was in no hurry. The weather was warm and the land beautiful. He now had Dulcie to himself, and he spent the days alone with her, postponing leaving, lazing in the cabin, enjoying her company. One afternoon as they lay on a blanket by the creek he rolled over to look down at her. Her blue-black hair was spread behind her head, her body golden in the dappled light, her eyes half-closed as she gazed at him.

"You're a good woman, Dulcie."

"And you're a good man, Dan Castle. Particularly in bed," she added in a throaty voice with a lusty note, as her fingers touched the corner of his mouth.

He chuckled and drew his finger along her shoulder. "Come into town with me and let's get married."

As her brown eyes focused on him, they widened endlessly, and her lips parted in shock.

4

Denver, January 1870

A windless snowfall sent a mesmerizing stream of flakes tumbling to earth, dusting men's shoulders with white, blanketing horses' manes and backs, banking in little piles on the broad brims of men's hats, and coating windowpanes with ice.

Inside the O'Malley boardinghouse, the hearty odor of beef stew, cooked venison, and hot bread mingled with the odor of smoke. A fire roared in the broad hearth of a dining room where Mary Katherine O'Malley moved quietly, eyes downturned, looking only at the thick white plates and bowls of steaming food while she served boarders and townspeople who regularly came there to eat, as well as the occasional customers who stopped on their way through town.

Keeping her gaze averted, speaking only when necessary, using mannerisms that brought the least attention to her from the rough men who came to dine, she nonetheless was aware of three men who watched her with more than idle interest.

Two brawny bull-whackers, slopping down their stew and letting it dribble into their black beards, watched her and tried to engage her in ribald conversation when she was at their table. Attempting to avoid them, she served a steaming bowl of stew to Herschel Windham, owner of the confectionery only a block away.

"That looks like it'll warm a man's insides right well, Miss O'Malley."

"It should. It's been cooking since five o'clock this morning."

"I have my little cold lunch back at the office, but today I thought I'd better come over and see what the O'Malley menu was and get some warmth on my insides. I gave Joel my dinner, and he's minding the store."

She placed a cup of hot black coffee beside his bowl of stew. "Can I get anything else for you?"

"No, thanks. No, this looks like all I need."

She relaxed, because Herschel Windham was an older married man with four small children. He was always courteous, never looking at her like she was one of the dishes she served.

On the other hand, a man seated alone by the kitchen was giving her such looks. He was a stranger, and at first glance he had reminded her of Silas, because his golden hair was as pale as straw, his blue eyes startling. He was handsome beyond measure, but his bold looks made her uneasy and she avoided him as much as possible. He sat at the table closest to the door to the kitchen, so she had to pass him constantly.

His conversation had been courteous, but his intent, curious gaze was not polite, and she would be glad when he was through and gone, because she found him disturbing.

Dan sipped strong coffee and watched Mary O'Malley move around the dining room. When she had first appeared, he barely noticed her, dismissing her as hired help, until he heard a man speak to her and address her as Miss O'Malley. Dan had taken another look, and a mild sense of shock struck him. After listening for several years to her praises and hearing her extolled as a nonpareil of beauty, virtue, brains, and disposition, he realized that beauty was indeed in the eye of the beholder. She was pathetically thin, looking as if she never sampled her own cooking. He sat near the swinging doors and was constantly afforded a peek into the kitchen as she passed back and forth. He realized she was the sole worker, serving as cook, dishwasher, waitress, and hostess. His gaze flicked over her swiftly in another appraisal, and surprise continued to ripple in its aftermath. She was pale,

with a smattering of freckles across her nose, thin to
the point of boniness, wide-eyed, and youthful. He
couldn't remember what Silas had said about her age,
but Dan suspected she couldn't be a day over fifteen.
Silas was in love with a baby. And not a beautiful baby
at that.

Sinking his teeth into a slice of hot, fluffy bread,
Dan ate the delicious food while he watched her. One
thing was certain, though: she could cook. It was the
best food he had ever eaten, including Dulcie's cooking. Maybe Silas had fallen in love with Mary O'Malley for her culinary achievements. There were worse
reasons.

The town boasted a one-room school, and this waif
looked as if she should be running across its play-
ground with the other children instead of managing the
kitchen and dining room of a boardinghouse.

Two bull-whackers were giving her difficulty, and
she seemed terrified of them, avoiding answering their
questions or looking them in the eye. After a few more
minutes' observation, Dan realized he was making her
nervous. Uneasily he recalled his promise to Silas to
take her out. He wasn't one to go back on promises,
but he had no desire to spend time in her company,
and he suspected she would refuse, no matter how
much he coaxed. How could Silas have fallen in love
with her?

Dan knew there was no explaining people's tastes.
She walked with a slight limp, as Silas had said. Her
hair was in braids tightly wrapped around her head in
an unattractive manner that added to her plainness, yet
if the plaits had hung down on either size of her head,
he would guess she wouldn't look a day more than
twelve years old.

He should have known better than to promise Silas
to take her out. He shoved that thought aside, deciding
he would deal with his obligation sometime in the future. There was no hurry. She certainly wouldn't be
besieged by suitors. She was timid, shy, and frightened of the strangers in the dining room. He had yet
to see a real smile cross her features, much less a

laugh. He would give her the money Silas had sent, because it was obvious she could use it on the boardinghouse. The place was spotlessly clean and neat, but the cheerful yellow curtains on the windows were faded and worn, and the straight-back chairs were scarred from years of use. Her dress was a few inches too short, a rough brown poplin that was faded from washing and surely couldn't be as warm as wool.

Silas, you should have told me the truth about Miss Mary Katherine O'Malley, Dan thought, scraping the bowl for the last delicious bite of stew.

While he ate, Mary escaped from the dining room, relieved to get away from the scrutiny of strangers. She entered the steamy warmth of the kitchen with its stew bubbling on the big wood-burning stove, loaves of freshly baked bread on the counter, and venison roasting in the large oven. Water boiled in two kettles, one in readiness for another pot of coffee, the other to scald the dishes. Pans hung from the ceiling and on the walls, and coals burned in a fireplace at one end of the room. She hurried to place dishes on the counter and stir the stew.

An hour later there were only three customers left in the dining room—the burly bull-whackers and the pale stranger with golden hair. The presence of the three men made her nervous, because they had long since eaten and were dallying over coffee.

She stirred the stew, wondering if she should announce that the dining room was closed so the men would have to leave. While she debated, she heard the soft whisper of the swinging doors open and close.

The burliest of the two dark strangers stood only a few feet behind her, arms akimbo on his hips, a grin on his face.

"Sir, you don't belong in my kitchen," she said, facing him, her heart racing.

"Now, miss, don't be so unfriendly. It's a cold day outside. My friend and I want a place to stay and a little kindness shown to us. We're good men, with plenty of gold dust lining our pockets. We can have a little party."

"Get out of this kitchen."

"As I see it, there's no reason for me to go. Come give me a little kiss."

"I'll scream. Get out!"

"You're not going to scream," he said softly, "and get that one fellow hurt. If you yell, he'll come through those doors, and then he's going to get hurt. You don't want that on your conscience." He grinned as he talked, moving closer to her. Heart pounding, Mary backed up. His hand shot out and caught her left wrist.

"Leave me alone!" She ground out the words. He laughed and began to pull her closer.

She reached back, her fingers closing over the handle of the kettle of boiling water. She picked it up and flung it at him.

He screamed, jumping back, while she picked up a second kettle, steam curling up from it.

He let out another yell and ran for the back door. His friend burst into the room and stared at Mary, who held the kettle of boiling water. Dodging and swearing, he dashed through the back door as she tossed the water.

Water arced across the kitchen, splashing harmlessly over the floor in a sizzling stream while the back door banged against the wall. A blast of cold air and snowflakes tumbled inside.

"I don't guess you need any help," drawled the blond stranger who stood in the doorway to the dining room, laughter bubbling in his voice.

She whirled around. Her nerves were stretched thin, her patience gone. She raised the empty kettle. "Customers don't belong in my kitchen. Get out, mister. You've paid and eaten. Now, go!"

"Hey, Irish, wait a minute," Dan said, laughing as he confronted her.

"Get out of here, I said," she ordered, throwing the kettle.

"Hey! Dammit!" He ducked, and the kettle clanged on the wall behind him. Instantly she lobbed another at him, yanking them off the wall and throwing with all her strength. He sidestepped and yelled, waving his hand at her as she heaved the third and fourth pans.

"Hey! I just want to talk. Silas—"

A skillet banged over his head and hit him as it fell. He swore, and she yelled at him again.

"Get out!" Mary's temper boiled. Everyone in town knew Silas had promised to marry her, and this wasn't the first stranger to try to use Silas as an excuse to meet her. She flung two pans. "Get out of my kitchen." She yanked up the butcher knife.

He swore and jumped back through the swinging doors. "To hell with it!" he shouted. She heard a clatter of boots, and silence.

Trembling seized her as she locked the kitchen door. She pushed open the swinging doors. Her father stood in the empty dining room, his blue eyes round, his nose and cheeks as red as holly berries, tufts of white hair showing beneath his cap.

"Is dinner over?" he asked, swaying slightly.

"Oh, Pa. Dinner's been over for ages. It's half-past two now."

"Well, Mary, love, I was delayed on my way home. Now hunger tears at my insides. Seems the last customer left in a bit of haste."

"That he did, Pa," she said with resignation. "Sit down. I'll bring you some stew."

He bumped into a table and sat down. "That's a lovely idea, darlin'. Something hot to warm a man's cold insides on a wintry day."

She returned to the kitchen to rinse her hands in a sink full of water. Beyond their plot of land she could see a wedge of street and shops. The blond stranger was striding away, his hat pulled low, his collar turned up. She remembered his laughter and regretted her temper. He had mentioned Silas, but she doubted if he actually knew who Silas was. He was a handsome one, that blond, and she wondered how many women were in his life.

In the biting cold, Dan strode along a street empty of its usual traffic of wagons and carts and carriages. He still hadn't told Mary O'Malley about the money—

something he had procrastinated about too long, but his time had been spent with Dulcie and building houses. He liked Denver and he saw the promise in it. His long legs stretched out while he alternately fumed about the hot-tempered Mary O'Malley and questioned Silas' taste in women.

Six blocks farther along, he began to pass the sporting houses. One stood at the end of the street, its fresh coat of pale blue paint looking lovely with snow on the roof and windows. The ornate gingerbread trimming was appealing. A porch circled the house, with scrollwork along the overhanging roof and posts. Dan felt a swift stab of pride. He had designed and built it himself, hiring four men to help him. It was the first house he had built when he came to Denver, and it was the best work he knew how to do. He had gotten the job to build the Potter house because of it. Lester Potter had liked the house and asked Dan to build one for him. Thinking about the Potter house, Dan glanced up at the sky, wondering how long the snow would fall. He couldn't work outside in this kind of weather.

He strode up the porch steps and stomped snow off his feet before going inside. When he opened the door a bell jingled and a maid appeared, a smile breaking forth when she saw who it was.

" 'Afternoon, Arletta. Is Miss Dulcie in her office?"

"Yes, sir. You go on back, and I'll bring you some hot coffee."

He strode down the hall, still looking around and admiring the house, wondering when he would stop feeling proud of it. It had been his first real effort, and he had been so terrified of failure that he still had to study it as if to make certain that he had actually accomplished what he had set out to do. The door to Dulcie's office was open. She sat with her back to him, her black hair piled high on her head, wearing a red woolen dress. A cheroot lay smoldering in an ashtray to her right as she shuffled through papers on her desk.

"All work and no play makes a very dull day," he said. She turned, laughing and coming up out of the chair as he closed the door behind him. She crossed the room straight into his arms, and he caught her up to kiss her fully on the mouth.

She returned his kiss for almost two minutes before she wriggled away. "Brr. You're wet and cold!"

"That's what usually happens when I walk in the snow."

"You haven't been working, have you?"

"No. Merely admiring your magnificent house."

Her brown eyes twinkled warmly. "It is magnificent. And so is the man who built it. I love it, Dan. How can I ever thank you enough?"

He shrugged. "Maybe there are one or two things you can do."

A throaty laugh came from her as she took his hand and crossed the room. She placed the cheroot between her teeth and handed him one. "Here, have a smoke. Did you give Miss O'Malley Silas' money?"

"The money! Damn, I completely forgot."

"Forgot? How can you forget fifteen thousand dollars?"

He sat on a chair, hooking his knee over the arm and letting his foot dangle in the air. "I can't imagine Silas coming back to her."

"That doesn't matter. You promised Silas—"

"I know. I'll give her the money. But I don't want to take her out, and she isn't going to want to go."

"Why not?"

"She's a baby. She looks fifteen years old."

"Fifteen? She can't be! Did you ask Silas how old she was?" Dulcie asked, coming to sit on his lap. He swung his leg off the arm to hold her, playing with one of her midnight locks, looking at her slender throat.

"Marry me, Dulcie."

Her head turned and her brown eyes surveyed him tenderly. "You're sweet."

"The hell I am."

"I'd be a rock around your neck." Dulcie studied him while her heart constricted with pain. Each time, from that very first proposal in Montana, she had wanted to accept his offer and damn the consequences.

But for the first time in her life, she was truly in love, and she wanted Dan Castle to have the life he deserved. He was twenty-one; she was almost thirty now. She was eight years older, and a soiled dove. Denver held a promising future for Dan, and she didn't want to pull him down or cause him to be ostracized by a society that would otherwise welcome him and let him live peacefully. She studied his thickly lashed blue eyes, his handsome triangular face with prominent cheekbones and slightly crooked nose from being broken in a fight. He was handsome beyond measure, so good to her, and she loved him until it hurt.

"The answer is still no. Ask me again in a month."

"Dulcie," he said, his voice becoming hoarse as his arms tightened around her waist, "I want you. You're good for me."

"And you're mighty good *to* me. Look at this, Dan," she said, gazing around her. "You built this house for me and gave it to me so I could go into business. It's the nicest, prettiest, fanciest sporting house in the West, and I didn't have to pay you a greenback for it."

"I wanted to give it to you, and it's good business for me. Half the town's leading citizens come here," he said dryly.

"Maybe not half," she answered, "but some do. That still doesn't mean you didn't do all this for me. I don't need marriage. This is enough."

"No it's not. I want a home and family, and you're a good woman, Dulcie. A damned good woman. In bed and out."

She wiggled impatiently and picked up her cheroot. "Tell me about Miss O'Malley," she said, to get his mind elsewhere. "Other than being fifteen—and I don't think she is—why can't you take her out? You could take out a fifteen-year-old."

"You're changing the subject."

She blew a stream of smoke in his face, and he turned his head, swearing. "Dulcie!"

"Miss O'Malley."

He picked up his cheroot in self-defense. "She's shy,

and doesn't seem to like men. She's plain as a stick and has a mean temper.''

"You made her angry?''

"No, I didn't, but two strangers did. One of them followed her back to the kitchen. I was close enough to the door to hear him. A big, burly fellow who wanted to kiss her. I was just getting ready to go to her rescue when I heard a bellow. His friend rushed to the kitchen, and I followed. She threw boiling water on the bull-whacker.'' Dan paused, frowning at Dulcie. "It isn't funny.''

"You're not a woman and you don't understand how it feels to be mauled by some big ruffian who outweighs you by a hundred pounds! Good for her!'' Dulcie exclaimed happily.

"That's what you think! By the time I entered the kitchen, she wouldn't listen to reason. She threw pots and pans and skillets at me. Stop laughing!'' Dan snapped. "It wasn't funny, dodging iron skillets. How that little thing could heave those skillets across a room, I don't know.''

"Did you tell her you knew Silas?''

"I said his name and tried to tell her, but she picked up a knife. I didn't wait to discuss it with her. I'll go back and tell her about the money. It's all safe in a bank right now,'' he said, kissing Dulcie's throat.

"Dan.'' She pushed against him. "A Mr. Corning was here. He wanted to know who designed and built the house. He's a railroad man. He's moving here because of the line they're building.''

"Benjamin Corning?'' Dan asked, sitting up, eagerness in his voice.

"I gave him your office address and let him look the house over.''

"Did you show him the cornices and the bay windows?''

She smiled and stroked his cheek, taking his cheroot and hers and stubbing them out in an ashtray. "Yes, I showed him everything, just like you instructed me to do,'' she said, her voice dropping a notch, her hands fluttering across his chest.

His features softened as he gazed at her mouth and leaned forward to kiss her.

Late that afternoon Dan left Dulcie's to go to his room at the hotel. He was in the process of building a house for himself, something he had temporarily halted to complete the contract on the Potter house. He hunched his shoulders as he stomped through the snow, frowning, his thoughts on the party he was invited to tonight at the home of his banker, Charles Shumacher. It was Dan's first big social event in Denver. He was torn between elation and anger. Eagerness filled him because he wanted to belong to Denver society, and he wanted to build houses for people here. At the same time, he wanted Dulcie for his wife. He knew full well why she steadfastly refused him. He didn't think she would be a hindrance, but if she was, they would go somewhere else to live and she could start anew just as he had.

He was so wrapped in his thoughts he didn't watch where he was walking. Suddenly there was a dark blur before him, and he collided head-on with someone.

Both lost their balance and fell into a drift. Dan reached out to brace himself, a feminine yelp coming from the soft person beneath him.

5

Dan gazed down into wide eyes that were a deep shade of lavender. The woman's thick black lashes were laced with flakes of snow, and her cheeks were pink from the cold. Dan grinned.

"Sorry, ma'am. I wasn't watching my step, and I do apologize."

Her lashes fluttered, and a smile came that took his breath away. "Maybe you should move away."

"Oh! I guess I should at that," he said, grinning and standing up to pull her to her feet. She was tall and willowy, with an upturned nose.

They gazed into each other's eyes and laughed. Someone yelled, and she glanced over her shoulder at a waiting carriage. "I must go." She began to hurry away.

"Wait a minute," he called after her. "What's your name?"

She smiled over her shoulder as she ran to the waiting carriage. A man helped her inside and the door closed as the horses pulled the carriage down the street. Dan stared after it in consternation, her image flaming in his mind. She was breathtakingly beautiful. He wondered who she was, and if the waiting man had been a husband.

He hunched his shoulders again and went striding to his hotel, unable to get the woman out of his mind, and determined to find her.

He bathed and dressed carefully for his first dinner party in Denver society. The invitation had come as an afterthought one day when Dan was leaving the bank. He banked with Shumacher and had had several friendly conversations with him. When Charles discovered Dan was a bachelor, he casually mentioned he had a daughter. At one time Dan knew he would have looked forward with eagerness to meet Shumacher's daughter. Now, however, with heartaches still plaguing him from his time with Melissa Hatfield, and with Dulcie in his life, he had little interest, but he was delighted to be invited for dinner. It would be a good opportunity to mix with the powerful men of Denver society, and Dan knew he would need them if he was to succeed as a builder.

Pulling on a coat and setting his broad-brimmed hat squarely on his head, he gazed at his own image in a mirror, startled to see himself dressed in such finery. He gave his reflection a cocky grin and left, striding outside, where snow continued to fall in tiny flakes, sparkling on the ground like millions of bits of glass tossed against a white blanket. He climbed into his carriage, taking up the reins and turning down the lane.

The Shumacher house was one of the fine new houses in Denver. Set back from the street, it was a tall stone structure with leaded-glass windows, a porch circling the house, and bays in both front rooms. Dan turned the reins over to a groom, climbed down from the carriage, and went up the steps to stomp the snow off his boots. The door opened and a servant smiled at him, offering to take his coat and hat.

His bald head shining and his thick black mustache drooping over his full mouth, Charles Shumacher came forward to greet Dan and introduce him to his slender, dark-haired wife, Hortense. "Come into the front parlor, Mr. Castle," Hortense Shumacher said in a high voice that Dan suspected could grow tiresome. "I'll introduce you to our friends." He moved beside her, realizing the party was larger than he had expected. Two parlors were filled with people, and the wide double doors between them were thrown open, fires burning in the hearths in both rooms. His gaze swept over the crowd recognizing certain prominent men he had already met, sighting many whom he didn't know at all. There were three banks in town—the Kountze brothers', the First National Bank of Denver, and the Shumacher bank—and men from all three were present tonight. The Knelvilles, father and son, who ran a land office, were there, also Emily Parsons whose father owned a freighting business. Dan's gaze moved over new faces.

He almost missed a step. Across the room, standing near the blazing fire, was the beauty he had tumbled with into a snowdrift hours earlier. His heart skipped a beat and began again at a more erratic pace. She was laughing, looking at three men clustered around her, her profile to Dan. She wore a blue dress that looked like it was the latest fashion. Her hair was looped in braids over her dainty ears, and the front was crimped and curled above her forehead.

She turned her head and gazed into his eyes, and for an instant Dan felt as if an invisible current bound the two of them together, wrapping them in a world shut away from everyone else in the room. Her lashes fluttered and a pink flush rose in her cheeks. He nodded, giving her a crooked smile.

"Mr. Castle—"

"What? Oh, sorry." Dan turned to meet four businessmen. He wanted to talk to them, but was relieved when his host moved him on to meet more people.

He curbed the urge to ask to go directly to her, trying to shake hands, smile politely, and talk briefly with people as he was introduced. Dan and Charles slowly moved around the room. As they circled to the point where his back was no longer to her, Dan was pleased to see that she had moved also, standing where she could easily observe his approach. Now Charles paused before five men, and Dan was introduced to whiskered gentlemen who looked prosperous and gazed at him with curious eyes. One, Benjamin Corning, said, "I've heard your name. You're the fellow building the new house on Sherman."

"That's right. I'm in the building business."

One of the men laughed, his voice dropping to little

more than a whisper. "You're the fellow who built Miss Dulcie's house."

"Yes, I am."

"Fine house." He cleared his throat and raised his voice to a normal level. "How's progress on your own house?"

"This snow has me stopped," Dan said, aware that the black-haired beauty had turned and was openly listening to his conversation. His pulse beat faster in anticipation. She must have felt something extraordinary too, or she wouldn't be paying such close attention to him.

"I've heard about your house on Sherman," the one named Forester said. "I'll have to ride past and take a look. Even Mrs. Forester has talked about it."

"You can talk to him about it later," Charles Shumacher said. "I want him to meet all my guests."

Then Dan finally faced her, seeing her smile coyly at him, a twinkle in her eyes, which were the most unusual color, a clear lavender blue like wild hyacinth.

"Louisa, may I present Mr. Dan Castle, a new arrival in our city and a new customer of mine. Mr. Castle, meet Miss Shumacher, the light of my life."

"Your daughter?" Dan asked in surprise, and he smiled. "How do you do, Miss Shumacher?" he greeted her, relieved that she was not already married.

"And meet the swains, Gerald Rathway, Manfred Bliss, and Reuben Knelville."

Dan shook hands with the three men. He turned to take Louisa's arm. "Sir, thank you for introducing me to your guests. Mrs. Shumacher was looking for her daughter, so I'll take Miss Shumacher to her, if you gentlemen will excuse us."

Charles Shumacher reflected one second of surprise in his blue eyes; then it was gone and he smiled and nodded. "Of course, Mr. Castle. We'll talk later."

They moved away, and she laughed. "What a liar you are!"

"What are you talking about?" he said, threading his way through the crowd toward the hall.

"My mother didn't tell you to come searching for me! My mother doesn't know you!"

"She does now," he said happily, steering Miss Shumacher into the hall. "I met her when I arrived."

"And she sent you to fetch me?"

He looked down at her and grinned. "Of course not. I wanted you all to myself."

"You're a bold man, Mr. Castle. First you knock me flat in the snow, next you whisk me away from everyone!" she said. "We shouldn't leave the party."

"No, but we're going to," he said, taking her arm again. She resisted, but he gazed steadfastly down into her eyes and she yielded.

"Do you always get your way?"

"I hope so," he said, stepping into a lighted library and closing the door. She moved on, turning to face him and raising her eyebrows.

"You'll scandalize me and get thrown out of Papa's house!"

"I don't think so on either count. We'll go back in a few minutes, but I wanted you alone so I could talk to you," he said, leaning against the door. "Otherwise I would have to share you with a wagonload of men, and I don't care to do that."

There was a moment of silence and he moved away from the door, stepping closer to her. "Louisa—"

"You'll scandalize everyone if you don't address me as Miss Shumacher."

"Is there any one man?"

She gave him a teasing, coy look that also held speculation. "Perhaps I see one more than the others. But Reuben isn't the only one."

"Good. I'm going to ask your father if I can take you to . . . What does Denver have in the way of events where I can be your escort?"

She laughed, a musical sound, and he drew a sharp breath. He wanted to hold her in his arms. She reminded him of Melissa—dazzlingly beautiful, obviously intelligent—and he was intrigued with her in a way he hadn't been with anyone else.

"You are the most brazen man I've ever met! You

want to take me out to an 'event,' but you don't even have an event in mind! All you want—'' She blushed and closed her mouth.

"Go ahead and say it," he drawled in a husky voice, moving a step closer, his pulse racing.

"I don't know about *events*," she said, suddenly sounding uncertain and young. "There's the church social next Friday evening. Emily Parsons is having a taffy pull in two weeks on a Saturday night."

"What's happening tomorrow night?"

"I'm going with my parents to a party given by the Montroses."

Dan filed the name away in memory. Her breathing was fast, her gaze sliding away from his and back with nervous curiosity. He was drawn to her like a freezing man to warmth, and he couldn't resist reaching out to touch a silky curl. As she drew a swift breath, he gazed into her eyes.

"We had better join the others," she said somberly, all her playfulness gone. "I don't want a scandal."

He nodded, watching her, knowing her pulse was racing as much as his. "We'll go back, but before the month is up, I'm going to hold you in my arms and find out what it's like to kiss you," he whispered.

"Sir, you are too bold!" She swept past him for the door. He reached out to spin her around to face him again.

She gasped, her breast straining against her bodice, her lips parting, her eyelids drooping as she raised her mouth, looking as if she expected him to steal a kiss now. Dan gazed down at her, wanting to kiss her, knowing he could, but also wanting to set himself apart in her mind from the flock of men who were after her.

"And when the time comes, you're going to want to be kissed," he said softly.

It took two heartbeats for her to realize he wasn't going to kiss her now, and to absorb his implication that she would be as eager as he when he kissed her. Her cheeks flooded with a pink glow, and she tilted her head to gaze up at him, momentarily flustered. She could see the teasing glint, the blatant desire in his

eyes, and she regained her composure, smiling at him.
She was accustomed to men losing their balance, and
she wasn't usually the one thrown off stride. Dan Castle was an interesting man she wanted to know better.

She gazed boldly back at him. "You're as confident
as you are brash. Perhaps someday, Mr. Castle, you'll
meet your match!"

He laughed, feeling sparks dance between them,
wanting to haul her into his arms right now, knowing
it would be best to wait.

"I'm sure that by this time my mother actually will
be searching for me!" Louisa Shumacher continued.
"She doesn't allow me to single out acquaintances and
slip away with them during parties." Dan watched her
leave, giving her time to return to the party alone. He
didn't care to share her with a host of eager men, each
hanging on her every word, and he had no doubt that
was exactly what the rest of the evening held in store.
Instead, he glanced at the books on the shelves, taking
one down and hearing a faint crackle of pages when
he opened it. It looked as fresh as the day it had been
placed on the shelf, and he guessed that no one in the
Shumacher family had actually read the elegant
leather-bound volumes on the shelves. His gaze ran
over them, and he remembered for just an instant his
childhood and his mother, Hattie, who had loved to
read. She had taught him the same fascination for books,
spending hours reading to him when he was small,
making certain he received a new book each Christmas and each birthday. They were always treasured
items. He ran his fingers along the books. Someday
he would have his own library, his own leather-bound
books, and enough time in his life to read.

He sauntered toward the hall without realizing he
hadn't once thought of Dulcie in the past few hours.
A twinge of guilt plagued him as he joined the party,
deliberately avoiding Miss Shumacher as he moved
from group to group. When he went to dinner, he was
surprised to discover he was seated to her right. To his
left was Mrs. Byers, wife of William Byers, who published one of Denver's newspapers, the *Rocky Moun-*

tain News. Dan spent his time talking to her about the newspaper.

"It seems we're together again," he said once, leaning close to Louisa Shumacher.

"Yes, perhaps Mama placed me next to you to welcome you into Denver society, since she knows you're new in town. I hear you build beautiful houses."

"I hope so. I'd like to show you mine."

"I'd love that, but I don't think Mama will consent." She smiled as she slanted her head to study him. "But you'll probably find a method to win her agreement. I suspect that most of the time, people do as you want, Mr. Castle."

He grinned in return. "Time will tell," he said, lowering his voice.

Her lashes fluttered, her smile becoming coy. "I suppose it really depends on what it is you want people to do. And how you go about charming them into it," she said, her own voice becoming a throaty velvet that made him burn with heat. She was sophisticated and beautiful, flirting with him, answering his every challenge with one of her own, and he wanted her. He flicked a glance beyond her at the head of the table, saw her father engaged in conversation with the woman on his right, and then looked back at Miss Shumacher, letting his gaze drop to her bosom, looking at the soft rise of lush breasts that strained against the blue silk, the lace that fluttered against her pale skin with each breath. With an effort he raised his gaze and met hers, staring boldly without banking his desire, wanting her and deciding he would have her.

She blushed, her lashes fluttered, pale pink suffused her cheeks, and once again he realized he had jolted her. He was glad. He wouldn't be satisfied the way the other men were, fawning over her and waiting for crumbs of her attention.

She turned her head. Her dinner partner on the left was engaged in conversation, the back of his head to her, and she stared straight ahead, picking up a crystal goblet of wine. Dan watched her lips touch the glass, and he leaned close to her ear. "Today and tonight

have been special. I won't forget them.'' He let his
breath tickle her ear, wanting to touch her slender
throat.

"Sir, you will stir gossip with your brazen behavior.''

"Smile, Miss Shumacher,'' he whispered easily,
glancing at other guests, catching Reuben watching
them with smoldering eyes. ''If you smile, they will
think I'm merely telling you some gossip.''

"Sir—''

She sounded annoyed and breathless. He turned
away to say something else to Mrs. Byers, ignoring
Louisa Shumacher for the remainder of the meal until
he helped her from her chair, offering his hand. The
moment her slender, soft fingers were placed in his,
he felt a fiery tingle from her touch.

"What an unforgettable dinner,'' he said softly,
gazing down at her with a faint smile.

At a loss, Louisa stared up at him. She should have
thanked him. It was, after all, a Shumacher party, and
she was a Shumacher, but the tone of Dan Castle's
voice had implied something entirely different, giving
his casual statement a personal meaning.

"Thank you,'' she answered after a moment's hesitation, and was instantly annoyed with herself. He
disturbed her. Lord, he was handsome! His blue eyes
seemed to bore into her and nail some part of her to
a wall, leaving her under his scrutiny for as long as he
pleased. She expected him to accompany her from the
dining room. Instead he turned to take Mrs. Byers'
arm.

As he moved ahead, Louisa stared at the back of his
golden head. She couldn't understand him. He wanted
her. He was blatant in his desire, far more blunt than
any man of her acquaintance. And far more sure of
himself than most men, although Reuben was another
exception. The exciting thought of pitting Reuben
against Dan Castle tingled through Louisa. Contem-
plating the two men, she went to the front parlor with
the ladies while the men shut themselves in the library
for brandy and cigars.

Marvella, one of her best friends, pulled her aside. "Louisa, I saw you with him!"

"With whom, Marvella? I've talked to every man under forty here tonight."

"With that new Mr. Castle. Isn't he the most handsome man you've ever seen!" Marvella rolled big brown eyes, her golden curls bouncing as she jiggled her head.

"He *is* handsome," Louisa admitted, glancing at the closed parlor door that separated them.

"Has he asked you out?"

"Well, yes."

"I knew he would," Marvella said with a sigh, and her eagerness vanished so swiftly Louisa had to laugh.

"If you're interested—"

"Of course I'm interested, but I'm sure he's interested only in you."

"I don't think so," Louisa said, realizing she meant it. For once, she couldn't tell. At moments he had seemed taken with her, and she knew he wanted her. Yes, he wanted her. He wasn't even polite or careful about letting his desire for her show, but at other times he seemed to forget her existence, something bachelors never did, particularly bachelors she had encouraged. "I don't know what he feels," she said, more to herself than to her friend.

"You—uncertain?" Marvella asked in amazed disbelief, and Louisa blinked with annoyance.

"I don't care whom Mr. Castle likes or what he does! I do think he's making Reuben jealous," she said with satisfaction. She thought about Reuben, who was so handsome with his thick brown hair and broad shoulders. Yet Dan Castle was at least equally handsome.

"Louisa, I do believe you've met a man you can't wind around your little finger," Marvella said, studying her friend openly. "That's amazing."

"Don't be absurd! Are you going to the taffy pull?"

"Yes. If you shun Mr. Castle for Reuben, I hope he'll look my way. He is the most exciting man in Denver in ages! The way he looks at a woman just makes you want to curl up and melt. Doesn't it, Louisa?''

"I wouldn't know," Louisa answered stiffly, hating the fact that she couldn't control her blushes.

"They say he's from Texas, that he has relatives in San Antonio.''

"I'm weary of hearing about Mr. Castle.''

"La, la, la!" Marvella teased. "I'm tired of Mr. Castle," she said, mocking Louisa. "I saw you watching him before dinner and flirting with him during dinner. Did you have your mother seat him beside you?''

"Good Lord, no! Do you suppose he thinks that?'' Louisa asked, aghast.

"Of course not," Marvella answered. "What will you wear to the party?''

Louisa answered perfunctorily, her stormy thoughts on Mr. Castle and whether that was exactly what he would think. If he thought she had asked to have him placed next to her at dinner, how humiliating it would be!

"No, I couldn't have!" she blurted belatedly, realizing she had interrupted Marvella and Elsabet, who had just joined them.

"Couldn't have what?'' Elsabet asked politely.

"I'm sorry. Never mind. I didn't mean to interrupt," she said, blushing with embarrassment.

Marvella studied her intently. "You couldn't have had him seated next to you?'' she asked with exasperating clearness.

"No, I couldn't," Louisa answered stiffly. Dan Castle was causing her an inordinate amount of discomfort, and she intended to put a stop to it. Until now she hadn't met a man who constantly stirred her embarrassment, and she didn't intend to let him succeed at it.

At that moment the parlor doors opened and the men rejoined the ladies. She saw Dan stroll into the room, a brandy still in hand. He was talking to Mr. Byers and laughing, his gaze flicking over a bevy of women, then returning to Mr. Byers. They paused with a group of men and women standing close to the fireplace while Louisa was absorbed by a group of young men who plied her with questions, each trying more than the other for her attention. Reuben eased himself through the group until he was at her side.

"And now, Louisa promised to show me her father's new rifle. Excuse us, gentlemen," he said, and propelled her away from a cluster of disappointed men.

She laughed. "You fool no one. Every party we have, you have to see Papa's new rifle!"

"Why were you seated by that man at dinner? Did you request that arrangement, Louisa?"

"Of course not!" she snapped, angered that everyone must assume she had.

"Next time, check your mother's seating arrangement. I'm sure you could persuade her to put you close to me."

Her anger melted as she slanted him a glance. "You're jealous, Reuben!"

"I don't care to share you with some unknown newcomer."

"He asked me out," she said, twirling around to smile at Reuben, delighting in the scowl on his face. He was far too sure of himself where women were concerned. A little jealousy would do him good. "I think he's quite charming."

A sardonic smile curved Reuben's mouth. "Louisa, you're a kitten with claws. You're trying to provoke me." He tucked his arm in hers and strolled into the empty hall, moving to an alcove, where he paused and put his arm over her head, standing close to her and hemming her in. "Where did Castle ask you to go?"

"To Emily's taffy pull," she said, knowing he had done no such thing, but deciding it would be nice for Reuben to think so.

"You're going with me."

"No, Reuben. Didn't you hear—"

He leaned down to kiss her, his arm slipping around her waist and pulling her close against him. His tongue thrust into her mouth in a delicious foray that sent tremors through her. Louisa knew they might get caught, but she loved Reuben's kisses, especially the

way they made her hot and breathless. He was the
most daring man she knew, but visions of smoldering
blue eyes danced in her mind and her response to Reuben faded until it became annoyance. She pushed
away.

"You're going with me."

"You would have me tell him no after saying yes?"

"I would."

She flashed him a smile. "Perhaps this once, Reuben!"

He studied her, burning desire plain in his expression. "Good, Louisa," he whispered, running his
finger down her throat and letting his hand slide along
the plunging neckline of her dress. His fingers were
warm, tantalizing, and she wanted to close her eyes
and let him fondle her, aching for more, but she knew
she shouldn't. For an instant she yielded to the sensations his caress stirred; then she caught his wrist and
looked up at him.

"This is scandalous, Reuben!" she exclaimed, and
flounced past him into the hall, turning for the front
parlor. He was at her side in seconds.

"There's no need to run," he drawled. "Calm
yourself or they will take one look at you and know
what you've been doing."

She slowed her walk to a sedate pace, regaining her
composure and smiling up at him. "They'll think I've
been showing you a rifle."

He laughed and tucked her arm in his as they rejoined the party. Within minutes she stood in a cluster
of men again, Reuben at her side as they talked.

She moved where she could cast surreptitious
glances at Dan Castle, but she couldn't ever catch him
looking her way. Exasperated, she turned her back,
and before long guests were taking their leave. The
next time she glimpsed Dan Castle, he was at the door
with his coat in hand, bidding good night to her parents. She gazed at him, and his head turned. He
winked and was gone.

It was so swift, she almost wondered if she had

imagined the wink—and, if it was real, had it been intended as a silent message to her?

When the last guest was gone, she stood beside her parents in the hallway.

"Did you like my new customer, Mr. Castle?" her father asked.

"Mr. Castle?" Louisa tried to sound unconcerned. "Oh, yes. He was nice."

"I think he found you nice too," her father said dryly. "He asked if he could call on you tomorrow."

"And what did you tell him?"

"I said yes, of course. Every other eligible young man in Denver calls on you."

"Charles, is that wise?" his wife asked. "From what I understand, he's quite new in town. How well do you know him?"

"I know him many thousand dollars well. The man has a fortune in the bank."

"And how did he earn it?" Hortense Shumacher asked, her pale brow furrowing. Louisa studied herself in the hall mirror, smoothing her braids, waiting to hear her father's answer.

"In gold. He found a vein in Montana Territory. And he's got a career ahead of him. He's a builder, and they say he's good. He's building his own house on Sherman, and they say it will be something to see, one of the best in Denver."

"He's seems terribly young. And there are some lovely homes here now."

"We're going to have a lot more," Charles said solemnly. "We're growing. And I think Dan Castle is going to grow with Denver. Besides, he'll keep Reuben on his toes."

"Papa, you always worry about Reuben. I'm not ready to settle down with him," Louisa protested, although the exact same thought had crossed her mind.

"I don't suppose you are," her father answered dryly. "Especially since he hasn't asked for your hand."

"When I marry, it will have to be a man who can give me the opportunities my parents have," she said, kissing his cheek. She turned to study herself in the mirror, smoothing a lock of hair. "I want to be a leader in town. I already am, with my group of friends. I want society to follow in my footsteps."

"You have lofty ambitions, Louisa," her mother said.

Charles Shumacher smiled and put his arm around her waist, standing beside her and gazing at her fondly in the mirror. "I'm glad you have lofty ambitions. I want my little girl to marry a man who can give her more than her papa did. I hope you do lead Denver society."

"Charles, you put ideas in her head! And if that is what you want, then you had better smile more often at Reuben Knelville. His family is one of the wealthiest here."

"Mother's right," Charles said, becoming somber. "The Knelvilles are wealthy, and Reuben is a shrewd young man. He'll go far."

"I'm not ready to settle yet with Reuben."

"Perhaps that's a good thing, since he hasn't asked for your hand," Leonard repeated dryly, moving toward the staircase.

Ignoring her father's reply, she turned to her mother. "Mama, next time there's a new man in town, don't seat me beside him at a dinner party. It appears I arranged it."

"Nonsense!" Charles said from the steps.

"I told you, Charles, we shouldn't put the child next to him."

"Mama, please. I'm not a child."

"He couldn't possibly think you arranged the seating," Charles went on, unperturbed, "because the two of you had never met until tonight."

"I hope you're right," Louisa said, turning away to go upstairs to bed, mentally comparing Reuben Knelville to Dan Castle.

Dan rode toward his hotel in euphoria over Louisa Shumacher. He could remember everything about her: her thick black lashes that framed her luminous eyes . . . He glanced up a side street and saw a young

girl trying to avoid the dark shadows of the buildings
as she walked toward a saloon. He tugged on the reins
and slowed his horse, knowing the child shouldn't be
on the streets at such a time, suspecting she might not
be warmly clothed for a snowy night either. She carried a large crooked stick in her hand, but little good
it would do her against a man. Dan guessed she had
been sent to fetch a drunken father, and he watched
her progress, wondering if she would wander on beyond the blocks of saloons to the shanties at the end
of the street.

He saw he was right when she stopped and moved
close to the lighted window of a saloon to gaze inside,
as if searching for someone. As he rode past, she was
lost to sight. He tried to get his thoughts back on Miss
Shumacher and forget the child, but his conscience
nagged at him. No waif should be out in the snow at
this hour, searching taverns for a drunken father. With
a sigh, silently calling himself a fool for meddling in
another's business, even if she was a child in need of
help, he turned the horse and went around the block.
Back on the street of saloons, he saw her another block
up the street, gazing into a window. He turned his
horse in a wide circle and had started down the street
toward her when two men emerged from the saloon
and began talking to her.

She fled, and they raced after her. Dan yanked on
his reins, vaulted down from the seat, and ran toward
them as they grabbed her and pulled her into a darkened alley between saloons.

"Hey!" He knew his yell was probably drowned out
by music from the saloons. He hadn't worn his revolver since his first week in Denver, and he swore as
he dashed past a saloon.

With a bellow of pain a man flung out of the alley-
way into the snow. Another followed, careening into
Dan and knocking him aside.

"Hey! Damnit!" Dan shoved past him and raced
around the corner. Something hit him in the middle
with a resounding blow that doubled him over. He
glanced up to see the waif with the knotty club raised

in her hands, and he lunged forward, tackling her, his arms locking around her middle. Both of them catapulted back into the snow as she came down with the club, striking his head and shoulder.

He yelled with pain as the club went flying. He felt as if he had wrapped his arms around a wildcat. She kicked and bit and fought and scratched until his anger exploded and he shoved her down, sitting astride her flailing body, pinning her arms, astounded at her strength.

"Dammit! I'm trying to rescue you."

"Go to hell, mister! I didn't ask for your help!"

He recognized her voice and the faint Irish brogue. "Holy hell. Mary Katherine O'Malley!"

6

"Who're you?" a stunned voice asked, and for the second time in less than twenty-four hours Dan found himself on top of a female in the snow. Only this one wasn't as round and soft as the other. She felt tiny and frail. A total illusion.

"I'm Dan Castle," he said dryly, standing up and pulling her to her feet. He rubbed his shoulder. "If I had known," he said almost to himself, "I'd have ridden like the demons of hell were after me. Did you hit those men with the club too?" he asked, looking at the thick gnarled club in the snow.

"I'm sorry," she said, sounding truly contrite as she retrieved the club. "Are you hurt badly?"

"I'm going to live," he said, touching the side of his head gingerly and pulling away his hand covered with warm blood.

"Oh, my goodness, you're bleeding!"

"Your goodness is not the way I would describe the past few minutes," he snapped, and fished in his pocket for a handkerchief.

"I'm sorry. I thought you were one of them. Why are you always around when I'm in trouble?"

"That's a question I was just asking myself," he said. "Damn, I can't find my handkerchief."

"Here's my muffler. Maybe we should get you to the doctor. You might need to be sewed up."

"No, I don't need to be sewed up!"

He felt dizzy, and it added to his anger. "If there is one thing from this night I hope I learn, it's to mind my own business!'' She took his arm and they staggered through the snow back to the street. Yellow light spilled from the frosty saloon window; muted music and laughter could be heard. "What the hell were you doing? Hunting for your drunken father?" He turned to confront her, and gazed down into a face filled with fear. His anger fled.

"I'm sorry. Can't you find your father?" he asked gently.

"I'm not looking for Pa. I'm looking for Brian," she said, a distraught note coming to her voice. "My little brother."

"You think he's in a saloon?"

"I don't know." He heard the uncertainty in her voice, watching her lift her chin, and he had to admire her. "I would feel terrible if you had an ugly scar," she said. "Please, let me go with you to see Doc Felton. He stays up all hours of the night. He isn't married and he plays keno at the Lazy Dog until after two in the morning. You should have told me who you were."

"I didn't exactly have time." In his two brief encounters with her, she had managed to get under his skin and work on him like a thorn. Minutes before, his sympathy had been stirred; now annoyance returned. "What about your brother?" he asked.

A frown creased her wide brow. As she glanced toward the light, he was afforded a clear look at her profile. With a furry cap fastened around her face, her severe hairdo and plain clothes hidden, he saw she had pretty features, with thick eyelashes he hadn't noticed the first time he met her. "He should have been home hours ago," she said.

"I'll help you find him."

"You don't need to do that, and besides, you're bleeding."

"Head wounds bleed, and I'll be all right. I've been hit in the head before." But never by a waif who shouldn't be able to kill a fly, he thought, studying her slight figure and wondering how she could wield such a blow. "Where have you looked?"

"All the saloons in the block behind you, and I just looked in this one. He's not in here."

"All right. Let's go look in the next block."

"Why don't I take one side of the street, and you take the other?"

"I don't know what your brother Brian looks like and I don't think you should wander around alone. I don't want to have to come to your rescue again."

"I told you I was sorry. And I'll take care of your doctor bill."

"Thank you," he said, amused by her offer. He took her arm and they moved down the street. "What does Brian look like?"

"Like me. Everyone says we look alike. He has red hair, freckles, and hazel eyes. He's seventeen years old, and too young to be gambling. Besides, he had chores at home, and he was supposed to return long ago. I sent him to the store, and he was going to see his friend Newton."

"Have you asked Newton about him?"

"There's not much use," she said with a sigh, crunching through the snow. "Newton lives with an uncle who gambles day and night, so he doesn't care where Newton is or what he does." They paused in front of a saloon and she rubbed the window, standing on tiptoe to look through a spot that hadn't frosted over.

"The window isn't as frosty higher up. Let me hold you up."

"Oh, no! You needn't," she answered, sounding uncertain.

Ignoring her protest, he took the club from her, closed his hands around her waist, and lifted her. She was feather light and she grasped his wrists to steady herself. There was a tiny ledge at the bottom of the window where she could rest her toes. When he was near her, he realized she smelled like roses, and in the middle of winter it gave him a strange yearning for summertime. She was tiny, and he was amused that his holding her flustered her, until he remembered how long Silas had been away and how plain she was. She probably knew next to nothing about men. He glanced up at her, unable to see her face, feeling her fingers clamped tightly around his wrists.

"He's not here," she said, and he set her down. Instantly she moved away from him toward the next saloon. In spite of her coat and the lightness of his touch, Mary knew the moment his fingers closed on her arm. He walked beside her and her heart beat rapidly. He made her nervous, and the fact that she had almost split his head open added to her worries, but Brian was the prime concern now, and with each saloon her fear mounted.

They reached the next block, with only three saloons left. Dan held Mary O'Malley high again, where there was a clear circle in the frosty panes.

"I see him! There he is!" Her voice was filled with relief. "Thank you for your help!" she exclaimed when he set her down. She shook his hand vigorously. "Good night to you, sir," she said, and he heard the faint touch of Irish brogue to the "sir."

"Wait a minute, Miss O'Malley," he said, laughing at her instant dismissal of him and finding it strange to address her as Miss O'Malley after listening to Silas calling her Mary. "You can't go inside a saloon alone at this hour."

"Oh, I've done that before."

"Wait right here. I'll go get your brother," he said firmly, holding her shoulders. "If he really looks like you, I can't miss him."

Dan strode inside, wishing he had his six-shooter at this late hour. The saloons at the end of the street were the rowdiest, with the most fights. He paused inside, blinking in the bright lights, his gaze sweeping over the warm, smoke-filled interior. He spotted Brian O'Malley without difficulty. He looked like his sister, and except for broad, bony shoulders, he looked fifteen years old too. Dan's jaw clamped shut grimly. He didn't know the age of any of the O'Malley children, but they all needed a ma and a pa who would keep them at home out of trouble. Dan decided he might have a talk with Paddy O'Malley.

As he threaded his way through the crowd, his anger mounted, that the young sapling would gamble and stay out late and worry his sister. He needed his hide tanned for such foolishness. Dan strode up to him without a pause and dropped his hand on Brian's shoulder.

"Gentlemen, the kid is out past his bedtime, count him out of the game. Brian O'Malley, you belong at home in bed."

Dan yanked him up by the back of his shirt. There was one moment of stunned shock, and then, if Dan thought he'd had a wildcat in his arms when he tackled Mary, now he felt as if he had yanked a grizzly out of its winter slumber.

Brian O'Malley exploded into fists and feet and teeth until Dan was lifted into the air and tossed out through the front door of the saloon. He sailed over the steps, landing facefirst in the slushy snow, the breath knocked from his lungs.

"Oh, holy saints," Mary O'Malley mumbled, kneeling beside him, trying to turn him over. "Mister! Oh, saints preserve us! Please answer me! Mister, I'm sorry. Did Brian—"

"Yes, Brian did!" Dan ground out the words. "How old is he?"

"He's seventeen and a little high-tempered. Let me help you to a doctor."

"Hell, no." Dan sat up in the snow and glared at the saloon door.

"Are you all right?"

"I'm just dandy," he said, standing up, steadying himself by clutching her shoulder while he took a deep breath and gritted his teeth. Throbbing pains seemed to come from several places on his body at once. "I'll be right back."

"Oh, no!" She caught his arm. "Mister, I'll go get him. You go home before you get killed." She stomped toward the doors of the saloon, and rage burst in Dan. He caught her shoulders and turned her to face him.

"You wait right here! No seventeen-year-old kid is

going to throw me out of a saloon into the snow and get away with it! I'll bring your brother out.''

"I should have warned you, but I was so relieved to find Brian alive—my brother is scrappy.''

"Yeah. Well, so am I.'' Dan stormed past her into the saloon. Heads turned as he crossed the room. Brian O'Malley looked up, saw him coming, and stood up.

"Not again! Haven't you learned to leave me alone?''

Dan put his head down, lunged, and knocked Brian O'Malley to the table. It crashed to the floor, and several men toppled over and tried to get out of the way while the two fought. Dan pulled back his right arm and threw a punch with all his weight behind it, connecting squarely on Brian's jaw. It popped Brian's head back and sent him sprawling over another table. Dan yanked him up, charging to the front door. When he was right in front of the door, Dan stepped back and kicked, his foot landing squarely in Brian's backside and sending him flying through the door into the snow. Dan followed, to see Brian get up and shake his head, Mary clinging to his arm.

"Brian, come home.''

Dan strode to him, giving him another swift hard kick in the backside, sending him sprawling facefirst in the snow. "Get up and go home like your sister says.''

"Who's he, Mary? I'm going to kill him,'' Brian ground out, pushing himself up on hands and knees and shaking his head.

Brian started to get up, and Dan kicked him in the rump again. "You belong at home, not in a saloon. Don't you know you could get your sister hurt badly? She shouldn't be out hunting for you.''

Brian bellowed in rage. This time when he came up, Dan faced him.

"I can kick you all the way home and give you the beating you deserve, or you can go peacefully with your sister. Which will it be?''

"Brian, come home.''

"Mary, who is he?" Brian asked, staring at Dan with clenched fists.

She looked up at Dan. "I don't know," she said, suddenly realizing she didn't know his name.

"I'm Dan Castle. I'm a friend of Silas'."

"You really know Silas?" she asked in amazement.

"Yes. I'll stop by your place someday and we can talk about it. Right now, it's snowing again, my head is throbbing, and I'm freezing. Let's go home."

"Are you sure you don't want to go to the doctor?"

"Aw, Mary, I didn't hit him that hard," Brian interjected, looking from one to the other with a puzzled frown.

"I did," she said, and Brian turned to stare at Dan.

"I don't need a doctor. I need to go home and get out of the cold." And away from the O'Malleys, he added silently.

"Thank you for your help, sir," she said, and Brian snorted derisively.

"You're welcome."

"Good night." She took her brother's arm and the two turned around to trudge away in the snow, Brian protesting her interference. Dan was going the same direction, so he shook his head in resignation and called to them.

"Miss O'Malley."

"Yes?"

"Come get in the buggy. I'll take you two home."

"Oh, we don't want—"

"Get in," he said curtly, "before my toes freeze off."

"Aw, hell, we can walk—" Brian began.

"No. We'll ride," Mary answered with dignity, and Dan reached out to help her into the buggy. He climbed in beside her, Brian getting in the seat behind them. Snow fell, tumbling in tiny flakes as they drove through a silent, deserted street. As he approached the boardinghouse, he saw smoke curling from the chimneys.

He tugged the reins and the team halted. Brian jumped down and strode into the house without looking back.

"Mr. Castle, thank you again. I do appreciate your efforts," she said in a soft voice.

"You're welcome, Miss O'Malley."

"I'm sorry you got hurt."

"I'm going to be fine," he said, trying to hold on to his patience.

She nodded solemnly, and suddenly he wondered if she ever laughed. With the family she had, and with the boardinghouse, she had little to laugh about. Silas hadn't said too much about it, except that he didn't want her to work so hard. On impulse, Dan jumped down and helped her out of the carriage. She raised her face to gaze up at him as solemn as ever while snowflakes caught on her thick lashes.

"Good night, Mr. Castle," she said again.

He watched her walk away, noticing her slight limp, wondering how she could wield a club or a skillet with such strength. He climbed back to drive to his hotel, wondering the same thing about Brian O'Malley, who should have been as easy to handle as a child. He was almost six inches shorter than Dan, and several pounds lighter. Dan had been in enough fights in his life to make him a match for almost any man, except perhaps his brother-in-law Noah McCloud, but tonight when Brian O'Malley had started fighting him, it had been fierce.

His head throbbed, a pounding pain that made him swear under his breath and heap his anger on Silas' absent person. Suddenly he grinned. The O'Malleys were a handful! He thought about Mary O'Malley sending the two rowdies running in pain. She didn't need anyone's help to defend herself. He chuckled, rubbing the back of his neck. He wondered how many boarders she had. There had been several influential men eating in her dining room that day he had been there. It was easy to guess why—she was the best cook he had ever crossed paths with, including Dulcie. It was the first time he had thought of Dulcie all evening, and a twinge of guilt plagued him. But he had to admit that he wanted to see Louisa Shumacher again, wanted

to take her out. He wanted more than that. He wanted
her in his bed.

He clamped his jaw down grimly, worrying about
Dulcie, knowing he wasn't bound to her in any way—
Dulcie had seen to that—but in spite of her continual
rejections, he felt guilty.

He kept his team of horses and his new carriage at
Dulcie's place. She had a small buggy and her own
horse, but the roomy stable gave her customers a place
to leave their carriages or horses out of sight in back
without tethering them on the street. Dan had ordered
an Excelsior Top Carriage when he arrived in Denver,
but it was too open and chilly for Colorado winters.
He already had an order in for a new Brougham Rock-
away, costing him over six hundred dollars, far more
than the Excelsior, but it was roomy, just right for
winter, and due to be delivered this week.

Shivering, he hurried along on foot from Dulcie's.
The only sound was the crunch of his footsteps in the
snow, and when he paused, the world was silent.
Snowflakes fell on his face, and he gazed at the town,
wrapped in the soft beauty of white that cloaked the
unsightly posts and wagons. Dan gave a silent prayer
of thanks that he had this chance to start again with
another name in a town where he felt safe. He was
becoming acquainted with honest men who worked
hard for their living, who had been fortunate in silver
or gold or been shrewd in business. He was no longer
on the wrong side of the law, riding with thieves and
renegades, and he had a chance to become friendly
with women like Louisa Shumacher.

He strode on toward the hotel, glad he would move
into his new home within the month. A clerk dozed
behind the desk, and Dan tiptoed across the lobby and
up the stairs to his room. He peeled off his fine clothes,
looking at bloodstains he would have to get out of his
shirt and coat, shaking his head again and swearing
over the O'Malleys. Yet at the same time, he couldn't
keep from laughing to himself. Mary and Brian
O'Malley should go on the road as boxers. They would
earn a fortune.

* * *

As soon as she shut the door, Mary faced Brian. "How much did you lose tonight?"

"Why do you think I lost?" Brian asked. "Stop worrying about me and leave me alone. I'm a grown man."

"You're seventeen," she said, hurting as she faced him. "Brian, do you know how worried I was about you?"

Suddenly his scowl vanished and he crossed the room to place his hands on her shoulders. "Aw, Mary. All you can see is your little brother. You used to call me your baby, and that's the way you still see me."

His abrupt change from anger to coaxing pleasantry was disarming. She ran her hand across her forehead. "Brian, don't try your charm on me. I was so worried!"

"Mary. Look at me. I'm growing up."

"You're too young and too poor to be gambling away your wages in a saloon at night."

He tried to grin, winced, and rubbed his jaw. "Who was that fellow? He really packs a wallop."

"So do you. You hurt him badly."

"Evidently I wasn't the only O'Malley who hurt him. What happened?"

"Brian," she said, trying to hold on to her stern feelings before he made her completely forget his earlier behavior, "you're changing the subject. I don't want you in saloons."

"Okay, okay. I won't stay so late, but, Mary, I'm a man now. I'm seventeen and I have the right. Michael started before that age. And Pa—"

"We can't help what Pa does, and he certainly doesn't set an example. And I think Michael was older than seventeen."

"He wasn't. You just didn't go out and hunt for him like you do me. Admit it, Mary, I'm still your baby."

She gazed into wide green eyes and a faint smile, and she couldn't maintain her scowl. "Brian, don't worry me so!"

"I won't. I'm sorry for that," he said softly.

"And don't make empty promises. You're so quick to say you'll do what I want, and as soon as the words are spoken, you promptly forget them and do just as you please."

"Come on, now, you know better than that. My head is throbbing. What can I put on my eye?"

"I'll get a cold cloth and we'll clean up your cuts."

He followed her as she went to a bucket of water and placed it on the floor. She wrung out a washcloth. "Sit down so I can reach you."

"I'm getting taller. You used to be able to reach me without any difficulty," he said happily as he pulled out a straight-backed chair and straddled it. "What did you do to that man Castle?"

"You should apologize to him, Brian."

"Balderdash! I'm not apologizing. What did you do to him?" he repeated.

"I was looking in saloons for you when two men bothered me." She dabbed at a cut on the side of his head, his thick auburn hair matted with blood. She cleaned it, the unruly hair springing away in waves.

"Mary—Ouch! Someday you'll have to let me go."

"Someday is after you're eighteen years old."

"I'll be eighteen next December."

"Almost a year, and all too soon. If you had good sense and were an adult, you wouldn't go into saloons."

"Bosh! Silas went to saloons. Michael goes. Anyway, how'd you get rid of the two men?"

"I took a stick along."

He tilted his head and gave her a crooked grin. "I'll bet you sent them flying."

"That I did, and Mr. Castle too. He saw the men and he intended to come to my rescue. I didn't know it was someone trying to help, and I hit him over the head."

To Mary's chagrin, Brian burst out laughing. "If the man was coming to your rescue, I suppose I'm going to have to be nice to him."

"He was. And he does know Silas."

"Why are you waiting for Silas? You haven't heard a word from him in years."

"I'm going to marry him," she insisted stiffly, feeling a deep ache that came every time she thought of him.

"Yeah. Well, I hope you don't have white hair when you do." He chuckled. "I'd like to have seen what happened."

"It was dreadful. Hold still."

He jerked his head away to look into her eyes. "Don't send a stranger after me again, Mary. I didn't know he was with you. How'd you find out he knows Silas, and how did he know it was you in that alley?"

She blushed, hating to admit the truth. "We've met before. He ate here once."

"Seems like he would have told you more about Silas then." He twisted around to glance at her.

"There, you're done. Off to bed with you, Brian."

"You're blushing. How come you didn't talk to him before about Silas?"

"I was busy."

Brian tilted his head to one side, squinting at her out of his good eye, holding the cold cloth to his puffy, darkening eye. "Mary, you can't lie worth a pig's tail."

"We had a little disturbance here and he left without our talking."

"What kind of disturbance?" He stepped in front of her, blocking her way. "I'll keep on until I find out. What happened? Did Castle do something to you he shouldn't have?"

"Oh, no! Actually, there were two strangers who started trouble. I threw scalding water on one, and they ran away."

"Yeah? What did you do to Castle, Mary?" Brian asked, and his one eye sparkled with gleeful curiosity.

"I just threw things at him until he became angry and left."

"And tonight you clubbed him over the head." Brian laughed. "He'll learn to leave the O'Malleys alone! I'll bet he's home nursing his head and his aches

right now." Brian rubbed his jaw. "He knows how to
fight, I'll say that for him, so I guess he's no coward.
I'm going to bed, Mary."

"Good night, Brian," she said, watching him stride
down the hall. Her heart ached because she did view
him as her baby and knew the time was quickly approaching when he would be a man and she would
have to let him go completely.

In two weeks' time Dan had called on the Shumachers twice and encountered them elsewhere half a dozen
times. While he hadn't yet been alone with Louisa, he
was getting to see her. It was easy for him to get invited to Emily Parsons' party. He had become friendly
with Cyrus Blakely, who worked at his father's smelter,
and Thad Robeson, both friends of Emily's, so when
Dan received an invitation, he accepted with alacrity.
To his satisfaction, he ran into Louisa during the week,
stopping by her carriage to chat with both Emily and
Mrs. Parsons. When Saturday night came, eagerness
bubbled in him. He wore his best black pants and linen
shirt. It was another snowy night, although at least the
snow from the weekend before had melted away during the week. Now the ground was covered again with
a layer of pristine white, and flakes drifted silently
down, melting on his shoulders as he stopped on Grant
Street to pick up his friend Cyrus, who came bounding
out to climb up beside him.

"Thanks for the ride."

"Your house is along the way."

"When you get your house finished, you'll live close
to us."

When they reached the Parsons' house, Emily wel-
comed them at the door, her brown eyes sparkling, a
faint scent of lilac assailing Dan as he stood and talked
to her while a servant took his topcoat. Emily led him
into the back parlor, where a fire blazed and guests
stood talking in clusters. It was a party for young people. There were no elders or married couples, and Dan
had already met most of the people present. It took
only seconds to see that he had arrived before Louisa,

and he stood where he could watch the door while he chatted with Emily and her friends. He heard Louisa's laughter before she came in sight. She was in front of Reuben, and was talking to Emily, who had moved back to the front hall to greet her guests. Dan's gaze swept over Louisa, taking in the soft pink woolen dress with velvet trim. He knew little about women's clothes, but he knew the dress was costly, with fine lace around the collar and cuffs, bands of darker pink velvet circling the skirt inches above the hem, and a belt of velvet around her tiny waist. Her hair was combed in the latest style, her eyes sparkled and he was dazzled by her. For a moment he lost his awareness of everyone else in the room.

"Excuse me," he murmured to the group where he stood, and moved away, his gaze on Louisa.

She turned her head then to look directly into his eyes, and Dan felt as if she had reached out to touch him. Her lashes fluttered and he drew a sharp breath, threading his way between guests while keeping his gaze locked with hers. Reuben stepped to her side, his gaze sweeping over the crowd and pausing on Dan.

Louisa's gaze held sparks of excitement, while Reuben's scowl held unmistakable anger. Dan didn't care what Reuben felt. He wanted to push him away from her and be left alone with her, but he knew it was impossible. The pair moved into the room, and she paused in front of him.

"Good evening, Miss Shumacher, Mr. Knelville," he said without taking his eyes from her. Her cheeks became pinker as she smiled up at him.

"Good evening, Castle," Reuben cut in. "Louisa, we need to say hello to everyone. And Bessie's waiting to talk to you."

"Excuse us, Mr. Castle," she said softly.

He nodded, watching them move away. There would be plenty of time for him to see Louisa later on, and he didn't want to get involved in any embarrassing scene with Reuben, who was firmly established in Denver society.

He didn't talk to her again until they began a game

of musical chairs. Emily's brother played the fiddle while everyone walked around in a circle. Three people were between Dan and Louisa, and when Patrick Parsons lifted his bow from the fiddle and silence descended, Dan sat down instantly, crowding Elwood Deakens out of a spot. In three more turns Dan was next to Louisa, carefully dropping to a chair when the music stopped, but careful to avoid taking Louisa's, eliminating a player on his right so Louisa could remain on his left. They bumped shoulders, knees, and arms, and everyone laughed as the excitement of the game mounted. The losing spectators cheered the others on as they stood in a ring behind the players.

Once, as they sat down quickly, Louisa laughed, looking up at him. Dan gazed down into her eyes and wished he could get her alone, all to himself. She was the most beautiful woman he had ever known—including Melissa Hatfield and Dulcie.

The child's game made everyone relax, and chatter filled the room when the game ended, until Emily clapped her hands for the next game. They progressed through two more games, before finally adjourning to the Parsonses' large kitchen, where two cooks were stirring kettles of taffy that had cooled sufficiently to pull. All the guests were given aprons, and Dan moved quickly, scooping up a mound of taffy, turning to Louisa and thrusting it into her hands.

"Pull with me, Miss Shumacher," he said, watching her.

She tugged on the taffy, laughing at him as they both worked.

"Careful or you'll have hands that hurt tomorrow," he cautioned. "This isn't good for delicate skin."

"I'm not that delicate," she said. "I survived our fall in the snow."

"Yes, even though I landed on top of you," he said softly, watching her reaction as she looked down quickly. He caught her hands, causing her to stop.

"You'll get blisters if you pull vigorously. Just hold and I'll pull," he said, conscious of his hand still over hers. He released her, watching her steadily as he

tugged at the candy. Finally they were finished, and
everyone had bites of taffy and adjourned to the parlor
again for food and more games.

He took Louisa's arm as if to lead her toward the
dining room, but then instead stepped outside onto the
back porch, where it was quiet and dark.

"Mr. Castle, we have to go back inside."

"We will. Call me Dan, Louisa. You and I are going
to know each other well. There's a barn dance in two
weeks, on Friday and Saturday nights at the new livery
stable. Go with me Saturday night."

She nodded. "I'll have to get permission from
Mama, but she'll agree."

"Good. We have another minute," he said, and
glanced through the kitchen window at the last of the
taffy pullers, still lingering and getting more bites of
taffy. He moved closer, holding her upper arms.

"You look beautiful tonight."

"Thank you," she said breathlessly, her face upturned. Dan looked at her full lips and bent his head,
his mouth brushing hers, pressing, and opening her
lips, which parted easily. Her tongue thrust against his
as his arms closed around her, and he pulled her
against him. His heart slammed against his ribs. She
was soft and fiery and breathtaking.

She pushed away, her breath coming in shallow
gasps. "We have to go inside."

"I want to hold you in my arms and peel away all
your fancy finery, your ribbons and lace and dress—"

"Sir!" she gasped, but he could detect no anger in
her voice. She hurried inside and he followed, glad
that Reuben hadn't started searching for her yet.

He took her arm again. "I'll pour you some punch.
Come with me."

"There you are," Reuben said, moving to the other
side of her, his gaze snapping back and forth between
Louisa and Dan. "Mr. Castle, this is one of your first
parties in Denver, isn't it?"

"One of the first."

"Oh, yes. You were invited to the Shumachers' because you do business with Louisa's father. I've forgotten. What business are you in?''

"I design and build houses," Dan said as he poured a crystal cup full of pink punch and handed it to Louisa with a smile at her.

"That's right. You did the . . . house on Holladay Street, didn't you?''

"Yes, I did," Dan said evenly, expecting Reuben to cause trouble.

"So you're a good friend of the . . . *lady* of the house?'' he asked, laughing. Louisa blushed and looked away as if seeking another conversation, yet Dan knew she was listening.

"It was good for my business. Right now snow is hampering my work. You don't have to worry about such things, do you, Mr. Knelville?''

"No. But someday, if you're ever successful, you won't either. Where are you from?''

"Texas," Dan lied, having rehearsed the answer before. "And where do you hail from?''

"From Pennsylvania. You—''

"Louisa," Dan cut in smoothly, "where were you born?''

"My family came from Kentucky.''

"Do you remember Kentucky?''

"Oh, yes. I remember fancy houses and lots of trees and flowers.''

Dinah Mason joined them. "Louisa, my hands are red! I pulled taffy so much that my fingers feel as if they're on fire. Look, Reuben!'' she said, holding out her hands for his inspection.

"While you two look at hands, excuse us. I promised Louisa one of the teacakes.'' Dan moved her away from them and she laughed.

"Shame on you! You promised no such thing.''

"Well, now I will. Louisa, I promise you a teacake.''

"Reuben is going to be angry with you.''

He gave her a searching glance. "You don't mind.''

A smile hovered on her face. "No, I don't. Reuben's far too sure of himself.''

"While on the other hand, I lie awake nights worrying whether I will get so much as a hello from you tomorrow."

"You do no such thing! I doubt if you've thought of me since the party at my house."

"That's not true at all," he said softly. "I was teasing. But I *am* awake at nights thinking about you, wondering when I can kiss you as long as I'd like."

"Sir, you shouldn't say such things! We're in a crowd."

"You know no one can hear me. Do you sleep peacefully at night, Louisa? Or have you had one or two thoughts about me?"

His pulse jumped as she looked away and caught her full, soft lower lip in her teeth. She realized she had waited too long to answer.

"So you do think of me when you're in bed," he said, giving his observation all the innuendo he could. "Think of our kiss tonight."

"You're the most brazen man!"

"I won't do anything I shouldn't—yet. Shall we join the others?" He tucked her arm in his, closing his hand over hers and running his finger along her knuckles. Emily was calling to everyone, motioning them to gather close to sing. Dan slipped his arm around Louisa's waist, turning to watch her as they sang an old ballad, her soprano voice mixing beautifully with his bass.

He ached to be alone with her, to pull pins out of her precise hairdo, to unfasten the fancy pearl buttons and untie the velvet ribbons. As they sang, Louisa's cheeks became a deep rose, as if she knew exactly what he was thinking.

Finally they broke up, and the late hour was signaled by the departure of the first guest. Reuben was at her side instantly. "Louisa, we should get our coats. Your father will be watching for you."

"You're right, Reuben. Good night, Mr. Castle."

"Good night, Miss Shumacher, Mr. Knelville," he said quietly. Then he slowly moved away, knowing Reuben would leave with her.

Soon Dan thanked his host and hostess, then left with Cyrus and two other friends, taking them home in his carriage. He rode home, listening to the steady clop of the horses' hooves while his thoughts were tangled with images of Louisa. The memory of her kiss burned as hotly as a fire in his memory.

He was on Grant Street, having left Cyrus at his family's imposing two-story house. A carriage approached, and Dan knew it belonged to Reuben Knelville, who had just taken Louisa home.

As Reuben turned up the lane to his house, his carriage halted and Reuben stepped down. The carriage then moved ahead toward the Knelville carriage house.

Reuben walked into the road, standing off to one side, his fists on his hips.

"Someday, if you're lucky, Castle, you'll be able to afford a driver. If my father doesn't like your work as a builder, he can influence many of his friends."

"And he'd do that for a son who is afraid of me?" Dan asked softly, ready to take on the irritating man.

"Damn you. If you think I'm afraid of you, you're just kidding yourself." Reuben strode to the carriage and Dan dropped to the ground, raising his fists as Reuben swung.

Both vented their anger. Reuben's punch barely glanced off Dan's jaw before Dan came back with one that connected and sent Reuben staggering backward. Reuben feinted, then his right fist shot out and Dan's head jerked back upon impact. Dan shook his head, protected himself against a flurry of blows, and then slammed his fist into Reuben's middle.

There were shouts behind them. Cyrus and his younger brother, Cole, ran out of their house through the snow, jumping a hedge to try to pull the combatants apart.

"Stop it, before my pa finds out and there's real trouble!" Cyrus snapped, looking back and forth between the two men, who glared at each other.

"Stay away from her. I'm warning you now," Reuben said. He shook free of Cole's grasp easily and stomped away.

While Cole ran back home, Cyrus faced Dan. "What brought that on?"

Dan wiped blood off the corner of his mouth. "Man's a mean fighter."

"I guess he is. He boxed for his college team. He can probably beat almost anyone in the territory."

"That's what you think!" Dan answered, his anger evaporating. "Thanks for stepping in. You probably saved me some teeth. My teeth and I thank you."

Cyrus didn't smile, but stood frowning at Dan. "You've made a bad enemy. He's powerful, wealthy, and self-centered, and he always has the pretty ladies with him. Look at him now—he's squiring Louisa. Oh!" Cyrus exclaimed as Dan cast a sharp glance toward him on the last statement.

"Oh, no. You should forget Louisa Shumacher. Her father's very particular about the men in Louisa's life, and Reuben is her beau. You'll lose more than teeth if you tangle with Reuben. And you've told me you want to settle in Denver and have the leading townspeople accept you. You won't succeed if you cross him. His father is on the new board of directors of the Denver City Water Company. Colonel James Archer and Ralston Knelville are best friends. Knelville's also good friends with Manfred and Elwood. He's part of Benjamin Woodward's Musical Union."

"I know he knows everyone. What's the Musical Union?" he asked, brushing snow off his clothes and walking back to his carriage.

"Mr. Woodward came out here for his health after the Civil War. He's with the Pacific Overland Telegraph Company and he's interested in music. He started the Denver Musical Union and they're the ones who are putting on the cantata next month."

Dan nodded, his thoughts still on Reuben. "So if I'm to move in Denver social circles, I'll have to step carefully around Reuben Knelville."

Cyrus grinned. "You will until you're firmly established yourself. Then you can drop him down the well.''

Dan laughed and clasped Cyrus on the shoulder. ''Thanks for coming to separate us. It saved me some trouble.''

Cyrus stepped back and Dan flicked the reins, waving as the carriage drew away.

The next morning he stopped at Dulcie's to eat breakfast, following her back to her bedroom afterward.

Dulcie brushed her hair, watching him in the mirror as he moved restlessly around the room and stopped in front of the window.

''Snow again! I can't get anything built in this kind of weather. I'm glad we have a roof on the Potter house so at least we can work on the inside.''

''All you talk about is work,'' she said quietly.

''I'm getting behind schedule.'' He stood with his back to her, his wool shirt pulled tautly across his broad shoulders. His hands were hooked in his hip pockets as he stared outside. She moved across the room to the bed and shrugged out of the silk wrapper. She wore lacy underclothes and long black stockings with blue satin garters. She scooted back on the bed.

''It's snowy. It's early. You don't have to go to work,'' she said in a seductive voice. ''Dan . . .''

He turned around, a frown furrowing his brow. His gaze swept over her and his frown vanished. A month ago he would have crossed the room eagerly. Now he stood and gazed at her.

''You're beautiful, Dulcie.''

And you have someone else, she thought, keeping her smile in place. ''Come here, Dan.''

He came across the room and sat down on the bed. She wrapped her arms around him, knowing she was losing him and afraid it would be permanent. She knew him so well and she knew that once he fell in love it would be lasting and deep. There wouldn't be a place for another woman in his life.

''Dulcie—''

She stopped his faint protest with her kiss as she

rubbed her body against him. He was a man of strong appetites. He wouldn't be able to resist her touches for long, but she suspected this might be the last time she would coax him into her bed. The thought of losing Dan made her cling to him desperately, using her wiles to hold him. Her fingers tugged free his shirt while she rubbed her bare thigh against his arm.

"Dulcie," Dan whispered, starting to raise his head.

She kissed him passionately, pushing him down and stretching out beside him, sliding her leg over his and caressing him. Dan's arms wrapped around her and lifted her, sliding her over him. She clung to him, moving her hips against his, knowing in her heart their relationship had changed.

An hour later he moved restlessly around her room as he fastened the buttons on his pants. A cheroot was clenched between his teeth, and a spiral of smoke surrounded his head.

"I thought you'd be here last night," she said as she lay back and watched him.

"I went to a party," he said in an offhand manner, moving to the window. "Damned if it isn't snowing again."

"You're moving up in society."

"Dulcie, I love it here. I think Denver will be one of the major cities in the West. The more I get to know the people and learn what they're doing and have done, the more I have to admire them. Before we came, the railroad was going to bypass Denver and run north of here through Cheyenne. When these people learned they would be cut off from the railroad, they did something about it—they incorporated the Denver Pacific Railroad and Telegraph Company, and now the first train is scheduled to arrive here from Cheyenne this summer. The people in this town raised the money themselves. That all happened in 1867. Do you realize how much money they must have had to raise in such a short time?"

Dulcie's mind wasn't on railroads. She wished she could get Dan back to bed with her, just to hold him. She didn't want him to walk out the door and leave her, because she was afraid of how long it would be before he came back. And it plagued her to wonder who the new woman in his life was.

"How was the Shumacher party? You never did tell me about it."

"It was nice," he answered quietly, and Dulcie noticed the change in his voice.

"How is Miss Shumacher?" she asked blandly, sitting up to pull on her wrapper. She had no idea whether there actually was a Miss Shumacher or not.

"She's beautiful," he answered, and Dulcie looked up at him.

"Describe her. I can't remember if I've seen her or not. I get the ladies mixed up."

He gazed out the window, and his voice softened as he answered, "She has black hair and big blue eyes."

Dulcie stared at him, knowing now who was replacing her in Dan's affections. It had been a mere guess, asking about Miss Shumacher, but she knew without question that it had been an accurate guess. "I don't recall seeing her. I don't know the Shumachers," she said, knowing Mr. Shumacher didn't patronize her house.

"You wouldn't forget her, Dulcie." He turned around to look at her, stamping out the cheroot.

"You're in love with her, Dan," she said, wishing she could hold back the accusation, yet unable to do so. She didn't want to let him know how badly it hurt. She stood up, trying to sound brisk. "I knew you would fall in love with some little simpering slip of a girl someday. It was inevitable. There'll be others after her. You can come back to me between them."

As she glanced in the mirror at him, he laughed and shook his head. "Haven't you ever given even a little piece of your heart to a man, Dulcie? If you weren't so good and kindhearted, I'd think it was impossible for you to love."

"Love is for the princess in the fairy tale," she said haughtily, hoping her tone hid the hurt she felt. She wanted to cry out that she had a heart and it belonged to him. She loved him as she had never loved anyone else, but that was exactly why she couldn't tell him the truth. She loved Dan and she wouldn't ruin his life or stand in his way.

"She should help you move into Denver society."

He laughed. "I have to move into Denver society to get her to give me the time of day!"

"Oh, Lord, I hope she isn't one of those prissy women!"

Dan shifted impatiently, yanking up his coat. Dulcie was beginning to bother him with her questions about Louisa Shumacher. "I'm going to work."

"Sure, hon," she said, lifting her face for a slight brush of his lips on her cheek. He looked down at her and patted her fanny.

"You're fun, Dulcie." He winked at her and left, his footsteps fading as he went down the hall.

She closed her door and moved to the window. In minutes she watched him stride away, walking briskly, bareheaded. Most people were hunched over from the cold, but Dan was swinging his arms as if it were a May morning while snow sprinkled his shoulders. Tears stung her eyes. "Oh, Dan, my love. I hope she's a good woman. I hope she deserves you and can make you happy. And I hate her." She wiped at her tears. "Louisa Shumacher," she said aloud, determined to get Lyle Workman, who ran a general store, to point out Miss Shumacher to her.

Three mornings later Dulcie entered Lyle's store. She shivered, smiling and nodding at the group of men clustered around the glowing potbellied stove.

"Howdy, Miss Dulcie," two of them said in unison.

"How're things at the house?" another asked.

"How's Silver Lady?" a regular customer of her house asked.

"Silver's fine, Thomas. Everything's fine, except this cold spell has me freezing when I have to go out."

"Come over here, Miss Dulcie, and we'll warm you up," Jake Clozen said, and guffawed, while the others grinned at her good-naturedly. She laughed and passed them. There seemed to be only a few other females in the store. Three young ladies dressed in finery stood at the counter talking with Lyle, and another was shopping, gathering potatoes out of the barrel. She looked up as Dulcie approached, and smiled.

'' 'Morning,'' she said softly, and Dulcie gazed into wide green eyes.

'' 'Morning,'' she answered in return. The woman surprised Dulcie, because few of the town's women would speak to her. But one sweeping glance told her this young woman wasn't in Denver society. She was far too plain. Dulcie moved on to the counter, where the three young women turned to stare at her.

'' 'Morning, Miss Dulcie,'' Lyle said. ''I'll be with you in a minute.''

One of the ladies drew herself up. They were dressed in the latest fashion, and Dulcie knew they would never speak to her or even so much as nod.

''Now, ladies,'' Lyle said, ''I can order—''

''Mr. Workman,'' one of the women said in frosty tones, ''we'll come back another time.''

''Miss Shumacher, I'll be happy to take the order. It won't take more than a few weeks.''

''We'll be back another time,'' she said emphatically, looking at Dulcie, who stared back defiantly, her gaze sweeping over Louisa Shumacher's blue velvet coat trimmed in ermine, her fancy bonnet, her eyes flashing with annoyance.

The ladies turned and swept out as Dulcie watched them. The hurt she had felt earlier was growing stronger, because she didn't want Dan to love a cold, snobbish woman. Louisa was beautiful, but not any prettier than beautiful women Dulcie had known. Louisa didn't deserve someone like Dan, but men were foolish where beautiful women were concerned. Dulcie turned her attention to Lyle, who shrugged.

She leaned on the counter and lowered her voice, ''Sorry, Lyle. I ran them away.''

''Oh, hell, Miss Dulcie, that's all right. These uppity ladies are a pain in the ass if you ask me, which you didn't. Your gals and you do enough business here, I don't want you going to my competition. Those three will come back.''

"I'll hurry so I don't run off your other customer."

"You won't run her off. What can I do for you?"

Dulcie got out her list, and a half-hour later she had gathered all the supplies she needed. Lyle helped her load them into her carriage, and she went down the boardwalk, heading toward the shoe shop. Planks had been put down across the wide, frozen street of hard-packed snow, glistening now because the weather was finally beginning to warm.

Dulcie had started to cross the street when she slipped. She yelped as she went down, striking her hip sharply on the ice. One man laughed, and another whooped as her skirts flew high. She sat up and started to rise as a hand reached down. The girl who had been in the store helped her up. She looked no older than sixteen.

"Are you all right?"

"Yes. I don't have any dignity left to ruin, and the rest of me is all right. Thanks for your help, miss."

"O'Malley."

"You're Mary O'Malley! I knew Silas. I'm Dulcie Hazelwood."

"How do you do," Mary said, smiling.

"Miss O'Malley, you shouldn't stand here and talk to me. Some of the ladies won't approve of you if you associate with me."

To Dulcie's surprise, Mary O'Malley laughed and her eyes twinkled. "I'm not worried about town ladies disapproving of me!"

Dulcie liked her instantly, and remembered Dan fuming about her, talking about her throwing skillets at him. Dulcie smiled. "Maybe we have some things in common."

"I'd like to hear about Silas. You should stop at my boardinghouse sometime. It's on Larimer Street."

"I might do that. Thank you, Miss O'Malley."

Mary nodded and strode on. Dulcie glanced at the men calling out to her to give them another good show. She grinned, hiked up her skirts, and crossed the street carefully, walking on the planks and avoiding the ice.

7

Dan strode through the snow up the steps to the boardinghouse. He had taken time from his job and had
made an appointment to see Mary O'Malley at three
in the afternoon. It would take only minutes to tell her
about the money, and his conscience bothered him that
he hadn't done so sooner. He let the knocker fall with
a thud against the door as he noticed a crack in a front
window and the worn, weathered boards.

The door opened, and Mary faced him. Her cheeks
were flushed, and wisps of unruly tendrils escaped
from the tight braids wrapped around her head. "Come
inside, Mr. Castle."

"Thanks. It's freezing today." Stomping the snow
off his boots, he followed her into a warm front parlor.
The furniture was well-worn, but there was a coziness
to the braided rugs and a simplicity that was refreshing
in a time when styles dictated fancy frills and crowded
rooms.

Mary motioned to a chair as he shed his thick coat.
His golden hair was tousled and in disarray, and once
again she thought how handsome he was. While she
sat down on a chair, Dan Castle sat facing her on the
settee. He withdrew papers from his coat pocket and
leaned forward, his hands on his knees.

"You never have told me how you met Silas."

"He saved my life." Thickly lashed blue eyes gazed
at her steadily while he related how renegades had
captured him and intended to rob and kill him, when
Silas rode into sight.

"Silas is an unusual man," Dan added.

"Yes, indeed, he is," she said, her features softening and a yearning coming to her voice.

"We rode away from the bandits and later split up. Silas headed north to the gold fields while I turned south," he said, noticing how intently she listened to him. She leaned forward slightly, sitting as still as a tiny bird on a branch as she gave him her full attention. "I hadn't ridden long when a band of Comanche made me reverse my path. I had to go back the way I came, and this time I saved Silas from an ambush."

Fright flared in her features, and Dan hastened to reassure her. "Don't worry, he's all right. We traveled together, and he talked me into prospecting with him. We struck a vein in Montana."

"You did!" Her eyes seemed to widen endlessly, and Dan saw hope flare in her expressive features. "He'll be coming home?"

Silently Dan cursed Silas for not writing to Mary and for not returning to the Colorado Territory. He knew his next words would hurt her. "Sorry, Miss O'Malley. He wants to come back to you a millionaire, and we didn't do that well."

Mary felt a pang that hurt more than she would have guessed. After all this time without word from Silas, she thought she had grown accustomed to his absence, and had prepared herself for the fact that he might not come back, but for a moment her hopes had soared. Now they plummeted back to reality, and it hurt badly to know that money was of more value to Silas than her love.

Dan suspected she was trying to hide her hurt, but it was pitifully transparent. The money should help a little.

He leaned closer and detected a sweet scent of roses, and he noticed that except for the smattering of freckles across her nose, she had creamy, flawless pale skin. "Silas rode back to California to see if he could make another strike. He said he wasn't one to write letters."

"I know he's not," she stated quietly, winding her

fingers together in her lap and still keeping her face averted as she stared out a window.

"But he saved what he made in Montana. That's why I'm here. He wanted me to give half to you." Dan waited to see the surprise and joy in her eyes as he watched her turn to stare at him. He smiled at her. "It's a lot of money."

Her face flushed and her high small breasts strained against her bodice as she drew a deep breath. "Silas sent me a lot of money?"

"Yes, he did," Dan said. He wondered if money were so important to Mary O'Malley, just as it was to Silas, but then remembered that she probably needed it badly to keep the boardinghouse going. His gaze went around the room swiftly, taking in the slightly threadbare furniture, and he was pleased to think Silas had made this provision for her even if he hadn't returned to her.

"I've put the money in the bank for you. I made all the arrangements, and it's in your name. You can draw it out as you please." Dan rustled the papers in his hand. "I'm sorry I didn't get it to you sooner," he said with another twinge of guilt. "If you remember our first meeting, you didn't give me much of a chance. Nonetheless, it's yours and in the bank. Silas was firm—"

"You can take that money to Old Harry and build a fire with it!"

Startled, Dan looked up as she stood and pointed to the door. "And you may leave, Mr. Castle. The next time you see Silas, you tell him it isn't money that's important to me. How could he send money and not write or come home?"

"Hey! Wait a minute, Irish! The man's in love with you!"

"Love? What kind of love is this?" She put her hands on her hips and glared at him. "I haven't seen Silas for years!"

"He loves you so much he doesn't want to come home until he's made a million and can treat you royally. He sent you a fortune. Now, here are the papers."

Grasping the proffered papers, she ripped them apart. "That's what I think of the money!"

"You don't even know how much it is."

"I don't care how much," she snapped, torn between anger and sorrow. Tears began to well up in her eyes, and she was mortified at the thought of crying in front of this stranger.

"You have to care," Dan said, his patience slipping. "It's fifteen thousand dollars."

Mary's jaw dropped, and she stared at him. *Fifteen thousand dollars.* Even when Silas had made thousands, he still wouldn't return home to her! Hurt and anger engulfed her. "Get out of my house!"

"Look, you need those papers. We can glue them back together or I can go back to the bank and talk—"

"I don't want a penny of it! I won't take it!"

"It's in your name and it's yours."

"I won't touch it."

"I know you can use it. That's obvious. And Silas wants you to have it," Dan argued. Her reaction astounded him because he couldn't imagine anyone who would turn down money, particularly someone as badly in need of it as Mary O'Malley. "That's your damned stubborn Irish pride talking."

"It isn't pride! If he had that much and he . . ."

Dan realized what she had been about to say. If Silas had really loved her, he would have come home to her. "Look, Silas is a man with a mission, but he loves you. You were all he talked about. He told me about your favorite foods, your favorite song, and your favorite time of the year. I have heard him sing your praises by the hour!"

She shook visibly as Dan Castle's words made it more difficult for her to stop the tears from falling from her eyes. "I won't take a cent!"

"You don't have to. It's yours already."

"It'll rot in the bank!" she exclaimed, mortified that she might cry.

"Now, that is just bullheaded cussedness!" Dan snapped.

She drew herself up and glared at him. "We're through with this discussion. Get off my property, or I'll send for the sheriff!"

"How he fell in love with a woman who is as fiery and stubborn as you, I'll never know!" Dan wanted to shake her. She was too tiny and too young to cause so much confounded trouble.

"There are some things about women you don't understand." Scooping up the papers, she stepped to Dan's side, took his arm firmly, and propelled him toward the door.

"I'm sure when you think about it, you'll be reasonable and take the money. Silas loves you. He did it for you."

She opened the front door and handed Dan his coat. "Good day, Mr. Castle." She flung the bank papers at him and slammed the door in his face. Dan stood there staring at the door.

"Irish, you are stubborn as an old bandy-legged mule," he said, his fists on his hips. He was torn between kicking open the door and arguing further, and ignoring the papers and leaving Miss O'Malley to her poverty-stricken life. Suddenly he laughed and shook his head.

"Silas, you didn't warn me that the woman you love is a little firecracker!" he said softly, picking up the torn bits of paper. He smoothed them out and glanced at the total: fifteen thousand two hundred dollars, actually. His gaze went over the cracked pane and the worn boards, and he remembered Mary O'Malley's patched dress. He sighed and jammed the papers in his pocket.

Early the next morning Dan stopped to see Dulcie. "I finally got around to calling on Mary O'Malley to give her the money."

"Well, it took you long enough!" Dulcie said. She sat in a chair facing him and her heart beat swiftly. He had come rushing in from the cold and he looked so

handsome. His face was flushed, his hair tangled, and
the thick sheepskin coat emphasized his broad shoulders. She wished she had known he was coming, and
worn something more revealing. She ached for him,
and with a painful twist remembered Louisa Shumacher, who was cold and unfriendly.

Dulcie had known all along that someday a woman
would come along and catch his fancy, but now that it
had happened, it hurt badly. He paced up and down
the room, and it was difficult to resist going to him
and putting her arms around him.

"I thought she'd be overjoyed." He whirled around.
"Wouldn't you be overjoyed?"

"Of course I would, sweetie," she answered dryly.
"If a man gave me fifteen thousand dollars, I'd be
delighted."

"Then why isn't she? She ripped up the bank papers."

For the first time Dulcie began to pay attention to
what he was saying instead of to Dan himself. "She
what?"

"I've been telling you, Dulcie, she tore up the papers and threw them at me."

"I'll be damned!" Dulcie threw back her head and
laughed.

"It isn't funny either."

Instantly she sobered. "I know it's not. Just momentarily, the vision of her flinging all that money in
your face astounded me." Silently she praised Mary
O'Malley for having enough spunk to defy both Silas
and Dan.

"She needs the money. Silas wants her to have it."

"Doesn't that fool Silas realize this girl wants his
love, not his money?"

"I tried to tell him that. But she can still want him
while she uses the money he gave her. If she marries
him, he'll spend it on her anyway."

"I met her. She looks young."

"She looks fifteen years old, but sometimes she acts
as if she's one hundred. Dammit, I could just shake
her!"

"So now what will you do?" Dulcie asked coolly, enjoying the situation.

"I don't know, dammit. If she didn't need it so badly, I'd forget all about it."

"No, you wouldn't," Dulcie said softly. "You're too softhearted to forget it when it concerns Silas or her."

"She wears patched dresses, and the boardinghouse looks as if it will fall down on her head. She is the most stubborn little snippet—" He ran his hands through his hair, and Dulcie bit back a smile. It was seldom that a woman had Dan tied in knots. So far she couldn't think of any since the fabulous Melissa Hatfield.

"And what's worse," he said, pausing suddenly in front of her, "I think she loves him and she's hurt by the money. I swear I think she tried her damnedest to fight tears. That Silas! I'll knock him flat when I see him again, for getting me into the middle of this."

"The money will keep. Just forget it, Dan."

"I want to forget it, but then I think about Silas wanting her to have it so badly that he would risk life and limb, and I look at her needing it so badly . . . Dulcie, would you—?"

"No. I know exactly what you're thinking, but ladies in town don't talk to me. And frankly, darling, if there is a woman on earth that you can't persuade to do something, she isn't going to listen to me."

He laughed, and a momentary smile crossed his face. Dulcie knew she wasn't in his thoughts at all except as a friend to hear his worries.

"I met Mary O'Malley," she said. "I slipped on the ice and she helped me up. She's nice, Dan."

"She's a fiery-tempered baggage!"

Dulcie wanted to cry out that she had been nicer than Louisa Shumacher, who wouldn't even stay in the same store with her, who wouldn't have helped her in her fall if she had broken her arms and legs. Instead, she was afraid to speak out against Louisa, afraid it would send Dan away, and she realized how vulnerable she was. She had let her heart grow warm by loving Dan. Now she would pay for it.

"I'll try again," he said with another long sigh. "Dammit, she's difficult! She looks as if the first big wind would blow her right through town, but she can handle bull-whackers and renegades as well as a man."

"If I didn't know you so well, I wouldn't believe you."

"I'm going to work, Dulcie. I'll be back later," he said casually, brushing her cheek with a kiss. But she knew he probably wouldn't return for several days.

"You work too hard, Dan," she said, sliding her fingers along his shoulder. "Your crew won't be at work for another two hours."

"I want to make a place for myself here, and hard work will eventually give me what I want."

It was still early in the February morning, an hour before most people would be stirring. Snow crunched beneath Dan's feet, and as he strode down the street, he thought about the town and his future. Denver had a population of over five thousand people now, and it seemed to be growing daily. Dan's home, the one for Lester Potter, and Dulcie's wouldn't catch the attention of the men in town who could afford the type of house Dan longed to build. But Benjamin Corning had contacted him, asking him to draw up plans. A six-bedroom house, it would be one of the fanciest in Denver when finished, and Dan prayed he got the contract.

A man and woman hurried across the road ahead of him. With a perfunctory greeting, the couple passed him and hurried away, but for an instant Dan thought of his mother, Hattie. It had been weeks since her last letter, and he wondered if she would ever reconsider returning home to the ranch in New Mexico Territory. His thoughts went back to his childhood, and he could remember the countless times he had seen Javier, his father, return home and swing Hattie up in his arms. She would laugh, her hands on Javier's shoulders as he set her down and kissed her. A wave of sadness overcame him momentarily, because Dan hated to think of Javier alone. He was a man meant to have a woman at his side, a man deeply in love with his wife. Yet Dan could understand the rage and hurt Hattie had felt when she discovered Javier had given away Hattie's daughter so many years ago. Dan frowned as he thought about the pain his family had experienced, April's years of growing up without her family, Javier's regrets and guilt, and Hattie's fury. There was no way to undo the past. And Dan prayed his was buried forever.

Dan squared his shoulders, his stride lengthening as he thought about the house his men were completing. He wanted it to be the best possible. He had no patience with slipshod methods. He had discussed the matter with each man he hired, making sure they had some experience, and checking their work to see if it met with his standards.

He rounded the corner and studied the carriage in front of the Potter house. Dan quickened his step, wondering who had stopped and why. He took the front steps two at a time and stomped snow off his feet before opening the door and entering. A man stood in the front parlor, his back to Dan, but he turned at the sound of footsteps. His tall beaver hat was dusted with snow.

"Good morning," Dan said, offering his hand. "I'm Dan Castle."

"Mr. Castle. I'm Edward Ringwood. I hope you don't mind, but I wanted to look at your work."

"I don't mind at all. Can I show you around?"

"I've already looked around," he said, turning to study the Victorian Gothic mantel. "Very nice touches. I like your mantelshelf," he said, running his hand along dentils in the bed molding, the decorative pilasters and turned woodwork. He looked around the room, glancing up at the coved ceiling and the wide polished mahogany both above and at the base.

"That's nice wood. Very good job," he observed.

"It came from Santo Domingo. I order some of my wood from a company in South Carolina."

Edward Ringwood's black eyes finally focused on Dan. "We share the same liking. I have a preference for Victorian. It's eye-catching. Thank you for your time, Mr. Castle."

"Yes, sir. Anytime you want to come look, feel free to do so," Dan said, shedding his coat.

"You work early."

"I'm shorthanded. I get more done if I start early."

"There are plenty of men for hire in town."

"I'm particular when it comes to my houses," Dan said. His pulse raced. He wanted to grasp Edward Ringwood's arm and show him every inch of the house, the high ceilings and ample fireplaces, the Vermont slate used in building the fireplaces, but he resisted the impulse.

"How many houses have you built, Mr. Castle?"

"Two others here in Denver, and I'm presenting plans to Benjamin Corning. I've also worked on houses in California."

Ringwood nodded. "Good day, sir." He left, striding out to his carriage, where a coachman sat quietly waiting. Dan watched him drive away, wishing he would come back and ask Dan to build him a house. Edward Ringwood had made a fortune in silver before he settled in Denver. He had opened a smelter, and he was just the type of man Dan hoped to acquire as a customer. Young, wealthy, married with two small children, Ringwood could afford a fancy mansion.

Dan gathered up his tools and went to the hall, and his thoughts of Ringwood vanished as he concentrated on his task.

Two hours later his men worked in two rooms while Dan nailed cove molding in place beneath the tread on a riser on the stairway. In spite of the pounding of hammers, the shattering of a loud blast was heard and all hammering stopped. Dan ran out on the porch, glancing up and down the street.

A column of smoke rose above roofs near the center of town.

"Fire!" Dan yelled.

His men ran outside. Only one man had his horse, which was tethered at a rail. "Come on, Dan, I'll give you a ride," Hiram Veck said. Dan swung up behind him while Willie North waved them to go ahead. They could follow the rising cloud of smoke to the fire. The town's two-thousand-pound bell began clanging; a fire brought all able-bodied people. Dan knew Denver had burned in the spring of 1863, and people were acutely conscious of the hazards of fire.

As they rounded a corner, Dan's eyes narrowed and he swore. It was the O'Malley boardinghouse. One corner was ripped away, and flames and smoke billowed out. Mary O'Malley was pumping water furiously, and a bucket brigade had already formed, winding from the pump around the corner of the house to the fire. Denver Hook and Ladder Company was only a few blocks away on Lawrence Street, so the hook-and-ladder crew was already at the boardinghouse when Dan arrived. Men pumped vigorously as they poured a stream of water on the fire. Dan jumped off the horse and ran to Mary. He pushed her away from the pump, taking the handle to pump faster. "I'll do this." As he talked, he shed his coat. "Put on my coat."

"I've got to help," she said, starting toward the line. Dan grabbed her arm, throwing his coat around her shoulders.

"Put on my coat," he snapped, and she slid her arms into the sleeves. As he pumped, Mary called to one of the men to move the horses. In addition to the bucket brigade, men on the porch had wet gunnysacks to beat at the flames. Mary ran toward the porch, and Dan swore. "Jed, man this pump!" he called, running to catch up with Mary. He yanked the gunnysack from her hands as she beat at flames.

"Get back where it's safe," he ordered.

"Mr. Castle, it's my house!"

"Dammit, Irish, get back there or I'll carry you and hold you, and two of us won't be any help!"

"Mary, where's Pa?" Brian asked. Mary and Dan turned to face Brian. "I can't find him."

Mary looked at the burning house. "Holy saints preserve us."

Dan stepped in front of her as her brother ran ahead. "Get off the porch, Mary. Let the men do this. I'll go with Brian."

Brian and Dan raced inside the house, Dan winding his handkerchief over the lower part of his face and following Brian upstairs. The fire burned in the front parlor, a gaping hole torn in the wall, and Dan wondered how the hell this had happened, but then his mind was on the O'Malleys.

Paddy O'Malley sat on the top step, bottles clutched in his arms. Blood streamed from a cut on his temple, and he smiled at them.

"Brian, I must take care of my bottles."

"Pa, the house is on fire. Get out." Brian and Dan each took Paddy's arms and led him down the steps. He coughed violently, tears streaming from his eyes. Dan's eyes burned and he felt as if he were suffocating as they tried to hurry Paddy O'Malley along.

"Careful, boys, the bottles."

"Pa, come on." Brian coughed, his voice a rasp.

"Boys, we have to go. The blasting powder is in the front parlor," Paddy warned.

"Pa, it blew out the side of the house."

"Brian, only one bag blew a hole in the house."

They reached the foot of the stairs. Brian gave Dan a horror-struck look of shock. "Pa, there's more?"

"Yes, my boy. There were two bags," he said carefully, his words slurred in spite of his efforts to pronounce them distinctly.

"Let's go!" Dan snapped, and they rushed Paddy out. "Get off the porch!" Dan shouted. "Blasting powder! Fire in the hole!" he yelled, knowing every miner would understand. He grabbed Mary around the waist, scooping her up while Brian pulled Paddy along. Men dropped buckets and ran.

"The fire—" Mary protested, pulling back.

Dan tightened his grip as he ran, while she clung to

his neck. The blast shook the ground, and Dan dropped down over Mary, trying to protect her from flying boards. Something hit him across the shoulders.

Silence came, and in spite of all the turmoil, the fire, and the explosion, he was aware of Mary's soft body beneath his. He turned his head to look directly into her wide green eyes. "Are you all right?" he asked, noticing that her skin was beautiful and as smooth as porcelain.

"Yes."

"I didn't mean to hurt you."

"Are you hurt?"

"No." There was one long heartbeat of time when neither moved. He rolled over and stood up, pulling her to her feet. Black smoke rolled and billowed skyward. Men were getting up all across the yard and street, but no one seemed seriously injured.

"It blew out the damned fire," Dan said, looking at what was left of the boardinghouse. Only two-thirds of it remained. The front corner of the structure was missing. Rubble was strewn across the yard. Men stood in shock as they stared at the house. A small flame flickered beneath the floor, and Dan yelled, "Get the pumper going! We can control it now."

Men worked swiftly, and in another quarter-hour, the last ember had died. Dan set down his bucket, glancing around to locate Mary and Brian. He thanked everyone who had helped out, while Paddy sat on the unburned portion of the porch, bottles clutched in his arms.

Dan told his men to go back to work while he picked up debris and stacked it on the porch. He covered his mouth again and ran inside, opening windows to clear the smoke. By the time he came downstairs, Mary and Brian stood in the front hall and the smoke had cleared. A stranger stood talking to them about his room.

"We'll find our boarders other places to stay until we can get things fixed," Mary said. "Lonnie and Jen McGruder said we can send two men to their house. You can take your things there now if you want."

"Thanks, Miss O'Malley. Is it safe to go upstairs?" Nolen Parker asked, his white beard covered with cinders.

"Yes, unless your room was in the corner that burned or adjacent to it," Dan answered, joining them. "Don't get near that part."

"No. My room is at the back," Parker said. "Miss O'Malley, your pa has got to do his inventing in the shed," he said.

"I know, Mr. Parker," she said, and he ambled toward the house.

"I can stay this afternoon," Dan said. "Four of the men said they would help today. Jeb Long said he'd send a wagon with lumber, and we can start repairs."

"Thank you," she said, sounding sincerely relieved. She ran her hand across her brow. "I don't know where to begin."

"Once the smoke is out of the house, you can shut off the parts that didn't burn and get some heat back."

"Fortunately, the front rooms are unoccupied at the moment. Only two of the men should have to vacate."

"I'll help with repairs," Brian said. "I work at the livery stable, and Henry said I could take the rest of today to help here."

"Good. See the tall black-haired fellow, Will North? He works for me and he'll give you my tools to bring back here."

Brian left, and the neighbors who had volunteered to stay began picking up debris in the yard. Paddy sat on the stairs, singing softly to himself.

"Put all the costs on a bill," Mary told Dan. "I'll have to pay you as I can."

"You don't have to pay me at all," he said firmly. "You have money."

"That is Silas Eustice's money. If you want your money now, you can take it from his and I'll repay him."

Dan nodded, knowing he wouldn't take a cent. "What the hell was your pa doing with blasting powder in the house?" He wished he hadn't asked, because her eyes seemed to cloud over with worry as she glanced at Paddy.

"Pa always thinks he's going to invent something the world will want. I don't know what he had in mind this time. Two years ago he blew away the toolshed. He said he was trying to build a device to enable miners to blow holes beneath the ground efficiently so they wouldn't have to dig. He might have gone back to that. He doesn't let things go if they don't work out. I don't know what he was trying to do, and right now, I doubt if he does either."

"He doesn't seem to be hurt badly. The second blast blew out the fire, and since no one was hurt, I suppose it was just as well."

"I appreciate your help," she said stiffly, and he grinned.

"You appreciate it, but you wish it weren't me."

"It's not you personally," she said. "I don't like to have to take men's time and aid."

"Unbend a little, Irish," he said softly, looking closely at her again. Her face was smudged, and his coat made her look more childlike than ever, as her hands were completely hidden by the long sleeves. He brushed a speck of dirt off her cheek.

"Here's your coat. Thank you."

"Keep my coat. It's still cold in the house." He walked over to Paddy. "Sir, let me have one of the bottles, please." Gently he pried one of the bottles from Paddy's hands. Paddy smiled and continued to sing softly while Dan walked back to Mary. He worked the cork free and led her into the dining room, closing the door behind him.

"You need to get away from people, the fire, and the problems for a few minutes. The world will keep right on turning, Miss O'Malley. Have a sip of whatever this is. I'm sure it'll warm your insides."

"I don't—"

"But this time you do. Take a drink," Dan said, thinking he wanted one himself.

"No, thank you."

He leaned closer to her, and in spite of the smell of

cinders and soot, he could catch a whiff of rosewater. "Irish, I know what's best. Drink this." Big green eyes glared at him; she blinked, and reached for the bottle.

"Take a big drink."

She tilted the bottle, letting the fiery liquid drain down her throat, coughing and sputtering as she handed the bottle back to him. "That's horrible! How can Pa consume such vile liquid?"

"Paddy doesn't think it's a vile liquid," Dan said dryly. "We'll try to get walls up as quickly as possible. If you shut off the burned rooms, can you continue with your dining room and boardinghouse?"

"It looks as if I can, with the exception of the two boarders." She noticed a cut on his cheek and reached up to touch him. "You're bleeding a little."

He pulled out his handkerchief. "Where?"

She took it from him and dabbed at a cut on his cheekbone while he studied her. Mary glanced at him, disturbed by his watchfulness. "It isn't bad. Mr. Castle, I still want to pay you and the men."

"Look, accept help when it's offered. Soon enough we'll be gone, and you'll have to hire men to do the rest. I'd guess you've helped others in emergencies."

She blinked. "Sorry, I didn't mean to sound ungrateful."

He patted her shoulder, thinking she looked as if she ought to be in the small schoolhouse nearby. He closed the windows, striding around the dining room. "And for a few minutes, sit down and relax and let us worry about the boardinghouse. I think it's aired out sufficiently, so we can start getting some heat in here again."

The fiery liquid had burned her throat, but it warmed her. She watched Dan Castle move around the dining room and was relieved to have someone else to take charge, because it was a unique experience.

"Thank you for your help."

He paused and grinned. "You're welcome, Irish. I think your pa's whiskey mellowed you."

She blinked at him, and suddenly he regretted his

teasing. He crossed the room to take her chin in his hands. "I was teasing."

"I know. I do appreciate your help." She sighed and stood up. "I better mop up the water."

He caught her arms. "You can mop anytime tonight. Sit down here and relax." He sat her down and sat down with her. "You've had a shock. Here, have a little more whiskey."

"I'll be as tipsy as Pa."

"Long as you don't blow off more of the house, I can't see that it would hurt."

She laughed, and he felt better. He liked to see her laugh, because she was the most solemn person he had ever known. "That's good, Irish. You're pretty when you laugh," he said, touching her dimple.

She blushed and looked down, and lashes feathered above her cheeks. She took another drink of the whiskey and coughed. "I don't see how men can love this stuff."

"Like a woman, it becomes more important with time and familiarity."

She laughed again. "It would take a long time and a great deal of familiarity for me to love this!"

"Now, you sit right here and let me go to work. Promise you won't move for another ten minutes or so."

"I promise," she said, smiling at him. He winked and patted her knee, then moved away to go outside and join the men working there.

Mary waited as she had promised. She looked down at Dan's coat that hung off her shoulders and thought about things he had said to her, and she smiled until she walked out into the hall and looked at the damage.

While she mopped up water inside, closing off the damaged rooms and trying to clean the hall, she heard Dan calling out directions. Brian worked side by side with him, and with the men working, she saw that some repairs would come about swiftly. Within two hours they had a framework up along the corner of the parlor. She went outside at nightfall.

"Mr. Castle, I have supper ready, if you and the

men would like to eat now. You can wash up in back if you want.''

''Thanks. We'll be there in a few minutes.''

As he ate at a long table across from Brian, Mary served the workmen as well as her regular customers. ''To sit in here, you wouldn't know anything had happened today,'' Dan remarked, watching her move between tables.

''It's a blessing the wind wasn't high so the fire didn't spread.''

''And somewhat of a blessing your father had two bags of blasting powder. If you ever want a job building houses, I could use a worker like you,'' Dan told Brian.

Brushing thick red curls out of the way, Brian raised his head, giving Dan an amused, scornful look. ''You don't hold grudges, do you?''

''Nope. I see no reason to hold grudges where you're concerned.''

''Thanks about the job, but I'm learning to be a smithy. I want my own livery stable.''

''You're a good carpenter. I watched you today.''

''Thanks,'' he said, looking pleased. ''I learned that from Michael.''

By the time Mary served them slices of steaming apple pie, the remaining customers in the dining room had finished and gone.

The men who had helped thanked her for their suppers, Brian went back to work, and finally Dan was the only one left in the dining room. As she cleared the table of dishes, he watched her.

''Have you eaten?''

''Not yet, but I will.''

''Get your dinner and come join me while I eat my pie.''

She nodded and carried a stack of dishes to the kitchen. In minutes she reappeared with a steaming bowl of stew. Dan stood and pulled out her chair, and she sat down facing him. ''How's your father?''

''He's fine, I'm sure. He's gone now, probably down

to the saloon. That's where he is most of the time. It was good of you to take time from your work."

"Glad to," he answered. "There's no reason you shouldn't use the money."

Her green eyes widened. "Of course there's a reason. The money belongs to Silas and not to me."

"He's given it to you. It's a gift, already given. I can't keep it because it wasn't given to me. If you want to save every penny of it for Silas, you can do that, but you have to take it."

"Why do you care?"

"Because I promised him I would give the money to you. I keep promises."

"This one you shouldn't have made without knowing what you were saying," she said with an unyielding note of determination that stirred his anger, until he remembered the fire.

"You've had a bad day, Irish. I'm not going to argue with you tonight." Impulsively he leaned forward. "Do you ever have fun?"

She looked startled, gazing up at him with wide eyes, and he noticed how thickly lashed and beautiful they were.

"Of course."

"Doing what?" he persisted, suspecting she wouldn't know fun if it exploded in her life like Paddy's blasting powder.

She shrugged, looking at the flames dancing in the hearth. "I used to take the boys out when they were little. We have a favorite place along Cherry Creek north of town, and we'd have a picnic."

"Do you dance?"

"No," she said quickly, shaking her head. He remembered her limp and was sorry he had asked, but then he remembered seeing her running, so he decided the limp might not be the reason. "I like to read."

"So does my mother," he said.

"Where does your mother live?" she asked.

"In San Antonio."

"Do you have other relatives?"

He answered her questions with the story he had

decided to tell others, trying to stay close enough to the truth to be able to remember easily what he had told people, yet far enough from it that no one would suspect his identity or background. While she plied him with questions and listened to his answers, she refilled his cup with coffee twice. It was over half an hour later that Dan realized he was doing most of the talking.

"You've let me talk like I haven't seen another person for the whole winter. You're a good listener, Irish."

"You're an interesting man, Mr. Castle," she said forthrightly, and he wondered if she had ever flirted with a man in her life. But Silas' deep attraction to her still puzzled Dan. "Thank you for taking time from your work to help me today," she said. "And for getting Pa out of the house in time, although he has a knack for coming through trouble."

He stood up and she walked him to the door, handing his coat to him. His hand brushed hers, feeling her cold fingers. He caught her hand in his. "You're cold."

"I'm fine," she said softly, trying to withdraw her hand.

He held her tighter. "Your hand is cold."

"I'll get warm in the kitchen," she said, withdrawing her hand this time.

"Good night, Irish. We'll have your boardinghouse back in order in no time."

"Thank you, Mr. Castle."

He left, striding away, thinking he was getting farther behind schedule on the house he had contracted to build for Lester Potter.

For the next few days he worked in the mornings on the Potter house, then in the afternoons at the O'Malley boardinghouse. They framed in the damaged walls and floors, then laid the floors and put in the roof. As days passed, the volunteers quit and went back to their regular jobs, until Dan and Brian were the only ones working. Then Dan came only in the evenings, cutting into the time when he could call on Louisa. Each evening Dan ate dinner in the O'Malley dining room, staying later to talk to Mary O'Malley, and sometimes Brian as well. She was a quiet, intelligent, capable woman who always seemed to amaze him. She could take charge better than Dulcie, and got things accomplished quietly. One evening when he was telling her about the books he had read and liked, he paused to ask, "What's your favorite?"

"Charles Dickens' *Great Expectations.*"

"Why?"

"Miss Havisham is eerie, and I can't help but want Kip to succeed."

"I haven't read it. My ma was going to get it on a trip"—he paused and went on smoothly—"on a trip, but she never got around to it." He realized he had come close to saying on a trip into town, contradicting his careful story that his mother lived in San Antonio and that was where he had grown up.

"I have it. Would you like to read it?" Mary asked him. Moments like this, when he sat and talked to her, she enjoyed his company, beginning to look forward to this time each evening. And she was happy to find someone to talk to about her books.

"Yes, I would."

"I'll get it now. Come with me." He followed her down the hall into a back parlor that was filled with furniture as threadbare as that in the front parlor. It was a cozy, inviting room, though, with plants growing on the windowsills and blue curtains at the windows. Bookshelves lined two walls, and she paused in front of one, studying the titles.

"Here's one of my mother's favorites," he said, withdrawing a book by Sir Walter Scott.

"I like that too. I love to read and forget the boardinghouse and Pa's inventions."

"Maybe you should see to it your father doesn't keep blasting powder."

"I can't rule Pa. It's getting to the point where I can't even control Brian any longer."

"That's part of life," Dan said quietly, leaning against the bookshelf and studying her. Her hair was

the color of fire and he wondered how it would look
down across her shoulders.

"Do you ever laugh, Mary Katherine?"

She gazed up solemnly, and a twinkle came into her
wide green eyes. "Occasionally, on my birthday."

They both laughed, and again he marveled at how
it changed her face. She had dimples in both cheeks
and white, even teeth. "That's better. You've had a
bad time with the fire."

"No one was hurt. The boardinghouse will get repaired, thanks to you. I'm sorry I threw a skillet at
you that first day."

He laughed and tucked a wispy tendril of hair behind her ear. "If you knew how Silas sings your
praises. Right this minute he probably has someone
pinned down listening to him talk about Mary Katherine O'Malley."

She looked down at the book in her hands. "I wish
he'd come home to me instead of telling people about
me," Mary said quietly, the old hurt surfacing.

"I understand. I wouldn't want to wait for someone
to find a strike," he said gently. "But he loves you
very much."

She gave him a fleeting smile and placed the book
back on the shelf. "If you want to read any of my
books, you may."

He turned to look at them. "Where'd you get all the
books?"

Dan glanced at a bracket on the wall holding a lamp.
It was canted at an angle and he reached up to touch
it lightly.

"That's broken."

While Mary watched, he pulled a straight-backed
wooden chair beneath it and climbed up to look at the
fixture. As he stepped up, her gaze ran down his flat
middle, his slim hips, and long legs. She blinked and
looked away quickly, unable to resist glancing back.
He reached into his hip pocket to remove a screw-
driver. "I can fix this. I need a longer screw."

"I don't have any."

"I do, in my box of tools."

"I'll go get it," she said before he could climb down. "Where is it? In the front parlor?"

"Yes." He removed the broken fixture, studying where it had pulled loose from the wall. In minutes she handed him the box and he hunted until he found what he wanted. "Hold that for me," he said, dropping two long screws and a metal plate in her hand.

Mary stood close, watching him work. A lock of golden hair fell over his forehead. His sleeves were rolled back, revealing muscular forearms. Her gaze ran swiftly down his length again, looking at his dusty black boots. "You like to build, don't you?"

"Yes," he answered in an offhand manner, concentrating on his work. "You can see what you've accomplished when you're finished. I like sheep ranching too, but you can't see what you've done. You do the same thing over, season after season."

"I thought you grew up in a city."

Dan paused, glancing down at her, realizing there was something so disarming about Mary Katherine O'Malley that he dropped his guard completely when he was around her. "I worked on a sheep ranch once."

"I've seen the house you're building. It's going to be beautiful."

He heard a wistful note in her voice and paused again. "You could fix things up here very nicely if you'd use the money Silas gave you."

"Mr. Castle, I won't use one cent of Silas' money. When I think about that money, I just get angry," she said.

"Irish," he said as he went back to work, "you're as stubborn as a Missouri mule."

She laughed, a merry sound that startled him and made him look down at her. He grinned in return, thinking Silas had good taste. Mary Katherine O'Malley was quite a woman when it got right down to it. Not so pretty, but very nice, very capable, and very intelligent. He studied her as she gazed up at him, and reassessed his appraisal. She was pretty, just not beautiful.

"Maybe I should call you names more often," he

said, teasing her while he leaned forward to put a screw in place. "Stubborn, balky . . ."

Mary was accustomed to horseplay with her brothers. She smiled and reached out to give the chair a gentle shake. "Beware, Mr. Castle! I can tumble you right to the floor."

"Hey! Damn, I dropped the screw." He looked down and laughed. "Irish, you shake my chair again," he said as she dutifully handed back the fallen screw, "and I'll come down and get you."

She placed her hand on her heart. "Mercy me, Mr. Castle! I'm terrified!" she said, making him laugh.

He grinned and went back to work, finishing the job and dropping down off the chair. "Got anything else that needs fixing?"

"You'd be here until next year."

"What's broken?"

"So many things, but nothing that won't be manageable."

"I don't have another thing to do tonight. What's broken?"

The second window won't raise."

Dan fixed the window, a broken cabinet door in the kitchen, and a loose tread on the stairs, while Mary followed him around and stood quietly talking to him. She liked watching him work and he was fun to talk to, more interesting than anyone she knew. There were moments when she was relaxed with him, and then suddenly she would become intensely disturbed by him. Throughout the evening, she was unable to understand the mixed reactions he stirred in her.

As he replaced a broken baluster on the stairs, Mary sat two steps below and watched him work.

"Michael used to fix things around here, but he's got gold fever and has gone into the mountains now. Sometimes I think Silas talked him into it. I hear you're building your own house."

"That's right. I'll show it to you sometime if you'd like to see it."

"Yes, I would. When we came to Denver, it was actually two towns called Auraria and Denver. They consisted of only a few tents and buildings, mostly saloons. We were here during the fire and when Cherry Creek flooded the town. Pa built a boat, but by the time he had it ready—actually it was a raft with a sail—the waters had gone down. The boys had fun playing on it until they hauled it down to the river and set sail. It crashed into the bank and broke up.''

Dan laughed. ''How'd your brother get to be such a scrappy fighter?''

''When we were kids, we had to fight. Pa's different from most men. He builds strange contraptions and odd inventions, he drinks too much, and he does all that whittling. Other kids used to tease us a lot, and all of us fought. I suppose we didn't have a mama to tell us we shouldn't. And on a frontier town in the early days—well, it isn't easy being a woman, even if you're young and lame and not very pretty.''

She said it as matter-of-factly as if she was talking about the weather. Dan turned around to glance down over his shoulder at her.

''Michael is the real fighter. He can whip Brian with one hand, and I haven't—''

Dan scooted down the steps and tilted up her chin. ''Don't ever say that again about being lame and not pretty,'' he said quietly.

Startled, she stared at him, her reaction switching to a volatile awareness. He looked angry, and she couldn't imagine why he would care. ''It's true.''

''You limp a little, but it's barely noticeable.'' He remembered Silas asking him to take her out, and his promise that he would. ''There's a barn dance at Simpson's new livery stable Friday night. Go with me. Silas wanted me to take you out. Just a brotherly thing. Brian can go with us.''

''Thank you, but I can't dance.''

''You can learn. Come here.'' He took her hand and led her down the steps to the hall, shoving the braided rug out of the way with his toe. ''Sing something. I heard you singing in the kitchen, so I know you can.''

''Mr. Castle, this is absurd,'' she said, embarrassed.

"Sing, Mary," he said.

"I can't dance. I'll step on your feet," she said, remembering Dewar Logan. "I don't—"

"If you don't sing, I'll have to and you'll wish you had."

She laughed and sang, and he took her hands, holding her at arm's length. "Watch my feet. You're singing a waltz, that's good. Now, left foot, step. Step, step. One, two, three, one two three, I'll count and you sing slowly and we'll master this in no time."

Mary followed his lead. She had danced with Silas and she knew how, and in minutes she didn't have to watch Dan's feet. She looked up to find him watching her as she sang softly. His eyes were blue, thickly lashed, and he was watching her with a faint smile on his handsome face. For a moment she tilted her head back and enjoyed dancing, thinking how nice it was to have him insist they dance, how easy he was to talk to. She suspected the woman he loved wouldn't have to wait years for him. Her gaze drifted down to his mouth, which was wide, the underlip full. He had a sensual, masculine mouth that made her heartbeat skip. Her cheeks grew warm and she blinked, looking away, trying to change her thoughts.

"Hey, you *can* dance," he said softly, watching her cheeks become pink.

"I haven't for years."

He laughed. "Years? You can't even be eighteen!"

"I am! I'm twenty this year. For mercy's sake, how young did you think I was?"

"Seventeen," he lied, adding two years, because he suspected the truth would make her more annoyed. He was amused at her bristling over being thought young. She had forgotten her dancing, forgotten to sing, yet she continued to follow his lead, and Dan continued to waltz, watching her, thinking she was as quick-changing as mercury.

"You dance as well as the best of them. Sing some more," he said in a deep voice, watching her solemnly.

She began to sing again, and Dan slipped his arm

around her waist, really dancing now, and watching her intently. He realized she was as light as a feather, and graceful, following his lead as if she had no limp.

Mary gazed up into his eyes, feeling caught in a spell while she danced, wanting to go on dancing. Since Dan had come into her life there were moments when some of her responsibilities seemed to fall away, and she realized he was beginning to be a true friend.

"What are you thinking, Mary?"

"It's nice having you here."

He smiled with a flash of white teeth. "You don't need lessons. I'll come for you around eight o'clock."

"You don't have to take me to a dance."

"No, but I'll do this for Silas. You should get out and see people."

"I see people every day."

"You need to have fun," he said, determined to see that she did, even if it was only one evening.

The front door opened and a tall thin man entered. " 'Evening, Miss O'Malley."

"Good evening, Mr. Lewellan. This is Mr. Castle. Mr. Castle, meet the boarder who has been with us the longest, Mr. Lewellan."

"Yes, sir. I came to stay one night, and that was five years ago. I've been through a lot here, but this is the first time your pa has blown off half the house. I'm right happy I wasn't in bed at the time."

"So am I, Mr. Lewellan."

"He was trying to make a mine blaster. He told me about it. Fill a container just like a giant bullet with blasting powder, same principle, trigger it off and let it shoot right through the earth. Save men lots of digging. Good idea if it had worked. My first wife, Mrs. Ella Lewellan, always had big ideas she couldn't get to work, God rest her soul. At least she didn't try to put them into practice. Nice talking to you young folks. If your pa comes in anytime soon, tell him to come up for a game of checkers."

"Yes, sir," she said as Mr. Lewellan climbed the stairs.

"Your pa likes to play checkers?"

"Yes, that's his favorite pastime, next to whittling."

"What's he whittle?"

"You haven't been to Pa's room? I'll show you." She led him down the hall, lighting a lamp in a back bedroom. "See? Pa likes to whittle."

Dan stood in the center of a bedroom filled with bottles and dozens of wooden figures.

"He carved all these figures?" he asked, picking up one and recognizing tiger maple in the wood, a fine, artistic wooden horse with a flowing mane. "Mary, he's good!"

"I suppose. He's productive—that I know."

Dan touched a wheel that had a wire that ran across the room to more wheels and levers beside the bed. "What's this?"

"I don't know what all the inventions are. Pa has one that brings him his shoes when he pulls on a string. That little box with wooden rollers—he runs his feet over it and says it relaxes the muscles. His has all sorts of inventions."

Dan spent a quarter of an hour prowling around Paddy's room, engrossed in the oddities. Finally he turned to Mary. "Guess I'll get my coat and head home."

"It's a cold night. I'll fix you a cup of hot cider before you go."

"You won't get any argument about that," he said, and followed her to the kitchen. He walked around looking at the large iron stove. He ran his hand along the edge of the stove as she poured cider into a pan to heat it. "You've put your earnings into the kitchen."

"I think it's only good business. I have to run the boardinghouse. They say we'll have gas piped into houses within the year, and water within two years."

He gazed at the immaculate counters and spotless floor and marveled again at her, thinking he hadn't ever known a woman quite like her. Dulcie earned her keep and now ran her own house, but she didn't work as hard as Mary O'Malley.

"Sit down and let me do that," he said, taking her hand and pushing her toward a chair.

She laughed. "Why is it you're always trying to get me to stop working?"

"You work too hard."

"That's not true. Getting cups of cider isn't work."

"Do you ever just sit and gaze into space and watch clouds float past?"

"I guess I don't very often," she said, watching him as he sat down near her. "But I have an idea that you don't either."

"I have done it. Especially in my sheep-ranching days. I used to lie back and watch clouds change shapes and dream." He looked down and caught her staring at him, and realized his shirt was open at the throat and the old scar was showing.

"I got hurt one time when I was ranching," he said quietly.

Mary's cheeks burned, and she was embarrassed that he had caught her looking at his scar. "I'm sorry. I didn't mean to stare. I have my own scars. It looks as if you were hurt badly."

"I was," he said solemnly with a strange note in his voice, and she realized he didn't want to discuss it.

"I have a scar from Michael trying to shoot a bow and arrow at the spring house. Instead, he shot me."

"Badly?"

She laughed and shook her head. "No, but he did the cooking for me for two weeks afterward."

Dan grinned. "Where's your scar?"

Suddenly she wished she hadn't brought up the matter. Her cheeks flamed and she looked down at her cider. "You can't see it."

"Oh? Sort of unmentionable?" he teased.

"Michael likes to box. I don't know why my brothers are so . . . physical. I hope if I ever marry, I have little girls."

"Well, the scar can't be on your foot, or you'd show me," he persisted.

"Mr. Castle, I'm sorry I mentioned it!"

He looked at her, and they both laughed, because

she knew he was teasing her. "Where was the sheep ranch?"

"In New Mexico Territory," he said, deciding he could trust her. There was something disarming about her, and he couldn't imagine she would gossip.

"Tell me about San Antonio."

Dan was thankful he had ridden through there once and could talk about the town. It was one in the morning when he finally told Mary good night. She followed him to the back door, feeling a forlorn longing for Silas. It had been good to have a man in the house, to have someone her age to talk to.

"Good night," he said. "Silas will come back before you know it."

"Thanks for your help. You're a good man, Mr. Castle," she said.

"I'll remind you of that next time you toss a skillet at me," he said with a grin, and winked at her. She watched him stride away, thinking Silas had chosen well to send money home with someone like Dan. He was good, and she was grateful to have the house rebuilt, knowing it was taking him away from his regular work. She smiled and closed the door, and then remembered Dan's remark about her age—seventeen! What a child he must think she was. Humming the waltz, she rinsed their cups, then dried her hands and waltzed around the kitchen with her hands held out, remembering how nice it had been to dance with him. She smiled to herself while she recalled his blue eyes and golden hair.

Each evening Dan stayed and did repairs on the O'Malley house. He spent one evening with Brian at his side while both worked on the house, and another with Paddy singing and telling him stories of his childhood in Ireland. Sometimes Dan and Brian would hammer boards into place while Paddy whittled, scraps of wood falling at his feet.

With the work on the O'Malley house still going on, Dan was spending all his waking hours on construction. He stopped once in the morning for breakfast at Dulcie's and told her what he was doing, but otherwise he hadn't been to her place in quite a few days. He was getting in before midnight and leaving before sunup. He had moved into his house now, and although it was sparsely furnished, he was happy to be in it. His new brougham carriage had been delivered and he would use the topless buggy to get about town easily when the weather was good. Friday he got ready to go to the barn dance, knowing that Louisa Shumacher would be there with Reuben and that on Saturday night she would go with him.

He dressed in a dark blue woolen shirt and blue denim pants. The weather had warmed and the snow was melting. He took the O'Malley steps two at a time and raised the knocker to let it fall.

Brian opened the door. "Come in, Mr. Castle. Mary will be here right away. I was just leaving," he said, setting a flannel cap on his head. "See you at the dance."

"Sure, Brian."

Mary looked at herself in the mirror. She didn't want to go to a barn dance, and the memories of that first terrible dance after Silas left still plagued her. She didn't want to draw attention to herself, and had dressed as plainly as if she were going down to work in the kitchen. It wasn't as if she were going with Silas. She could imagine Silas extracting a promise from Dan Castle to take her out, and if she hadn't come to like Dan and consider him a friend, she would have flatly refused. As it was, she would go to please Dan and Silas, and it would be over and done.

She ran her hand across the braid that wrapped around her head. She wore a blue gingham dress that was two years old, still in good condition, but not her best by any manner. Taking her cape, she went down the hall. "Brian?"

"He's gone, Mary," Dan Castle answered in a voice several notches deeper than Brian's tenor.

"I'm sorry. I didn't realize you were waiting."

"You look pretty," Dan said politely, wondering if she ever let her hair down or if she slept with a braid wrapped around her head.

"Thank you." She paused in front of him. "I know you're doing this for Silas. And you really don't have to, you know."

"I agree with him that you need to get out. I don't think you have much fun, and while you'll have all the fun you want when he gets back, it doesn't help now. I'm a poor substitute, but I'll do my best," he said with a grin, making her laugh.

"You're a fine substitute."

He helped her into a woolen coat and took her arm. At the barn, music played and people mingled and danced on the hard dirt floor while potbellied stoves warmed the air. Dan took her coat, placed it on a stack of garments, and they sauntered toward the crowd. A man blocked their way, and Mary's heart seemed to miss a beat as she looked into Dewar Logan's dark eyes.

8

"Well, if it ain't little Miss O'Malley with a new beau," Dewar said, his gaze sweeping over Dan.

"Mr. Castle, this is Dewar Logan. Mr. Castle is a friend of Silas'," she said stiffly. Neither man offered to shake hands with the other.

"Sure thing. Right cozy. You can take in his friends as boarders and go dancing with them."

"If you'll excuse us," Dan said coolly, and Dewar's gaze snapped back to him.

Dewar moved sideways, his gaze raking insolently over Mary. "There's just no understanding some men's tastes in women," he said quietly.

With her hand on his arm, Mary felt Dan's muscles tense. She clutched his arm and tugged. "Please, ignore him."

Hearing the plea in her voice, Dan relaxed. "What's between you two? Or is he that way to everyone?"

"He's probably that way to women who have refused him," she said stiffly, spots of color flooding her cheeks, and Dan realized Mary had a hard life in more ways than just working long hours running a boardinghouse. Once again he silently cursed Silas for refusing to return to her until he was a millionaire.

"I'll forget him, Mary, if that's what you want. Or I'll go back and—"

"No! Please. I can't bear another scene with him!"

"Oh? He's caused you trouble before?" Without waiting for her answer, he wound his fingers in hers and headed toward the dancers. "There's a nice slow waltz. Come dance with me."

For the first turn around the floor, he remained silent, letting her concentrate on dancing, but halfway around the barn, he realized she was doing fine, following his lead effortlessly. He saw Louisa dance past across the floor, and he winked at her, receiving a smile in return. She was held close in Reuben's arms, and Dan longed for the evening to pass and Saturday to come, when she would be in his arms. When he looked at her, all the other women at the dance seemed plain.

Mary glanced up and saw Dan wink. Following his gaze, she discovered Louisa Shumacher looking back at him with a smile. Mary found Louisa Shumacher to be unfriendly and as beautiful and cold as the moon, but perhaps Louisa had another side she presented to men. A mild regret stirred in Mary, that Louisa was the woman who had caught Dan's fancy. He deserved better, Mary thought, until she silently laughed at herself. Louisa was the most beautiful woman in Denver, and every man in town would be happy to have her attention. There was no need to feel the slightest stir of sympathy where Dan and Louisa were concerned.

"You dance like you've been doing it every week all your life," he said, smiling at her.

"Thank you. I love to dance. When I hurt my leg in a wagon accident years ago, I thought I wouldn't be able to do anything, but I was determined I could, so I tried and tried, and finally I could run and dance. I still have a limp, but it doesn't bother me."

The musicians began a schottische. "Shall we?" Dan asked.

"I'm not as sure about this."

"I am. You'll do fine."

Across the room Louisa watched them, wondering why Dan Castle had brought someone like Mary Katherine O'Malley to the dance. It annoyed her, and made her less anxious to go with him Saturday.

As if he could read her thoughts, Reuben voiced them aloud. "Look at that. The best the man can do is take Mary O'Malley from the boardinghouse. No doubt where he's staying.''

"He moved into his new house, which is only six blocks from us. And he told me he came to Denver because of Silas Eustice. He's probably brought Mary O'Malley tonight because of the friendship with Mr. Eustice.''

"Hah! He's brought her because she's the only woman who would consent to come with him.''

Anger suffused Louisa and she turned to face Reuben. "Look around the room, Reuben. Half the young women here watch him constantly and would have come with him if he had asked.''

"That's not so, Louisa.''

"Look at Marvella right now. And Carrie. They're practically following him.''

Reuben's face flushed and his scowl deepened. "I've heard he lives with one of the soiled doves in town.''

"Reuben! You shouldn't tell me such things.''

His annoyance vanished and he gave her a sardonic smile. "Louisa, you love gossip more than any woman I know.''

She was annoyed, but equally curious. She watched Dan swinging Mary O'Malley on his arm, then part with her as they danced.

"Who is she?''

"Who? The soiled dove? She's a very beautiful woman. Dulcie is her name. Castle built her house for her.''

The last statement sent a ripple of discontent through Louisa. She didn't care to share any man with another woman, yet at the same time, Dan Castle was exciting. The fact that he had a woman who was beautiful and a harlot only added to his mystique.

"Dulcie? I know who she is,'' Louisa said, remembering seeing her in the store. "She's much older than he is. She's not so beautiful,'' Louisa said carefully, remembering seeing Dulcie fall on her backside on the ice, her skirts flying high and revealing trim ankles.

Reuben laughed. "She's startlingly beautiful. I've

seen her. You can't admit there's another beautiful woman in Denver, Louisa.''

"If you don't stop, I'll wave to Mr. Castle and dance with him the next dances!"

Reuben smiled and took the cup of hot rum from her hands. "No, you won't." He moved through the crowd, his hand firmly on her elbow as he steered her beside him. They stepped outside, away from the others, and Louisa's pulse began to race because she liked Reuben's kisses. He turned her into his arms, the warmth of his body protecting her from the cold.

"You won't dance the rest of the dances with him, Louisa, because you like what I can give you. You know the woman I decide to marry will lead Denver society, and she'll live like a princess. A man like Castle can never give you all I can." Reuben bent his head to kiss her, his arm banding her waist, his other hand plunging beneath the neckline of her dress to fondle her.

She murmured and struggled, but he held her tighter, his fingers brushing her nipple, his kisses deepening until she sagged against him and finally tightened her arms to kiss him back. He released her, gazing down at her with smoldering eyes.

"You're meant to be mine, Louisa. Don't ever forget it."

"You're an arrogant man, Reuben Knelville," she replied, but there was a breathlessness to her voice, a flirting taunt in her words that made him smile.

"We'll go back now."

"And everyone will know you've kissed me. And that's just what you wanted, isn't it, Reuben? You want Dan Castle to know you've kissed me."

"Don't ever use him to tease me, Louisa," he said coldly, and she bit back a reply. There were moments when Reuben frightened her, yet his arrogance and strength and threats excited her. And she wanted him to fight Dan Castle. It seemed the most exciting thing in the world to have two handsome men fighting over her.

"Don't be afraid of the man, Reuben! It isn't like

you," she said, teasing him, knowing it would infuriate him.

"You little witch. Just for that, Louisa, I'm going to dance the next dance with Marian Comber. Excuse me, my dear," he said, and left her.

Instantly two young men appeared at her side, and while Louisa smiled at them and politely entered their conversation, she silently fumed over Reuben's self-assurance. She would like to bring him to his knees, to have him pay homage to her like other men in town, like Darrell and Wayne, who were talking to her now, hanging on her every word, obeying her slightest wish. She watched Reuben waltz with Marian. He laughed with her over something, and anger streaked in Louisa like lightning. Her gaze fell on Dan and she gave him a wide smile. He took Mary O'Malley's hand and stopped dancing, crossing the floor to join Wayne, Louisa, and Darrell. Louisa nodded coolly at Mary O'Malley, who gave her a brief hello in turn. They talked about the cold weather, and when someone asked Mary to dance, Dan turned to Louisa.

"Louisa, may I have this dance?"

"Of course," Louisa said, delighted, fighting the urge to see if Reuben were watching. They moved to the dance floor and she smiled up at Dan.

"I can't wait for tomorrow night," he said softly. "Then I'll be here with the most beautiful woman in the West."

"Thank you! I'm surprised to see you with Miss O'Malley. She doesn't go to dances."

"Silas is my best friend. I promised I'd take her out sometime. A brotherly task," he said.

He whirled her around and she looked for Reuben. To her amazement, she didn't see him, and as she conversed and danced with Dan, coyly flirting with him, she realized Reuben was nowhere in the barn. The only place he could be was outside, and the only reason to be outside was to kiss Marian! Rage momentarily shook Louisa. She was furious with Reuben. She tried to remember to pay attention to Day, to smile at him, to laugh at the right moments, but it was difficult to keep from leaving the dance floor to search for Reuben.

"Did you attend school in Denver?"

"Good heavens, no! Denver's so new. I went to school in St. Louis after my family moved here. I think in a few more years we'll have fine schools here."

"Someday, Miss Shumacher, I'll make you stop searching for Reuben Knelville."

Startled, she gazed up into his solemn features, a smoldering desire blatant in his blue eyes, and her heart skipped several beats. "I'm not searching for him."

"Tomorrow night seems years away."

"Yet actually it's only hours."

"I'd like to dance you right out that door to my carriage and take you away with me," he said. Amusement shone in his eyes, and she didn't know if he were merely flirting, telling the same thing to other women, or if he meant it.

"You would be hauled back to Denver and locked in jail if you did. Or worse."

"Someday, Miss Shumacher, someday . . ." He let his words trail away, but the intense, searing look he gave her made her breathless. His voice changed and a smile lifted the corner of his mouth. "And in the meantime, I have finally made you forget him."

"So I did! Reuben has a temper, Mr. Castle. Be careful you don't irritate him."

"I'm not afraid of Reuben Knelville."

"Perhaps you should be. Most of the men here are for one reason or another. He's a good fighter, and his father is a powerful man in town."

"Speaking of fathers, I talked to yours for a long time tonight."

"Did you really? Where was Miss O'Malley? I can't imagine Mama spending idle conversation on that child."

"That child is a very capable woman," he answered with amusement, wondering if Louisa Shumacher had the slightest idea what kind of life Mary O'Malley led. "Actually, Mary was talking to two of her friends at the time."

The music ended, but Louisa gripped his arm. "We'll dance once more."

"So you can make Reuben jealous," Dan said, not caring what reason she had, happy to have her in his arms.

"Perhaps," she said, giving him a smile.

"Or perhaps . . . ? What other reason?"

"I shan't say another word!" A schottische commenced and they danced too fast to talk. Her eyes sparkled and her cheeks became pink from the exertion. He longed to crush her in his arms and kiss her until she succumbed to him. He glimpsed Reuben standing on the sidelines watching them, a frown furrowing his brow. Dan knew he would have trouble again from Knelville, but he didn't care. Louisa was worth the trouble.

When the dance ended, he returned her to the sidelines, where Reuben claimed her at once. Dan found Mary talking to two of her friends.

"Sorry I was gone so long," he said.

"I didn't mind. You may dance with Miss Shumacher the rest of the night if you like."

He laughed. "You're generous with my time, Mary."

"Miss O'Malley, may I have a dance?" Dewar Logan blocked their path.

Before she could answer, Dan said, "I'm sorry, Mr. Logan. She's promised me every dance for the rest of the night. If you'll excuse us . . ."

"Let me hear the lady say it. Is that right, Miss O'Malley?"

"The lady has promised, and I'm holding her to her promise," Dan said cheerfully, and he stared evenly at Dewar. The two men glared at each other and Mary held her breath, afraid of what either might do, but then Dewar nodded and moved past Dan.

"Go ahead and dance with the shanty Irish."

Dan clamped his hand on Dewar's shoulder and spun him around. "Apologize to the lady," he said quietly.

"Mr. Castle, no!" Mary exclaimed in embarrassment.

"She heard me," Dewar said, clenching his fists. "Get your hand off my shoulder."

Dan squeezed, pressing on a muscle, and Dewar swung. Dan stepped back, ducking, then followed with a lightning right that connected and sent Dewar sprawling. A woman screamed and men moved back as Dewar yelled and lunged back at Dan.

"There's your gentleman," said Reuben scornfully, pausing on the dance floor to watch the fight.

"Everyone knows what a troublemaker that Logan is," Louisa said, watching the fight, gratified to see Dan handling Dewar easily. "It looks as if Mr. Castle is able to protect himself. He must be terribly strong."

In minutes order was restored, while Dewar Logan lay unconscious on the floor and Dan took Mary's arm, moving her away from Logan.

"You're hurt!"

"It's nothing," he said, dabbing at his bleeding lip with his handkerchief while she told him about that long-ago dance when Silas first left Denver and how she had refused to leave with Dewar.

"Serves Logan right. I should have given him a swift kick for good measure."

"You've made an enemy."

"It won't be the first one," he said dryly. "Let's dance. People won't talk as much if you look as if nothing has happened."

She laughed. "You're the most patient man I've ever known. You don't have to be here doing any of this. You didn't have to defend me."

"Oh, I know that, Mary Katherine O'Malley! You could have handled Dewar Logan and me at the same time."

She laughed up at him as they waltzed. "I've had a good time tonight. I'm sorry he caused trouble and that you're hurt, but it's been fun."

"It has been fun, and you dance as well as the best of them."

His words made her warm and she smiled at him. It was divine to dance with him, to move with the music and forget her responsibilities. "You were a good instructor."

"When Silas returns, will you both stay in Denver?"

She gazed into the distance, her profile to him. "I don't know." Green eyes met his. "Tomorrow doesn't exist for me. I never think about the future."

"You think about his returning to you, don't you?"

"Only that he will, not when or how. There's really only today and yesterday."

"And sometimes it would be nice to get rid of yesterdays," he said, thinking about his past.

"Your yesterdays weren't good?" she asked, wondering who the women or woman was in his past.

"They were good when you were with Silas. I'm sorry I asked. I didn't mean to pry."

"You can ask me anything you please," he said gently, smiling down at her, and she thought there couldn't be a more handsome man in the entire country. She was aware of the women who had watched him all evening, including Louisa Shumacher. But what was nicer than his appearance was the man himself. He was fun and capable and kind. And even though she should have released him from his promise to Silas to take her out, she was glad he had, because it had been the most fun she had had in a long time.

They danced half a dozen or more dances and finally she knew the hour was late and Dan had gone far beyond the call of duty in dancing with her all evening long. "We should go home now," she said as the dance ended. "You've carried out your duty beyond measure."

"It wasn't duty. It was fun," he said, running his hand lightly along her jaw. "Silas is a fortunate man."

She smiled. "Said by the man who has had half the women here tonight watching him all evening."

He laughed. "That's absurd! Let's stay a little longer. I like to dance." And, he thought, he liked to watch Louisa, to be near her. There might be an opportunity for one more dance with her.

By the time he helped Mary into his carriage, it was

half-past midnight. They sang on the way home, Dan's bass sometimes warbling off-key, Mary's lilting voice carrying the melody in spite of his monotone.

When they reached the boardinghouse, he jumped down, lifting her down with his hands on her waist.

"It was fun, Mr. Castle. And I appreciate your carpentry on my house," she said, gazing at the new walls.

"It was fun for me too, Mary. I ought to ride out after Silas and bring him back here."

"You would have to do so at gunpoint, I'm afraid," she said with a sad note of longing, and Dan silently vowed to avoid mentioning Silas unless she brought up the conversation herself.

He ran his hands beneath her coat collar. "Someday soon, I'm going to show you my house."

"I'd like that," she answered.

"I never dreamed I'd be a builder, and it still amazes me. I like it."

"You're very good at it. And you've been so good to us," she said softly, knowing there was to be another barn dance tomorrow night and that he would take Louisa Shumacher.

He gazed into her large eyes, and he didn't want to tell her good night. He liked to be with her, just to talk to her, and now, gazing down on her in the dark night, he felt drawn to her more than ever. On impulse, he kissed her cheek. Her skin was soft, and she smelled sweet.

"Good night, Mr. Castle," she said, gazing up at Dan, tingling where his lips had brushed her cheek.

"See you Monday," he called, and turned to go.

She lay in bed that night, for the first time in several years thinking about a man other than Silas. She remembered dancing in Dan Castle's arms, hearing his laughter, watching him talk to people, dance, and laugh. She gazed into the moon-splashed darkness and wondered why he didn't want to remember his past. What had happened to him that was so bad? She remembered his remark about sheep ranching and the strange brief look that had crossed his face when she quizzed him about it. Many men who came west hid their pasts, and she suspected Dan Castle was one of them.

April Danby McCloud, Dan's sister, lay in bed, her golden hair spread over the pillows behind her head while she watched her husband, Noah, shave. He was bare to the waist, his thick black hair curling on his forehead.

"Noah, I had another letter from Javier yesterday."

"Mmmm," Noah said, preoccupied with shaving.

"I worry about him. And I worry about Hattie."

"April, you can't do anything about your mother and stepfather. It's her decision to leave him and never go back."

"But it was over me, and I've forgiven him."

Noah turned, blue eyes softening as he studied his wife. "You're generous, April."

"I can afford to be. I'm the happiest woman on earth," she said softly.

"Stop that or I won't be able to finish shaving," he commanded in gentle tones.

"It's the truth. I want her to go back to him. He said he's regretted for years that he took me away from her and gave me to the women in Santa Fe."

"He separated you from your family, your mother, your half brothers, Luke and Dan, for all your growing-up years. It's difficult to feel sympathy for Javier Castillo."

"But he and Hattie love each other."

"Loved. Past tense." Noah rinsed his face and wiped off his razor before carefully putting it away. April watched him, her eyes moving over his strong muscles, his smooth tanned skin and slim hips. He was tough, so strong, and exciting to her.

She patted the bed. "Noah, come here."

He rubbed his jaw with a towel and glanced over his shoulder at her and tossed down the towel. "Sure thing, April," he answered. He sat on the edge of the bed, placing his hands on either side of her. Her bare shoulders showed above the covers, and he studied her.

"Noah, can we go to San Antonio and see Hattie, let me talk to her again?"

"If you'd like."

She ran her hands along his strong arms. "You're good to me."

"You're good to me and good for me," he answered in a husky voice, desire burning in his eyes.

"Can you get away?"

"Yes, you know I can. Duero can run everything."

"You're going to have one of the biggest hotels in the West soon."

"I wish Dan were building it. At least the plans are his."

"Between the saloons and the hotel, you're going to be a busy man."

"I have good men working for me who can take charge if I'm not there. When do you want to go to San Antonio?"

"As soon as you can. Noah, I'd like to bring Hattie back with us if she'll come. I think Luke keeps her angry with Javier."

Noah drew his fingers along April's bare shoulder, his mind only half on their discussion. "Your brother Luke is a hard man. He had a hard past and he's unbending about Javier. I can't say I really blame him. I don't know why you're so forgiving."

"Because Dan has told me how much in love Hattie and Javier were. I understand that. I couldn't live without you, Noah."

The last vestige of interest in their conversation vanished. He gathered her into his arms to kiss her. When he released her, she gazed into his eyes, her fingers trailing over his bare chest. "If she's here and sees that I can forgive Javier, perhaps she can."

"Away from Luke's influence, she might relent. You can try, honey, but I wouldn't interfere too much."

"I won't interfere. Look at Luke. He doesn't have a kind word for Javier. It's torn the family apart. It hurts Dan because he loves his father as well as his mother. I hate it, because I know Hattie isn't happy. It keeps Luke angry." Her thoughts switched to Luke and the latest letters from his wife, Catalina. "I wonder if Luke will ever run for governor."

"I've told you—he talked to me a long time about it. Men want him to run, but he says he won't, and I don't think he'll change his mind. He doesn't want all the family secrets aired, particularly anything about Dan."

"Or my past either. I hope Luke doesn't really want to be governor, because Dan and I will keep him from it."

"I don't think he does. He likes the law practice, he's happy with Catalina and his family."

"How soon can we go? I'll write to them."

"As soon as you like," he said softly, drawing his hand along her shoulder. "We can leave Friday."

"I'll see Luke's best friend Ta-ne-haddle and Lottie again. It's impossible to think of them settling into a house."

"Not half as odd as Ta-ne-haddle becoming a rancher."

"Lottie probably rides with him."

"Lottie is chasing their children. How's it feel to have a little one named for you?"

"Very nice. If Hattie comes home with us, I'm going to write and tell Javier."

"You and Luke both should stay out of it. Let her make up her own mind."

"I won't beg her to return. I just want her to know that I've forgiven him. It doesn't accomplish a thing to make him suffer now. Aaron will be excited about going. He thinks his uncles are the most wonderful men in the world. Next to you, I think the man he loves the most is his Uncle Luke."

"For a stern man, Luke is good with children."

"Noah, that brings up something else." She ran her pale fingers along his tan arm. "I didn't have any family when I was growing up. I want Aaron to have brothers and sisters."

Noah's eyes darkened as he looked into hers. "You want another baby?"

"Don't you?"

He pulled her to him to kiss her, giving her his answer in his embrace, while April wrapped her arms around his neck, temporarily forgetting her family's problems.

Three weeks later they arrived in San Antonio, coming in along the wide green river, passing the missions that were almost two centuries old now. April could ride into town without painful memories. When she thought of the boy she had first loved, Emilio Piedra, it seemed so distant, something that had involved two children who were in love. She turned to touch Noah, thankful for him, adoring him. He kept her happy and he was a wonderful father to Aaron. And she prayed they would have another baby. She wanted children, lots of babies. Noah glanced down at her, draping his arm around her shoulders. The wagon slowed and halted, and he climbed down, swinging her to the ground as the relatives poured out of the house to greet them.

April marveled at how unchanged Hattie stayed, looking very much as she always had. Her yellow hair was now sprinkled with gray, but her skin was unlined, tanned from San Antonio's warm sun.

April hugged Catalina and Luke. Ta-ne-haddle and Lottie had also ridden to town and Ta-ne-haddle scooped April up in a tight hug. Next she turned to Lottie, who wore her black hair in one long braid. Her skin was dark as teak as she squeezed April and held April's namesake on her hip. The child gazed up with black eyes so different from April's wide blue ones, and April had to hold her.

After quick perfunctory hugs, Luke's boys wanted Aaron to go with them to look at a cave they had dug. They ran across the field, Dawn's black hair flying in the breeze. Knox and Jeff were growing tall, promising to be as tall as their father, and Aaron struggled to keep up with the older children.

It wasn't until almost suppertime, when Luke stood up and said he would go find the children, that April saw a chance to talk with him alone. She stood up quickly, excusing herself. "I'll join you, in case Aaron wants to argue," she said, smiling because she knew her gentle son wouldn't argue with his Uncle Luke.

As they left the house, Luke draped his arm across her shoulders. "Noah's good for you."

"I adore him, Luke. I can't imagine life without him."

"We're lucky, April. I worry about Dan, though. I hope his past is buried forever."

"You need Catalina just as I need Noah. Luke," she said, moving in front of him to stop him, "I want to take Hattie home with me."

"You want her to go back to Javier," Luke said quietly.

"Yes, I do. I know you can't forgive him, but I can. I couldn't live without Noah."

"Noah wouldn't do to you what Javier did to Hattie. He hurt us all."

"He regrets it."

"The hell he does. He regrets losing Hattie. What would you do if Noah took Aaron from you and abandoned him? Answer me!"

"I can't answer a question like that."

"Yes, you can. You couldn't forgive him."

"I don't have to answer that. This isn't Noah and Aaron and me. It's Hattie. I forgive Javier. We can't undo the old hurts, but why keep Hattie and Javier apart now? He loves her deeply. Do you honestly think she's happier here than she would be with Javier?"

"Of course I do. I'm not keeping her chained here. She can go home anytime she wants."

"You know you stir up her anger with him."

"No, I don't April. Probably I did when we were first reunited with them and when she came home with us, but I don't now. It's their problem, not mine. I know that."

"Then let me ask her to come home with me."

"Sure, April. Go ahead and ask, but how you can forgive him, I'll never know."

"He's Dan's father, and Dan loves him. This hurts

Dan. It hurts Hattie. The children are growing up without knowing their grandfather.''

"I can't forgive him to that extent. If she goes back to him—"

"You let Knox, Jeff, and Emilio visit Hattie. Don't separate them from their grandfather.''

He patted her shoulder. "You're good, April. A lot more loving than I can be.''

She kissed his cheek. "Thanks, Luke.''

"And don't get your hopes up," he added. "She won't read his letters or answer them.''

"When are you and Catalina coming to visit?''

He laughed. "I don't know. We stay so damned busy. We talk about getting away, but then something always comes up. Hold your ears, I'll whistle for the boys.'' He whistled, a long sharp whistle that was answered in minutes by two short whistles.

"They're coming. We can go back.''

"Is there still talk you'll run for governor?''

"Sometimes, but it isn't serious. I won't do that. I don't want to. Catalina doesn't want the public life. And because of Dan, I don't think I should.''

"I think he's doing well in Denver.''

"I think so too. I'd like to come visit you, leave Catalina and the family there, and go on to Denver and see for myself how he's doing, but I wouldn't want to jeopardize the life he's established.''

"You wouldn't. He has a new name and a new identity.''

"It's safer if I don't." They heard footsteps and turned around to see the children running toward them across an open field behind the house.

"How they've grown!''

"If I can talk Catalina into it, I want to send Knox east to school in a few years. I want him to have a good education. He has the mind for it.''

"I couldn't bear to give up Aaron.''

"I haven't talked Catalina into it yet. Aaron isn't as old as Emilio. I'll miss him too. He's my companion. Emilio is the cowman. He spends half his time at the ranch with Ta-ne-haddle.''

"What about Dawn?" April asked, watching her run with the boys. "She's beautiful, Luke."

"She rides like Ta-ne-haddle, just like she was born on a horse's back. It's good to have you here, April. San Antonio has grown. I'll have to show you around, let you see some of the changes."

"Right now Aaron is too young to remember, but someday I want him to see the missions."

"There'll be time for that. All he's interested in now is trailing around behind the boys. If we had Dan here, everything would be complete. Do you ever hear from Melissa Hatfield?"

"Occasionally. She has three children and she never mentions Dan. I hope he finds someone to love as much as he loved Melissa."

"He will."

"You make it sound as if women are abundantly available."

"What's this about abundantly available women?" Catalina asked, stepping down to meet them, her gaze on Luke, a smile playing on the corners of her mouth.

"I said beautiful women are abundantly available. Look how many there are at my house!" Luke drawled.

"Abundant is one thing, Mr. Wordy Lawyer. *Available* is something else."

He laughed softly and hugged her against him, his features softening. Once again, April thought how lucky they had been.

9

On Saturday night, excitement rippled through Dan as he approached the Shumacher house. He leaned forward to gaze out the window of his new, elegantly carved, full-plated carriage with gracefully scrolled irons and English steel springs. He had hired a driver, Grizzly Jones, one of Dulcie's men, who kept peace at her house when necessary. Dan had never known if the name Grizzly came from the man's thick brown hair and beard or from his large size; he had carefully given instructions to Grizzly about what he wanted him to do. Usually as Dan drove through the new section of Denver, he noticed the houses, and studied their details, but tonight his mind wasn't on the imposing two-story or its dormer windows or shingled roof. Instead Louisa filled his thoughts, and his anticipation was rampant. It was the first opportunity he had had to escort her to a party. Stella, the Shumachers' maid, opened the door and ushered Dan into the front parlor, where Charles Shumacher waited. In minutes Hortense Shumacher joined them, and finally Louisa appeared in the doorway.

Dan felt as if the temperature jumped as he gazed at her. She was a vision to fill dreams, her black hair shining in the soft light, her cheeks pink. Her dress of blue gingham was cut in the latest fashion, clinging to her high, full breasts and her tiny waist. He longed to be alone with her, but as it was, all he could do was smile politely and greet her conventionally.

"Good evening, Miss Shumacher. You'll be the

most beautiful woman at the dance, without question.'' He turned to shake hands with Charles Shumacher. ''Sir, we'll go now and see you and Mrs. Shumacher at the dance.'' He turned to smile at Hortense Shumacher, who gazed back with a cool, level look, and he knew there was still one Shumacher whose approval he needed to win.

He followed Louisa into the hall, where Stella held their coats. Dan took Louisa's and held it, letting his hand brush across her nape, catching a whiff of a sweet scent of rosewater. In the carriage he pulled a lap robe over their knees, scooting close beside her and draping his arm around her shoulders.

''Cold?''

''A little,'' she said, gazing up at him intently and allowing him to pull her closer.

''I've been waiting for this evening.''

''I might as well warn you, Reuben may cause trouble. He's green that I'm going with another man tonight.''

''Reuben has full claim on you?''

''No! And it's time he realized it.''

Dan didn't care at all about Reuben Knelville. He touched Louisa's collar, letting his hand slide to her throat. Her skin was silken. ''You smell like roses.''

''I heard you and Reuben had an altercation last week,'' she said with a sly note of pleasure in her voice.

''It was nothing. Cyrus stopped us.'' He leaned down to kiss her throat, sliding his hand beneath the heavy coat to slip his arm around her waist.

''Mr. Castle!'' she whispered, yet Dan thought it was a perfunctory protest. She didn't resist or pull away.

''It's Dan. Call me Dan, Louisa.''

''That's much . . . too forward,'' she said, her words slowing as he kissed her ear, his hand caressing her nape. His blood drummed in his veins because she wasn't stopping him. She liked his kisses and he was thankful beyond measure he had instructed Grizzly to take a long route to the dance. And he was careful to avoid touching her hair, knowing she wouldn't want a hair out of place. He kissed her throat and she turned her head, looking at him with a smoldering gaze. "You shouldn't . . . I shouldn't let you."

"You like it, Louisa," he whispered gruffly. "Say my name."

"Dan," she said, closing her eyes.

He let his hand slip around, moving higher, feeling the soft thrust of her breast. His thumb slipped over her full breast across her taut nipple. She gasped, but she didn't push his hand away, and he continued to caress her, his manhood throbbing. He wanted to crush her against him, to push away the heavy coat and kiss her.

"Someday you'll be mine, Louisa. I'm going to kiss you all over."

"You shouldn't say such things to me," she whispered.

"Yes, I should, because you like it when I do. You like this, don't you?" he persisted, fondling her breasts.

She moaned softly, and he felt on fire. It was the first time since Melissa Hatfield that he had wanted a woman so desperately, refusing to face the fact that this one might be unattainable to him. He kissed her throat, then moved his lips to the corner of her mouth to touch her mouth with the tip of his tongue.

She moaned again and leaned away. Her breathing was rapid, her gaze lethargic. "You must stop. I can't go to the dance looking as if you tumbled me in the carriage."

He gazed down solemnly. "You won't look as if I had, because I'm being very careful. I'm not doing what I really want to do. I want to take down your hair and kiss you until you're on fire."

Her eyes closed as he talked, and he bent his head, nudging open her coat to kiss her breast, knowing she would feel his hot breath through the thin material of her dress and chemise. "I want to do this when you're bare in my arms."

"Dan," she said, and moved away with obvious reluctance. "You're a bold man. I don't want to arrive in your arms."

He gazed at her with amusement as she straightened her clothes, which weren't even slightly awry. She smoothed them with her hand, and suddenly Dan realized she was teasing him as she slid her hands beneath her breasts, watching him with narrowed eyes. Her cheeks turned pink as she gazed at him, because his desire was plainly evident.

He leaned forward, his hand brushing across her nipples. "You're as aroused as I am, Louisa," he said softly. He sat back, looking at her with a mocking smile. She leaned toward him, her eyes half-closed, expecting more caresses. She looked up, and blushed, scooting away and drawing her coat closed over her dress.

"You're a rascal, Dan Castle! You're much too bold."

He laughed, knowing she wasn't really protesting at all. The carriage slowed, and he turned, raising the leather flap to gaze out as they halted in front of the lighted barn. Dan climbed out and turned to swing Louisa down, holding her waist and pausing to smile at her. "Ready?"

As she nodded, he tucked her arm in his, striding to the barn, where a fiddler was playing. The sound of music and voices floated in the air.

They danced, and he was oblivious of others around him. They stopped once between dances to chat for a time with her parents, and Dan caught a glimpse of Reuben Knelville staring at him.

Louisa flirted with Dan constantly, making his pulse race. Her hands brushed him continually when they danced. He danced to the far side of the barn, where they were out of sight of her parents, took Louisa's hand, and hurried away to slip through the open back door.

She had stood in the same spot the night before with Reuben. Louisa gazed up at Dan, thinking he was the more handsome of the two men and the more exciting.

But Reuben was more powerful, and he was wealthy, something far more important.

"We shouldn't be out here."

"I want you, Louisa," Dan whispered, leaning forward, bending down to kiss her, stopping her protests. He crushed her to him, holding her close. One hand slid down her side, then up again over the full softness of her breast. She moaned and clung to him, sagging against him as he held her and kissed her passionately.

"Sir!" She pushed away. "I must go inside. If Papa caught me out here, I'd be in trouble forever."

A dark shadow appeared and Reuben paused in front of them. "Damn you, Castle. Take your hands off Louisa!"

He pushed Dan away from her, his fists clenching. Dan stepped back. He didn't want the scandal of a fight with Reuben, because it could ostracize him from society as a troublemaker.

"Reuben!"

Dan heard the note of pleasure in Louisa's voice and could have groaned, because it would only encourage Knelville.

"I won't fight you here," Dan said softly.

"You coward," Reuben said with a sneer.

"I won't unless you force me to," Dan rejoined, knowing he would either look terrible in Louisa's eyes or have to fight Reuben, because the man wasn't going to let it drop.

"Shall we go inside, Louisa?" Dan asked.

"Stay away from the silly coward, Louisa. She's coming with me."

"All right, Knelville," Dan said softly, stepping forward, his left fist shooting out. Knelville feinted, but Dan was ready, throwing a right that sent Knelville spinning. Instantly Dan's hand closed over Louisa's wrist. "Come on, Miss Shumacher."

He pulled her inside, expecting Reuben to catch up with him at any second. He swung Louisa into his arms to fall in with the dancers. A half-smile curved her lips.

"So you're not such a coward after all. I believe you knocked Reuben unconscious."

"No, I didn't," he said, thankful Reuben hadn't caught up with him before they reached the dance floor. "And you liked every moment of it, you wicked little beauty," he said softly. "You provoked him, Louisa."

"Who, me?" she asked with round-eyed innocence.

"And I'll make you pay for that," he threatened in a husky voice. "When we're in the carriage on the way home, you'll see what happens when you provoke sleeping lions."

Her eyes sparkled and her cheeks flushed. She laughed. "Should I be terrified?"

"It won't be terror I'll make you feel," he said, glancing over her shoulder to see Reuben standing on the fringe of the dancers. Except for a cut on his cheek, the only evidence of their brief altercation was the burning look of rage in Reuben's eyes as he gazed at Dan.

"Now I have a strong and powerful enemy."

"And does that frighten you?"

"You already know the answer. I do believe your parents are leaving."

She turned to glance over her shoulder as her mother waved. Louisa waved in return. "I have Papa's permission to stay out until midnight."

"We have an hour," Dan said. After two more dances, he led her to the door.

"We're going home."

"We have lots of time," she said with a pout. "The dance isn't over."

He held her coat. "We're leaving now, Louisa."

Louisa's heart fluttered. Dan Castle was an exciting, forceful man. The fight with Reuben had barely started before it was over, and she had no doubt that Reuben would retaliate in some manner. Reuben would be furious and jealous, and perhaps he would lose a little of his masterful arrogance. She gazed around the barn

and saw him watching her. She turned, giving Dan a
full smile.

"I'm ready."

Dan followed her glance, looking at Reuben, and a
little twinge of anger came over him. Louisa Shumacher was a troublemaker. But what a beautiful, exciting one! He slipped his arm around her. Grizzly had
been summoned, and waited with the carriage, and
Dan stepped up to the box to whisper instructions to
him before helping Louisa inside.

She gazed at him intently, and he realized she actually thought he was taking her home. For a moment
he credited Reuben Knelville as a man of little imagination. The carriage began to move, and Dan turned
so his knee pressed against hers.

"You wanted us to fight."

"Of course not!" she denied primly.

He rubbed his knee against hers, and pressed his
calf against hers while he laughed softly. "Of course
you did, Louisa." He leaned forward. "You didn't
care what kind of trouble it caused, as long as we
fought over you. You like to have power over men,
don't you?"

"Of course not," she answered breathlessly, her
hands pressed against his chest.

"Remember what I told you. You're not to goad
Reuben into fighting me again. Can you remember
that?"

She tilted her head to study him. "And if I do, what
then?"

"You may be the one destroyed, Louisa," he whispered, bending down to place his lips firmly on hers,
opening her mouth and crushing her to him while he
kissed her deeply. Her struggle was brief, gone almost
as swiftly as it started. He kissed her throat, and his
hands slid to her breasts to push away the soft material.

She gasped and clutched his wrists, but he bent his
head to stroke her nipples with his tongue, and she
moaned, all resistance stopping. He pushed away her
lacy chemise and kissed her, sucking and biting gently,

while he slipped one hand beneath her skirts to her thighs.

"Dan, please stop. You mustn't touch me."

"Oh, yes, Louisa. I must touch you. You set me on fire and I'm going to do the same to you. I want to touch you all over." His knees nudged hers apart, moving between them. In minutes she was gasping, crying out, clinging to him, and returning his kisses wildly.

"Marry me, Louisa," he asked all at once, gazing down at her. He wanted her, and marriage was the only way he could have a woman like Louisa Shumacher.

"I can't."

"Yes, you can. Marry me," he whispered, kissing her breasts, his hand moving between her legs. Marry me so I can love you night after night. Marry me."

"Yes, oh, please. Yes."

He stopped all at once and tilted her face up. "You mean it. Look at me, Louisa. Will you marry me?"

She raised her lashes. Never had Reuben made love to her like Dan Castle. His kisses had never been as fiery, and he wasn't as forceful or as seductive. For a moment she forgot about wealth and power. "Yes, I mean it," she said, knowing if she changed her mind, she could get out of the engagement later. Right now, she wanted him to kiss her again. She burned with longing for him.

"Oh, Louisa," he said, feeling as if he would burst with happiness. "You are the most beautiful woman on earth!"

"Kiss me now, Dan. Please . . ."

He kissed her, pulling her onto his lap, pushing her skirts away to caress her legs, touching her intimately, making her cry out with ecstasy, yet knowing she wouldn't allow him to possess her until they were married.

Finally she pushed against him and scooted away. "You are a rascal. How can I go home disheveled like this? Mama waits up for me."

"We can stop. I'll show you my house and you can get your clothes in order."

"I'll be scandalized if I'm caught in your house at this hour."

"Be daring, Louisa. You won't be caught. We'll go in the back."

He hadn't planned on bringing her to his house, but he instructed Grizzly of the change. A fire still burned low in the grate, and Dan drew the heavy drapes. "This will be your house someday, Louisa."

He pushed her coat off her shoulders while she gazed around. "It's beautiful," she breathed, thinking it truly was one of the grandest houses in town. He had little furniture. There was a horsehair sofa covered in blue velvet, and a wooden rocking chair. He carried her to the sofa. "We still have half an hour before midnight. Let me look at you," he said. He untied the ribbons to her bodice, unfastened the pearl buttons, and pushed away her dress. He bent his head to kiss her, and she gasped, winding her fingers in his hair. She watched him through narrowed eyes. He was exciting. Her parents would never consent to his proposal when they had known each other for such a short time, but she was still interested in him. He had an elegant house, a better one than Reuben could build at present. Dan's hand slid beneath her skirt and she lost her train of thought. She succumbed to his caresses momentarily, until he pushed her skirts high.

She scooted away so quickly she almost toppled him off the settee.

"No! We have to stop!"

Dan wanted to push her down and seduce her, but he understood why she wanted to wait. And for the first time that night, he heard the unmistakable note of firmness in her voice.

He watched her in a steady gaze while she dressed.

"Dan, I can't go home looking like this."

"There's a pier glass in my bedroom. It's the last room in the hall on the right."

She left, and he moved around the room as he tucked his shirt into his pants. He was engaged to Louisa

Shumacher. He would have to ask her father for her hand, but she had consented. He had asked in haste, and she had consented in haste, but he wasn't going to worry about that. He wanted her, and he would have to marry her to get her. He thought he would float off the earth with happiness. She was all he had ever dreamed of, exciting, educated, and beautiful. She was the envy of Denver society, and if they wed, he wouldn't have to worry about his future.

But at the moment he couldn't concentrate on his future. All he could think about was her breathtakingly beautiful body. He ached to possess her, praying there wouldn't be any reason for her father to refuse to allow the wedding.

She reappeared. "I'll be late getting home, and Mama will be furious."

"You look beautiful and you don't look as if you've been so much as kissed on the cheek."

"Whereas we've actually done much more," she said, assessing him, her eyes drifting down below his belt.

He crossed the room to her, reaching for her, but she stepped back. "Oh, no! I'm all neat and ready to appear for Mama's inspection."

He laughed. "We're engaged, Louisa. Do you remember you promised to marry me?"

"I remember," she said. She was charmed by him, and wondered if her father would be too. "My father may have something to say about it."

"I'll talk to him as soon as possible. You'll be mine soon."

Tingles raced through her as she remembered the past hour and listened to his words. He was exciting beyond measure. Her mother would be enraged, but she would consider her daughter's wishes in the matter. Her father would be more likely to approve. She glanced at the house once again, thankful it was so elegant.

"Mama wants me to marry Reuben."

"And your father?"

"I hope you can persuade him."

"I will," Dan said confidently, knowing he would do anything to marry her. He wasn't going to let the second love in his life slip away.

"I must go home."

He held her coat, turning her to face him. "We'll have fun. I promise you."

She laughed. "When Reuben learns about this, he may come to fight."

"To hell with Reuben," he whispered, kissing her. "I don't want to stop touching you."

She pushed away. "If you don't, I'll appear mussed." Her mind raced over how to break the news to Reuben. She wanted to be the one to do it. Engaged. It was both frightening and exhilarating, and she couldn't stop thinking of Dan Castle's lovemaking.

"My father will want to meet your family. You have a brother, don't you?"

"Yes, in Texas," he said, wondering if he would ever be able to reveal his past to her, to introduce her to Hattie or Javier.

When he took her home, he stepped inside. Charles Shumacher appeared at the door of the parlor.

"You're ten minutes late," he said, gazing sternly at his pocket watch.

"Sorry, sir, we were stuck in a drift of snow as we left the dance. "Thank you, Miss Shumacher, for a lovely evening."

"You're welcome, and thank you, Mr. Castle."

"Mr. Shumacher, may I have a word with you?"

"Of course. Step into the parlor."

"Good night," Dan said again to Louisa, his voice softening. He followed Shumacher into the parlor and waited while he closed the door to the hall.

"Sir, I'd like a word with you privately. If this is a poor time because of the lateness of the hour—"

"No, Mr. Castle. Go ahead. Why did you want to see me?"

"I like Denver and have a thriving business started."

Charles Shumacher stopped stoking the fire and turned to study Dan. As he looked at Dan's broad shoulders, he wondered if the young man wanted to borrow money, to build a house for them, or to ask for his endorsement among his friends.

"I know you do. I've heard about your work," he said, poking the coals, watching sparks dance up the chimney. He put away the poker and faced Dan.

"I expect to settle here, to be successful here. I think my prospects are good, because I think the town's prospects are good."

"True enough."

"I'd like to ask for Louisa's hand in marriage."

Charles Shumacher's jaw dropped, and Dan realized the man hadn't expected such a request at all.

"I can provide for her well, and in the manner to which she is accustomed. Frankly, sir, I expect to have a successful building career."

"You've surprised me, young man. You and Louisa barely know each other."

"That's true, but I know my feelings are strong for her."

"I'll have to think about your proposal, discuss it with Louisa and her mother. I'm a father who wants his daughter to be happy."

"Yes, sir. I rather imagined you were."

"We'll talk it over among ourselves, and you and I'll talk further on the matter. Mr. Castle, we know nothing of your family. As you know, Louisa has been squired by Reuben Knelville for some time now. The Knelvilles are family friends."

"My parents are gone," Dan said. He hated lying to everyone, and for an instant he was tempted to reveal the truth about his past to Charles Shumacher. But he had grown too wary of people to relent so easily. "I have a brother who is a lawyer in Texas. He's been a United States marshal."

"A lawyer. What's his name?"

"Luke Danby. We're half-brothers."

"I see. It makes it more difficult when we don't know your family. We're protective of Louisa, but as I'm sure you realize, she is our only daughter and she is a beautiful young woman. I expect her to marry well.''

''Yes, sir.''

''And you haven't known her long. I would insist on a long engagement.''

''Yes, sir. Whatever you say,'' Dan said, wanting to groan. He wanted Louisa now, but if he had to wait, so be it.

''Why don't we discuss this in a week. Say, next Thursday afternoon at four?''

''Yes, sir. That would be fine,'' Dan said, determined to be agreeable, no matter how difficult.

''I've heard rumors you and Reuben have fought. I don't want a breath of scandal attached to Louisa.''

''Yes, sir.''

''And she must not be late arriving home again.''

''Yes, sir. I take full blame for that.''

''Yes. Well, until Thursday, Mr. Castle.''

''It's Dan, sir,'' he said, crossing the room and shaking hands with Shumacher. ''I would take good care of her, sir. I adore her.''

''We'll see. Good night, Mr. Castle.''

Dan left, aware that the Shumachers might be more of an obstacle than he had thought. He wanted to shout with joy, yet he was half-afraid to, until next Thursday, when he talked to Charles Shumacher.

He jumped up on the box and gave Grizzly a squeeze. ''It is a beautiful night, Grizzly, old friend, and if anyone asks you, we got stuck in a drift at the dance and that's why Miss Shumacher was a few minutes late arriving home.''

''Yes, sir.''

Dan laughed. ''Shall we go home? I'll drop you off at the house.'' For the first time he thought of Dulcie. He would have to tell her about Louisa Shumacher. He dreaded it, yet Dulcie had steadfastly refused every marriage proposal presented to her.

He paid Grizzly and strode toward the back door. Music wafted from the house, smoke spiraled from the chimney, and suddenly Dan thought he should tell Dulcie now. Music and laughter came from the two parlors, and the deep voices of the men mingled with the high laughter of the women. Dan saw Dulcie leaning against the piano. Her gaze met his, and she smiled, crossing the room to him.

He felt a pang. Dulcie was a friend above all else, but he couldn't explain that to Louisa. Dulcie could no longer be part of his life, and he dreaded breaking the news to her.

"Hi, stranger."

"Hi, Dulcie. I brought Grizzly home."

"And did you and little Miss Shumacher have fun?"

To his surprise, he realized Dulcie was slightly tipsy. He had never seen her that way before. "Yes, we did," he said evenly. "I'll come back tomorrow, Dulcie."

"Relax, Dan. Come down to the room and have a little brandy with me."

"I'll be back."

She linked her arm in his. "Come on. You can stay with me a few minutes."

He shed his coat while she closed the door. He poured two brandies and handed her one.

"To old times, Dan."

"To old times, Dulcie," he said, gulping down the brandy, feeling the fiery liquid burn his throat.

She poured him another. "Tell me about the dance. Which ladies were there and what did they wear?"

He moved around the room, wishing that he hadn't stepped foot inside her house. "Oh, hell, Dulcie, I don't know what they wore."

"You know what Louisa Shumacher wore."

"Yes, I do know that," he said. He remembered how her dress felt beneath his hands, the soft material and ribbons and buttons unfastened and pushed away. His desire was rekindled, and he sipped the brandy. "She wore some kind of soft blue material that had ribbons here," he said, his voice getting husky when he thought about those ribbons.

Dulcie crossed the room to him and put her arms around him. "Dan," she said, moving her hips against him.

"Dulcie, it's late."

"Love me, just this once. I'm older than Louisa Shumacher and her friends. I'm not the beauty I once was," she said in a trembling voice.

"Dulcie, you're one of the most beautiful women in Denver," he said.

"Just kiss me," she whispered, winding her arm around his neck. Her hand slid down over his hip and thigh. He bent his head, kissing her, feeling her softness press against him, and suddenly he yielded to the passion that had been so fully aroused only hours earlier.

He carried her to bed, stretching out beside her as her hands unfastened his pants and removed his paper collar. He pulled his shirt over his head.

Dulcie stood up, peeling away her few garments. "Is my body getting old, Dan?"

"That's the most absurd question," he said, pulling her down into his arms. As he kissed Dulcie, Louisa was forgotten.

When he woke in the morning, she was asleep beside him. He disentangled himself and slipped out of bed, washing and dressing quietly. As he gazed at Dulcie, he had no regrets about their night together. They would have to part soon now, but he wasn't married yet, and they had wanted each other badly last night.

Dan felt kindly toward Dulcie, and was grateful that she hadn't accepted his proposals. He peeled two one-hundred-dollar bills from his billfold and left them on her desk before picking up his boots and coat and slipping out.

Wednesday morning of the next week, as Dan rode around the corner toward the Potter house, he saw Edward Ringwood's carriage once again parked in front. Dan urged his horse to a trot, swung his leg over, and dropped down to run up the front steps.

Dan burst into the house. "Mr. Ringwood! Oh, sorry, sir."

Edward Ringwood smiled as he stood only yards

away. "I thought I'd find you here. I've heard you're rebuilding the O'Malley boardinghouse for them."

"Yes, sir. I work on the boardinghouse in my spare time."

Edward Ringwood laughed. "I wonder how much spare time you have. When do you expect to finish both places?"

"This house should be done in three more weeks if the weather holds. The work on the O'Malley boardinghouse is going slowly because I work odd hours on it, and most of the men who volunteered at first have quit helping now. I should finish it within a month."

"I see. Well, when you have more free time again, I would like to see some plans for a house. I bought a lot on Grant Street."

"Yes, sir!"

"If you'll come to my office on Larimer sometime this week or next, whenever you can work it into your busy schedule, I'll go over what I would like with you, give you some specific ideas."

"Yes, sir. I can come anytime you like."

Ringwood gave another frosty smile. "I thought you might work it into your schedule. How about four o'clock today?"

For one brief instant Dan had been afraid Ringwood would say four o'clock Thursday, and he would be faced with a terrible dilemma.

"Yes, sir! Today at four would be grand."

"Good. I'll see you then."

Dazed, Dan watched Ringwood climb into his carriage and drive away.

Dan gave a whoop of joy. Suddenly he wanted to tell someone. He couldn't call at this hour on Louisa. If he called on Dulcie, she would coax him into bed again, but he could safely go tell Mary O'Malley. The more he thought about it, the more he wanted to. He might even get breakfast. He strode outside to mount his horse and head for the O'Malleys'. They were all at breakfast when he entered.

"Good morning," Mary greeted him cheerfully.

"I didn't mean to intrude," Dan said, "but I thought

I would stop for a few minutes before I start working.''

''You can have some breakfast,'' Paddy said, pushing out a chair while Brian stood up and carried his plate to the sink. ''I'm leaving for the stable. I'll help you tonight, Dan.''

''Fine.''

''My boy,'' Paddy said, leaning forward, ''I am building something that will make your eyes dance. You must come out to the shed and see the windmill of the future. It will transform the desert into a land of abundance, with water pumped from the ground far faster than now.''

''Yes, sir. I'll look after breakfast.''

''And if you'll excuse me, I'll go back to work on it.''

''Yes, sir.''

They were left alone, and as Mary served him a plate of eggs, biscuits, and ham, he caught her wrist. ''Have you eaten? If you haven't, come join me. I want to tell you something.''

''Yes. Just a minute, Dan.''

When she had filled a plate, she sat across from him and leaned forward, her arms on the table. ''Now, tell me. You look as if you found a rainbow.''

''Better than that. Edward Ringwood stopped by this morning and he wants me to draw up plans to build him a house.''

''Oh, Dan, how wonderful for you,'' she said, looking at the sparkle in his eyes and wondering if she had ever seen anyone look quite as happy.

''Between that and the Corning plans, I see the promise of a real future. Mary, this will mean others will come to me. This is the job I need to get my real start here.''

''I'm so happy for you.''

''Can I tell you a secret?''

''Yes,'' she said, laughing at his excitement.

''I've asked Louisa Shumacher to marry me.''

Mary stared at him, suddenly losing all her merriment. Louisa was a cold, haughty woman. She was

She laughed and picked up her milk to clink her glass against his, wondering if he realized he had left both Louisa and Silas out of the toast.

He finished breakfast and stood up as she removed the dishes. "Thanks, Mary, for listening. You're a friend as much as Silas."

"I'm glad, and I'm happy for you." He placed his hand behind her neck, stroking her lightly. "He'll come home to you before you know it," Dan said gently. "And you'll forget all about the years when he was gone."

She nodded, intensely aware of his fingers moving on her neck. He seemed so filled with vitality and exuberance that she didn't want him to leave. She had to admit she enjoyed his friendship and understood why Silas liked him.

He winked and left, shrugging into his coat, mounting his horse, and riding away while she stood on the porch and watched him. Her neck still tingled from his touch, and she realized she was beginning to watch for his arrival every afternoon, cooking special dishes because she knew he would be there at night. She leaned her head against the doorjamb and thought about Dan's sparkling blue eyes and his bubbling happiness. She felt a pang of loneliness, an empty ache. Straightening her shoulders, she went back to work, pausing once to stop in the parlor and look at the new woodwork Dan had done.

Promptly at four, Dan was at Edward Ringwood's office. He listened carefully as Ringwood described what he liked and wanted, and Dan made notes.

"You seem to have a penchant for Victorian," Ringwood said. "I particularly like Victorian Gothic."

Dan nodded. "It's a beautiful style and I can build you a house you would be proud of for years to come."

"I want six bedrooms upstairs, one bedroom downstairs."

Dan nodded. Eagerness flooded him at the size of the house Ringwood was describing. Half an hour later he was riding to the O'Malleys'. Ringwood had paid him a fee and Dan had promised to draw up plans.

He ate dinner after Mary's customers had finished, sitting across from her and talking to her about his plans. Suddenly he realized how he had monopolized her time. "I've talked all through dinner. What a good listener you are!"

"It's interesting and exciting. If I could do something like building houses, I'd be very excited to have Mr. Ringwood hire me. I like hearing about it, Dan."

He didn't remember when she had switched from calling him Mr. Castle to Dan, but it had been sometime since the dance. "What kind of house would you like, Mary?"

She smiled at him. "That's another one of those things that belongs to tomorrows, and I never think about it."

"Surely you have a preference."

"No. This is what I have," she said, looking at the dining room, "and I don't look beyond that."

"Have you ever seen a house you thought was special?"

"Yes. The nicest place was the house we had when we lived back in Tennessee. It was long, with a wide center hall, a sloping roof over the porch, big rooms, wide windows, and high ceilings. Breezes blew through it and sunlight came in and I thought it was grand."

"There aren't any houses around here like that," he said, hoping Silas came home with his million. "Maybe I can build one for you and Silas someday."

Her dreamy-eyed look vanished, and he mentally swore at himself. He vowed he would try harder to remember to avoid mentioning Silas. "I don't know about that. Right now, I'm grateful beyond measure you've put a roof back over our heads," she said abruptly, and stood up to clear the table. He rose and caught her arm, and she looked up sharply, drawing her breath.

"He'll come home, and I think he'll bring his million."

"I'm not so sure I'll feel the same, years from now."

"The impatience of youth," he said softly, half-teasing her.

Her features softened as the anger left her eyes. "It's difficult to imagine you angry with anyone, until I remember our first two times together."

He tucked a stray lock of her hair behind her ear. "Do you ever let your hair down?" he asked casually.

"I did when I was ten years old," she answered, and he gave her a startled look.

For an instant he believed her, until she saw the mischievous look in her eyes. "Of course I take it down," she said, and carried the dishes to the kitchen.

He laughed and went to work, hammering diligently, putting finishing touches on the inside molding. She came to inspect his work and stayed to talk to him. Paddy also joined them after a time, to sit and whittle while he talked.

"Mary showed me all your carvings," Dan said, smoothing a board. "I talked to Lyle Workman, and he said he could carry them in his store."

"You mean sell them?" Paddy asked with a quizzical smile.

"Yes, if you'd like."

"I don't think people would pay for these," he said, holding up a wooden cat. "They just help me while the time away when I'm not working on one of my inventions."

"Why don't you let me take some to him and see if they sell?"

"Sure, Dan. Help yourself."

"You pick them out. I might get a favorite."

"Mary can help you." He stood up. "I told the men I'd come down to the Lazy Dog for a little while. Don't work too hard, my boy."

"I won't," Dan answered.

In minutes Mary knelt beside him, her plain brown calico skirt spread on the floor. "I can do that if all you're trying to do is smooth the surface."

"Fine," he said, giving the task to her and moving

to work on the windows. Once he glanced over at her, seeing her head bent over her work, auburn hair shining in the light while she worked diligently. He smiled at her. Silas was very lucky.

He went over to pull her up and take the tools from her hands. "You've worked enough for one day. Let's pick out some of Paddy's carvings."

"Do you really think people would want them badly enough to pay for them?"

"Yes. They're good, Mary. You're accustomed to them and probably barely notice them."

They walked down the hall and she was aware of Dan, of his height and his nearness. They made selections and put them in a box. When Dan returned to work, Mary did too.

He put down his hammer. "Mary, stop working. You and Brian work every minute you're awake," he said, taking her by the shoulders. "Sit here and talk to me."

"If I work, this will be done sooner and you'll be free to spend your evenings the way you want."

"I'll get it done in due time. It bothers me to watch you work constantly."

"Said by a man who works nights for no pay! That's ridiculous, Dan." She laughed.

He grinned while he worked. He had rolled his sleeves high, and muscles in his arms bulged as he planed a board.

"You haven't known Louisa Shumacher very long. You must make up your mind very quickly."

"I'm not one to sit long weighing matters in my mind."

"Maybe you should, when it comes to marriage. That's a lifetime promise."

"I know what I want. How long did—" He broke off. "How long did you live in Tennessee?"

"I was seven when we moved from there. We moved to several places before we came here. That wasn't what you started to say. You can talk to me about Silas."

He paused to study her. "I forget. I know it makes you sad."

"I'm accustomed to his absence. I knew him for six months."

"That's not so long either."

"Oh, yes it is, compared to you and Louisa!" she said, laughing, and he shrugged.

"I'm impulsive."

"You're patient too. That's a contradiction."

"We're all full of contradictions, Mary. Look at you."

"How am I contradictory?"

"You can be so sweet and so much fun," he said, bending down to squint at the bottom side of a windowsill.

"And," she prompted.

"And so fiery-tempered," he said, straightening up to face her with amusement twinkling in his eyes.

"Is that so?"

"Admit it," he threatened playfully. He enjoyed her laughter, and thought she did far too little of it.

"I'm just plain—what was it you said, sweet and fun. I haven't been fiery at all tonight."

He was on his knees, and he put down the plane and leaned forward to catch her by the shoulders and look her squarely in the eye. "Remember our first meeting? And our second?"

All her playfulness evaporated as she looked into his blue eyes, only inches from her face. "Yes, I remember," she said quietly.

"And what do you call those times?" he persisted playfully.

"I guess I was . . . defensive."

"Defensive, my foot! C'mon, Mary, admit it."

"Maybe I was fiery," she said quietly, her attention drawn to his mouth. His full wide lips were masculine and appealing, and Mary wondered how they would feel to touch.

"Mary, I didn't really make you angry, did I?" he asked, suddenly solemn.

She blushed, hoping he would never guess what had

run through her mind. "I might just show you *fiery,* mister!" She laughed at him, and to her relief, he grinned and tucked a lock of hair behind her ear. "Someday, I may just take those long braids down and see what you look like!"

"I'd look just the same, only with long braids down over my back."

He bent back to work, locks of golden hair tumbling over his forehead, and she wondered how it would feel to run her fingers through them. "How old were you when you lived on the sheep ranch?"

"Young. It seems like a long time ago. Now I don't miss it so much, but I like the mountains. Ever ride out to the mountains, Mary?"

"No. The boys have, and of course Paddy has, but I've always been right here or back east of here. They look beautiful, and I used to think I'd get on Blackie and ride up in the mountains all by myself."

"Sometime I'll take you. We can take Brian and Paddy and Louisa."

She laughed. "Louisa might not approve of this family you've adopted."

"Yes, she will. She'll like what I like."

"How on earth do you know? You barely know her."

"She likes what I like now. She will, you'll see."

"I'll bet the ladies always like what you like!"

He grinned at her. "All except one little lady, who tosses skillets at me!"

"There should be at least one in your life, Dan, who doesn't succumb to your charm," she remarked, wondering if she hadn't already succumbed.

"I've had more than one, I'll assure you of that," he said, driving a nail into place. For a moment they were quiet while he pounded. He stood up, holding a board to nail it in place, stretching his long arms.

"Here, I can hold that," she said, standing on tip-toe and holding the board. "Now you can nail."

He worked quickly and she went back to sit down. "Did you build when you were growing up?"

"Sometimes Pa showed me how to do something. I

helped around the place. Sometimes I built little things off by myself. When you grow up alone out on a ranch, you have time to do things.''

''I thought you had a brother.''

He looked up and she saw the startled expression in his features, and realized something was amiss. ''I'm sorry, Dan. I shouldn't have asked.''

''You can ask, Mary. I don't tell people about my life much,'' he said.

''Neither did Silas. He didn't like to talk about his past. I didn't mean to bring up something bad.''

''It wasn't bad. My brother didn't grow up with me. We were separated. He was in a wagon-train ambush. We got together after we were grown, but I don't usually tell people all that.''

''I won't either, then,'' she said, gazing into his solemn blue eyes.

''I'm quitting for tonight,'' he said, and stood up.

''I'll go cut a piece of cherry pie if you'd like.''

''I'd like that very much. I'll wash my hands.''

They sat in the kitchen and talked until after midnight, when he stretched and stood up to go, pulling on his coat and jamming a broad-brimmed black hat on his head. She walked toward the door with him, and Dan draped his arm casually across her shoulders. ''Thanks for the food.''

''Thanks for the house,'' she said, acutely conscious of his arm. ''I know why Silas trusted you with his money. He wouldn't have trusted most people.''

Dan laughed and turned to face her, his hand sliding to her shoulder. ''Trustworthy, impulsive—maybe the good outweighs the bad.''

''If sweet outweighs fiery!''

''Indeed it does. And the best cook this side of the Atlantic Ocean.'' He patted his flat stomach. ''My, you can cook!''

She laughed at him, standing in the dim light. ''Why don't you come for breakfast.''

''I thought you'd never ask!'' He bent and brushed her cheek with a kiss. ''Good night, Mary.''

He strode out the door and she followed, watching him mount up to ride away.

At four the following afternoon, as he strode up the walk to the Shumacher front door, his nerves were stretched raw. He wore his best black suit and his best linen shirt. His hair was neatly parted and combed down and he tried to rehearse what he would say to Charles Shumacher.

10

Louisa let the lace curtain fall back in place as she watched Dan stride up their walk. It had taken hours of pleading and tears to get her parents to listen to her arguments, but they had relented. She smiled, thinking she had what she wanted for the time being.

She would decide soon whether she really wanted Dan or Reuben. At the moment she wanted Dan. When she thought of his kisses, of being in his arms, she forgot all other considerations. He set her afire in a way no man had. On the other hand, she thought of Reuben's wealth and the power she would have as his wife, whereas Dan Castle was merely getting started and his future was far more uncertain. Her father said he was a wealthy man and was beginning to get contracts for homes. His own home was beautiful, so she knew that he could provide for her sufficiently and allow her to be the belle of society. Her parents worried about his past, but Louisa didn't give it a thought. The past was over; what she wanted to consider was her future.

She moved to the mirror to study her image, thinking what a marvelous pair they would be with her dark hair and his golden hair. They would turn heads everywhere they went. She smoothed the tendrils of hair already pinned neatly to her head. Tingling with anticipation, she thought about telling Reuben. He would fly into a rage, perhaps fight over her with Dan Castle. She wanted to be talked about, to have men fight over her. She looked at her image and smiled, turning her head to find the best view. Reuben's jealousy would stir him to kiss her, kisses she had enjoyed until she met Dan Castle. She slipped out of her room and moved soundlessly down the stairs to pause outside the parlor door. She shouldn't listen, but if she were careful, no one would know.

Inside the parlor, Dan shifted impatiently. "Sir, I understand that you know little about me, but I have a good start here. I've built a comfortable home. I love Louisa and will provide for her. To wait three months to get to know each other better seems unnecessary."

"This engagement might not work out, Mr. Castle. You're a stranger in our midst, and I cannot in good conscience promise her hand to someone I don't know. Get to know each other better. If all is satisfactory three months from now, in June, we'll announce Louisa's engagement to you."

"And when can we set a wedding date?"

"It'll take Louisa and her mother months to get the dresses and the plans ready. Mother and Louisa think a fall wedding would be nice."

"Next fall?"

Shumacher's voice was deprecatory and amused. "It sounds like a long time to someone so young, yet it's nothing. And you'll have to wait if you want Louisa's hand."

Dan hated the proposition put to him by Shumacher, yet he had no alternative. He thought about Louisa stretched on his settee, her clothes peeled away, and he drew a sharp breath. "Very well, sir. I don't have any choice except to agree."

"I might as well warn you, Reuben Knelville will be unhappy over this. Reuben hasn't talked to me, but his father has told me that he expects Reuben to ask for Louisa's hand."

"I'm not concerned with Reuben Knelville," Dan said.

"Perhaps you should be. You want to succeed in Denver. To do so, you'll have to have the acceptance of the Knelvilles, father and son."

"I'll manage without Reuben Knelville's help."

"Let me give you a word of advice. Louisa doesn't like scandal, nor do we. Reuben has less to lose if there is a fight over Louisa than you do."

"I'm aware of that, sir."

"So far your altercations have been kept to yourselves. You should see that they continue so. Better yet, you should try to placate Reuben Knelville."

Dan was impatient to see Louisa, and Charles Shumacher was beginning to grate on his nerves. "Sir, fall is a long time to wait. A lot can happen in that time."

"True, but by then you should know each other better."

"Yes, sir," Dan said. He intended to know Louisa better long before a month was up. "May I see Louisa now, sir?"

"Oh, of course. I'll call her." He stepped to the door, "Lou . . . Oh, there you are. Mr. Castle is here. Would you come in. Mother."

All the Shumachers filed into the room. Louisa's eyes sparkled and her cheeks flushed. As soon as the ladies were seated, Dan sat back down. Charles Shumacher stood in front of the fire, his hands clasped behind him. "Mother, you know the decisions we reached. Louisa, Mr. Castle has asked for your hand, and you've indicated this is your choice in the matter. Since you have barely met, your mother and I have discussed this. You're to get to know each other better, and if you feel the same three months from now, we'll announce the engagement."

Louisa listened to what she had discussed at length with her parents. She flashed Dan a broad smile.

Dan didn't know what was expected of him. All three stared at him, and Hortense Shumacher's gaze was cold. He crossed the room to Louisa to take her hands in his. "I love your daughter and I'll do my best to make her happy."

"There is no engagement yet. You both must understand that clearly."

"Yes, ma'am," he answered, continuing to gaze at Louisa.

"Mother, we should leave the young people to themselves. We'll talk later," Shumacher said to Dan and offered his hand.

Dan shook hands with Charles, feeling as if he had just entered a contest. The elder Shumachers left, and Dan reached out to quietly close the door. He turned to pull Louisa into his arms. "Do you know how long they want me to wait for you?"

"Three months."

"Three months plus an engagement that is to last until next fall," he whispered, bending his head to kiss her. He had no intention of waiting that long to possess her.

She twisted her head and smiled. "Darling, it'll take months to get ready for a wedding and the parties I want to have—don't deprive me of it!"

He bent his head to kiss her hungrily, tightening his arms around her. In minutes she moved away. "Dan, Mother will be back in minutes."

"Now you go out only with me," he said in a husky voice, mentally stripping away her fancy dress.

"Except tomorrow night I have to tell Reuben, and I've already promised to go with him. Reuben has a right to know."

He nodded. "I told Mary O'Malley I had asked you to marry me."

"Why that O'Malley person? Oh, you knew the man she's to marry."

"Mary's nice, Louisa."

"There's something else I want to know about." She gave him a coy look, batting her eyes and smoothing her dress.

"What is it?"

"I don't know how to say this. I've heard things. I know men do things."

"What are you talking about?"

"Reuben says you have a woman, her name is Dulcie."

Silently Dan cursed Reuben and wished he were crossing paths with him that night.

"She's a friend."

"I don't approve. I don't want my husband to be attending a bawdy house."

"Louisa, I've known—" He thought about the last time he had stopped to see Dulcie and had ended up spending the night in Dulcie's bed. "You're right. I won't see her anymore."

"Good. It isn't right, and I don't care to share you with another woman."

He was on the verge of telling her if she didn't want to share him, she shouldn't make him wait almost a year to get married, but he bit back the words and pulled her close again. His hand roamed over her breasts, and she gasped and strained against him while he kissed her.

"Louisa!" came a call from the other side of the door.

"Coming, Mother. I have to go now."

"I won't see you anymore tonight?" he asked, startled that he couldn't take her for a carriage ride or stay to visit even if it meant chatting with the whole family.

"No, sorry. Mama said we must not. She wants me to go with them to the Claridges'."

He kissed her long and hard. "Good night, Louisa."

He felt as if his feet didn't touch ground on his way to the O'Malleys'.

Mary had become accustomed to seeing him come in through the kitchen, where he could always find her and tell her he was starting work. Tonight she watched him dismount and tether his horse. When Dan strode to the back door, her heart seemed to skip a beat. He was dressed in a fancy black suit and silk tie, a white linen shirt, and he looked incredibly handsome.

Dan entered the back door with a rush of cold air as he pulled off his coat. She wore an apron over her blue gingham. "Come inside. I'm cooking for tomorrow. All the diners are gone." Tempting aromas of chicken assailed him.

"Her parents said we can become engaged in three months." He laughed and squeezed Mary, turning her to face him. "I'm going to be an engaged man soon."

"You have to wait until summer?" she asked, re-

turning to stir a kettle of chicken and noodles while
Dan followed her into the room.

"They said we hadn't known each other long
enough. And don't give me an I-told-you-so look,
Mary Katherine!"

"What will you do about Reuben Knelville? She
goes most places with him."

"Louisa is going to tell Reuben, because he'll want
to know why she suddenly won't go out with him any
longer. Maybe Charles Shumacher will relent in a
month when he sees that I'm reliable. Aren't I reliable,
Mary?" he teased, happy with the world.

"You're incredibly reliable," she said. "You took
me out, just as you promised Silas."

"Hey, I almost forgot. Paddy's carvings are selling.
Edward Ringwood is going to contact him to do some
special ones for him."

"You can't be serious!"

"I am. You'll see."

"Isn't that amazing. The thing that Pa gives the least
attention to is something worthwhile. Thank you, Dan.
This is because of you," she said, standing on tiptoe
to kiss his cheek. She stepped back quickly, her cheeks
flushing. "You've been so good to us!"

"In spite of having skillets heaved at me and almost
getting my skull split open," he teased.

"Oh, please! I'm sorry."

He laughed. "C'mon, Irish, let's celebrate my engagement. I brought a bottle of brandy. Have a little
drink with me."

"The only time I drank brandy was when the house
burned."

"Just this once."

He poured two drinks. "Shouldn't you be doing this
with Louisa Shumacher instead of me?"

Startled, he focused on her. "I'm delirious with
happiness. Yes, it should be Louisa, but her family let
me know when my visiting time was over."

Mary gazed at him, trying not to care, but Dan was
too good for people like the Shumachers. They

wouldn't appreciate him until he had wealth and position in the community.

"Here's to our happy future."

"Futures, Dan," she said softly, wanting to reach up and stroke the lock of yellow hair that fell across his temple.

He lowered his glass. "Well, I might as well go to work now," he said.

"You're dressed in your best clothes."

"I'll go home and change and then come back."

"Before you go, you can sit down and eat."

"Do you still have customers?"

"No, the last one has finished and gone."

"Have you eaten?"

"Yes, but you sit here in the kitchen and I'll talk to you while I work."

"Fine." He felt that nothing could mar his happiness tonight. They talked for over an hour before he realized how late it was getting and rode home to change his clothes.

While he worked, Brian joined him. Dan hammered with fury to give vent to the restless excitement that gripped him. He wanted Louisa to be with him, and his thoughts veered constantly to her, imagining her in his arms and in his bed. He talked to Mary and Brian over cups of hot tea late that night, and he finally pulled on his coat and left, waving good-bye to Mary from the edge of the yard. He intended to go straight home, but he still felt wide-awake and full of energy. He was happy beyond measure. He went to Dulcie's without giving it a thought.

She moved away from a crowd in the parlor the moment Dan appeared in the door, and they went back to her room.

"Want to drink a brandy with me?" he asked soberly, knowing he was going to miss Dulcie in his life.

"Sure, Dan. She said yes, didn't she?"

"Yes. Her father put conditions on his consent, though." Dulcie poured two generous brandies and handed one to Dan.

"Here's to your marriage, Dan Castle. I hope you're supremely happy."

"Dulcie, you're a good woman," he said gently, moving forward to give her a squeeze. "God knows you turned me down enough, it's time someone accepted."

"Yes, it is." They both drank, and when she lowered her glass, she refilled his. "What are the conditions of this wonderful engagement?"

"We have to wait three months before we can become engaged." He took another long drink of brandy and sat down on the settee. "Her parents are scared I won't be able to support her. Her mother doesn't approve. She's barely said two words to me. Her father knows more about my potential. If I get to build the houses for Corning and Ringwood, my future will be secure here."

"Did you just leave Louisa?" Dulcie asked, lighting a cheroot and exhaling a stream of smoke.

"No, I've been with Mary. You know, when Silas comes home, I'm going to knock him flat. She's sweet, Dulcie, and damned smart. That Silas is a fool."

"Men can sometimes be obtuse," Dulcie said dryly, removing her shoes and unbuttoning her bodice. She crossed the room to refill his glass with brandy.

"He should have come home and married her, taken her with him. Or he should have at least stopped here for a time before going prospecting."

"No one is going to take her away from him, from what I understand. She's plain and stays at home."

"She's not so plain. She might not be plain at all if she'd take her hair down. I asked her once if she sleeps with it braided. She runs that boardinghouse all by herself."

Dulcie studied him while he talked and sipped his brandy. "What about her father? Everyone in town laughs at him, and this last peccadillo—blowing away half his house with blasting powder—that must make it uncomfortable for her."

Dan swirled his brandy and chuckled. "Paddy is one of a kind. He whittles, Dulcie, and he's good at it. I took some of his carvings down to Workman's store. Lyle's sold some, and Edward Ringwood wants to commission Paddy to do some special ones for him."

"I'll be damned. That must make the O'Malleys happy."

"Paddy is always happy. I wish Mary would have more fun, though. I get angry with Silas every time I stop to think about it."

"Silas should have come home to her," Dulcie said, sitting down on his lap. "How's the house building?"

"The weather's good now and I just hired another hand. Hiram is a good carpenter. People pour through this town on their way west or on their way back east, so they're only here a few weeks. It makes it difficult to keep regular help."

"It makes for abundant help, though."

"With the train coming to Denver, this ought to become a center of activity for the West. I wish Noah could build a hotel here."

"You miss your family."

"I worry about my ma and pa," he said, his voice changing as she leaned forward to refill their glasses. Her unbuttoned bodice revealed an enticing glimpse of soft curves, and Dan bent his head to trail kisses across her flesh. She smelled like lilacs and was soft and beautiful. He pushed away her silk dress and stroked her full breasts. Her hands fluttered across his chest, down over his belly as she leaned forward to kiss him on the mouth.

Early the next morning, he lay with his arm around her in bed, a cheroot between his teeth while he talked about the O'Malley boardinghouse. "Once I'm through working there, I'm going to miss the best meals I've had since we lived in Montana. I know when Silas comes back, I'll build a house for them, but Mary won't say what kind of house she likes. She says she never thinks about tomorrow. She barely even remembers her mother."

"Dan, do you think she really loves Silas?" Dulcie asked quietly, studying his profile.

"Of course she does. She wouldn't wait for him if she didn't."

"Maybe she doesn't have a choice about waiting. She's plain and she limps."

"Her limp is barely noticeable, Dulcie. It doesn't keep her from dancing at all. She's as graceful as a ballerina and light as a feather to dance with. And she's not really so plain. Her eyes are downright beautiful. No, she loves him. I've seen men stop to eat and try to cozy up to her. She won't give them a second's attention."

While he continued to talk about Mary, Dulcie studied him. She was aware that he had talked five times as much about Mary O'Malley as he had about Louisa Shumacher. Dulcie made a mental note to try to encounter Mary O'Malley again. "Dan, are you sure you're ready to marry? To live with Louisa Shumacher for a lifetime?"

"Yes, I am," he said, growing quiet.

"Do you realize you've talked more about Mary O'Malley than Louisa?"

He rolled over and sat up, looking down at her. "I see Mary O'Malley every day. For Lord's sake, Dulcie, she's Silas' woman!" He threw back the covers and crossed the room. Her gaze ran down his length, and Dulcie thought he was the most handsome man she had ever known. She was curious now, and she loathed Louisa Shumacher. She sat up, watching him, wishing she hadn't stirred his anger, because now he would leave.

"Come back here, Dan. Just relax and let's talk a little longer."

"I should go, Dulcie. I have too much to do to waste away the morning."

"Waste away dawn is more like it." She pulled on her wrapper and slippers, watching him as he washed and dressed.

"You can stay for breakfast."

"I'll go by the O'Malleys'—" He broke off and looked at Dulcie, scowling suddenly. "Dulcie, Mary O'Malley is Silas' woman. She loves him. I'm engaged to Louisa Shumacher, and it isn't Mary O'Malley who . . . Never mind.''

She shrugged, knowing he was angry and would leave, no matter what she said. ''Marriage lasts for a long time. And you sure do talk about Miss O'Malley.''

''That's all it is, talk. She's a friend and she's going to marry my best friend. And she's a little plain. Not real plain, just a little.''

''You're arguing with yourself. Earlier you told me she wasn't plain at all.''

''She's not, Dulcie,'' he said evenly. ''I'm in love with Louisa Shumacher, not Mary O'Malley!''

''Sure, Dan. I hope you like Louisa as well as Mary.''

''Of course I do! I just don't see her as often. I see Mary every night, and we talk a lot. She's a friend. She's one of the best friends I've had. So are you. We talk. I'm in love with someone else; she's in love with someone else. She's a friend.'' Suddenly he relaxed and grinned. ''And she's a damned good cook! Almost a match for you.''

She laughed, wishing she could get him back in a better humor. ''And does Louisa cook?''

''I'll hire a cook. I should get dressed and go to work.''

She crossed the room to him, and he rested his hands on her shoulders. His gaze lowered to the half-open wrapper and he ran his fingers along her bare flesh, pushing the folds of silk farther apart.

''You're one of the most beautiful women in the world, Dulcie,'' he whispered, and kissed her. ''If I don't leave now, I'll be late to work,'' he said in a husky voice.

''It's all right with me if you stay.''

''I won't earn my living if I don't get going. See you later, hon.'' He winked and left, and she moved to the window to watch him. She wondered how many times she had watched him go and wished she could hold him. She stared at his golden head, his broad shoulders, and wondered if he really loved Louisa Shumacher or was simply dazzled by her beauty and her body. He talked about Mary O'Malley constantly, too much to simply be a friend. Dulcie had known many men and women, and to her it looked as if Dan Castle was falling in love with Mary O'Malley, whether he knew it or not.

She watched him and thought of the cold Louisa. And Silas. Silas and Dan were best friends and Silas was wildly in love with Mary O'Malley. Dulcie leaned against the cold windowpane. She hoped that Dan wasn't headed for years of heartache if he married the wrong woman, but men were fools where beautiful women were concerned.

Eight hours later, Reuben Knelville was ushered into the Shumacher house to escort Louisa to the new Denver Musical performance. Louisa took his arm, gazing up at him as they left the house. She wore her red taffeta, hoping to stun Reuben and catch the attention of everyone tonight. She was excited beyond measure because she could tell Reuben of her engagement to Dan. Once in the carriage, Reuben turned to her, caressing her throat. "You look beautiful, Louisa. And you look as if you have a secret."

"I do have! How amazing you'd guess, Reuben!"

"So what is this great secret?"

"It's a secret, so I shan't tell you," she said, and his amusement vanished.

"You think you'll tease me all evening, Louisa?"

Her heart skipped because she heard the underlying threat. "And if I do?"

"I'll have to punish you," he said, catching her wrists and holding her arms behind her back while she struggled playfully, wiggling and pressing her breasts against him.

"Set me free, Reuben!"

"Tell me, Louisa. Tell me!" He kissed her forcefully, stroking her, and she gasped. She finally felt his hand release her wrists, and she wound them around his neck, grinding her body against his, hearing his sharp intake of breath. She kissed him wildly, relishing his kisses, forgetting briefly her purpose.

Suddenly he turned her chin up. "Tell me," he ordered.

"I'm about to become engaged to Dan Castle. This is the last night I can go out with you." She had meant to wait and torment him for hours before revealing her delicious secret, but now it was out.

Suddenly he threw back his head and laughed. "You little liar. You don't have a secret. You did that so I would kiss you!"

Her annoyance quickly deepened to anger. "It's so. This is the last time I'll go out with you. I'll marry Dan Castle next fall."

As Reuben's smile faded, she felt a glimmer of satisfaction.

"You can't be serious."

She slanted him a look, a tickle of delight coming. "I'm very serious."

He grasped her arms painfully and turned her to face him. "Your parents won't want you to wed a man like Castle! Our fathers have discussed a union between you and me."

"Nonetheless, I'm about to become engaged to him."

"You don't love him. You barely know the man."

"I love him."

Reuben stared at her and suddenly yanked her to him, kissing her passionately until her head was spinning and her desire flamed once more. He stopped as abruptly as he'd started, "Tell me you love him and can kiss me like that, Louisa! It's me you love, isn't it?"

"No, Reuben," she whispered. He kissed her again, pushing her down in the carriage, fondling her. He raised his head. "Say you love me."

"I love you," she whispered, loving to be kissed. "I think I love you both."

"You can't. You need to be married, but to me, not to a man no one knows, who has nothing. He's a penniless builder."

"He isn't penniless. He's going to build a house for Benjamin Corning!"

"Corning? I don't believe it."

"He is. And he has thousands of dollars in Papa's bank!"

"Is he already commissioned to build the Corning house?"

"No, but Corning asked Dan to draw up some plans." She lay on the seat of the carriage and realized she had allowed Reuben to gain the upper hand. She was at a disadvantage, disheveled beneath him. She pushed at him, trying to sit up, but he pushed her back down as a frosty smile crossed his face. "When is the engagement to be announced?"

"Let me up, Reuben."

"Answer my question. Maybe there isn't actually an engagement after all."

"Yes, there is." She squirmed as he kept her pinned down. "Reuben, I shall look—"

"As if I tumbled you in the carriage. Answer my question before I do something you don't like."

"We can get engaged three months from yesterday."

"Three months! So why won't you go out with me during that time? Either you're engaged or you're not. And you're not." Reuben laughed again, moving away. "A damned postponed engagement, and you melt with my kisses! Your parents don't want you to marry him. They're biding for time to prove he's the wrong man for you. And why you want this engagement, I can't imagine. The man is nobody, drifting in out of nowhere. You know nothing about him. He can't take care of you, Louisa. And beware, in three months I may forget all about you."

She drew herself up, angry with him. She had wanted a different reaction. She had expected Reuben to grovel and beg and hang on her every word, not gaze at her with sardonic amusement lighting his eyes. "Dan will be wealthy when he builds Benjamin Corning's house, because if Corning's house is good, others will flock to him to build."

"Time will tell," Reuben said coldly, making a mental note to have his father talk to Benjamin Corning. He gazed at Louisa. She was the most beautiful woman in town, and damned if he would hand her over to Castle! He would deflower her first. He could control her. She was determined to be a leader in society, and she was sensual, beautiful, educated. He expected to marry her, and now that a threat loomed, he realized he did want to marry her. He wasn't going to allow a drifter to come into town and take Louisa right out of his arms. Her eyes sparkled with mischief, and he suspected she relished trying to stir his jealousy. "There are other beautiful women here," he said calmly. "Marian Comber, for one."

Louisa drew a sharp breath. "Dan Castle is dashing! He makes me faint with his kisses. He knows what pleases women."

Reuben's amusement vanished while his gray eyes flashed with anger. He leaned close.

"You're playing a dangerous game, Louisa. Your future is at stake. You don't act as if you find disfavor in my kisses either. Perhaps you're just a beautiful little slut who likes all men to handle you."

Enraged, she reached out to slap him. He caught her wrist and twisted it, making her gasp.

"No, you won't strike me. I know what you need, Louisa. And it isn't a long trial engagement." He bent down to kiss her breasts, holding her while she struggled and called him names. Finally her struggles ceased and she closed her eyes. She relished his kisses, wishing she could marry tomorrow. She wanted to be kissed and held and touched. Her senses were stormed by Reuben as his hands were everywhere, daring to touch her in places he never had before. His hands slipped beneath her skirts, stroking her legs, moving between them.

"No! Reuben, stop."

His hands moved over her, touching her. She grasped his wrists and twisted away to sit up, gasping as she straightened her clothing. "You shouldn't have taken such liberties."

He sat in his corner watching her. "For all practical purposes, you're engaged to be engaged. That's absurd."

"I won't go out with you again."

"Three months. We'll see how successful your Dan Castle is while you're engaged, Louisa. If he isn't one of the leading men in Denver, you know your father won't allow the engagement. If you don't break it off first."

"I shan't. Dan Castle will succeed. You'll see."

She saw the dark anger burning in Reuben's eyes and felt a flash of excitement.

As Dan worked, his chisel slipped. He swore, shaking his hand, turning around to see Mary enter the room.

"What happened?"

"I cut my hand." He pulled out a handkerchief and she came across the room to take his hand and look at it. "Come here and let me wash it and bind it up for you."

"It's all right."

"Come along. You sound like Brian."

"Yes, ma'am," he said with amusement as she took his wrist and walked down the hall to her room. A fire burned low in the grate, and as she washed his cut, he gazed around the room and was surprised at how cheerful it was, more so than the rest of the house. A blue-and-white quilt served as a coverlet on the iron bed. The curtains were pale blue, plants grew in the windows, and there were bright cushions on the rocking chair. One wall was lined with bookshelves. He turned his attention back to her.

"You have a nice room."

She stood close beside him, his arm tucked against her side as she worked. Her fingers were warm and soft. He looked at her lashes, which were feathered shadows above her cheeks. Her nape was bare, her neck slender and delicate, and he felt a warmth toward her.

She finished wrapping his hand, tying the strip of clean cotton cloth. "There. You'll be well in no time."

As he looked into her eyes, he thought she had beautiful eyes, more so each time he paused to gaze into them. "Thanks, Mary. This room is different from the rest of the house."

"It's my own special place when I have to get away from the others."

"I used to have a place like that, only mine was outside on a mountain."

"Why did you leave home?" Instantly she frowned, her straight reddish-brown brows drawing closer together. "I'm sorry. I don't ever mean to pry."

"If there was ever anyone on earth who could keep a secret, I'd guess it's you. I got in trouble and had to leave."

"I didn't mean to ask," she said, putting her hand on his wrist. "And I'm sorry."

He was aware of her nearness, of her wide eyes searching his, her sweetness. "It was a long time ago," he answered abruptly. "I should get back to work. Thanks for the bandage. Come talk to me while I work." Afraid he had sounded harsh or angry, he smiled, placing his arm casually across her shoulders. She walked with him down the hall and sat to watch him as he returned to work. In minutes she was helping him.

The last week in March, Dan had letters to post. He usually took them to Lyle Workman's store, where the mail service was located. This time, as Lyle weighed a package Dan was mailing to San Antonio, Dan stood talking to him about the fall weather and the new businesses that had just opened. Dan glanced down at two stacks of posters tied in twine that were the new mail that had just arrived. His blood ran cold as he saw the picture and name on a poster—Tigre Danby Castillo. The room seemed to spin, and he took a deep breath and glanced at Lyle, who stood with his back turned while he adjusted the scales.

Dan looked at his picture. It was a drawing of him

with long hair, a beard, and a mustache. He wore the bear-claw necklace, and his hat was pulled low over his forehead. He wondered if anyone could see the resemblance. After all this time, he had almost forgotten the past. He felt safer in Denver than he had anywhere since he had started running, and now there would be a poster of him in the sheriff's office, perhaps in the store.

"That will be seventy-five cents."

"Fine. How's business?" he asked, barely knowing what he said, wishing he had turned over the stack.

"Going right along. Every time new travelers arrive, I sell more goods. I may expand. I'm thinking about moving from here by the stage depot over to the new train depot. Sold three more of Paddy's wooden animals this last week. And someone else wants him to do a special carving. I told them to hunt him down in the Lazy Dog or the Missouri House. Here's your change."

"Thanks, Lyle." Dan left, striding out into warm sunshine, wondering how much risk he faced. He barely knew the sheriff, steering clear of lawmen if possible.

"Well, I do declare, aren't you the busy man!"

11

He looked up to see Louisa seated in an open carriage. "Louisa, Sorry, I didn't see you."

"I know," she said, smiling. "You were about to walk right past me without so much as a good-afternoon."

"Sorry, my mind was on business. We go to the Gaithers' dinner party tomorrow night. I won't be able to be alone with you because your parents are going too."

"You might," she said, smiling at him. Although he was usually captivated by her, today Dan couldn't keep his attention on her. At the moment he was disturbed over the poster and he wished he could confide in her. Somehow he couldn't imagine Louisa being anything except shocked, because she had led a sheltered, secure life. Even so, he wished he could unburden himself to her.

"Today a new shipment of goods arrived from the East, and Papa bought Mama and me two beautiful new pairs of shoes and material for the most gorgeous dresses. This has been a perfect day so far. Who's going tomorrow night?"

"I don't really know, Louisa."

"I know Annabelle and Emily both will be there. They'll turn green with envy when they see my new shoes."

Dan couldn't keep his attention on ladies' shoes. He nodded to her. I'll see you tomorrow night." He winked and strode away, realizing he could tell Dul-

cie, but not Louisa. Dulcie understood trouble. Louisa
had never known any, and Dan knew he shouldn't expect her to understand a past like his.

His thoughts shifted to his plans for Ringwood and
Corning. Every time he thought of the two entirely
different types of houses he was designing, his blood
raced in anticipation. If he could build those two
houses, his future was secure. He mounted his horse
to ride to work.

It was late when he stopped at the O'Malleys'. He
washed his hands at the pump outside, and was glad
Mary had the luxury of a well and pump at the back
door and didn't always have to rely on the water wagon.
Spring was in the air. It was a pleasant time of year
as the days grew longer. He had put in a long hard
day, and realized for the first time how dusty his clothing was. He knocked and stepped inside the kitchen.

"Mary?"

"I'm here, Dan," she called. The lilt in her voice
gave him renewed energy.

She came into sight, a dish towel in her hand.

"I washed at the pump, but I'm dusty all over," he
said, holding out his arms. "Will you let me in like
this? I can eat back here if you like."

"Come in," she said, laughing. "You're no more
dusty than some of my customers. And they're all gone
anyway. Go sit in the dining room."

"Let's eat here in the kitchen."

"I have yours and mine ready. Want a glass of
milk?"

"Yes." Hunger attacked him as he smelled the
tempting aromas of roast turkey and hot bread.
"Brian's been turkey hunting, I see."

"Yes. Brian keeps meat on our table and he helps
with my garden in the summer. I know I can't expect
him to stay here for too many more years, and I don't
know what I'll do when he goes. He's more of a help
in many ways than Michael ever was. Michael was the
one who did repairs."

"Does Michael ever come home?" Dan asked. He
sat down across from her, relaxing as he watched her

move around the kitchen. She set plates and a platter piled high with slices of turkey on the table.

"He hasn't in over a year now. He's like Silas, off chasing dreams."

"What are your dreams, Mary?" Dan asked, serving her turnips and dressing.

"I don't have time for dreams. Maybe for a little while, when Silas was here—" Abruptly she bit off her words. "I know what you dream. You want to build the biggest, finest houses in Denver."

"You're right. I dream about that and about a family." His thoughts shifted to the wanted poster and he became quiet, eating in silence.

"Did you get the order of lumber you've been waiting for?"

"Yes. It came in late yesterday afternoon," he said. He couldn't stop thinking about the poster. He had hoped all traces of the past had been left behind and he wouldn't have to live his life constantly watching for bounty hunters and lawmen. In a few more minutes he realized how quiet he was, and that Mary had grown quiet also.

"This is the best dinner I've ever eaten."

She laughed, a merry sound that made his spirits lift a notch. "How many times have you told me that!"

"It's true. Dinner gets better and better. I mean it every time I say it."

While he ate, his thoughts shifted to work, but visions of the wanted poster still plagued him. The milk was cold, the turkey tender and succulent. It was so delicious, Dan wanted a second helping.

Mary cast surreptitious glances at him, finally watching him openly because he was so preoccupied he didn't notice. Something was worrying him. He always talked to her, either idle chatter or talk relating to his day at work and his plans for houses. He never sat in brooding silence, oblivious of her presence, his blue eyes full of worry. His hair was tangled, and the shoulder of his shirt was ripped. He was as dusty as he claimed, but he looked wonderful. She worried

about him, though, because it was obvious that something had disturbed him badly.

"How's the cut on your hand?"

"It's fine. I had to get rid of the bandage." He
lapsed back into silence.

"Have you had a bad day?" She sat quietly leaning
back in her chair. Her helpings were always tiny and
she was finished, her plate clean.

He shrugged. "No, just a lot of hard work."

"Something's worrying you, and I'm sorry," she
said.

Startled, Dan lowered his glass of milk and stared
at her. "What in sweet hell makes you think something is worrying me? I guess I've been quiet," he
added, as if answering his own question.

"Whatever it is, I'm sorry," she said gently. "Is
there anything I can do?"

"No, there's nothing," he said, smiling at her. "I'm
tired and we had problems crop up at work." He studied her, shocked that she could tell so easily that
something was wrong, while Louisa hadn't had an inkling. "No. I had a long day at work," he lied.

Her gaze slid away and she flushed. "I'm sorry.
Once again, I wasn't prying," she replied, realizing it
was none of her concern, and she shouldn't have
quizzed him. Perhaps he had had cross words with
Louisa or had difficulties in his business. She had gone
beyond the bounds of her slight friendship with him
by asking personal questions, and she felt hot with
embarrassment.

Dan drew a sharp breath, realizing she had taken his
answer as a rebuff.

"Mary," he asked quietly, and she met his gaze.
"How did you know something was bothering me?"

"I'm sorry I asked. It wasn't my place."

"I've had bad news and I'm worried about it."

"I'm sorry. Is there anything I can do? Do you need
funds?"

"Now I answered your question. You answer mine,
because I want to know. How did you know I was
worried?"

"There are several reasons," she answered forthrightly, realizing it was important to him, but unable
to fathom why it would be. "You're acting differently tonight. You're eating in silence, your thoughts seem
to be elsewhere. You look worried."

"Ahh, so that's how," he said, leaning back to look
at her.

"Yes, and I didn't mean to pry. Would you like some
cobbler?"

"Do you need to ask?" he answered.

She stood up to take their dishes. He stood and took
them from her hands. "I'll wait on you tonight," he
said.

"We'll both do it, and it'll be faster," she said. She
dished up two bowls of steaming golden apple cobbler
and turned around. "Would you like cream on yours?"

He came to her and braced his hands on both sides
of her on the counter, standing close and hemming her
in. Mary gazed into his eyes as he leaned down slightly
toward her. Her heart pounded because he stood so
close to her. She pressed back against the counter until
she was unable to retreat any farther.

"I want you to understand something."

"Yes," she said breathlessly, wanting to tell him to
move away, yet embarrassed to say so because she
didn't want him to realize how his presence disturbed
her. He did disturb her, though, and she was fully
aware of it.

"I'm glad we're friends and that I had a chance to
get to know you," he said softly, studying her.

"It's been nice for me too," she replied. Her nerves
were stretched raw by his proximity. As she gazed at
him, she wondered if any woman could ever become
accustomed to his handsome features or if the women
in his life stayed permanently awed by them. A faint
blond stubble was beginning to show on his jaw.

"You work too hard, Mary. I want you to take Silas'
money and use it."

"I've been thinking about that," she said carefully. "I'll take enough to pay you for your work, because—"

"No," he said with a lopsided grin. "You're not paying me, and I don't want to hear another word about it."

"And I won't take Silas' money, and not another word about that," she retorted, raising her chin defiantly. They both laughed at the same time, and she relaxed a little.

His smile vanished and he gave her a searching look that made her heart thud. She was afraid to move, because she would bump him if she didn't stand completely still. Her hands were at her waist, holding a spoon.

"I'm going to miss coming here every evening."

"You can come when you like. Paddy and Brian and I will always be glad to see you," she said, knowing it was only herself, not Paddy or Brian she was thinking about.

"You have to take the money. Silas is liable to tear me to pieces when he gets back and finds out I failed him."

Dan saw the flash of fire in her eyes and knew he was battling a hopeless cause. "Silas Eustice will hear from me about just exactly why I wouldn't take his money! Money isn't the only thing in the world that brings happiness."

When it got right down to it, he had to admit there were times when it was easier to talk to Mary than Louisa. There were even occasions when it was easier to talk to Mary than Dulcie. He shared many interests with Mary, like their books and the work on the house.

"Why are you so easy to talk to? You're easier than Louisa sometimes."

Mary wasn't sure she wanted to hear that he enjoyed talking to her sometimes more than Louisa. On the one hand it frightened her, yet at the same time she felt a rush of pleasure.

"Louisa will be easy to talk to. You've spent more time with me lately, that's all. You'll enjoy talking to Louisa."

"If I can ever get the chance. Her parents won't leave us alone." As he stared into Mary's wide green eyes, he lowered his gaze to her mouth. If he hadn't known better, he'd have sworn she was so innocent she hadn't even been kissed. There was a naiveté to her that made her seem untouched by a man. Right now she stared back at him like a trusting child; yet as he studied her, he knew she was no child. She was a warm, intelligent woman. His gaze lowered to her mouth again. Her pink lips looked soft and inviting. He felt a pull. "Mary, you're the best friend I have."

"Thank you," she answered solemnly. Her eyes were wide, holding his gaze. He looked at her mouth again and his curiosity stirred. He wondered what it would be like to kiss her. His gaze met hers, and as he realized the direction his thoughts were moving in, he turned away from her abruptly. "I'll get the cobbler," he said, picking up both bowls to place them on the table.

They ate cobbler and Dan went to work installing one of the windows. His concentration centered on the task at hand and he forgot about all the women in his life. Late that night, before he left, he sat and talked with Mary.

They spoke softly, sitting in the kitchen where wood still burned in the cooking stove. She had a shawl around her shoulders, and in the soft light of a single lamp, dark shadows filled the corners. Paddy had gone to bed, Brian was out, and they were alone.

Dan talked about the plans he was drawing for Corning and Ringwood. He leaned forward to rest his arm on the table while he talked.

"That's exciting, Dan. The Shumachers should be pleased."

"I suppose they are."

"I'm sorry that working here has cut into your time to be with Louisa."

He shrugged. "If I go calling in the evening, I spend the whole time with Louisa's parents, and Mrs. Shumacher's cold stares aren't conducive to an enthralling evening."

"You'll be with them a long time once you're married."

"We won't live with them. I should take Paddy with me the next time I visit them. With his tales of Ireland, he would liven up the conversation a bit. He might even stir Mrs. Shumacher to a few words."

They both laughed, and impulsively he reached out to touch her cheek. "You're so damned easy to talk to."

She shrugged. "So are you. I don't have time to see my friends much. Sometimes Bessie comes over, but not often now."

"I'll bet you told Silas everything, and he told you everything."

"He told me a lot about himself that I don't think he shared with others."

"I don't think I can share some things in my life with Louisa. I suppose it doesn't matter. I love her and want to be with her."

"I imagine you can share everything with her," she said gently. She hated to think about Dan marrying Louisa Shumacher.

"No, I can't," he said somberly, studying Mary. He knew that what he really wanted was to have one trusted friend in town. And he was sure he could trust Mary with anything. "I can tell you what I can never tell Louisa," he said, voicing his thoughts aloud. "As far as my life is concerned, my secrets, Silas knows them, and someday he'll tell you anyway."

"Dan, if it's because I asked earlier, I apologize again. When I'm with you, I say whatever pops to mind."

"And that's the way I want you to be. That's what friends are for. They can say whatever they want to each other without stopping to consider consequences." He caught her hand in both of his and held it. He watched her, debating for another few seconds about whether or not he should share his problems with someone or keep them to himself as he usually did. Impulsively he decided to tell her. "Mary, I saw a poster in the store today. It had just come in with the mail. It's a wanted poster."

Mary listened to him, intensely aware of her hand

held in his. She didn't think he was aware of what he was doing. He looked lost in his thoughts while he rubbed her knuckles with his fingers. And she realized two things at once: he was going to tell her what bothered him, and it was a wanted poster that disturbed him. Her gaze ran over his features, and she saw him in a new light. He had seemed gentle, peaceful during most of the time he spent with her, but she had suspected that beneath, there was a strong, tough survivor, and now she was sure of it.

"Whose picture was it?" she asked, holding her breath. He met her gaze directly.

"Mine."

She closed her eyes for an instant as if she had received a blow. She had guessed that would be his answer, but had hoped against it. It hurt to think he would be *wanted* anywhere.

Dan was startled by her reaction, and suddenly regretted telling her. She looked shocked, as if she found the news repugnant.

"Mary, I'm going to have to ask you to keep this to yourself. Silas knows, so in time he would have told you," he said, releasing her hand.

"Oh, Dan, I'm sorry! Will you have to leave town?" she asked. She sounded so grieved that his dismay vanished, and he let out his breath, realizing he had misinterpreted her reaction.

"I don't think so."

"Can anyone recognize you easily from the poster?"

"I didn't look like I do now. Of course, I can recognize my own picture, but I don't know about others. I wore a bear-claw necklace and a hat with feathers. My hair was long and I had a mustache and beard. In the picture I'm wearing a hat."

"That doesn't sound the same," she said slowly, with doubt in her tone.

"I did look different."

"You're so hand—" She bit back her word, suddenly blushing.

"Thank you," he said quietly, surprised that she found him handsome. She seemed to pay little attention to him, and he supposed she wouldn't notice any man except Silas.

"I killed a man in self-defense," he said, wanting her to know what he had done and why. "He tried to slit my throat."

"That's how you got the scar," she said. She was leaning on the table, and she reached the short distance to touch his throat. She pushed down the shirt just enough to touch the white line in his flesh. She was acutely conscious of touching him, of hurting for him and she began to fear for his safety.

"They were going to string me up without a trial, and I escaped. I was innocent, and was only protecting myself, but when I ran, it put me on the wrong side of the law. I'll have to admit, I've done a lot of things I shouldn't have. I've robbed banks and trains."

She placed her hand on his arm. "I'm so sorry."

"My full name is Tigre Danby Castillo. I took the name Dan Castle while I was with Silas. He saved me from bounty hunters. I'm wanted dead or alive," he said harshly. "It doesn't matter which, and the reward is larger than ever."

"That's dreadful," she said. She was acutely aware of her fingers on his arm and as she felt the hard muscle through his cotton sleeve, she tried to imagine how his life had been.

"I don't think I can ever tell Louisa. I think she would be repelled."

"Surely you can. If she's going to marry you, she must love you very much." She thought about Louisa and frowned, looking down at her fingers on his arm. "But it would probably be wiser to wait to tell her. There may never be a need to do so."

"No, but I'd feel more honest if she knew."

"It won't matter to her, Dan. It won't matter at all," she said, but there wasn't much conviction in her voice. In fact she suspected it might matter a great deal to a woman like Louisa Shumacher.

"You're a little liar," he said softly in gentle tones. "It wouldn't matter to a woman like you, but it will matter to my Louisa. I don't fault her for being that way. Louisa has high standards and she knows little about adversity."

"Do you think there are bounty hunters after you now?"

"No, not since I left Silas. The more responsible I can become here, the less likely I'll be bothered. I don't have any enemies here. Except Reuben Knelville."

"Reuben Knelville is a powerful man, from what I've heard. He's Ralston Knelville's son, isn't he?"

"Yes, but he won't be studying the wanted posters."

"Just be careful. And you made an enemy of Dewar Logan, although Dewar stays out on his ranch most of the time."

Dan found relief and comfort in talking to her, and he patted her hand, picking it up again in his and idly touching her fingers with his other hand. "I'll be all right. It's something I've lived with for a long time now."

"I'm sorry. A man like you should have a chance for a fair trial. And you should have a chance to start again. So many people came here with hidden pasts, and now they're fine citizens. If you ever need help—"

"I know where to go," he replied with a smile. "I should leave now. It's past midnight," he said, always surprised by how swiftly time passed when he was with her.

"Dan, your secret is safe with me."

"I know that. If I trust Silas, then I trust you.

He stood up and pulled on his coat, carrying his dishes to the counter. "Good night, Mary. You lock up after me, and be careful."

Impulsively she stood on tiptoe and kissed his cheek. She stepped back quickly. "*You* be careful. I'm so sorry about the trouble you had."

"I feel better just talking to someone about it. I guess it shook me, because I thought I was safe in Denver, so far removed from bounty hunters and my past. I guess I'm stuck with it, just like my shadow."

''But shadows can't hurt you.''

He smiled at her. ''Thanks for everything. If I didn't sit and talk and eat so much, your boardinghouse might be finished by now.''

''This is more fun,'' she said, smiling and revealing her even white teeth and dimples.

She watched him ride away and went back inside, feeling the grip of fear. Wanted for murder, bank robberies, and train robberies! How different could the drawing look? And Dan had enemies now, powerful ones. She cleaned the kitchen and turned out the lamps on the way to her room. She was restless as she remembered their conversation. She remembered even more clearly when he had stood so close at the counter and she looked into his blue eyes. It was far into the night before she fell asleep.

The next night Dan had one of the best times he had had since the night he asked Louisa to marry him. There were moments he got her to himself, in the closed front parlor away from the other guests. Their stolen kisses set him aflame with desire, and on the ride home in the carriage she allowed him more liberties than ever before. After he kissed her good night, Grizzly drove to Dulcie's, where he climbed down to let Dan take the reins. Dan glanced at the house with all its lights pouring forth and went inside. He intended to see Dulcie for only a little while, but it was two hours later when he left. He was riding on empty roads, winding past the bordellos and saloons, when he saw a familiar figure standing in front of a saloon. He swore under his breath and shook his head. He flicked the reins, pulled his team to a halt, and jumped down.

Mary glanced around, saw him, and turned.

''Dammit, Mary, you shouldn't be out. Which one are you looking for, Paddy or Brian?''

''Brian. I'm worried about him, Dan, and I've looked in every saloon in town.''

Dan thought of Dulcie's house, and of how he had spent the past two hours. ''Mary, has it occurred to you that your brother is old enough to be in one of the sporting houses?''

Even in the shadowy light spilling from the saloon, he saw her blush and her mouth form a round O. He had to bite back a smile. He took her arm. ''Let me take you home.''

''I didn't . . . Brian's a baby.''

''Brian is a man. He's young, but he's a man and you're going to have to accept that fact. You're a sister, and whether you're sister or mother, he's grown, Mary, and you have to let him go.''

She ran her hand across her forehead and didn't answer him. After a few glances at her, he wondered if she might be crying. He put his arm around her and pulled her close, patting her shoulder. ''He'll be all right. Don't worry about him. You can't keep him locked up at home.''

''I'm so worried,'' she said so softly he had to bend close to hear. She looked up at him: ''Dan, he leaves home in the night, and I don't know where he goes.''

She sat only inches away, her face upturned, and he realized how tiny she felt with his arm around her thin shoulders. ''How do you know all that?''

''I followed him one night.''

He groaned and shook her lightly. ''You're in more danger than your brother! Dammit, you shouldn't trail around town at night after him.''

''I had to see what he was doing. I'm so scared. Where can he be going?''

''Mary, it's his business. Not yours.''

She twisted her fingers together and finally looked up at him again. ''I found money in his room, Dan. I haven't told anyone, but he has two thousand dollars hidden in his room. He doesn't earn money like that at the livery stable.''

''Lord, no! Two thousand dollars?'' he said, frowning at her. There wasn't an honest way a kid like Brian O'Malley could earn such money. All too well, Dan knew the ways Brian could get it.

''I'm so scared about what he might be doing,'' she

said. Dan squeezed her close and turned her against him.

"When does he go? Is it at regular times?"

"I don't know. He went out last month, and now he's gone tonight."

"Same time last month?"

She straightened up to look at him. "I guess, now that you ask, it was. I didn't think about that. Dan, I'm terrified he's robbing a stage or worse."

"Was he alone when he left?"

"Yes. He wasn't home at all the next day or night. He told me he slept at the livery stable. Sometimes he does sleep there, but I know he didn't that time because I followed him. The next day I went to look for him, and Henry told me Brian had asked for two days off from his job to tend to chores for Paddy."

"He couldn't be doing anything for Paddy, could he?"

"No!"

Dan mulled over what to do, and reluctantly came to a conclusion. "I guess if you discover he's going, come get me. I hate like hell for you to run around town late at night, but that's the only thing I can think of to do. I'll follow him and see where he goes."

"I don't want to put you in danger, and I'm afraid he's doing something dangerous. Otherwise he wouldn't hide it."

"I don't know what the hell it would be. I haven't heard of any robberies around this area in the past two months, except for that one of the stage, and the two men responsible for that were shot and killed."

He stopped in front of her house and swung her down. "I'll come drink some brandy with you. You're not going to sleep now anyway. First you go look in his room and see if he's there."

She hurried inside, leaving him to build up the fire in the front parlor. In minutes she returned to stand beside him as he poked coals and sent sparks crackling up the chimney.

She was shaking from the cold, holding her hands in front of the fire. He poured two brandies and brought one to her. "Sit down here," he said, pulling her down beside him on the floor. "Drink your brandy and turn around. I'll give you a back rub—that will help you relax."

Mary knew she should say no. It was highly improper for Dan to rub her back, no matter how many layers of clothing she wore, but she couldn't get out the refusal. Instead she did as he said, drinking the brandy and turning, feeling his hands squeezing her shoulders, pressing on her back as he rubbed. Slowly she relaxed and relished his touches.

He turned her to face him and smiled at her. "Better?"

"Much better, thank you."

He touched her chin. "Now, don't worry about him. Just come and get me the next time he leaves. Promise me you won't follow him and you'll stop going to saloons late at night to search for him."

She stared at the fire and debated whether she could promise such a thing. "Dan, I have to see about him."

"Mary, he's grown. He's a man. On the frontier, boys become men sooner than eighteen. My half-brother was ambushed by renegades when he was sixteen. They took my mother and shot Luke and left him for dead."

"Oh, no!" she exclaimed, turning to face him.

"Luke is my half-brother. I also have a half-sister, April. I have a different father from them, Javier Castillo." He told Mary briefly about his family. Then, "Enough about my problems. Back to your brother. Promise me you'll stop going out late at night to saloons in search of him."

Her gaze slid away and she caught her lower lip with her white teeth. "I suppose I should promise you, but it's hard."

He squeezed her shoulder. "I know it's difficult."

"Yes, I promise. I know I shouldn't follow him, but he isn't eighteen yet."

"Mary, accept the fact that he's a man now." Dan was suddenly tempted to reach up and pull the pins out of her hair and see what she looked like with it down. He reached out, realized what he was about to do, then merely brushed her shoulder and turned toward the fire. He had no right to take pins out of Mary's hair. He was almost engaged, and she was all but engaged. He tried to get his thoughts back to Louisa, to think of her dark beauty, yet all the time he was acutely conscious of the sweet scent of Mary's clothes, of her sitting only inches away. And his interest in Mary wasn't caused by any unsatisfied passion stirred by Louisa. He had calmed that storm at Dulcie's. He glanced around at Mary. She had her slender arms wrapped around her knees and was gazing into the fire. In the firelight her skin looked golden, her lips rosy. She slanted him a look.

"Thank you for taking so much time with me."

He studied her, really looking at her, and he wondered once more how she would look with her hair down. Her gaze met his and caught. Dan felt ensnared by her green eyes. He was unable to tear his gaze away, and in the silence, attraction sparked between them with a tug on his senses he couldn't ignore. Her skin was smooth, a smattering of freckles sprinkling her nose, and her wide eyes were luminous and beautiful.

He leaned toward her, realized what he was doing, and stood up abruptly. "I need to go home now."

She followed him to the door, and both of them were silent. Dan was shaken by what he had seen and felt. She was Silas' girl. His best friend. And he would soon be engaged, but at the moment it was difficult to think of Louisa. He yanked on his coat.

"Good night, Mary," he said abruptly, and left.

"Good night," she answered quietly. She was aware that he had felt the same thing she did. She watched him ride away, and closed the door. In the parlor she gazed into the fire. "Silas, you should have come home to me," she whispered, feeling an empty longing, knowing the man in her thoughts wasn't Silas. It was Dan.

12

For the next week Dan avoided the O'Malleys. They
had four walls, floors, and a roof. He still had to take
care of the finishing touches on the inside of the house
and the porch, but he found one reason after another
to postpone going to work there. And he wouldn't
think back about the last evening with Mary. When
she came to mind, and she did with astounding regularity, he put her abruptly out of thought.

On Friday evening during the first week of April, as
he stood in the parlor of the Parsons' home near the
fire, he swore to Louisa as he watched Reuben approach: "Dammit, Reuben Knelville is your shadow.
That ends when we marry."

"Jealous?" Louisa asked with a pleased smile.
"Hello, Reuben."

"Hello, Louisa, Mr. Castle. Will we meet your
family at the wedding, Castle?"

"You'll meet some of them."

"Oh, I didn't know you had relatives here in Denver. As a matter of fact, I didn't know you claimed
any relatives."

"Of course he has relatives. He has a brother in San
Antonio who's a lawyer," Louisa said smugly.

"What's this I hear about a horse-car line to some
of the new homes?" Dan asked.

"There's talk about it," Reuben answered. "It's
proposed to run from the center of town on Larimer
out to Twenty-sixth or Twenty-seventh and Champa.
So you have a brother who is a lawyer," Reuben said,

returning to the subject. His eyes were bright and curious, and Dan wanted to swear. The last thing he wanted was Reuben Knelville checking into his background. It wouldn't take long for him to uncover the truth.

"I know some San Antonio lawyers. What is his name? I can't recall one named Castle."

"It's a half-brother," Louisa said. She seemed happy to throw the information in Reuben's face, while Dan wished she would let it drop and avoid telling Reuben anything.

"Oh, and what is this half-brother's name?" he asked in a haughty tone.

"Luke Danby," Dan answered, wondering if his future would hang on his reply. If Knelville investigated Luke's life and asked enough questions, he would soon know all about Dan's past. And with Hattie living in San Antonio with Luke, discovering the truth would be even easier. "And where are you from, Reuben? Denver hasn't been here long enough for you to have grown up here."

"We came from St. Louis. My father was one of the first to find silver. Real estate is his keen interest now, of course."

" 'Evening, Marvella," Dan said, catching her arm as she passed.

She smiled at him, her eyelashes fluttering. "Mr. Castle! Hello, Louisa, Mr. Knelville."

"And where are you from, Marvella?" Dan asked, knowing Marvella would be unable to resist pouring her attention on Reuben. Tall and willowy; with a long nose and a high voice that sounded more like a two-year-old child, she gave her attention to Reuben. And he seemed happy to give his attention back to her. In minutes Dan was able to ease Louisa away from Reuben, but several times during the evening Dan caught Reuben's curious eyes studying him.

On the way home in the carriage, Louisa turned to him. "Where are your thoughts?" she asked. "They're not on me."

"I'm sorry," he said, turning to pull her into his

arms. "I was thinking about work. And you've had all the attention you could ever dream of wanting tonight. Reuben couldn't leave your side. If men still fought duels, I'd have already had one over you. Reuben would have challenged me or given me a challenge I couldn't have refused."

"I think a duel would be incredibly exciting!"

"That's because you're a bloodthirsty little witch," he said softly in a husky voice, kissing her throat.

She murmured and wound her fingers in his hair. Suddenly she pushed him away and pouted. "You can't touch me or come near me, Dan Castle, if you call me names like bloodthirsty witch!"

He chuckled. "Bloodthirsty," he whispered, leaning forward to kiss her. "Witch," he said, trailing his kisses to her throat. He pulled her on his lap, and was thankful he had had the foresight to buy such an elegant carriage that gave them complete privacy. He kissed her passionately, pressing her against him. His hands worked at the fastenings on her dress until finally her breasts were free and he could fondle her.

"Dan! You mustn't," she protested. She sat up and moved to her corner, but Dan knew her protests were merely a game. He leaned forward, slipping his fingers beneath her dress at the neckline, pushing aside the material before Louisa could button it. Dan cupped her breast, his thumb flicking over the nipple, and she gasped, closing her eyes. He leaned forward to kiss her, pushing her back against the corner of the carriage, his hand slipping beneath her skirt to caress her legs.

By the time she sat up and told him to stop, he was burning with passion. As he watched her straighten her clothes, he tried to imagine her without them on. And as he watched Louisa, he thought of Mary, who would never tease and torment him simply for her own enjoyment.

He kissed Louisa good night, then turned his carriage toward Holladay, unable to resist going to see Dulcie.

* * *

The following Monday, Dan had a meeting in which he would present his plans and drawings to Benjamin Corning. He had already finished Lester Potter's house, and had appointments to discuss plans with Edward Ringwood and Jay Varner.

As he rode in his carriage, excitement gripped him. Sunshine spilled over the busy, prospering town. The saloons and the stores were filled with customers, and businessmen strode along the street. Dan found Denver exciting. There was a transient population of prospectors, of disillusioned men returning home, and of travelers headed east or west. Dulcie's house did a lot of business, and Dan hoped this was the start of a successful career for him in this city. The only troublesome aspect was Reuben Knelville, who could so easily unearth Dan's past. He pulled his carriage to a halt to jump down and tuck the rolled drawings under his arm.

As he was ushered into Corning's office, Dan took a deep breath. He felt as if his entire future depended on this man's decision. If Corning and Ringwood both refused his services, he didn't think other wealthy men would seek his business.

Tall, black-haired, and solemn, Corning came forward to greet him, shaking hands and offering Dan a chair. His manner was brisk and cool.

"How's your work going?"

"Fine. I've just finished Lester Potter's house."

"How did you get into this business, Mr. Castle?" Corning asked, sitting down behind his desk.

"I've worked with others in California."

"Where's your home?"

"My family—what's left of it—lives in Texas," he answered evenly. He wondered if Reuben had talked to Corning, because never before had he inquired about Dan's past.

"Why didn't you want to stay in Texas?"

"I wanted to prospect, and when I hit a vein, I gathered up enough funds to go into business. Silas Eustice mined with me, and he constantly told me about the glories of Denver. So I decided to come here and see if it was all he claimed.''

"I really prefer to have references from places you've worked in years past.''

"I can give you Lester Potter's reference. Other than that, I'd have to write to people I worked for long ago in California.''

"Mr. Castle,'' Corning interrupted with barely a glance at the plans, "to save time, because I know you're a busy man and I'm busy, I'll pay you for your services to date. Mrs. Corning and I have decided to wait before we build.''

Dan thought of the hours of labor he had poured into the plans and drawings, and the expectations he had for this project. He wanted to argue, to show every irresistible detail to Corning, but he knew the uselessness of such a gesture.

"I'd like an opportunity to at least show the plans to you.''

"Sorry, but I'm not interested.''

"Would it help to send to California for references?'' Dan asked in a quiet voice.

Corning shrugged. "I need to know more than that about a man before I invest my money in his work. It's a matter of trust,'' he said coldly.

"I'll send you a bill, sir.''

"Fine.'' Corning stood up, signaling the meeting was over.

"I'd appreciate your business and would like to discuss plans with you when you do decide to build.''

"Of course.''

"Good day to you, sir.''

Outside, Dan wanted to smash the plans and grind them into the dirt. He wondered if Reuben Knelville was behind the difficulty. He swore under his breath, flung the plans into his carriage, and had started to climb up when he glanced across the street at a saloon. He turned around and strode over, going into the darkened interior of the Missouri House. He spotted Paddy O'Malley at the bar and went to stand beside him.

"Good morning, Paddy. I'll have a whiskey,'' he

told the barkeep, who set a tumbler of water, a bottle of whiskey, and another tumbler on the bar.

"Good morning, my boy. Mary sent me out early this morning. Today she shops for supplies. I've already gotten my supplies." He patted his middle, and Dan saw a bottle tucked into his waistband. "That's fortification. This can turn the coldest day into spring."

An hour later Dan rode home to go back to work on plans he had drawn for Edward Ringwood and Jay Varner.

Five nights later he paced in Dulcie's room. "I will wager Knelville is behind this. Neither Corning nor Varner would even look at my drawings. They paid the fee and said no."

"Dan, there are other men in the world besides Benjamin Corning and that Varner. You said you're drawing up plans for another wealthy man."

"Yes. I hope Knelville can't influence him."

"You didn't tell me about Reuben Knelville before tonight."

Dan paused, lowering his glass of brandy to the table. He had a blanket wrapped around him, and Dulcie lay propped against the pillows, covers to her waist, her breasts bare.

"There wasn't any reason to tell you about him. Do you know him, Dulcie?" Dan asked, studying her. She averted her gaze, something as uncharacteristic of her as fainting spells.

He sat up, and a prickle ran across the back of his neck. Dulcie knew everything about him. "You're seeing him."

She didn't answer, and he moved to the bed to sit down. "Look at me, Dulcie. You're seeing him."

"Yes, but I didn't know he knew you or wanted information about you."

"Did you give him any?"

"No. Dan, I swear I didn't. I wouldn't ever do that."

"What did he want to know?"

"He wanted to know if I had known you in the past—"

"You're seeing other men now, aren't you?" He gave her a level look as he interrupted her.

She raised her chin and stared back at him. "Yes. I was meant to have a man around, and you're not here often."

He turned away, running his hands through his hair. "Sorry, Dulcie. I don't have any claim on you. I forfeited that when I asked Louisa to marry me."

Silence stretched between them, and finally she spoke. "You could have a claim again, Dan."

He turned to look at her, seeing the longing in her eyes. He thought of Louisa and stroked Dulcie's cheek, gazing beyond her as he thought of Mary O'Malley.

"To hell with you," she said mildly, pushing him away. "You're in love. I can see it."

"Go ahead and tell me about Reuben."

"He asked me about when I met you. How and where. I told him Montana in the gold fields, but that's all." She sat up suddenly to hug him. "Dan, I'll never give away your past."

He hugged her, feeling her softness. The blanket fell away when he released his grip on its folds, and Dulcie's body was warm and bare in his arms. He pushed her down on the bed. "Don't tell Reuben Knelville one damned thing about me."

He kissed away her answer, hoping he was safe with her, knowing a mere promise wouldn't bind her.

Monday night Dan went to work at the O'Malleys'. When he came in the back door, the night was chilly and a fire burned on the hearth. Mary turned to greet him, her eyes lighting and her cheeks turning pink.

"Dan! This is a surprise!"

"Sorry, I've been busy on other things, and I know you have four walls and won't freeze. How are you, Mary?" he asked quietly, his gaze sweeping over her. She was self-conscious with him and he felt a sense of restraint with her which he didn't feel with other women. It was so good to see her, though, and he realized how much he had missed her.

"I didn't know you were coming."

"I don't need to eat."

"Oh, no! I can get it out quickly." She turned to open the cabinet and take down dishes. "I can heat something in just a few minutes," she said. Her heart pounded, and she didn't know what she was saying to him. He stood in the doorway watching her, arms crossed, a scowl on his face.

"I'll go to work, Mary," he said gruffly, and strode past her. She heard his boots fade and stared after him. It was so good to see him, but she knew his work would be finished soon and he wouldn't need to come back. She tried not to think about that, and turned back to put another log in the stove and bring covered bowls in off the cold porch to reheat food from supper.

She didn't eat with Dan, but served him. She stayed in the kitchen while he ate, staring at the door and wishing she were out there with him, yet knowing she shouldn't be. She picked up a pitcher of milk and went into the dining room.

"Would you care for more milk?"

"Sit down, Mary," he ordered. "You don't have anything to do in the kitchen. How's Brian?"

"He's fine. He's been coming home quite regularly now. I hear you're not building Benjamin Corning's new house."

"How in blazes did you hear that?"

"From the general store. You know, Mr. Workman hears everything. I should get back to the kitchen."

"Sit down," he ordered again. "Please," he added gently.

She settled back in the chair to talk to him until he went back to work. Then, instead of going to watch or help him work, she stayed away. She couldn't forget the last time he was there, the strong attraction she had felt and shouldn't acknowledge. She went to the back parlor to read. She held the book idly in her hands, but read and reread the same page until she heard boots on the hall floor and looked up to see Dan at the door.

"I'm quitting. Is Brian home tonight?"

"No, and neither is Pa, but they'll be along later."

She stood up, feeling awkward with him. His gaze swept over her, and he turned away, raking his fingers through his hair. "I'll finish tomorrow night. Actually, if you'll show Brian that molding around the floor—there's a piece that's broken. He can fix it himself. I'm all finished."

The words made her draw a deep breath.

"I knew you would be," she said, and he wanted to cross the room to her. "Brian will take care of the molding."

"Well, it's la—"

Both looked up as the thud of hoofbeats sounded. There was a pounding at the front door.

13

"Miss O'Malley?"

"Yes?"

A man stood in front of her, his horse directly behind him at the post. He turned his hat nervously in his hands. "I'm Clyde Jethro, ma'am, and I hate to come like this so late at night. Have you got parents here, ma'am?"

"No. Come inside, Mr. Jethro."

Dan moved closer, seeing the earnest look on the man's face and hearing his question.

"I can't stay. I came to get the doc. Ma'am, we were in the mountains at a mining camp. Your brother tangled with a bear. I'm taking the doc back with me, and Michael said to get you."

As Jethro talked, Dan put his arm around her shoulders. "I'm Dan Castle," he said, extending his hand. "We'll be ready. Get the doctor and stop back here, and we'll join you."

"Right."

"Do you know the way to the doctor's house?"

"Yes. I've been in Denver before."

"Mr. Jethro," Mary said in a quiet, strained voice that Dan hated to hear, "how badly is Michael hurt?"

When Jethro looked into Dan's eyes, Dan realized it was bad.

"Getting in a scrape with a bear, ma'am, ain't the thing to do." He held up his hand, and two fingers were missing. "See. Had my own run-in with a bobcat. Took my fingers clean off."

"You get the doc," Dan said, and moved toward the door to close it behind Jethro.

"I'll go with you," he said to Mary.

"Oh, no! You don't—"

"I'm going. You're not riding off into the mountains with a stranger, so don't argue, Mary. Get your things. It'll be a long ride, and we may have to camp. Take enough for a few days. I'll ride home and be back as soon as possible."

"Dan, you don't have to go with me."

"I'll get my friend Dulcie to send someone over to cook and stay here. Where's the most likely place to find Paddy or Brian?"

"I completely forgot the boardinghouse!" She ran her hand across her head. "Pa and Brian could be at the Lazy Dog, the Missouri House, or the Billiard Saloon. I don't really know."

"If I don't find them, we'll just have to go without them. Leave Brian a letter. Go get ready."

She nodded, her eyes round and her face pale. Dan ran to mount his horse, then raced to send a telegram to Luke in San Antonio, asking him to tell Ta-ne-haddle what had happened and see if the Kiowa could come help. Next he hurried to the Lazy Dog. When he couldn't find either of the O'Malley men, he hired a man to search for them. Next he rode to Dulcie's. She was in the parlor sitting on a man's lap. At the sight of Dan, she came across the room.

"I need your help," he said without preamble.

"What can I do?" She moved away from the parlor, where it was quieter.

"Mary O'Malley's brother was mauled by a bear. She's going to a mining camp in the mountains, where her brother is. Can you find someone to cook and keep the boardinghouse running while she's gone? Someone to go over there by breakfast time in the morning?"

Dulcie wrinkled her brow. "I suppose if nothing else, I can send my own cook."

"That temperamental little chef—do you think he'll agree?"

"Of course. I'll tell him what you said, that Mary

O'Malley is the best cook in the world. He won't be able to resist taking over her kitchen.''

Dan hugged her. ''Thanks, Dulcie. I knew I could count on you. I'm going with Mary.''

''You're going?''

''She doesn't know where Brian and Paddy are. I hired someone to search for them, but it could take all night.''

''One more time Silas should have been at her side. Instead she has you,'' Dulcie said, staring at him intently. ''You may be gone for days.''

''I'll go with her and come back tomorrow. If necessary, I can go back and get her later, but Brian will probably be with her. I'll pay for whatever the cook costs. Just keep the place running for her.''

''Silas can pay, Dan. Take it out of that money. Come here, before you go. I'll pack food you can take.''

In a few minutes she handed him two baskets of food. ''Run along, honey. I hope he's okay.''

Dulcie watched him stride through the door. She followed him out to the porch as he mounted and wheeled his horse around to ride away. He waved, and she waved in return, shivering in the cold. ''And did you think to tell Her Highness you're leaving town?'' Dulcie asked softly with only the sigh of the wind for an answer. Mary Katherine O'Malley. She had seemed quiet, sweet, innocent, and the least likely person to stir up a tempest, but if Dulcie knew anything about men, there was going to be a terrible tempest swirling around Mary O'Malley before long.

Dan rode to Louisa's house. Charles Shumacher opened the door in response to Dan's loud knock.

''Mr. Castle? It's far too late for you to be calling on Louisa. Do you realize what time it is?''

''Sir, I'm leaving town on an emergency and I wanted to let Louisa know.''

''She's in bed asleep. I'll give her the message.''

''Mary O'Malley's brother was mauled by a bear. He's at a mining camp in the mountains and one of the men came to get Mary and the doctor. We can't find her father or brother, so I'll accompany her to the camp.''

''I see. Sorry. Sounds bad. That Michael O'Malley is a strong one, though. He's not like the other O'Malleys. Big, strapping fellow who boxes. Is there anything we can do?''

''No, but thanks. Just tell Louisa. I hope to come back in the morning, but I may be delayed. I'd appreciate it if you pass word on to people for me.''

''Certainly.''

Dan hurried off the porch and mounted up, riding to his house to grab the clothes he thought he'd need. He strapped on his six-shooter and got down his rifle, then headed back to the O'Malleys'.

Long past midnight they rode away from town, headed west toward the mountains. The wind was chilly, and low clouds scudded across the sky. They rode until three in the morning, when Dan caught up with Jethro. ''I think we should stop. Mary can't ride straight through.''

Mary appeared beside him. ''Yes, I can. I don't want to sleep. It's up to Dr. Felton. Ask him.''

''Doc, what about it?''

The lanky, taciturn doctor said, ''I can ride. I can sleep in the saddle if necessary.''

Near dawn Dan noticed Mary nodding. He rode close beside her, placing his hand on her arm. ''Mary.''

She straightened up and looked at him. ''I'm fine.''

He lifted her to his horse. ''Ride with me and you can sleep a little.''

The doctor took the reins of Mary's horse, leading her horse behind his, while Dan settled Mary in front of him. ''Comfortable?''

She hooked her knee around the pommel. ''Yes,'' she said. She knew she should have protested and stayed on her horse, but she was exhausted and it was warm and comforting in Dan's arms. He held her tightly and she placed her head against his chest, closing her eyes. Without thinking about what he was doing, Dan bent his head to kiss the top of her head lightly, brushing his lips across the top of her furry cloak.

Dawn came and they reached the mountains. They rode upward on a narrow trail, and the wind whistled through pines and spruce. A fresh, woodsy scent that Dan loved filled the cold air, and the white trunks of aspen looked beautiful in the first light of dawn as the sun rose and streamed through the trees. Mary felt warm pressed against him, her arm wrapped tightly around his waist. They halted by a stream to wash and let the animals drink. Dan shook her gently, "Mary, wake up."

He dismounted and lifted her down. "I've got some dried beef and some cold biscuits."

In a short time they were traveling again. This time Mary rode on her own horse, but she could remember clearly how it had felt to be held tightly in Dan's arms leaning against the solid strength of his chest. As they wound higher up the mountains, there were patches of snow that became denser, until they reached the mountaintop, which was covered with snow. Sunlight splashed over them and Dan rode beside Mary, casting continual glances at her. Plumes of smoke spiraled up from the valley below, and Dan guessed it was the mining camp.

As they rode into camp, Jethro gave two long whistles, a signal, and Dan wondered why he would have to signal their approach. He felt a prickle across his nape, and hoped they weren't riding into trouble. Jethro turned in his saddle, dropping back to ride beside Dan.

"I think I should take Doc in first. Her brother ain't a pretty sight. And if I was you, I'd stay close to the lady. We got some tough ones in camp. I wouldn't want my sister there. The little lady looks nice. 'Course, the thought that Michael O'Malley might recover will keep most of 'em in line. He's as tough as they come."

"I don't doubt it for a second," Dan replied. "I sent a telegram to a friend who might come."

Jethro gave him a curious stare. "What kind of friend?"

Dan's suspicions that all wasn't right grew stronger. "A Kiowa. He nursed my brother through something as bad as this."

"You going to bring him back here?"

"Yes."

"You whistle before you ride into camp, just like I did," he said, and moved back in the lead. Dan turned to look at Mary, who was the last in line now, and he suspected she might have heard what Jethro said.

Mary had heard the soft-voiced conversation, but it caused her no worry because all her thoughts were on Michael. She prayed as she rode, thinking the ride seemed interminable. Dan wore a gunbelt and pistol on his hip, the first time she had seen him armed. It changed him, giving him a more formidable appearance. He wore faded denim pants and had a knife in a scabbard at his waist. It was reassuring to have him along, and she was thankful he had come with her. For the first time since Michael left home, she had someone around who really helped bear some of the burden of her problems.

As the sun rose higher in the sky, spilling warmth over the mountain, they rode down into a valley thick with spruce. Along the valley floor, log cabins had been built near a gurgling mountain stream. At one end were sluices, and the land was gouged where men were digging for gold. Jethro rode to a large cabin set off yards away from the others, where he dismounted. Men working paused to watch them, and waved at Jethro, who returned the wave.

"Doc."

Mary dismounted quickly, but Dan was down first and caught her around the waist. "Let the doc look at him first."

"I'm not going to faint. Let me go, Dan!" she cried, struggling against him. She pushed against his chest, but he held her tightly.

"Mary, please wait," he asked gently.

She felt a desperate need to see Michael, to know

for certain that he was still alive. For a moment she was bound to Dan. Arms like steel bands held her, and she couldn't break free.

"Let me go to my brother!"

"When Doc says you can, I will. Mary, they're trying to take care of him. Give them a chance."

She stopped struggling and sagged against him, resting her forehead against his chest. He stroked the back of her head. "It won't be long."

Growing calmer, she moved away, staring at the door.

"I know you're cold," Dan said, rubbing her hands between his. As he rubbed her hands, he looked around. Two men sauntered toward Dan, and the foreboding he had felt earlier returned. Their clothes were ragged, both wore gunbelts and pistols, and both had knives in scabbards. As they came closer, Dan studied the taller one, who had a curly dark beard and black mustache. The man had a pockmarked face where it wasn't covered with the thick mat of hair, and Dan felt a nagging twinge of recognition.

"Howdy," the man said. "You O'Malley's kin?"

"This is his sister, Miss O'Malley. I'm Dan Castle."

"Sorghum Baines, here, and my friend is Donner Moffit," the taller man said. Both of them studied Mary intently. "We're shore glad to have a woman here. You want to come have a bite to eat?"

"I'm going inside as soon as I can," she answered. "Thank you."

"The doc is in the cabin," Dan explained, draping his arm protectively around her shoulders. "We're waiting until he's ready."

"O'Malley and the bear about had a draw. Bear's dead. We skinned him."

"You a friend of the O'Malleys'?" Sorghum asked Dan.

"Yes, a very close friend of Miss O'Malley's father and of her fiancé."

Both men nodded. Behind them Doc Felton opened the cabin door. "Miss O'Malley." He stepped outside. "I've cleaned his wounds and you can come in now. I've done all I can do. I've sewed up the cuts and I've left laudanum and some ointments. I'd like to give you instructions on his care. I'm riding back to town. I have two babies due anytime now, and I've done all I can."

"Will he be all right?"

"I can't honestly give you an answer," Doc Felton replied.

As she moved past him, Doc Felton followed her inside. Dan glanced at Sorghum and Donner. "Glad to meet you," he said casually.

"Mister, we got a mine here, and it's off limits except to those who're working it. 'Course, the little lady can come talk to us anytime. We ain't had many women around here."

"We're just here because of Michael O'Malley," Dan answered evenly. And while he talked, he remembered Sorghum. The man had ridden with a gang in New Mexico Territory. They had robbed a train and had come into town to spend their money. It was a little Spanish town without a lawman. Dan had ridden with his own gang at the time, and they had stayed in the town because it was a safe hideaway from lawmen. He hoped Sorghum didn't remember any of that.

They turned away, and Dan watched them walk back toward the fire. Jethro came out of the cabin.

"I see you've met Sorghum and Donner."

"Yes. They warned me to stay away from the mine."

"Take their advice, mister. Those two are better off alone." He rubbed his neck. "Actually, Michael and I were about ready to pull up stakes and move on. We'd been discussing it. And keep your eye on the lady. I'd get her back to Denver as soon as you can."

"Thanks, I intend to." Dan wondered if they were hiding anything more than a mine. "Who's been caring for Michael?"

"I have," Jethro answered. "No one touched him since I left."

As Jethro walked away, Dan entered the cabin. The

man who lay on the bed bore little resemblance to Paddy, Brian, or Mary. He looked pale as snow, with a thick shock of black curls showing above a bandage. Even with bandages wrapped around his chest and arms and hands, some cuts were still visible. He was a big man, with broad shoulders and thick muscles, something Dan suspected would help him through the next few days. Mary lightly touched Michael O'Malley's hand.

Dan pulled a straight wooden chair beside the bed. "Sit down here, Mary." He moved away with Dr. Felton.

"I'm going back to Denver," Felton said. "You said you were coming along."

Dan shook his head and stepped outside with the doctor, closing the door behind them. "I'll pay the bill for this. I don't think I should leave her alone, though," he said, remembering fleetingly that in two days he had an appointment with Edward Ringwood. "What are Michael's chances?"

Doc Felton shrugged his broad, bony shoulders. "Can't say. I've seen men that weren't hurt that bad who couldn't survive. I've seen others who were hurt worse than that, and they were strong enough to pull through."

"I don't know him, but I know the family," Dan said, "and I'd wager Michael O'Malley is as tough a man as you'll ever meet."

Doc set his hat squarely on his head. "If that's the case, he'll make it."

"Thanks for what you've done."

Doc Felton's brown eyes swept the camp. "They didn't give you a big welcome, did they?"

"No. They warned me to stay away from their mining. If he does pull through, I want to get Mary back to Denver as quickly as possible."

"She ought to come now, and let someone else tend him."

"The moon would fall out of the sky before she would do that."

"Be careful. No one has been tending him. When I went in, he had his six-shooter in hand."

"Damn, he can't trust his cronies!"

The physician offered his hand. "Good luck."

"Thanks for everything, Doc." Dan stood with his thumbs hooked in his belt while Doc Felton mounted. Dan waved, his gaze shifting to the miners. The men were out of sight except for one standing over the sluices, and Dan could hear picks striking rock in the distance. He surveyed the area, glad their cabin was isolated and at the opposite end of the camp. The area reminded him of home, and he inhaled deeply, realizing his love for the mountains would always be part of him. They were in a beautiful valley surrounded by spruce-covered mountains, and a sparkling stream ran only feet away from the cabin's back door. He walked around the cabin, trying to get familiar with the cabin and the land, because he had a hunch trouble was brewing. He remembered tales about Sorghum; he was wanted for robbery and murder, and was known for gunning down people in holdups.

There was a privy in back, along with a pump, a well, and a small shed, where he put the horses. There were two doors to the cabin, one in front and one in back and he decided it had been built to serve as a home long before the other cabins were put up. Kindling was piled against the back wall. As a precaution, Dan filled buckets of water and a copper tub, so they would have a good supply inside in case they had to board up in the cabin. Mary didn't look around to see what he was doing, remaining as still as Michael, her hand over his while his chest rose and fell in quick, shallow breaths.

Dan went inside to build up the fire, glad they had brought plenty of provisions. He didn't think he could ride out to hunt for meat and leave Mary alone for so much as an hour. While he waited for coffee to brew, he glanced around, wondering if Michael had stayed in this cabin alone. It was larger than all the others, and inside there were four beds made of rough-hewn logs and hides. One was along the east wall, and Dan strung a rope and hung blankets around it to give Mary a corner to herself and some privacy. ''Mary, you sleep here,'' he said, and she nodded, turning her attention right back to Michael.

There was a wooden table in the center of the cabin, half a dozen stump chairs, two straight-backed wooden chairs, a plank floor, three windows, and two doors. Dan studied the high windows that had shutters. ''Mary,'' he asked softly, ''do you know how to shoot?''

''No. I've never held a pistol.''

Dan was surprised because they were a scrappy family, and he gave her a crooked smile before she turned back to Michael. A gunbelt with a pistol hung on one bedpost near Michael's head, and a rifle was propped against the wall beside the bed. Dan checked them both, saw that they were loaded. He moved the rifle.

''That's Michael's six-shooter.''

''Come here a few minutes and let me show you how to use it.''

Mary crossed the room to him and listened carefully, trying to concentrate, wondering why he would want her to learn to use a weapon. ''Are you leaving?''

''No.''

''You should go back to your work, Dan. I'll be all right.''

''Forget it. Look here. You load the pistol now.''

She did as he had shown her, and he nodded, looking satisfied. ''Now, aim at the coffeepot,'' he instructed. He moved behind her, steadying her hands. He wrapped his arms around her, holding his body close against hers, and she became intensely aware of him and his touch, his nearness. When he talked, his voice was soft and deep, his breath blowing lightly on her neck as he explained how to sight down the barrel. His voice changed and his words slowed.

''Hold as steady as you can and squeeze the trigger when you fire.'' He was intensely conscious of her as he looked at the back of her slender neck. He wanted to lean the few inches between them and brush her

nape with a kiss. The notion shocked him, and he
stepped away abruptly. "We can't practice, because I
don't want them to hear it. If there's trouble, go for
the pistol or rifle," he said, taking the six-shooter from
Mary. "Let me show you how to fire and load the
Henry."

He held the weapon in his hand, sighting down the
barrel, studying the rifle. "Michael must like these.
He's taken good care of them."

"I've seen him shoot blossoms off their stems. I
don't like fighting."

"There are grown men who would dispute that
statement," he said dryly, glancing at her. She wore
a worried frown and her gaze had returned to Michael.
Instantly Dan's sympathy was stirred.

"Mary, it's going to take time for him to heal."

"He's like my child."

"I know," he said gently, thinking the man in bed
looked older than she. "How old is Michael?"

"He's nineteen, just a year younger than I am, but I
raised him. And he wasn't bigger until just a few years
ago. It always surprises me how much he grew."

He showed her how to use the rifle, once again becoming acutely conscious of her. She was slender, and
the top of her head came to just below his shoulder.
She smelled sweet, and he felt protective toward her,
praying Michael survived. The rifle was heavy, but she
handled it easily enough. He squeezed her arm, feeling the small knot of muscle.

"How such a little someone like you can manage
rifles and clubs and skillets, I don't know."

"Look at Michael and Brian. I grew up scrapping
with them," she said, turning to look at him over her
shoulder. He stood directly behind her, his arms
around her to steady the rifle. Her face was only inches
away, and looking down into her eyes made him yearn
to wrap her in his arms and hold her, a notion that
entered his mind quite often. She drew a deep breath,
and both of them moved quickly, colliding.

He steadied her, and they gazed at each other solemnly. Mary was drawn to him, and the attraction was

constantly growing stronger. His kindness and consideration made him irresistible.

"I sent a wire to Ta-ne-haddle," Dan said in a husky voice, stepping away from her and setting down the rifle. "Maybe he'll come."

"Who's Ta-ne-haddle?"

"A Kiowa friend who nursed my brother through something like this. He lives on a ranch outside San Antonio."

"San Antonio? It would take a long time to get here. And he couldn't find us anyway, unless you return to Denver to show him the way."

"He can get here in a shorter time than you might think. And once in Denver, he'll find the doctor and ask where we are. He'll track us here."

"Track? He can't. It would be impossible."

"You're not accustomed to riding across country."

"Then I hope he does get here, and quickly," she said, moving back to her chair beside the bed.

"So do I," Dan said under his breath, watching her. He brewed coffee and took Mary a cup.

For the next hour she sat quietly while he looked at their cabin and supplies, stacking kindling inside. If trouble came, he wanted as much as possible in their favor.

He cooked potatoes Dulcie had packed, and dried meat. "Come eat, Mary."

"He hasn't stirred," she said. "I'm going outside to wash."

"Carry the pistol."

"You're right here. I don't need a pistol with you here."

"There may be snakes," he said, not wanting to worry her with his suspicions about the miners.

She picked up a gnarled stick from the kindling. "This will do."

He would have preferred her to carry a pistol, but he nodded. As soon as she was back, he dropped the bolt in place on the back door. "Has he stirred?"

"No. Stop worrying so much. Doc Felton tended his cuts and told you what to do. He said don't worry about feeding him today. Now, come eat so you have strength to care for Michael.''

She nodded and sat down at the table across from Dan. After a few bites, she shook her head. ''I'm not hungry.''

''Honey,'' he said gently, leaning forward to touch her arm lightly, ''you need to stay strong, and you won't if you don't eat.''

The term ''honey'' made her instantly aware of him. It was the first time he had ever said it to her. She knew his feelings had been stirred out of pity for her because of Michael, but it made her tingle. Dan's eyes were wide and full of concern as she gazed at him. And then she saw a flicker in their depths and a faint change in his expression. She felt caught in a spell, unable to look away, aware of a tension growing between them. She had felt the same thing sometimes with Silas, but not as strongly as now. She made an effort to shift her gaze, trying to think of Silas, but found it difficult to conjure up his image.

Michael groaned, and instantly she rushed to his side. ''Michael! I'm here now, Michael.'' She leaned over him while Dan approached the bed. ''I'm here, Michael.''

His lashes fluttered and he gazed at her. ''Mary?'' he whispered.

''You have to get well, Michael.'' Thick lashes came down over blue eyes.

''Maybe you can get a little broth down him,'' Dan said, going back to the steaming pot on the hot embers in the hearth. He ladled out a small bowl and returned to hand it to Mary. ''I'll hold his head.''

Dan moved him carefully while Mary talked to him. ''Michael, you must eat a little. Michael, it's Mary. I'm here to take care of you.'' His eyelashes fluttered and finally opened, and she began to spoon broth down him.

In a few minutes he turned his head. ''No more,'' he whispered.

''Michael . . .''

''Mary, he's gone to sleep,'' Dan said, lowering Mi-

chael to the pillows. "He ate a little broth, and it probably exhausted him. Let him sleep."

She nodded and sat in the straight chair, taking up
her vigil once more. Dan moved around the cabin,
putting away dinner things, closing the shutters, and
lighting lamps. He dropped the bars that secured each
door in place.

"I'll sleep over there," Dan said, pointing to a
rough-hewn bed of logs and hides. "Mary, if anyone
comes to the door, wake me. I'll sleep awhile, and
then I'll sit with Michael."

"I'm fine, Dan. Sleep all night if you want."

"Sure, Mary." He stretched out fully clothed, his
gunbelt hanging at his head where he could reach it in
an instant. His rifle was propped along the wall beside
Michael's. He was asleep in minutes after stretching
out on the bed.

During the night he stirred and sat up. Mary sat
with her back to him in the chair.

"Mary," he whispered, and she turned around.

"Go get some sleep now. I'll sit with him."

"I don't need to."

He placed logs on the fire and then crossed the cabin
to her to take her hand and pull her up. "I know you're
exhausted," he said gently, wanting to hold her, to try
to comfort her so the worry would be gone. Instead he
stepped back as if he needed to put more space between them. "Go on and sleep."

"You'll call me—"

"If there's the slightest change or if he wakes. I
promise."

She nodded and moved away while Dan sat in the
chair. He gazed at Michael and prayed he would survive. His breathing was regular and he lay still. In
seconds Dan became aware of the sounds of Mary
moving around. He glanced around and could see her
bare feet and dainty ankles below the blankets he had
hung on the rope, and he was mesmerized, as if he
had never seen a woman's feet before. He watched her
moving around, saw the calico dress she had worn
billow and settle around her feet. She stepped out of

the dress, and his imagination ran rampant. A white cotton chemise fell, and he could picture Mary standing there bare-skinned, slender, *desirable*.

A white nightgown dropped down, almost hiding her ankles from view. She scooped up the clothing, and he watched her moving around and heard the rustle of covers.

He pushed back his chair and stood up, walking to the center of the cabin, making no effort to hide the noise of his boots on the plank floor. "Mary, do you have enough covers? Do you want my coat?"

"I'm fine. His Michael stirred?"

"No. Go to sleep. I'll call you if he does."

"Promise?"

"Yes." He could picture her in bed, and in his mind, her head was still wound with braids. There was something so innocent and prim about her, yet—

His thoughts veered off the subject, and he felt guilty as he thought about Silas, remembering him sitting before a campfire and talking about Mary. Dan clamped his jaw shut and sat back down, but he turned to look again at the blanket, imagining Mary stretched on the bed. He sighed and shifted, propping his hands on his knees, staring at Michael O'Malley. The man was slashed badly, but the injuries didn't hide the solid muscles, and Dan expected Michael to survive. The O'Malleys were tough, and this one looked like the toughest, strongest O'Malley of all. He ran with bad company, though, and Dan suspected Brian did as well. For the first time, he wondered if Brian's disappearances from Denver might have something to do with Michael. He could be riding out to the mining camp.

Mary deserved better than she was getting from her father and brothers and Silas. Dan mentally swore. It was none of his concern what the men in Mary O'Malley's life did. Yet he cared, and he acknowledged that he cared too much. He twisted again to stare at the blanket. Restless, he stood up and moved to put more logs on the fire, building up a blaze.

He poured a drink of brandy and sat back down in

the chair. Time crept past, and Michael stirred and groaned.

"Water," he whispered.

"I'll get it, Michael," Dan said, standing up and moving toward the blanket. He hated to wake her, and it seemed unnecessary, but he had promised. He heard the rustle of clothing or blankets before he called her name.

"Mary," he said softly.

She pushed aside the blanket. Her eyes were round, her gaze going to Michael. "What's wrong?"

"He wants water," Dan said, his mouth becoming dry, barely able to get out the words. She stood in the flickering firelight in the white cotton gown that was buttoned to her throat. Her hair was down. It fell in a shimmering red cascade, wavy from the plaiting. The ends curled just above her waist, and it changed her appearance completely. He felt riveted to the floor, unable to move or breathe or stop staring. She was beautiful.

"Dan?"

"Yes?"

"Is something wrong?" Suddenly her face suffused with pink. "I didn't bring my wrapper, I packed in such haste, but I figure you've seen lots of ladies' nighties."

He couldn't stop the compelling urge to touch her hair, reaching out to stroke a silky lock.

She drew a deep breath. "Is Michael all right?"

"He asked for water. I'll get it."

She hurried past him to Michael. "He's asleep again, Dan."

"I'll get a cup of water and set it beside the bed."

"Mary," Michael murmured hoarsely.

"I'm here, Michael."

Dan handed her the cup of water and helped raised Michael so she could hold the cup to his lips. He drank slowly. Each swallow was an effort, and drops spilled over his jaw, which was covered in dark stubble where it wasn't bandaged. And all the while her brother drank, Dan was aware of Mary, her slender hands holding the cup, the locks of flaming hair falling over her shoulders, and the top button at the throat of her white gown that was unfastened.

"I'll get more," Dan said when Michael drained the cup.

"No. I'm sleepy." Michael closed his eyes and in seconds his breathing was even again. Dan felt his forehead.

"How is he?"

"Hot. Not too bad, though."

"I can stay with him."

"Go back to bed." Dan stood at the foot of Michael's bed. He picked up the cup and refilled it, and turned around. Mary stood beside the bed, watching her brother. She glanced at Dan and moved away, crossing the room to the fire.

"Now I'm cold. I want to get warm and then I'll go to bed." Her cheeks were flushed and she stared at the fire. "If you're tired—"

"I'm fine," he said without thinking about his answer. He ached to reach out and touch her hair. She held her hands toward the fire and glanced around at him.

Mary drew a sharp breath as she met his gaze. Men never looked at her the way Dan looked at her now, and it warmed her more than the fire.

"You're beautiful, Mary," he whispered, and her thoughts spun away. She stared at him, unable to move or breathe.

He reached out to touch her hair, the faintest touch, yet she seemed to feel it in the depths of her person. His gaze was riveted on hers, and a longing she had never known came over her. She wanted to reach for him. She wanted him to reach for her.

"Mary," he whispered, tilting her chin up. She watched him, drawn by a pull that was as strong as chains. He stepped to her and she felt as if all the air in the room had suddenly been withdrawn. His arm slipped around her waist, and he leaned down. His lips were warm and soft as he brushed hers. His mouth

settled on hers, parting her lips, and her heart pounded
with his kiss.

Dan tasted her mouth, finding in her kiss a sweetness and fire he wouldn't have dreamed possible. His
arm tightened around her, and he felt her high soft
breasts press against him. Her body was slender, her
waist smaller than he had thought.

As his arm tightened, Mary's hands rested against
his chest. For just seconds she was lost in a storm
created by Dan, pressing against him, clinging to his
broad shoulders. Then she remembered.

"No!" She twisted away and moved back, horrified
at how she had yielded to him so easily and forgotten
Silas so quickly. "Silas!"

"Dammit, I know that," Dan said, grinding out the
words, his hands clenched into fists.

She turned and hurried out of sight behind the blanket. Dan wanted to stride across the cabin and throw
back the blankets that hung on the rope. He wanted to
haul her into his arms and kiss her for hours. He stared
at the fire, his body burning. He swore, mentally be-
rating himself, arguing in his mind that it was the isolation in the cabin, the frustration stirred by Louisa's
teasing, the shock of finding that Mary could be beautiful.

"It isn't love," he whispered aloud. "It can't be."
He turned around to stare at the blankets. "Dammit,
it isn't!" His gaze shifted to Michael's still form, and
he swore softly again. The O'Malleys had turned his
life upside down. They all caused him trouble, each
and every one of them! His nerves were raw, his body
aroused, and he wanted to pull on a coat and go striding out into the night, to move and work off the frus-
trations building in him, but he had promised to sit at
Michael's bedside so Mary could sleep. *Mary asleep.*

He picked up the brandy bottle and took a long
drink, wiping his mouth and staring at Michael.
"Damn you, Silas," he said again, wishing he hadn't
crossed paths with the O'Malleys. He knew he wasn't
being fair, but he ached, and it was torment. And he
was in love with Louisa Shumacher, about to have their

engagement announced. *I cannot love Mary O'Malley.
I don't and I won't. I love Louisa, who is beautiful
and exciting and doesn't belong to my friend.* Yet while
he argued with himself, he thought of all the fun he
had with Mary, of the fact that he could trust her with
anything, ask her advice and expect a reasonable, intelligent answer.

Taking the brandy with him, he sat beside the bed
and stared at Michael, willing him to get well fast so
they could get the hell away from the mining camp.
"Get well, dammit," he whispered.

Mary lay shivering in the bed. Covers were piled on
her, yet she couldn't get warm. She tried to avoid
thinking about what had just happened, yet her ears
seemed to expand, listening to Dan move around the
cabin. She heard scrapes and rustles and silence. "I'm
going to marry Silas," she told herself in her mind
over and over, wishing she could sleep, or get warm,
or *forget*. Silas. She tried to think of times with him,
but now years separated her from those hours, and the
memories had blurred. She tried to remember Silas'
kisses, tried to blot out what she felt, but she couldn't
erase the memories of Dan's kisses.

She turned, huddled beneath a mound of covers,
shivering. She felt a longing that she didn't want to
experience, remembering kisses that shouldn't have
happened.

"Get well, dammit," Dan whispered, and Mary
raised her head. She heard him and frowned, biting
her lip. He was as unhappy over what had happened
as she. She thought of Michael and closed her eyes in
prayer.

Dan dozed and stirred, staring at Michael, who
groaned and shifted. His face was more flushed, and
Dan frowned. He leaned forward and felt Michael's
brow.

"Damn," he muttered, feeling the hot, dry flesh.
The man was burning up with fever. Dan went outside
to pump a bucket of cold water in the cool gray still-
ness of dawn.

"Mary," he called when he returned. She pushed

aside the blankets, her eyes round with fear. Once again the sight of her momentarily immobilized Dan, because her hair still tumbled around her shoulders and her feet and ankles were bare. Her calico dress was open at the throat to reveal pale, smooth skin.

"What is it?" she asked.

"Michael's burning with fever. We need to get him cool."

She rushed to the bedside, and Dan worked with her, wringing out cold wet cloths and trying to get Michael cooler. "I hope my telegram got to Luke, and Ta-ne-haddle is coming."

"San Antonio is so far away, Dan," she said, bathing Michael's forehead. "I don't see how your friend can find this camp anyway."

"Brian may know the way. Even if he doesn't, Ta-ne-haddle can track almost anything that has feet."

"I hope he comes, because I don't think we can get Dr. Felton back, and Michael is worse."

Dan helped her, wringing out rags, trying to bathe Michael's forehead to get his temperature down. Michael twisted and turned and talked, moaning softly. Dan silently prayed Ta-ne-haddle was on his way.

14

Hattie sat alone in the kitchen with Luke. She leaned forward, knowing he wouldn't take the news well. "I want to go home with April."

To her surprise, he smiled. "Fine. You know we love having you here, but I can understand why you'd like to visit April too. And I know she wants to see you."

"Luke, I still get letters from Javier."

"I know that."

"I used to leave them unopened, but lately I've been reading them. He said he's written to you and Dan, and that in his will he's leaving the ranch to April. He said that it's all right with both of you."

"I don't need it, and neither does Dan. I think it's a good idea to leave it to April."

"Noah is a successful man too, and April will always be well-taken-care-of, so it seems to me the ranch should be equally divided among all survivors."

"No. I want April to have it, and I imagine Dan does too. Judging from the last letter I had from Dan, he seems to be doing well. I think he's happy with Denver and is ready to settle there."

At the sound of a knock, Luke turned toward the door. In seconds a maid appeared. "Señor Danby, a man to see you. He has a message."

Luke moved to the door to take the telegram and tip the man. He closed the door and ripped open the envelope to read the message.

He stepped to the door. "A brother of one of Dan's

friends has been clawed by a bear. He wants Ta-ne-haddle to come. I'm going to ride out to the ranch and get him.''

"Where is he going? To Colorado Territory?"

"Yes. The mining camp is outside Denver," Luke said. Within a quarter of an hour he rode away from the house. Late that night, when the house was quiet, he returned. He moved through it on tiptoe, undressing and sliding into bed.

"I missed you," Catalina said in a throaty voice, winding her arms around him. He lifted her on top of him, relishing her softness and warmth, her full breasts pressed against his chest.

"I thought you were asleep."

She kissed his shoulder. "No. I was waiting for you. Has Ta-ne-haddle gone?"

"Yes. I started to go with him, but he said it wasn't necessary. Since it isn't Dan who's hurt, I decided to stay home." He kissed her shoulder, turning her head to kiss her deeply, crushing her to him, and rolling over so he was above her.

"Catalina, how I love you," he whispered. He pushed away the covers and shifted so he could trail kisses across her smooth flesh while he stroked her. He didn't think he could ever tire of loving her. Instead, he wanted her more and loved her more with the passing of time. His troubles faded from his mind as he lost himself in her soft flesh, feeing her legs wrap around him, his heart pounding with desire.

Later he held her close against his heated body, stroking her, murmuring endearments to her. After moments of silence, he said, "Mother is going home with April."

"I know. She told me. Luke, if she can find happiness with Javier, don't stand in the way."

"That's her decision."

Catalina sat up to gaze down at him, trailing her fingers along his jaw, feeling the rough stubble. "If she goes back to him, I want you to welcome them here if they want to come visit.''

"Dammit, Catalina, how can you welcome a man like Javier?"

"If Hattie goes back to him, I don't want our children shut off from their grandmother. She's a wonderful, intelligent woman and they love her. She's been good for them."

His scowl faded and he pulled her down into his arms. "You're right, as usual. I wouldn't want to separate her from them. So I'll tell her Javier is welcome."

"Good. I can sleep now."

"I'll bet you and April have discussed this."

"We might have," she said sleepily, curled against him.

He chuckled softly. "I'm glad I don't have to face you in the courtroom."

Her words were slow and languorous and she stroked his broad chest. "I have powers of persuasion your opponents don't have."

"Absolutely, hon." He smiled and kissed her temple. "I'm the luckiest man on earth, so I guess I should be charitable to Javier."

"Who did Ta-ne-haddle go to see in Colorado? A fried of Dan's?"

"A brother of a friend's fiancée."

"Sounds complicated," she whispered, and in seconds Luke heard her steady, deep breathing and knew she was asleep. He smoothed her hair away from her forehead, kissing her lightly before he lay back to stare into the darkness. He knew if Dan sent for Ta-ne-haddle, it was important.

A week later Hattie kissed him good-bye, hugging the children and Catalina before she climbed into the wagon with Noah and April and Aaron. They waved, and Hattie and Aaron rode in the wagon while April rode beside Noah. San Antonio had grown since she had first come with Luke, but the meandering river was still there, and the jacales and adobe houses, the cathedral, and the two busy plazas remained the same. Smells of food came from open doors, and laughter sounded as they passed cantinas.

April glanced up at Noah. His hat was pushed back
on his head, and his thick curls were tangled by the
wind. April felt a rush of love as she studied him, and
she hoped they had another baby on the way. She
placed her hand on his thigh, and he smiled at her,
draping his arm around her shoulders. He began to
sing, and she sang with him. Aaron and Hattie joined
them. As they wound away from San Antonio, she
thought about Noah's new hotel that would be so fine.

"Will we see Ta-ne-haddle?" Aaron called, and
Noah laughed.

"No!" he called over the rattle of the wagon. He
turned to April. "Stages should travel as quickly as
the Kiowa. Sometimes I don't think he requires sleep
at all. I've hunted with him and Luke, and it's all I
can do to keep up with them."

I've heard you say that, but I find it difficult to believe," April said. She knew all about Noah's strength
and his years of soldiering in the war.

"Luke's years with Ta-ne-haddle must have made
him adopt the Kiowa's habits. I'd hate to be on the
wrong side of them and have them tracking me."

"They're both peaceful men now."

"Until they're provoked."

"Said the rock about the stone," she said dryly.

"Who, me? You can't name the last time I had a
fight."

"June tenth, a Sunday afternoon."

"You made that up!" he said, laughing.

"I love you, Noah McCloud," she said, hugging
him. He squeezed her closer to this side.

"I've been thinking, April, we should add some new
rooms onto our house and make it larger."

"It's rather large right now," she said, thinking of
the sprawling abode they had.

"We only have three bedrooms. I think we should
have five. We should have a bedroom for Hattie, another for Aaron, and another for"—he paused and
smiled at her—"whoever's to come. I've been thinking
about how I'd like to do it."

She listened to his plans, happy with him, hoping

DENVER 241

that Hattie would see Javier when he came, because April knew he was coming.

Dan squeezed cold water out of the rags, and placed them on Michael where he wasn't bandaged. He noticed that some of the milder cuts had begun to heal. Mary kept crooning and talking softly to Michael, sponging his brow continuously. Suddenly Michael began to thrash and talk. Words tumbled out, making no sense, and then he gasped and groaned. Dan dropped the wet rags and tried to hold him still before he hurt himself. He shook violently and thrashed with a strength that Dan found hard to control.

"Michael O'Malley!" Mary said loudly, standing over him. "Michael, you have to get well! Michael!"

"Mary, he can't hear you."

"Yes, he can. Michael O'Malley, you listen to me. You have to get well. I'm telling you, you have to!"

As suddenly as the thrashing had started, it stopped, and he shuddered and gasped and lay still.

"Michael!" Mary said in a low, intense voice, clutching his hand. "Michael O'Malley, don't you do this. You have to get well."

Dan felt his throat for a pulse. "He's breathing."

"Thank heaven! Michael! Michael!"

He groaned, and to Dan's amazement, his eyelashes fluttered and his eyes opened. He gazed to Mary with a blank stare. "Michael, get well, darlin'. Do you understand?"

"Yes, Mary," he whispered.

"Lord," Dan said, amazed she had roused him. He lifted Michael. "Give him some water."

"Michael, you have to drink this," she said as Dan held up his head.

He swallowed, slowly drinking the whole cup. Dan looked up at Mary and saw there had been tears on her cheeks. He realized how difficult this was for her. He lowered Michael back to his bed.

"He's asleep again." Dan moved the wet cloths and water and went around the bed to place his hands on her shoulders. "You go get something to eat and put shoes on your feet. You'll get sick like that. I'll watch him.''

She turned to look up at him, and he saw she was on the brink of losing control. ''Mary, he's hanging on, and he looks strong as a bull.''

He started to reach for her. She looked as if she wanted to fall into his arms and cry, but the moment he reached out, he remembered the previous night. He saw a fleeting expression cross her face, but he suspected she remembered too, because her cheeks grew pink and she moved away.

''Thank you, Dan. I'm all right,'' she said in a breathless voice as she skirted past him, going in a wide circle and avoiding his gaze. He turned to watch here disappear behind the blankets, and pulled his coat.

''Mary, I'm going outside. You watch him.''

''I will.''

Dan went out back, inhaling deeply. He was glad to get out of the cabin and into the cold air. He could hear picks striking rock, and knew some of the men were working. He walked around the side of the cabin and thought he saw someone disappear around the corner. Dan quickened his stride, moving rapidly. No one was in front of the cabin, but he wondered if the person had merely circled on around it, because he could have sworn he saw a man move quickly out of sight. He glanced at the cabin and decided that for Mary's sake, he needed to wear a pistol.

Mary pulled on stockings and shoes, buttoned her dress, and went to sit beside Michael while she braided her hair. Michael breathed deeply and evenly, and when she felt his forehead, she didn't think he was as hot as before.

They spent the rest of the day tending Michael constantly, trying to keep his fever down. They took turns sitting with him through the night, and the next morning, to Mary's relief, Michael felt cooler.

She moved around the cabin, building up the fire and setting out a skillet to cook some of the provisions they had brought. She made another kettle of stew, and

poured them both apple juice Dan had brought. Her
thoughts were on Dan, and they were as stormy as
before. He came inside, and she glanced at him
quickly. She was aware of him every second, of where
he was, of when she caught him looking at her.

She knew she mustn't let anything happen again. It
had only happened because Silas had been gone so
long and because she and Dan were isolated with Michael. She repeated her arguments to herself all
through the afternoon, aware that Dan said little to her
all day. He stayed outside a good part of the morning.

"I think his fever has gone down," he said once.
Later Michael stirred, and together, she and Dan got
some stew and more water down him.

'That should help him," Dan said. He studied her,
noticed her hair was braided around her head again,
but he didn't think he would ever forget that first moment she had appeared in her white gown with her hair
down over her shoulders.

She looked up and caught him watching her. She
felt her cheeks grow warm and she glanced away
quickly. For the first time, she was at a loss for words.
She tried to forget, to ignore him, but she couldn't.
During the afternoon Dan said he would sleep so he
could sit up at night. He stretched on the bed across
the room, but he was opposite her, directly in her line
of vision, and it was impossible to keep from studying
his long lean body. Once both men slept peacefully,
and she threw a shawl around her shoulders and started
outside to the privy. Remembering Dan's warning
about carrying the pistol, she picked up a thick piece
of kindling and went outside.

" 'Morning, little lady," came a deep voice, and
she spun around.

Sorghum leaned against the wall of the cabin.

He smiled and came closer. "Sorry if I startled you.
How's Michael?"

"I think he's better."

"I thought I'd come see how you folks are doing.
Do you need anything?"

''No,'' she said, gripping the wood tightly. Sorghum's gaze dropped to the piece of kindling.

''Looks as if you're scared you'll meet a bear.''

''There might be snakes.''

''I'd be obliged to shoot them for you.''

''Thanks,'' she said, turning back for the cabin.

''I thought you just came out.''

''I did, but I forgot a bucket. I need to get water. It was nice to see you, mister,'' she said, trying to be polite, hoping he would go. He made her nervous, as his gaze constantly raked over her.

''Hello there,'' another voice said, and a man she hadn't met came around the cabin, moving to block her path to the door. She looked from one to the other of them and wondered if she should yell for Dan now.

''Dan and Michael are right inside,'' she said quietly, backing up, and wishing she had picked up a larger piece of kindling. Both men began to move closer. She took a deep breath. ''I'm going inside now.''

She heard a twig snap behind her. Before she could move, an arm clamped around her from behind, pinning her arms to her sides, and a hand clamped over her mouth. She kicked as hard as possible, and the hand was gone.

''Dan!''

''Let the lady go,'' came his deep voice, and he stood in the open doorway, Michael's gunbelt on, a pistol on his hip, his own tucked into his waistband.

In an instant two men drew on Dan. Quicker than Mary could see, he drew both pistols and fired, sending the other pistols flying from the men's hands. They stood staring at him in openmouthed wonder that Mary shared. She had never seen a man use six-shooters with the expertness Dan had just exhibited. No one moved a muscle, but Sorghum's eyes narrowed and he looked at Dan intently.

''Who the hell are you, mister?''

''You know my name. Come inside, Mary. Now, stay the hell away from our cabin. We don't have any quarrel with anyone. We just want to tend Michael, but don't come near Miss O'Malley. The next time, it won't be your pistols I'll shoot.''

Mary scurried past him. Her heart was pounding and she was still shocked and awed by his marksmanship. She stared at him as he bolted the door.

''Are you all right?''

''Yes,'' she said, nodding.

''I told you what I did before,'' he said grimly. Dan saw the shock in her eyes and wondered if it was the first time the truth about his past had become a reality to her.

''It's so unlike you,'' she said.

''Where's the pistol I told you to carry?''

''I don't know anything about revolvers, Dan.''

''If you want to go outside, I'm sure they're gone now. I'll stay in the doorway.''

She nodded and picked up a bucket. He took it from her hands, and his hands brushed hers. The slightest touch by him brought back memories of his arms around her, his lips on hers. He clamped his jaw shut and jerked his head for her to go outside.

She hurried to the privy while he pumped water and kept his eyes open constantly, watching for any of the men to reappear. Dan didn't think they would be so open about it again, but he knew he had made enemies. He wondered how long it would be before Sorghum remembered him.

Sunshine warmed the camp that afternoon, and they left both doors open to let in fresh air. Dan was getting restless, cooped up in the small cabin. He was conscious of every movement of Mary's and found the tension between them growing. She wasn't relaxed around him as she had been once, and her gaze avoided his often now. He watched her move around the cabin, stirring the stew that filled the cabin with an enticing aroma. He tried to blame his reactions to her on isolation, frustration, all sorts of reasons, but she was growing more desirable as he watched her.

Dan took the ax and split more logs for kindling, stacking them inside and working up a sweat in the sunshine, until he peeled off his shirt and tossed it aside. He enjoyed the activity after sitting in the confines of the cabin.

Mary stood by the window watching him. Sunlight played over his rippling muscles as he swung the ax. Her gaze ran over his long frame and down his legs. He paused, wiping his brow, and she realized how hot he must be. His chest was covered in golden curls. Unobserved, she stood quietly, studying him, his narrow waist and low-slung pants, the gunbelt hanging still lower. She turned away, picking up the dipper to fill a cup with cold water to take outside to him.

"Want some water?"

"Thanks," he said, glancing down at his hands, which were grimy from handling the kindling. He took the cup from her and drank, and she couldn't stop watching him. She tried to avoid the pull, but was unable to do so. She let her gaze slide down over his chest. She looked back at him to find him watching her as he wiped his mouth with his arm.

"Thanks, Mary," he said quietly, staring at her with that same brooding intensity that he had had all morning.

She nodded and hurried inside, her heart pounding. When she was near him, her heartbeat speeded up, her breathing changed, and she was acutely conscious of him. She heard the ax again. Michael groaned, and she went to the bed. It was impossible to hold him up without Dan, so she called to him.

He came at once, and she asked, "Will you help me?"

Dan filled the dipper with cold water for Michael. He held him while Michael drank. Michael struggled to sit up. Mary felt his forehead. "He's still feverish."

"Get me up," Michael whispered. Dan leaned down to help him, taking his weight. He realized Michael O'Malley was heavier and about two inches taller than he himself was, and he was solid muscle.

Each step was slow, an effort for Michael that made him wheeze and groan. "Mary, watch the cabin while we're in back," Dan said. He realized how vulnerable they would be if any of the men caused trouble.

Mary left them, hating to see Michael struggling so to walk, yet thankful for each step he took. She moved to the front door and brushed angrily at tears. It upset her to see Michael hurt. She went to the back door to meet them when they returned.

"Let's get him to the bed. This has exhausted him. If you can get some stew down him, it'll help."

She nodded, and finally Michael stretched out. They fed him, and he was asleep again as soon as he finished.

"He should be a little stronger after getting up. We need to change the bandages, Mary."

She laid out the clean rags and left Dan to work on Michael. While he worked, she pumped water to heat. Dan returned to chopping wood while she cooked. She cast glances out the window, watching him. She paused once, watching him work, aware of how much he was doing for her and her family, knowing his own work was suffering, and reminding herself that he did it out of his friendship for Silas. She had to constantly remind herself of Silas, and it was becoming more and more of an effort, because she was conscious of Dan in a way she had never been of Silas.

She went outside to talk to him. "I'm going to wash the bandages and bedclothes," she said, trying to talk to him without looking down at his bare chest.

"Have you heated water?"

"Yes."

"There's a tin tub. I can put it behind your blankets and you can bathe if you'd like. Then you can wash the clothes."

The thought of bathing while she was shut in the one room with Dan Castle made her face flood with heat, but she wanted a bath badly. She glanced through the open door at the blankets surrounding her bed and nodded. "I'd like that."

He nodded as solemnly. "I'll get it ready."

"Do you want me to wash any of your clothes?" she asked.

"I can wash them," he said easily. He moved away, getting out the tub, taking kettles of water and the buckets she had placed beside the fire to pour them into the tub.

"It's ready," he said, holding aside the blanket for her. As she moved past him, her shoulder brushed his chest very lightly, yet she was startlingly aware of it. He stood there watching her, smoothing the faded and frayed green blanket, running his fingers idly along the rope, and she was caught in an invisible current that held her.

"Would you like a little more water? There's still a bucket by the fire."

"No, I'm fine," she answered. Both of them stared at each other, and neither of them looked at the tub of water.

"If you need anything, call," he said, his voice sounding deep and gruff.

She nodded, unable to speak, feeling a pull that was intense. She wanted him to kiss her. Her heart thudded so loudly in her ears that she thought Dan couldn't keep from hearing it. His blue eyes were stormy.

"You'll take your hair down?" he asked in a hoarse tone that had dropped another notch.

She nodded slowly, trying to think about what he asked her, yet barely able to think at all. "Yes. I'll wash my hair," she said, and her voice had changed as drastically as his. She sounded breathless and uncertain. Finally her gaze dropped, trailing over his bare chest that was so appealing. Appealing and unsettling. She had seen men's bare chests all her life, and they had never been a particularly disturbing sight until now.

Dan watched her look at him, and her cheeks flushed again. Her breasts rose and fell swiftly with her shallow, quick breathing. He should go. He knew damned well he should go, but he couldn't move. She was only a few feet away, drawn by the same attraction that held him to the floor as if nails had been driven through his boots.

Mary battled with the powerful emotions that tore at her. Her longing for Dan and loyalty to Silas warred in her. She wanted to reach out and touch him, wanted him to reach for her, but knew she should not. She spun around, her fists clenched, her breathing ragged. "Dan, leave."

He blinked, sucking in his breath, looking at her stiff, thin shoulders. He knew he was causing her problems, yet he wanted to reach for her and pull her to him. *She is betrothed to Silas!*

He left, striding outside and picking up the ax to attack the wood with an energy that made chips fly and his muscles strain.

Mary heard him go, heard the ax, and she stepped back out from her corner to look at Michael. She drew a deep shuddering breath as she stood over her brother. "Get well, Michael, so we can go home, away from this place where reason and time vanish. Please Michael, get well."

He slept quietly, so she hurried back to undress and step into the tub of hot water. She let her hair down, sinking down in the water.

Dan paused to wipe his brow and heard the splash of water in the tub. He groaned as he thought of Mary, only yards away, sitting naked in the tub of warm water. It was the solitude, the confines of the cabin that made him feel this way, he argued with himself. She wasn't beautiful like Dulcie or Louisa. She was thin, and had small breasts, and was a little plain. He paused again and stared at the door of the house, hearing a splash. He couldn't fool himself. She was beautiful with her hair down. Her skin was smooth and rosy, and her eyes could hold his attention riveted on her. But it was more than that.

He swore and begun to swing the ax again. There was sufficient kindling chopped for months, but he couldn't go back inside now. He paused again, thinking about Sorghum. Dan set down the ax and walked around to the front of the cabin. He could see men coming and going, working at the sluices, moving in and out of the mine dug into the mountainside. He stepped inside the front door, where he was in the cool shadows of the interior, and pulled over a chair to sit down.

"Dan?"

"I'm right here. I thought I should keep an eye on the men, Mary. If I'm in back chopping wood, we wouldn't know if someone were coming."

"When I get out, do you want to bathe? The water's still warm."

"Thanks, I'll wash under the pump."

"That's ice water. You'll freeze."

"Silas and I did that all the time we prospected. You get accustomed to it after a time."

He heard splashing, and turned his head to stare at the blanket. Water splashed over the side on the floor, and he turned around quickly to stare outside. He could hear Mary singing. Every sound grated on his nerves. He stoop up and moved to the door to lean against the jamb. Damn the O'Malleys. He was missing work, he was drawn to his best friend's fiancée, and he felt as if he were enclosed in a cage in the small cabin. And worst of all, he thought it was only a matter of time until Sorghum recognized him. If any of the men knew there was a price on his head, Dan knew he would have real trouble from them. He turned and sauntered to the Henry, picking it up to check it again. He had all the pistols and rifles loaded, ready to use.

Michael lay still, and Dan hoped Ta-ne-haddle would come, because when he had changed Michael's bandages, some of the cuts looked infected and worse than before.

He heard a splash and turned. Beneath the hanging blankets he could see Mary's wet feet and a few inches of bare, wet legs. He sucked in his breath and moved to the door, turning his back to her to lean against the jamb again.

"Dan, sure you don't want to bathe now? If you don't, I'm going to wash the clothes."

"I'll wash outside, thanks," he said, knowing he sounded gruff.

"Want some of your things washed?"

"Yeah. I'll hand them to you."

"Wait! I'm not dressed. Just a minute."

He took another deep breath, clamping his jaw shut

as he moved to his things and pulled out clothing he had worn. He rolled it in a bundle and turned.

"All right, give it to me." She pushed the hanging blanket aside and stood waiting. She had another blanket wrapped around her, her wet hair was smoothed away from her face, and her lashes seemed darker from the water.

"It looks as if a pup washed, Mary. You splashed water everywhere."

"It felt good. I like a tub of hot water," she said. She was warm and relaxed. He looked into her eyes as she said the last words, and all her calm vanished as swiftly as if storm winds had swept through the open doors of the cabin and carried it away. Dan gave her a heated look of longing that made her heart skip. When his gaze raked over her, he looked at her as if he could imagine her without the blanket.

And suddenly it became a problem for her just to reach for the bundle of clothing he held against his chest. "I hope we can go home soon," she blurted, then immediately wished she could take back the words. She wondered what had possessed her to say them aloud. Her cheeks burned with embarrassment.

"I hope so too, Mary." He held out the clothing.

"Just set it down," she said, tightening her grip on the blanket. She wished she had dressed, but if she had done the wash with long-sleeved calico on, it would get splashed.

She made a motion with her hand. "I'm not dressed. I thought I'd get my dress wet," she said solemnly, and he nodded. "You can drop your things in the water if you want."

Watching her, he moved to the tub to let the clothing fall into it. He stood only a couple of feet away, close enough to reach out and touch her. "It's just because we're together so much," she whispered. "I love Silas."

"I know you do," he said roughly.

He didn't move, and her pulse began racing erratically. He reached out and she knew she should step back away from him, but she couldn't. He tilted her chin up while his gaze held hers locked with his. "You're a beautiful woman, Mary."

She was aware of his finger touching her chin, aware of the husky note of his voice, and was torn between wanting him and guilt

"Mary," he said in a husky voice. His arm banded her, and he kissed her. His mouth opened hers, his tongue thrusting deeply. It was wrong, but it was as necessary as breathing. Her arms were folded in front of her as she clung to the blanket.

Mary's heart pounded. She couldn't slip her arms around him, because she had to hold the blanket. She couldn't stop him because she wanted him to kiss her.

Silas and Louisa both seemed so distant. Mary was torn with conflicting emotions, but at the moment all she knew was that Dan was kissing her and she wanted him to. She leaned away finally.

"Dan, please go."

He moved away and she stared at him as he strode toward the door. Her emotions churned and she had to face the questions raised by Dan's kisses.

"Mary, when you're finished with the wash and can watch the miners, tell me and I'll shower," he called from the doorway. His fists were clenched and he wanted to stride right back to her, but he knew he shouldn't.

"I will." She washed furiously, trying to vent some of her feelings in her work. It was a tub filled with wet clothes and rags and sheets, yet Dan's things were all she could see. She pulled up a blue shirt she had seen him wear many times. It was like one of Michael's shirts. It was cotton, and it had a tiny rip on the sleeve, yet it was something of Dan's, and consequently, touching it was like touching a part of him. She ran her finger along the seam, thinking about the shoulder usually beneath it. Shaking her head, she plunged it into the water and scrubbed.

Finally she had a stack of wet garments. They were tightly wrung and ready to hang. "Dan?"

"Yes," he said, and came inside the cabin.

"These are ready. Will there be anywhere to hang them?"

"Sure." Dan pushed aside the blankets to get the wet clothes. He scooped them up and hurried outside, trying to ignore her. It seemed as if every time he came closer to her, his desire burst to life. He couldn't understand his reactions to her, but they were impossible to ignore and damn near impossible to control. He draped clothes over a rope he had strung from tree to tree, and in few minutes she appeared beside him.

"I can help."

"I'll do it. You go back inside and keep watch. I don't want anyone slipping up on us."

"You think they would ever try again?"

"Yes." He turned to face her and then wished he had kept working, because every time he looked down into her wide green eyes, he was as lost as if he had fallen over a cliff. With an effort, he resumed hanging the wet clothes, and without looking around he was aware that she had gone inside.

He washed at the pump with icy water, then pulled on his pants again. He had just buttoned them when Mary called.

"Dan, Jethro is coming."

Dan yanked on his boots and shirt and hurried inside. "Is he alone?"

Mary watched him suck in his flat stomach to tuck his shirt into his pants. "Yes," she answered absentmindedly, her thoughts on Dan.

He went out the front door to greet Jethro, who had come to see how Michael was doing. He came inside with Dan. " 'Afternoon, ma'am. How's your brother?"

"Maybe a little better."

"Good. If anyone could pull through a bear fight, it's Michael O'Malley. He asleep?"

"Yes," Dan answered. "Want to stay and eat with us?"

Jethro looked torn with indecision, glancing worriedly over his shoulder. Dan realized the camp might be angry with Jethro for befriending Mary and him.

"Thank you. I'd sure like a woman's cooking for a change, but I better get back." Suddenly he grinned. "I hear you sorta surprised the boys the other day."

"I suppose I did," Dan answered carefully.

"I warned you, they're a wild bunch. I don't think you'll have any more trouble."

"Why don't you take a bowl of stew back with you?" Mary asked, going to the fire to ladle some out into a tin cup.

"I'd like that mighty well, ma'am. Indeed I would," he said eagerly, going to take it from her hands. "Mmm, that does smell good! You folks need anything?"

"We may need a wagon to take Michael back to Denver later. Any chance of buying one here?"

Jethro frowned. "It's Willie's wagon. I can ask him. I suppose if the price is right, Willie would sell his right arm."

"See how much he wants for it or if he'll take something in trade in case I don't have the money. Tell him Miss O'Malley's brother, her father, and a friend of mine are coming from Denver. Tell the boys my lawman brother is coming too."

"You got a lawman brother?"

"Yes," Dan said evenly. "He won't bother anyone. All we want to do is get Michael back to Denver so he can get well."

Jethro nodded, and a worried frown creased his brow. "I'll ask. When are those folks coming and how're they finding our camp?"

"One of them is a Kiowa. He can track anything. He'll follow our trail out here as if we had burnt the grass all along the way."

"You joshin' me?"

"No. He'll get here quickly as you and I did."

"I don't think an Injun or anyone else can track like that."

Dan smiled. "You'll see."

"I better tell the boys. They get nervous and quick with their six-shooters when people start appearing at camp."

"You tell them. I don't want Michael's brother or father shot."

"No. We'll watch, but like I said before, keep 'em away from the mining. Thanks, Miss O'Malley."

"You're welcome, Mr. Jethro."

They moved to the door as he left, and without thinking, Dan draped his arm across her shoulders. Jethro turned back and waved to them, then went striding toward a campfire the men were gathered around.

"Well, you won a friend. He was so happy with your stew, he looked as if he would wolf it down right here." He turned to look at her as he talked, and then he realized he had his arm around her. She stood close to him, looking up at him solemnly. He wanted to pull her tightly against him and kiss her.

She moved away, crossing the room to the fire. They ate dinner in self-conscious silence, and Dan helped Michael to the privy once more, noticing this time that Michael could move a little better. As he held Michael and Mary fed him, Dan said, "He's better."

Instantly her gaze flew to his, seeking reassurance. "Do you really think so?"

"Yes."

Michael fell back into a deep sleep, seemingly exhausted by his efforts. Dan barricaded the doors and closed the shutters, thankful the cabin was strong and built to withstand attack. He worried now about Tane-haddle riding into the camp, yet he knew Tane-haddle could get around in dangerous places with amazing ease. And he wondered where Brian was, why he or Paddy hadn't appeared.

He built up a roaring fire, because once the sun went down, the air chilled. "I slept today, Mary. You go to bed and I'll sit with him."

She nodded, and once again he had to go through the same agonizing ritual of listening to her move around, watching her bare feet, and trying to fight his rampant imagination. He stood up, wanting to go to her, knowing he shouldn't. He crossed the room and stood beside the blankets, aware she had become suddenly still.

"Dan?"

"Yes."

"Did you want something?"

He stood there, knowing what he should answer, thinking: Yes, I want you. "No, Mary. I'm just tired of sitting." He moved away, walking to the fire. He drank some brandy and sat back down beside Michael, who seemed to be sleeping better than before. Dan dozed beside Michael's bed for a while until he heard Michael groaning.

"Water," Michael said, and Dan picked up the cup. Holding Michael's head, he helped him drink. He heard a rustle and looked around as Mary came across the cabin.

"Michael?"

"He wanted water," Dan answered. He studied Michael intently, trying to keep his attention away from her. She moved opposite Dan and felt Michael's forehead.

"I think he still has fever. Michael, do you want anything?"

"No," he whispered, and finished the cup. Dan helped him to lie back, and his eyes closed.

In a few minutes his breathing returned to normal. Dan looked at Mary as she sat beside her brother, her hand on his arm, her fiery tresses falling over her shoulders. His gaze lowered to the rise of her breasts beneath the white cotton gown. He moved away to the fire.

"He's asleep, Mary. Go back to bed."

She stood up, and he noticed she was shivering. She clutched her arms to her waist. "Dan, I'm cold."

"Come get warm."

There was a long pause, and then he realized she didn't want to come stand beside him at the hearth. "Come on," he said quietly. "I'll sit with Michael."

A sudden eerie howl came from outside. She jumped, and her eyes opened wide with fear.

"What's that?"

"I think it's probably a timber wolf out there close to our cabin," he said, moving to pick up the Henry.

"You're not going out?" she asked, sounding stricken.

"No. I just want to be ready in case it isn't really a wolf."

Mary shook with cold and fear. The haunting howl had unnerved her, and she was freezing from moving around barefoot in her gown in the cabin. She watched Dan open a shutter a crack to gaze out the back.

Another long howl came, and she shook violently. She moved to the fire. "Should I get a pistol?"

"Not yet. I think it's a wolf. It sounds like one, and I don't see anyone moving around." He crossed to one of the front windows and looked out. "It's a wolf. I see men building up the campfire."

"Why don't they stay in their cabins?"

"They'll go in if it's a wolf, but they probably just ate and are sitting around talking and drinking. It's tiresome to go off alone in a cabin if you don't have a wo—" He looked at Mary and bit off his words.

Another howl cut through the silence, and she jumped. Dan closed the shutter and placed the rifle where he could get it in an instant. He buckled on the gunbelt.

"I thought you decided it was a wolf."

"I did, but I like to be ready."

When it howled again, he saw how it was unnerving her. He walked over to her to console her, and he wrapped his arms around her. "It's a wolf, Mary. It can't get in here. I'm armed to the teeth." He moved closer to the fire, turning her so her back was to the flames because she felt like ice and she shivered violently.

"It sounds so eerie. You don't hear them in town. Coyotes are almost as bad. I don't hear them as often as I used to."

"No, Denver's become too civilized for them." He tightened his arms, letting his chin rest against her head. She smelled sweet and clean, and he knew he was only fooling himself if he thought he was holding her to comfort her. She felt marvelous in his arms, and there was only one layer of cotton covering her.

Her waist was so tiny he could almost circle it with his hands.

The wolf howled again and she covered one ear with her hand, placing her other ear against his chest. "I hate that. It scares me."

He smiled, brushed the back of her head. "You can single-handedly fight off big tough men, and yet you're afraid of a wolf's howl."

"It sounds so *alone*. And it scares me. It scares me for Michael."

"Honey," he said tenderly, "that wolf isn't going to make Michael any worse. The wolf is just a big shaggy animal howling in the wind."

She shivered in his arms and he realized she was terrified. He tightened his arms around her, holding her close against him. They were standing so close to the fire, he didn't see how she could continue to shiver. He bent his head to look at her, and was amazed. She seemed almost invincible, running the boardinghouse, tending her injured brother, riding hard through the night to get to the camp, dealing with Brian and taking her father's disasters in stride, yet now the simple howl of a wolf had undone her completely.

Mary clung to him, thankful for his arms tightly around her. She wanted desperately to shut out the long, lonesome-sounding howling that frightened her. It made the isolation of the cabin and Michael's injuries seem worse. She knew she was acting foolishly and she was embarrassed, but she couldn't stop shaking or stop her fear.

"Honey," Dan said, his voice a deep rumble as she pressed her head tightly against his chest, "Do you know what a wolf looks like?"

"I saw one once in a cage someone brought to town, and I've seen wolf skins."

"Then you know they look just like big dogs. And beautiful big dogs at that. Their fur is soft and thick. Some people keep wolves as pets."

While he talked, she remembered the wolf and how she had pitied the creature, hating to see it caged. And it had been beautiful. Her fear began to subside as she thought of dogs and remembered one they used to have at the boardinghouse. He had been shaggy and friendly and she loved to hug him and sink her fingers in his thick coat.

She became calm, but along with the vanishing of her fear came an awareness of Dan. She clung to him tightly and he held her hard against him. His hand moved over her back and his strokes that moments ago had been reassuring were now disturbing and tantalizing.

Dan became aware that she no longer covered her ear. Her shivering had ceased and she became silent. He stroked her back, feeling her warm flesh beneath the cotton, feeling her shoulder blades.

He held her tightly and he couldn't let go. He shifted, tilting up her face. Her eyes met his gaze and tension flared between them.

"Aw, Mary," he whispered, and bent his head to kiss her.

Mary let him, clinging to him. His lips felt so light on hers, and then they were firm, pressing hard. His tongue touched her lips and delved deep into her mouth, storming her senses. She yielded to the passion he stirred, clinging to him, feeling his hard arousal pressing against her. His kisses went on, and she wanted them to never stop.

His hand drifted to her shoulder, her nape and throat, and then down to her breast. She gasped and suddenly pushed against him. "No!" She stepped back, her eyes wide.

"Oh, damn, I'm sorry Mary." He ground out the words and spun around to stride to the far side of the cabin. "Sit there by the fire. I'll stay over by Michael." He pulled a chair beside the bed and sat with his back to Mary, his body burning with longing.

Mary watched him, standing and shivering again. She rubbed her hands together, and when the wolf howled again, she jumped.

Dan glanced over his shoulder at her. "Are you alright?"

"Yes. I'll be all right," she said, hating the howling. But now she was not quite as unsettled by it as she was by the reaction Dan's kisses had stirred.

He went·to her bed and came back with a blanket and her shoes. "Here, wear this. You can wrap yourself up in it and sit in a chair or go back to bed."

"I'm sorry I'm so foolish about the wolf, but it scares me."

He gazed at her solemnly. "That's all right. All of us are scared of something."

"What are you afraid of, Dan? I can't imagine you being afraid of anything."

"I guess the thing I've been most afraid of is hanging," he said, looking into the fire. His gaze shifted to her. "And that the woman I love won't love me in return."

"I'm sure you don't have much to fear there," Mary said quietly, thinking of Louisa and Silas, knowing her kisses with Dan were wrong. "I'm going to sit here by the fire for a while if you don't mind."

"No, stay there as long as you like," he answered politely, moving away from her. He sat with his back to her again.

"Dan, have you ever killed a wolf?"

"No."

"I wonder if they're vicious."

"Probably only if provoked. I don't now much about them," he answered softly, turning his chair to look at her. She sat in front of the fire, and the flames made her hair look more fiery than ever in the reflected orange glow.

"What have you hunted?" she asked after a time.

"Things we could eat. Venison, turkeys, doves, prairie chickens," he said, suddenly wanting to lift her heavy mane of hair and kiss her slender nape.

Another howl came, and she jumped, squeezing her eyes closed.

"You want me to come closer?" he asked.

"No!" she exclaimed, and then blushed, glancing at him and away. "It's so foolish. I know a wolf can't get in here after us. But why does he keep howling?"

"I don't know why a wolf howls," Dan answered

slowly, thinking he would like to howl himself. He felt keyed-up, tense, and disturbed by Mary, although he knew his feelings were caused by their isolation. "How'd you escape growing up in a frontier town without learning how to use a pistol?"

"Pa and the boys weren't about to teach me!"

"You're a beautiful woman, Mary," he said solemnly, knowing he shouldn't say it, but unable to resist.

She turned to look at him, her eyes wide. "Thank you."

He couldn't remember feeling this way about a woman before. He ached to touch her and he couldn't stop watching her.

They talked quietly for over two hours while the fire died down. The wolf had stopped howling long ago, and the wind whistling around the cabin was the only sound. Michael slept more quietly than he had any night since their arrival, and Dan realized that each day now, Michael was improving. He turned back to Mary and saw her head loll over and realized she was asleep sitting up in the chair. He crossed the room and picked her up.

She stirred and opened her eyes, stiffening in his arms.

"Dan?"

"You were asleep. You should be in bed."

He carried her to her corner, kissed her forehead, and set her on her feet. "Good night, Mary," he said quietly, and left without looking back. Mary saw him jam his hands into his pockets, and she stared after him, all sleepiness gone after finding herself in his arms. She spread the blanket over her bed and crawled beneath the covers, lying awake and listening to him move to the fire and put on more logs.

Dan stood watching them burn, thinking there was one thing about Mary that was different from Louisa and Melissa Hatfield: he never tired of talking to Mary. Even Dulcie wasn't as interesting as Mary. He couldn't remember spending much time talking to Melissa at all, and he couldn't remember enjoying conversations with Louisa, because the only time they talked were the long evenings spent in her parents' presence. Mary was fast becoming the best friend he had ever had.

The thought made him pause and turn to stare at the blankets surrounding her as if he could see her through them.

He sat beside Michael and dozed, only to waken when the fire had died and the embers had turned to gray ashes. Dan looked first at Michael, who still slept quietly. His gaze circled the cabin and he wondered what had awakened him.

A tapping came at the back door, and Dan got up cautiously. Mary appeared, a pistol in hand.

He motioned for her to remain quiet. He picked up the Henry and moved to the door.

15

Reuben Knelville stood before Sheriff Borden's desk discussing the robbery of the stage. "Can't you put a man on the stage when I receive the next order? I wired Kansas City, and they'll have everything ready to send in four weeks. I want a guard on that stage!"

"Sorry, Mr. Knelville. I told your pa that if you want someone to guard your own goods, you'll have to hire them yourself. Now, you can talk to a Pinkerton man if you want. I've got the name of one who works out of St. Louis."

"All right, give me his name, but remember, Borden, you're hired by the city fathers to control criminals. If you want to keep this job, see that it gets done!"

"Yes, sir!" Sheriff Borden snapped, his face flushing. He rummaged through his desk. "Just a minute. Maybe I stuck it in the cabinet." He pushed back his chair with a scrape and went to a scarred cabinet that stood along the back wall. A cabinet filled with rifles was mounted on the wall beside it, and wanted posters hung next to the gun cabinet.

Reuben's gaze drifted over the cabinet while his fingers drummed impatiently on the counter. Louisa was shopping and he wanted to be finished with the Sheriff in time to get back to talk to her. His gaze swept over the wall to the window onto the back, where the sheriff's horse grazed in a small area fenced by rope.

Reuben's gaze went back to the posters, and he stared at one. Something about it nagged at him. He looked at the name: Tigre Danby Castillo. Wanted for murder, theft, bank robbery. Reuben looked again at the picture.

"Here's the fellow's name, Buster Brawne, with his St. Louis office address."

"Doesn't sound like a real name."

Sheriff Borden shrugged. "Here's his card. Take it. No one else is interested in a Pinkerton man."

"Soon we can get things sent in here by rail. In the meantime, think it over, Sheriff. You might change your mind about putting a guard on the next stage. The election comes up in a few months."

"I'll keep that in mind, Mr. Knelville," he said in a tight voice.

Reuben left, letting the door bang shut behind him. He jammed the card in his pocket and climbed into his buggy. Life had taken a strange turn. Dan Castle had left town with the O'Malleys to tend the injured brother. Paddy was still in town, but Reuben hadn't seen Brian, although he assumed the young man had gone with Dan and Mary O'Malley. To Reuben's delight, the trollop, Dulcie, knew exactly where Dan was. Castle had taken time to tell her before he left, a bit of information Reuben might find useful.

As Louisa came out of a dry-goods store, Reuben slowed his team. "Good morning, Louisa."

When she turned, he was struck again by her beauty. Since she had all but actually become engaged to Castle, Reuben had been comparing her to other women he knew. In all honesty, the only woman who could come close to Louisa's beauty was the whore, Dulcie. And that amazed Reuben every time he stopped to think about it. Some of the whores he had known were pretty, some attractive, and some downright plain, but many of them looked as if life had been hard on them. Not Dulcie. She was beautiful. Naked or clothed. It pleased him to buy her favors, knowing she was Dan Castle's woman, hoping it annoyed Castle. He couldn't get much information out of her, but after the first time with her, he really didn't care. He was also amazed that his taste in women was exactly the same as Castle's. He supposed it was simply a matter of having an eye for real beauty.

Reuben's gaze ran over Louisa with what he hoped was a bold, blatant look of desire, because he knew how she loved to have him show that he desired her. He climbed down to stand beside her. "Shopping early this morning?"

"Yes, we wanted to finish before we made our morning calls."

"And tonight is the Haskinses' dinner. Have you heard from the wayward fiancé yet?"

Her eyes became stormy as she gazed up at him, her red lips pursing in anger. "You know I don't care to discuss that, and if you want to talk to me, Reuben Knelville, you will kindly change the subject!"

"And your father, who is so taken with Castle. Has he heard from him yet? Or is he still out in the woods with Mary O'Malley?"

"I'm going now."

Reuben laughed and took her hand, leaning down. "How I wished I were to be allowed to take you tonight. I'd steal a kiss, Louisa. A long kiss." His fingers tickled her palm while he whispered in her ear.

He saw the anger in her eyes change to a look of desire. She was as hot-blooded as that tart. Sometimes Dulcie was more of a lady in her own way than Louisa. And Dulcie wouldn't torment a man to death, something Louisa delighted in.

"Maybe I can escort you home if you indicate you'd like to let me," he said. "Just a few kisses, Louisa, before you're engaged."

She slanted him a coy look, and he knew she would let him take her home tonight. "Perhaps, Reuben."

"Perhaps you might like me to ask your mother if I can take you. Then I could steal two kisses?"

She laughed, a merry peal. "How could you talk Mama into that, when—" She stopped, and realized she had thought of Dan. The anger returned to her eyes and she lifted her chin. "You do that, Reuben. See if you can talk Mama into allowing it. Our carriage is right there in front of the confectionery."

He smiled. Louisa would be his, never Dan Castle's. He knew that when Castle returned he could make amends, but Reuben intended to cause such a wide rift between Dan and Louisa that Castle would never win her back. And Reuben had decided he wanted Louisa for his wife. She was the most suitable woman he knew.

"Very well, Louisa. You wait right here and let me talk to your mother."

"I'll go back into the store. You have five minutes."

He laughed. "Always, you want to make life more difficult for me in any little way you can!"

"Why, Reuben, you make me sound cruel."

"You *are* cruel like a little kitten who can cause only tiny scratches. I'll show you a sweet cruelty tonight, Louisa, when I put my hands beneath your skirts!"

"Reuben! Stop that this instant!" She frowned and spun away from him, but he had done it enough to know it excited her, and she liked for him to talk to her about forbidden things.

He strolled half a block to the Shumacher carriage and knocked lightly, stepping inside.

"Mrs. Shumacher, may I have a word with you? Louisa has stepped back into the store."

"Of course, Reuben. We're going to call on your mother shortly."

"She'll be happy to see you. I know she counts you as her best friend. Mrs. Shumacher, this is a delicate question, but you're an understanding woman and one whom I've known since I was a boy."

"What's troubling you, Reuben?"

"Under ordinary circumstances, I know you would refuse my request, but ordinary circumstances no longer exist. I'm invited to the Haskinses' tonight, as your family is also. May I escort Louisa?"

She drew a sharp breath and gazed out the carriage window. She was so much like his own mother that Reuben found it easy to be with her and usually easy to please her. He knew when to speak and when to keep his silence.

"Yes, Reuben, if that's agreeable with Louisa."

"It's agreeable. Thank you. Mrs. Shumacher. I know it's a delicate situation."

"Frankly, Reuben, I think the girl has such foolish notions sometimes. Simply because the man has become a bank customer, Mr. Shumacher has turned a blind eye to a ridiculous situation."

"If I were about to become engaged to your daughter, I wouldn't leave town with another woman, that I can promise you."

"I know, Reuben. You're reliable and trustworthy."

Reuben smiled, his purpose accomplished. "I see Louisa returning. Thank you."

He stepped down and strode across the boardwalk to take Louisa's elbow in his hand. "You'll ride with me tonight, and we'll do just what I promised."

"You're a scoundrel, Reuben, and how you have Mother fooled! She thinks you're a perfect gentleman. If she knew what you do to me, you'd be banned forever from my presence."

"But she doesn't know," he said, turning her to face him, looking down at her breasts. "You're beautiful, Louisa."

"And you're far too forward!"

"I'll call at six, and for a few hours I'll make you forget your betrothed."

"One thing, Reuben," she said, her temper suddenly flaring. "You're not to mention the name Dan Castle!"

He smiled and helped her into the carriage, closing the door and watching the carriage move down Larimer. *Dan Castle*. The words rang in his ears. And he thought of the name on the poster. *Tigre Danby Castillo*. "Danby Castillo," he said aloud under his breath, his gray eyes widening. *"Danby Castillo—Dan Castle."*

Reuben climbed in his carriage to ride back to the jail.

16

Hattie studied her dresses. Catalina had a marvelous seamstress who had made three dresses for Hattie. She studied the rasberry muslin, and amber crepon, and a deep blue grenadine.

She decided on the amber crepon and pulled it on. She then brushed her hair and began the arduous task of braiding it in the latest style, when she thought about Javier and how he liked it in a bun behind her head so he could take it down easily. She sat down on the rocker, running her hand across her forehead. Javier would be here this afternoon. It had been so long since they parted. Years of separation. And she finally answered his letter and agreed to see him. Since she had let down that barrier, memories had come flooding back, longings that she had tried to ignore. She was torn between burning anger that would never completely die, and a longing that would also be with her as long as she drew breath. She loved him. She couldn't stop. They had had so many good years together, perfect years. They had a wonderful son. Javier seemed truly sorry, and he seemed to be trying to make amends with April. With Luke it was impossible.

Luke was a hard man, but Hattie understood why. That terrible day of the ambush had changed their lives forever. They had molded into different people. Luke's gentle nature was tempered now by the hardness that had enabled him to survive. And she supposed the same was true of her.

Hattie unplaited her hair and twisted it into a bun, her fingers moving swiftly while her mind jumped to the present. She still didn't know what she felt for Javier. Anger and forgiveness. Yet it was becoming more and more difficult to cling to her anger when she saw how happy April and Noah were. April's life was full and good, and she had completely forgotten the past and forgiven Javier, so what was the point in clinging to something so far in the past?

Yet all of the lost years could come rushing back to Hattie so easily. And of all her grandchildren, there wasn't a girl baby. How she dreamed there would be one like April, but there wasn't. She adored the boys, and she knew the longing was simply for what had been lost to her long ago. If she stopped to remember, the pain returned, blurred, not as sharp as it had been in those first years, but unforgettable, and then she didn't want to see Javier or talk to him.

She started to put on the necklace Luke and Catalina had given her—emeralds set in silver—but she lowered it and opened a drawer, rummaging deep to pull out the old locket of gold that Javier had given her long ago. It had a tintype inside, of Dan as a child. Hattie held it in her palm a long time and finally put it around her neck. It lay above the neck of the amber dress in the cleft between her breasts. She dabbed rosewater behind her ears and on her wrists and realized she was as dithery as a young girl.

She moved to the window to look down at the road, and as if her thoughts had conjured him up, she saw the familiar wagon come into view. The driver was hidden by a broad-brimmed black hat, but his long legs and arms were showing, and her heart began to race.

"Javier," she whispered, watching the wagon turn into the yard. It stopped, and he jumped down, striding toward the front door and out of her sight, but she remembered well his long stride, his purposeful way of moving.

She went down the spacious hall, thankful for the grand house that Noah had given April. And now there were plans to enlarge it. Hattie suspected April and Noah wanted another baby.

When she heard Javier's voice, she paused. Memories flooded her mind. His deep tone seemed to reach out with invisible fingers and cling to her. She moved ahead more slowly, uncertain about their meeting. She turned the corner, and he stood talking to one of the maids. For an instant Hattie stared in shock, thinking it couldn't be Javier.

It was his voice, but the man only yards away had thick white hair.

"Javier?"

He turned. His mustache was as white as his hair, both thick as ever, his black eyes seeming to absorb her into their depths. He looked older, and it hurt to see the change in him. There were lines in his face that hadn't been there before, but he was as broad-shouldered and as masculine, and an undercurrent of excitement gripped her as she looked at him.

"Hattie!" he said, moving a step toward her and halting.

His one word set her pulse racing. Memories swirled like snowflakes, silent, constant, too many of them tumbling in her thoughts. "Come into the parlor," she said, barely knowing what she told him. "I don't know where April is."

"I will fetch her, Señora Castillo."

"*Gracias, María,*" Hattie said, and motioned to Javier. He stepped aside, and as she passed him, she was aware of his big body, the clean smell tinged with a faint trace of tobacco that was so familiar to her. In minutes April joined them. The rest of the afternoon and that evening were spent in pleasant but—it seemed to Hattie—strained conversation. April and Noah were at ease, but Aaron was shy around Javier. Finally Javier left the child alone until Aaron's shyness began to evaporate and he climbed onto Javier's lap.

Eventually April put Aaron to bed, and April and Noah said good night, leaving Hattie and Javier alone.

Javier moved to the mantel to rest his arm against it as he turned to look at her. He had shed his coat, and she saw how his shirt pulled across his shoulders. The muscles were still solid and powerful. "Hattie, I want you to come home with me."

Hattie had known this was coming, she had rehearsed answer after answer, yet she had never been able to say yes.

She clasped her hands together, turning the plain gold band on her finger. She heard a rustle and looked up as he leaned down to pull her to her feet.

"Hattie, I need you. I know I can't undo what I did, but we're both getting older. Is this the way you want to spend our last years?"

Her throat tightened as she looked at him, and tears welled up in her eyes. She couldn't give him an answer. She felt torn, for once in her life, caught in dreadful indecision.

He framed her face with large callused hands that she knew so well. "Hattie, you're my woman. I need you," he said hoarsely, his eyes growing red. "Even if you can't forget or forgive me, maybe you could forgive me enough to come back. When the memories make things too difficult for you, go away for a while, but come back for part of the time. Give me a chance." His eyes filled with tears. "I can't live without you. I don't want to be without you."

She wrapped her arms around him and cried. Instantly his strong arms enfolded her, crushing her to him while he poured out his love in a husky voice. He turned her face up to his and kissed her. She tasted salty tears and didn't know whether they were hers or his, or both, and it was wonderful to be in his arms again. Past hurts wouldn't vanish, but she needed Javier and she knew how much she had missed him.

She leaned back to look at him and he picked her up as easily as if she were a young girl and moved down the hall to his room which was in a separate wing from the other bedrooms. He carried her to the bed and went back to light the lamp and close the door. He moved to the bed to look down at her.

"Hattie, it's been so long. It's like you tore out my heart and took it with you," he said, unfastening his shirt and pulling it over his head. His body was hard and muscular as always, and her heart pounded as he stretched out beside her to pull her into his arms. "When it gets bad and your anger returns—I know it will—you tell me."

She nodded, feeling tears threatening again. She closed her eyes, leaning the last few inches to kiss him. Deep within her she knew that her anger would seldom return because it was such a senseless waste.

17

Dan moved closer to the door, his Colt ready, when he heard a bird's whistle.

"Mary!" came a faint call from the other side of the door.

"It's Brian," he said over his shoulder, holstering his Colt and unbarring the door to open it while Mary disappeared behind the blankets to dress. Ta-ne-haddle entered, followed by Brian. Dan closed and barred the door behind them, then turned to hug Ta-ne-haddle while Brian crossed the room to Michael's bedside.

"Thanks for coming," Dan said. "I thought you might keep Michael from getting scarred. He's still running a fever, and some of his cuts are infected. Come meet Mary." Dan shook hands with Brian as Mary appeared and hugged her brother.

"Mary, this is Ta-ne-haddle, Luke's friend. This is Mary O'Malley. I see you found Brian."

"How is he, Mary?" Brian asked.

"He's feverish and weak. Sometimes he doesn't sleep quietly, other times he does. He's been up with Dan's help."

"Let me look at him. Brian, why don't you help me change his bandages," Ta-ne-haddle said.

"You want to wake him?"

Ta-ne-haddle nodded. "I'll give him something that'll make him go back to sleep. I saw Doc Felton before we left Denver."

"I'll get clean rags for the bandages," Mary said, and for the next half-hour everyone in the cabin was

occupied. Dan built up the fire and made beds ready
while Mary brewed coffee and heated the stew. She
knew Brian would be hungry no matter how recently
he had eaten. She glanced at the men as they worked
over Michael. Ta-ne-haddle had him sitting up on the
side of the bed while he smoothed some kind of oint-
ment on Michael's wounds, and her hopes increased
that he would be better soon.

Michael settled to sleep while Ta-ne-haddle and
Brian ate. As they talked softly to avoid disturbing
Michael, Ta-ne-haddle told Dan family news.

"When I left, Hattie planned to go home with April
and Noah."

"Oh?" Dan asked, and Mary heard the hope in his
voice.

"April wrote Javier that Hattie would come home
with them."

"Do you know if Pa is going to Albuquerque?"

"No, I don't. The young'uns are growing." While
they talked, Brian sat warming his feet at the fire and
sipping brandy Dan had poured. Mary sat between
Brian and Dan, all four of them in a semicircle in front
of the fire. While the men talked, Dan reached over to
rest his hand on the back of Mary's chair, and within
a few minutes she felt him wind a curl of her hair in
his fingers. She didn't turn around to look at him, and
wondered if he was even aware of what he was doing.
Once while he was talking, she studied him. She felt
a yearning for him every time she looked at him, and
was relieved that they would no longer be isolated.
Yet, those same thoughts made her sorry too. Her
thoughts were in a constant turmoil and now questions
haunted her about her feelings for Silas.

"How'd you find Brian?"

"It wasn't difficult," Ta-ne-haddle said dryly. "He
had started here and I caught up with him."

"When did you get my message, Brian?"

"Henry had sent me to take a team of horses to
Silver City. I just got back and got your message. I
went to see Doc Felton, talked to Pa, and started out

here. Ta-ne-haddle caught up with me only about two hours out of Denver."

"I might as well warn you," Dan said, "we have a bit of trouble here." He told them about the prospectors, his fingers slipping beneath Mary's thick fall of hair and kneading her shoulder lightly. His touches were casual, yet she was intensely aware of them. His voice was deep and mellow, and she wished things were different. As swiftly as the idea had come, she rejected it. Silas would come home and marry her. And Dan was about to be engaged to one of the most beautiful women in the territory. Even if she were as free as a bird, Mary knew it wouldn't change his feelings. She wasn't beautiful, and she wasn't a part of Denver society, and Mary had known Dan long enough to realize this was important to him.

The time she had known Silas seemed like something that had occurred in her girlhood, a long time ago. Dan attracted her in a manner that Silas never had, and it disturbed her, making her question her future. She wanted marriage and babies more than anything else, but she didn't want to marry for the wrong reasons. And she realized she would never be as important to Silas as she would like to be to her husband. He wouldn't have left her for years without a word if she were important to him.

"Seems as if Miss Shumacher might be getting a little irate about your helping my brother all this time," Brian said, startling Mary, since that was the line of her thinking. To her surprise, Dan's face flushed.

"I'll have to explain to her when I get back. How do you think we'll be able to get Michael out of here, Ta-ne-haddle?"

The subject was changed, and Mary basked in the warm firelight, happy to have Dan beside her and wanting to be closer, to have more than his hand occasionally brushing her shoulders or her back.

"Brian brought a wagon," Ta-ne-haddle said. "It's about half a mile from here."

"You came the rest of the way on foot?" Dan asked,

and they nodded. "When can we move Michael home?"

"We may be able to tomorrow," Ta-ne-haddle said. "The sooner you get out of here and back to Denver, the better off you'll be."

"I'm going to bed now," Mary said, telling the men good night, and meeting Dan's gaze, which seemed intense and questioning.

"I'm exhausted," Brian said.

"Go sleep. I'll listen for Michael," Dan offered. Brian stretched out on the bed nearest Michael, and within minutes was softly snoring.

Mary slid beneath the covers and listened to the low murmur of the men's voices, thinking constantly about Dan. Without warning, hot tears flooded her eyes and she turned over to bury her face in her pillow because she faced the fact that it wasn't Silas she loved, it was Dan.

While Dan listened to Ta-ne-haddle talk about Luke's boys, he thought he heard a noise from Mary's direction. It sounded like a moan. He turned and glanced toward the dark corner where she should be sleeping.

"Just a minute," he said to Ta-ne-haddle. "Mary? Are you all right?"

He waited, and when there was no answer, he shrugged. "She must be asleep. I thought I heard a noise. Sorry, go ahead."

"I can talk about the little ones until the new moon rises. And to a bachelor, that's a tiresome subject. How much trouble do you expect when we leave?" Ta-ne-haddle asked.

"I recognized one of the men here, and I think it's only a matter of time until he recognizes me. If he knows there's a price on my head, which I'm sure he will, he'll want me all to himself. There are too many in camp for it to be profitable for him to share the reward money. I think he'll come after me if he thinks I'm alone with Michael and Mary."

"No one knows we're here."

"Brian can get the wagon and ride in here. We can load Michael on the wagon, and Brian and Mary can ride with him. I'll drop behind to follow, and they'll think I'm alone, bringing up the rear."

Ta-ne-haddle nodded. "I think it's best. I think we can move him tomorrow. Now, if you'll excuse me, I've been sleeping in the saddle for several nights now." He moved to a bed while Dan put another log on the fire.

Dan stretched out to sleep on blankets on the floor. He knew he would have to be alert for the ride home. He expected trouble and was thankful to have Brian and Ta-ne-haddle along. He gazed at Mary's corner, trying to bank a nagging sense of loss when he thought of returning to Denver.

At dawn, Brian slipped away only to arrive back midmorning with the wagon. Ta-ne-haddle had left before dawn and agreed to wait along the trail for Dan. Mary was self-conscious and constrained around Dan and he too was keenly aware they would part and their lives would go separate ways.

To everyone's relief, Michael seemed better. Mary was at his side instantly when he stirred. Dan helped him outside, noticing that Michael was able to bear his own weight now and needed Dan only to steady him. He ate better and sat up in bed, listening to them talk about riding back to Denver.

He looked from Mary to Dan. "You two have taken good care of me." His attention focused on Dan. "You must have been a damn close friend of Silas'."

Dan felt his face flush and wondered how much Michael had heard pass between Mary and him. "He saved my life."

"And Dan saved his," Mary added solemnly, her face as flushed as Dan's. Neither Michael nor Brian seemed to notice.

"There's a Kiowa going to ride with us?" Michael asked.

"Yes," Mary answered, "but your friends don't know it. Michael, we had trouble with them."

He swore and asked, "Which one? Sorghum?"

"Yes, but forget it now," Dan said. "You're in no shape to confront even an angry dog, much less someone like Sorghum."

"Give me my Henry. I can still sit up and shoot."

"And you might have to on the ride home. How good a friend is he to you?"

"Not at all, but we leave each other alone. He knows not to tangle with me, and he should know what I'll do to him when I get well."

"I'm not so sure they expect you to get well," Mary said quietly.

"I'm going to," Michael said with a stubborn thrust of his jaw that was becoming familiar to Dan. He had witnessed it in every O'Malley now.

"We'll load the wagon," Dan said, shouldering bundles and provisions. "Mary, you keep an eye toward the camp. I expect some of them to come soon, because they can see the wagon. Jethro will come to say good-bye."

"Jethro is my friend," Michael said.

Brian and Dan began to load the wagon, and in minutes Dan saw Jethro and two more men headed toward him. "Here they come."

He introduced them to Brian, and as he watched, he suddenly had a feeling they knew Brian. He felt like these were men who had talked before, and he sensed a charged feeling between Brian and Donner. Donner avoided Brian's eyes, shaking hands with him without once facing him directly, while Brian studied Donner with a look that should have sent the man fleeing for cover.

"You can go in and see Michael before we leave if you want," Dan said, watching Donner.

"You fellows go ahead. I wouldn't want to tire him. I'm going back to the camp. Wish you folks a good trip," he said, and turned to stride away, glancing back once over his shoulder. Brian was scowling at him, and Dan's suspicions became stronger. "You better go inside and make sure your brother doesn't lose his temper. Jethro hasn't caused any trouble, and it won't do Michael any good to get worked up."

"Yeah. I'd like to get my hands on Sorghum."

"Now's not the time," Dan said firmly. "Not with Mary along and Michael hurt."

"Yeah, I know," Brian said with reluctance, and went inside. Donner continued to glance over his shoulder and then broke into a lope, disappearing into a cabin. Dan would stake all he had that the O'Malley boys were involved in something that was going to hurt Mary. He felt angry that she had to struggle with them.

Within a quarter of an hour they loaded the wagon. Michael was stretched on skins and blankets in the bed of the wagon, and Brian held the reins. Dan went back inside the cabin to get Mary.

"They're waiting," he said, pausing a few feet from her. She stood beside her bed, clothing in her hands, her hair wound in braids. He felt as if they were saying good-bye forever to something that had happened between them.

"I'm ready," she said without moving. Her heart beat swiftly as she watched him, studying him intently, knowing she would see him less and less after this day, knowing she would return to Denver to watch him become engaged and marry Louisa Shumacher, and knowing she loved him. *I love you,* was all she could think as she looked into his eyes. His expression changed, and tension grew between them into a pull that was strong. It held them both immobile and silent.

Dan reached out slowly and stroked her cheek. "Let's go, Mary," he said, his voice husky.

She nodded and moved quickly past him, turning at the door to look back once and remember where she had stood in his arms and how Dan had kissed her. She glanced up to see him watching her with a stormy expression that looked as if he knew exactly what she was thinking.

Dan stared at her, aching to reach for her, gazing into eyes that revealed her confusion and longing. His gaze lowered to her mouth, and he remembered with perfect clarity when he kissed her.

Mary's face burned with embarrassment as she hurried to the wagon, and Dan swung her up on the seat.

He waved as they drove away, and he mounted to follow, letting the space between them widen swiftly. He stared straight ahead as if he didn't have a concern about anyone back at camp. He wore one pistol in a holster and one tucked into his belt. He and Ta-ne-haddle had discussed the ride home and expected trouble to come before they left the mountains. Once they were in the flat open land that stretched between the mountains and Denver, it would be far more dangerous for someone to ambush them.

Dan listened, letting the wagon get out of sight and hearing. He expected only Sorghum, or Sorghum and Donner at the most. It would be hours before they left the mountains, and as he rode, he constantly listened, hoping Ta-ne-haddle was where he was supposed to be, because Dan fully expected Sorghum to try to shoot him in the back.

He realized when he was being tracked. He heard a hoofbeat and the jingle of a harness and he realized that Sorghum might want more satisfaction than just shooting him in the back. Their confrontation at the cabin had come out poorly for Sorghum, and revenge might be as important as collecting the reward money.

Dan ran over his options in his mind, and when he heard a stream, he turned in its direction. He dismounted to let his horse drink, and moved away from the animal, trying to get the best vantage point for himself and for Ta-ne-haddle, riding up behind them.

He heard the jingle of harness and looked up.

"Don't move. Hands high," came Sorghum's order, and he walked into sight with six-shooters drawn. He was on foot, and Donner appeared leading Sorghum's horse. "Just stand right there, Castle."

Dan was surprised he was addressed as Castle and not Castillo. "What is this?" he asked loudly.

"You shouldn't have drifted back so far from your friends. Unbuckle your—"

Sorghum sagged, making a choking sound. Donner glanced at him, frowned, and drew his pistol. Dan shot it out of his hand and Donner yanked out a knife.

Dan squeezed the trigger again and Donner pitched forward on his face.

Ta-ne-haddle came into view and they stood over the two inert bodies, a bowie knife buried to the hilt in Sorghum's back.

"They had bad plans for you. I've been trailing them for two hours."

"Their plans are finished. Do we bury them or take them into town to the Sheriff."

"I say we leave them."

Dan nodded and watched Ta-ne-haddle put his foot on Sorghum's back and yank his knife free. He went to the stream to wash away the blood. "If he knew who you were, he wasn't telling his friend."

"He knew. Thanks," Dan said, thrusting out his hand.

Ta-ne-haddle shook, studying Dan. "You say your friend Eustice is marrying Mary O'Malley?"

"Yes, he plans to when he finds his millions in gold."

"Dan, you care about her."

"I'm about to become engaged to Louisa Shumacher in Denver," Dan said. "Mary is a friend because of Silas. He wanted me to watch out for her," Dan said, thinking he couldn't keep a strange note out of his voice, and he was fully aware how shrewd Ta-ne-haddle was.

"There's an old saying, I don't remember where I learned it: 'Love knows nothing of order.' And there's another one I remember: 'Friendship is constant in all other things save in the office and affairs of love.' "

"Silas saved my life and he asked me to take care of Mary."

The Kiowa merely nodded. "Her brothers are running guns to the Apache."

"Damn," Dan muttered, shocked at Ta-ne-haddle's news. "How in hell do you know?"

"Brian knows sign language. I trailed him to catch up with him and saw him with an Apache. They're getting rifles to the Indians. In turn, they're receiving stolen goods."

"Are they buying captives?"

"I don't know."

"Does Brian know you saw him?"

"Yes. I told him. He couldn't kill me; he's just a kid. He's young and doesn't know how to be sly enough to succeed at hiding what he's doing. He brings rifles out to his brother."

"So that's what they were hiding."

"The men have stolen goods. Some of them probably bring them into Denver to sell on occasion. I'm guessing about that part. Brian admitted furnishing the Apache with rifles. He said it wasn't his fight, and they got things from the Indians in return, and no one was hurt. Said they got hides from the Apache, but no one trades rifles for only hides. I promised I wouldn't relay this to Miss O'Malley. He loves his sister."

"That damn kid ought to be horsewhipped!"

"You can decide how to handle it."

"So now I get the pleasure of stopping the O'Malley boys without hurting Mary," Dan said dryly.

"You may find it hard to stop them unless you turn them over to the sheriff."

"I'll do it some way," Dan said with determination. "They're not going to hurt Mary."

"My friend, you have my sympathy," Ta-ne-haddle said solemnly. "Other than the complications in your friendships, how are things? Luke will want to know, and if the others haven't gone, they'll all want to know down to the last detail."

"I don't want to worry Ma. My business is good."

"And?"

"How do you always know what's in a man's thoughts? There's a wanted poster up in the sheriff's office," Dan said, distracted by his thoughts of Mary. "I'm getting contracts to build, and I like Denver. I want to stay there."

"Then stay, my friend. I leave you now and head south."

"You don't want to come home with me?" Dan asked in surprise.

"No, and Michael can be tended by the doctor now.

I've put something on his cuts that should remove the
infection. He won't be scarred like Luke. Particularly
his face. His legs and chest may be, though. He's a
strong man, so he'll pull through.''

"I can't thank you enough. I wish you'd come let
me show you Denver.''

Ta-ne-haddle shook his head. ''I want to be home
with my family.''

"I can understand. I wish I could return the favor.''

"Maybe someday you will.''

They shook hands and Ta-ne-haddle clasped Dan on
the shoulder and stood up in the stirrups to hug him.
''The Danby's are special to me. Luke is my brother,
therefore, you're like my brother. Sometimes I used to
think he was like a son, but as he has gotten older,
that feeling has changed. He was young and green
when I found him.''

"The Danbys have been damned lucky you did find
him. Now the O'Malleys owe you a debt.''

"Be careful, Dan. Brian is half-child, half-man. His
brother may be all man.''

Dan nodded. ''I pray Ma goes home with Pa. I'm
happy to hear that she went to Albuquerque with April,
because I know April wants them to go back together.''

"Farewell, friend. Stay out of trouble.''

Dan grinned. ''If you ever want a house built, I'm
not wanted in Texas.''

"I'll remember.'' He turned south and Dan watched
him go, thinking the Danbys had been very fortunate
to have Ta-ne-haddle. He turned and urged his horse
forward, knowing he needed to catch up with the others. His thoughts jumped to the problems that lay
ahead for the O'Malleys.

He caught up with them and rode a few feet behind
the wagon, brooding over what he could do. All the
time he had been in Denver, he had tried to stay out
of trouble. He had avoided creating enemies, avoided
drawing attention to himself other than as a builder,
but he knew if he hoped to stop the O'Malley boys

from their dangerous activities, he was going to risk trouble that could ruin his future in Denver.

He weighed the possibilities and courses of action riding in silence until they neared the town. Then his thoughts jumped to other problems. He studied Mary's slender figure as she rode beside her brother, and he ached with longing as he watched her. He vowed to himself that when he got into town he would put an end to the torment. His feelings for her were only the result of the isolation, because Mary could look beautiful and appealing, because she was such a marvelous friend. He had never had a woman who was a closer friend to him than a man. He had loved women, even adored them, but he hadn't been such friends with them that he could trust them with anything, discuss anything with them, or really want their judgment and opinions.

He swore silently, feeling an urgency to get home. He accompanied them to the boardinghouse and saw that they didn't need his help to get Michael inside. They thanked him, Brian rather perfunctorily, Mary with constraint. He left them and rode straight to his house, where he drew a steaming bath, washed, changed into his fine gray woolen pants and white linen shirt, pulled on his black coat, and rode to the Shumachers' to call on Louisa.

18

Dan sat in the front parlor trying to restrain himself, to make polite conversation with Louisa and Hortense Shumacher, while all he really wanted was to get Louisa alone. He studied her constantly while they talked, wondering why he didn't feel as if he were drowning in her beauty like he used to feel. In the past, every time he had looked at her, he had been dazzled and awed by her beauty. His pulse had skipped faster, and his desire burned simply from watching her. But now as he gazed at her, no matter how much he tried to conjure up his old feelings, they wouldn't come. It worried him, and he refused to accept that his feelings had changed. He studied her with an intensity that he suspected was the cause for the pink that had risen to her cheeks and for continual glances she cast his way. He had been away only a few days, but it seemed as if a chasm of time and place and emotions had opened between them. Her pink dress was beautiful, her hair shining and turned in curls, pinned up in an elaborate hairdo. He listened to them talk incessantly of their friends, of the party he had missed, and he found it difficult to respond to them with civility because he desperately wanted to talk with Louisa alone.

As if her thoughts ran along the same line, Louisa suddenly sat forward. "Mama, I haven't seen Daniel for days. I want to show him the garden and talk to him."

"Very well, Louisa," Hortense Shumacher answered. Dan wondered when Louisa had decided to call him Daniel. "Return within the hour, because I promised Maribelle we'd call this afternoon."

"Yes, ma'am," Louisa said, bouncing to her feet, her curls dancing as if they were springs, while Hortense Shumacher gave him a frosty stare.

He nodded and followed Louisa outside, where she took his hand. He knew they were in full view of the library, and her mother watched her daughter constantly.

"Louisa, where can we be alone?" An urgency gripped him that intensified by the minute. He felt as if all his dreams and plans would vanish if he didn't find what he had felt before with Louisa.

"We'll walk to the back of the garden, where there's an arbor and the springhouse. There we'll be out of sight of the house and Mama."

"Thank God," he said, and she giggled, a high sound that he couldn't remember noticing before, but which now grated on his nerves. Things weren't the same, and he kept trying to reassure himself it was because he hadn't been alone with Louisa, he hadn't held or kissed her in so long.

He listened to her prattle aimlessly, casting him sidelong glances and batting her eyes at him. They finally rounded a bend in the walk. Taking his hand, Louisa cut across the lawn to the springhouse, around the corner and out of sight of her house. "I declare, Daniel Castle, I don't think you've listened to one word I've said," she minced, her voice getting higher while she pouted and turned to slant him a teasing look.

His patience was frayed, his nerves raw, and he couldn't tease or cajole or pretend. He reached for her as if he were drowning and only she could save him. He hauled her against him roughly, his mouth coming down to kiss her hungrily with desperation.

His tongue probed and delved into her mouth, his hand ran over her breasts. She clung to him, grinding her hips against him while the image of green eyes and flaming hair danced in his mind. He wanted to groan. Louisa pushed away.

"My goodness! Aren't you the rough one! You'll
have me all messed up. Now I have to retie my ribbons, and I just simply can't tie a bow right. You're
the cause of this. You tie them for me," she said,
twisting her hips as she moved within inches of him,
running her fingers lightly beneath her breasts where
the tangled ribbons lay, decorating the bodice of her
dress.

"I can't tie ribbons," he said gruffly, thinking he
wanted a woman in his arms, not a teasing, playful
child. And if he married Louisa, that's what he would
have, a child bride who was seductive, beautiful,
trained in social amenities, and empty-headed. He
stared at her while he tied the ribbons. She had no
inkling about his feelings. He doubted if she cared.
She was pampered, and expected to continue to be
pampered, whether by father or husband. Dan had no
objections to that, but he no longer wanted to pamper
her. He knew if he kissed her long enough his body
would eventually respond, but he faced the fact that
the infatuation he had felt for her before was gone.

"Louisa," he said as he tried again, kissing her hard
and long, fondling her. He sat on an iron bench and
pulled her down on his lap until finally she stood and
moved away.

"Daniel, look at me. Mama will be shocked into a
fainting spell."

"Louisa, it's 'Dan,' not 'Daniel.' "

"I think 'Daniel' sounds more dignified. I want to
call you 'Daniel.' "

He let the matter drop. It really didn't matter. He
watched her smooth her hair and straighten her dress,
barely listening to her chatter, his emotions seeth-
ing. Whereas Louisa had charmed and drawn him before, now he found it difficult to be patient with her,
to listen to her. It was even an effort to kiss her. And
he couldn't get images of Mary out of his mind.

"We have to go back now. If you're going to be so
sultry and broody, I don't think I want to go to the
Parsonses' with you tonight."

"Sorry, Louisa. I'm exhausted from this week."

"Well, you're too grumpy to be with, staring at me like I have two heads! Except when you kiss me. Maybe we shall just have to slip away and spend the evening kissing," she said mischievously, but he couldn't rise to the bait.

"Are you listening to me, Mr. Castle?" she asked with a coy smile.

"Yes, Louisa, I'm listening."

"Perhaps I should go with Reuben. He was good enough to take me out while you were gone," she said, giving him a sly look, waiting for his reaction with a curious sparkle in her eyes.

"Good, Louisa, I'm glad you had fun while I was away."

"You're glad Reuben took me out?" For the first time, she lost her flirtatious manner and gazed at him with uncertainty.

"Your mother said to have you back within the hour, and it's past that now. Will she come searching for us?"

"Yes, she will. Do you want Reuben to take me out?" she asked, anger creeping into her tone.

"You're going with me tonight," he said, and she bit her lip, studying him with uncertainty. He took her arm and they walked back in silence through the garden. He couldn't think of one thing to talk to her about. His emotions were in a whirlwind, and polite conversation or teasing banter was beyond him.

After a few minutes of silence, Louisa tossed her head. "I think you're more than tired. You had better get rested up, because if you're like this tonight, I'll spend the evening with Reuben and let him bring me home."

Dan gazed at her in silence, and saw they were no longer alone. "There's your mother," he said.

Hortense Shumacher stood on the back porch, and for once in his life, Dan was half-glad to see the woman. He strolled through the house with them, told Louisa what time he would pick her up in the evening, and left. He mounted his horse and rode straight to

Dulcie's. The same sense of desperation gripped him, and this time he intended to lay it to rest.

She was in the back parlor talking to three men who sat at a table playing poker. Dan paused at the door and called to her. "Dulcie, may I see you?"

She laughed and leaned down to say something in an undertone to the men. They guffawed as she crossed the room to Dan, her hips swaying, her red taffeta skirt swishing with each step.

She linked her arm through his, looking up at him. "And how are the O'Malleys?"

"Better," he said, thinking Dulcie was a relief after Louisa. As soon as they closed and locked the door in her room, he pulled her into his arms. "I want you, Dulcie," he said, kissing her as passionately as he had kissed Louisa. His desperation mushroomed when he didn't feel what he wanted to feel. He reached out to unbutton her dress, his fingers tangling in the buttons, and finally he yanked at them in anger. He heard one or two pop, and Dulcie's eyes widened as she leaned back to gaze at him while he stripped away the taffeta and let it fall around her feet. He swung her into his arms and carried her to bed. She was naked beneath the taffeta, and in minutes he had shed his clothes. Dulcie watched him with a curious look while he knelt on the bed beside her, bending down to kiss her, finally stretching out to pull her to him. He made passionate love to her that was wild and rough and demanding, drawing it out until his body clamored for release.

Dulcie clung to him, raising her hips to meet his thrusts, knowing she had finally lost him. He had never loved her in such a manner, as if he were compelled to do so by an unseen force. She wondered if he were finally in love with Louisa, or finally engaged to her.

He sank down, rolling over to light a cheroot. He lay beside her smoking, and she sat up, twisting around to look down at him. "You just came from Louisa."

He slanted her a look and Dulcie caught her breath, watching him as he swung his long legs over the side of the bed and stood up, moving around the room restlessly. She pulled on a silk wrapper, tying it around her waist. She lit her own cheroot and sat down to watch Dan wash and dress. "Are you engaged now?"

"No, I'm not."

"But you finally love her," she said, blowing a stream of smoke into the air and watching him. "I knew someday you would and I'd lose you, at least for a time, and that day has finally come. What happened? Did absence make the heart grow fonder?"

"Something like that, Dulcie," he said, yanking his shirt over his head, raking his hair back off his forehead with his fingers. "I've got to call on Edward Ringwood and try to make amends with him."

Dulcie felt a stab of hurt. There would always be a part of her that loved him, but it was over. She didn't think he would be back, and she wondered why he had come today. He looked angry with her, and she wondered what devil he was fighting. She hadn't tried to seduce him, far from it. Yet he hadn't taken her in passion or love. Something else had been driving him, and she didn't understand what it was.

"I've known a lot of men, Dan, and you're singular."

He gave her a cynical smile. "How's that?"

"You're a complicated man. More so than any I've known. Silas was an easy man to understand. He had one driving goal, and his ambition took first place. Reuben Knelville is like a million other successful men—he has the same wants, the same passions. You're one thing one day, something else the next. You're a thinker, Dan, and the world can't always tolerate thinkers."

He laughed. "Hell, Dulcie, I go whole days without a thought. I work with my hands, not my brain."

"But your mind is always going. Should I? Shouldn't I? Why? And you design houses with your brain. So you're finally in love with Louisa?"

He turned around to face Dulcie, his blue eyes wide, angry, perplexed. And in turn, she was puzzled. "No," he answered flatly.

"You go riding off into the—" She stopped and

looked at him, and she felt a constriction around her heart because she knew what was wrong with him. "Damnation," she said quietly. "You love Mary O'Malley."

"No, I don't!" he snapped, raking his fingers through his hair.

"You're in love."

"I'm not"

"I can tell when a man is in love," she persisted, studying him.

"And it's none of your damned business!"

She turned her head, and instantly he was at her side, kneeling by the chair, his hands on her arms. "Lord, Dulcie, I'm sorry. I shouldn't have said that. You and I have been friends for a long time now. I didn't mean it." He said it so contritely that she forgave him instantly, as she looked into his eyes which were filled with worry. "I'm sorry."

"Forget it, Dan. I accept your apology. You've never been anything except good to me."

He pulled her to him and kissed her cheek. She placed her hand against his face as she looked into his eyes. She saw the answers to her questions and knew she was right. Now she understood why he was so distraught.

"I can't love her, Dulcie. Silas is my best friend. I just can't." He paced around the room.

"Silas was the world's biggest fool to leave her like that. No woman should be expected to wait without a word."

"Silas is my friend," Dan said in a tone of voice that stopped her. "I won't steal his woman. Right now, I'm worrying what to do about Louisa. I can't marry her."

At the thought of Louisa Shumacher, Dulcie almost had to bite back a laugh.

"Dulcie, I'm sorry," he repeated quietly.

"Honey, I'm a friend too," she said gently. "Don't be so hard on yourself. You've been better to me than any man I've ever known." Suddenly, to her amazement, her eyes brimmed over with tears. "Lord, I can't remember when I cried over a man."

He pulled her into his arms and held her while she clung to him. She kissed him hard on the mouth. "I've lost you to Mary O'Malley, dammit."

"I can't marry her, Dulcie. I'd never take Mary from Silas. Never."

Dulcie placed her hand over his mouth. "Shh. Silas may not be the best man for Mary. Don't forget that." She moved away. "Now, get out of here, Dan Castle, because I know you're going for good."

"Dulcie, you've been the best—"

"Get out!"

Dan stared at her a moment. He felt terrible because he realized he had hurt her. He turned and left the room, closing the door quietly behind him.

Dulcie heard him go and covered her face. She loved him and she hoped he had sense enough to marry a woman who was as good as Mary O'Malley.

Dan mounted his horse and rode down the street toward Edward Ringwood's office. As he rode, he was unaware of his surroundings, and his emotions boiled like water over a fire. He couldn't have changed so drastically in such a short time. It was as if he had gone off to a cabin in the mountains and been transformed into another person with different likes and dislikes. But when he faced his feelings honestly, he knew it wasn't something that had come about in the past week. It was from hours and hours spent with Mary, from dancing with her and eating with her and working with her. He had been infatuated with and proposed to three breathtakingly beautiful women— Melissa Hatfield, Dulcie, and Louisa—but it was Mary O'Malley who had won his heart.

He needed Mary. He needed her intelligence, her understanding, and her love. He respected her and he loved her. Clenching his fists, he silently vowed he would not take the love of his best friend while Silas was away from town. Dan's thoughts shifted to the dilemma of Louisa. While he couldn't love Mary O'Malley because of Silas, Dan also knew he couldn't marry Louisa and spend the rest of his life with her. It was almost May, and in another month their engagement would be announced. He had to break it off in a way that wouldn't embarrass Louisa.

It took only minutes to explain to Edward Ringwood why he hadn't kept his appointment during the week. He unrolled the plans, thinking how different Ringwood was from Corning. Short, freckle-faced, with a bushy red beard, he had a constant smile on his face and Dan found his own enthusiasm building as he showed Ringwood the plans.

"You had a preference for brownstone. This is mansard style or Second Empire, which has been in favor for the past few years. It has a mansard roof. This roof will give you a full story of space on the attic level. Now, there are several possibilities for the roof."

"I want something attractive and durable. Something that will last."

"One of the finest is Vermont slate. If you prefer, we can have colored wood shingles or we can use tin."

Ringwood nodded, and Dan continued, "As you can see, I've put in Palladian dormer windows to allow plenty of light into the upper story."

Both men bent over the plans, and it was over an hour later when Dan shook hands with him and left the office. He had a new contract, a fact that would have made him ecstatic only a week ago. He rode home, realizing how great the changes in his life had been in the short time since he left for the mountains with Mary. While he was glad for Ringwood's business, Dan's emotions churned over the problem that loomed largest in his life, and his thoughts were constantly on Mary.

Back at his home, he changed into his black suit, combed his hair, and left to pick up Louisa. He was early enough to go by the O'Malley boardinghouse for a few minutes to see how Michael was doing. He knew it was a time when Mary would be busy serving dinner, and he wouldn't be able to be alone with her. It would keep temptation out of his way, but as he rode closer, he longed to see her, to talk to her, and to spend the evening with her.

When he went up the front steps, the door stood open and people crowded the hall. Dan began to hurry, his heart lurching. Mary lay on the floor, diners and boarders clustered around her.

"Mary! What happened?" Dan knelt beside her.

"Dan, help me up."

"Maybe you should lie still, Miss O'Malley, until Doc gets here," Nolen Parker said in his slow drawl.

"Fell down the stairs, she did," Herschel Windham said. "Just fell right down. I saw her. Hurt her head and foot. Brian has gone for the doc," Herschel added.

"I'm fine, really. Just a sore ankle," she said. "Please Dan, help me up."

"You don't think anything else is hurt?"

She sat up. "Nothing except my ankle and head. My head will have a knot."

He picked her up easily. "I'll take her into the parlor, gentlemen. Send the doc in when he gets here, and go on with your dinner. Mary, is anyone in the kitchen?"

"Yes, Dulcie's cook is still here. You should know. You hired him."

Dan carried her into the parlor and kicked the door shut behind him. He gazed down into her face, and he wanted to kiss her. Instead he put her down, tossed off his hat, and knelt down beside her. "Let me get your shoe off," he said, working free the buttons.

Mary gazed down at his golden head bent over her foot, his hands gently tugging at buttons. She longed to reach the short distance between them and touch him.

Dan slipped her shoe off her small, slender foot.

"My ankle hurts."

"What happened?" he asked, looking at her ankle, which was red and beginning to swell.

"I missed the last two steps."

He looked up in surprise. "You walked off the steps?"

"I wasn't thinking about what I was doing," she

whispered. Mary was acutely aware of his hands on her foot and leg, of his proximity, of his handsome appearance. She had been thinking about him when she missed a step on her way down the stairs, and now he was here, rubbing her foot, gazing at her with a look of longing that was unmistakable.

"I have to pick up Louisa in half an hour," he blurted, wondering what had happened to his finesse.

"I'm fine." She wanted to touch his face, touch his golden hair so badly, and she locked her fingers together in her lap, fearful that she wouldn't be able to resist the impulse.

"How's Michael?"

"He's better. Dan, I'm so grateful to your friend."

"Ta-ne-haddle is special. So is Silas, Mary."

She drew a deep breath and gazed at him, wanting him to put his arms around her again, wanting to be held close to him, wanting to kiss him. She thought that it wasn't Silas who stood between them as much as Dan's future bride. "You better go so you aren't late to pick up Louisa," Mary said stiffly.

He nodded. "Do you want anything before I leave?"

"No, thank you."

He moved away and walked out without looking back. As he rode to the Shumachers' house, his thoughts seethed over the women in his life. Mary had walked off steps she had gone up and down nearly all her life.

He tried to shut her out of his mind as he strode across the Shumachers' porch and knocked on the door.

"Come in, my boy, come in," Charles Shumacher said, stepping forward to greet him. "Louisa will be down right away. I suppose it is utmost male foolishness to expect the ladies to be ready on time." He laughed at what he said.

"Here she is," Dan said, and gazed at Louisa, who descended the stairs. She wore a dress that Dan was sure must have cost a year's wages for many men. It made her blue eyes bluer, emphasized her tiny waist and lush breasts, and was stunning, yet she held no more interest to him now than the other women in town. With one exception. The image of Mary in her simple green calico pulled on his thoughts and heart far more than Louisa in her best finery. He smiled and moved forward, offering her his arm.

"Ready, Louisa?"

She nodded, taking his arm.

He had brought his smaller, light carriage and he would be busy driving. The top was removed, leaving them very much in the public eye, so he wouldn't be expected to try to kiss her. She paused a second when she saw which carriage he had brought.

"We won't have any privacy."

"We can enjoy the evening. It's beautiful."

She clamped her lips together and allowed him to help her into the carriage. "If you are as brooding and silent as you were today, I shall do exactly as I threatened and ride home with Reuben."

"Where did you get the pretty dress?"

He knew how she loved to talk about her dresses, and it was a short distance to the Parsonses'. To his relief, Louisa was busy with the subject of her clothing until he handed the reins to his carriage over to a waiting servant and helped Louisa down.

Half an hour later, when he had a chance, he took Louisa's arm and led her down the hall to a deserted solarium.

Her eyes sparkled and he knew she wanted to be kissed. Reuben was occupied with Marian Comber, and Dan wanted a few minutes alone with Louisa before Reuben interfered. "Louisa, I need to talk to you alone. May I call in the morning? Can we arrange some time and place where your mother won't disturb us?"

"I suppose," she said, slanting him a curious look. "Why?"

"Tomorrow will be a better time to tell you."

"I want to know now, and if you don't tell me, I'll go right out and find Reuben and stay with him all evening."

Dan leaned back against the piano and shrugged. "Go ahead, Louisa. Get Reuben to take you home."

Her eyes narrowed to slits, and her cheeks flushed. "Do you know what you're saying?"

"I think so. You threatened me. I don't want to discuss the matter tonight, so my only choice is to let you go ahead and carry out your threat."

"And I shall, Dan Castle!" She flounced out of the room, and all he could feel was relief. He wanted to leave the party, but he wouldn't do that, so he sauntered down the hall, studying the house, joining guests in the front parlor. Louisa stood beside Reuben, smiling at him, her hand on his arm.

Reuben turned to look at Dan, a searching look and one of smug satisfaction at having won Louisa to his side. Dan turned his back to converse with William Byers and Jay Varner. To his relief, he was seated several seats away from Louisa at dinner, while Reuben was at her side. From the moment he sat down to eat, he paid no attention to her, knowing it would fuel her anger and bring about the separation he wanted.

After dinner, as the men congregated for cigars and brandy, Dan conversed with Trent Waltham, who had only recently arrived in Denver. It was rumored that Trent had made a fortune in silver and was ready to settle. Half the people coming into town now, if they had a few dollars, were rumored to have struck it rich somewhere west of Denver.

"I hear you built the Potter house."

"Yes," Dan answered, exhaling a stream of smoke.

"I'd like to see some of your work."

For the first time in the evening, his worries over Louisa and Mary diminished a notch. "You can look at my house. I built it."

"When?"

"In the morning. Whatever time suits you."

"About seven. Is that too early?"

"No, sir."

"Do you have any house plans I can look at?"

"Yes, I do."

"I hear you drew up plans for Benjamin Corning and he rejected them."

"That's right."

"Tell me about them."

The doors were opened to the front parlor, and the men joined the ladies again. Dan talked to Trent for the next hour about houses, and when he finally moved away and looked around, he couldn't see Louisa. Once he looked into Hortense Shumacher's eyes and met a smile of triumph, and he realized Louisa had either slipped away from the party to let Reuben kiss her, or Reuben had taken her home. Dan hoped Reuben had taken her home. But Louisa and Reuben appeared back at the party within half an hour, Louisa's eyes sparkling. Her anger resurfaced when she looked at Dan. He moved through the crowd to her. " 'Evening Reuben, Louisa."

"How were the mountains?" Reuben asked.

"Michael O'Malley is going to survive. He's much better now."

"Dan, I'm going to ride home with Reuben," Louisa said smugly.

He nodded. "That's your privilege, Louisa, to do as you choose. I assume your mother is aware of your change of plans?"

"Yes, as a matter of fact, she is," Louisa answered, once again looking perplexed for a moment. "Emily, come join us," she called to Emily Parsons, who stood nearby. Emily and Letitia Hopper joined them, and for the rest of the evening Dan wasn't alone with Louisa. When she left, he told his host and hostess good night and walked out at the same time as Louisa and Reuben.

"I'll call in the morning, Louisa," he said quietly, "unless you want me to take you home now so we can talk."

She glanced up at Reuben. "Perhaps that would be better," she said, looking over her shoulder at the house. Dan knew as well as Louisa that her parents were old friends of the Parsonses and they would stay for another hour.

She looked at Dan. "Excuse us a minute, please," she said in haughty tones, and walked with Reuben to his carriage. Reuben looked almost as curious and puzzled as Louisa, and Dan suspected he had thrown them both off-balance. Reuben's usual hostility was missing, and his smugness had vanished.

In minutes she walked away from Reuben, who looked over her head at Dan. "Good night, Louisa. Good night, Castle."

Dan nodded and helped Louisa into the carriage, thankful for the chance to talk to her tonight.

"I can't imagine what you have to say to me, but your inattention tonight was inexcusable."

"Louisa, you left with Reuben, he's kissed you tonight, so I'm not altogether the only one at fault," Dan said quietly. He knew she felt no more for him than he had felt for her. He wondered if she had simply agreed to the engagement to stir Reuben to jealousy or a proposal.

She gasped and twisted around to glare at him.

"Don't deny he kissed you."

"No, I shan't," she said, drawing herself up. "He's fun and very attractive, and he likes me. And you are like someone only half-alive since you came back from the mountains!"

He thought perhaps she was exactly right. He felt only half-alive, shaken by his discovery. He slowed the team and jumped down in front of the Shumachers' home. As soon as they entered the house and the maid left them, Louisa led the way into the front parlor, where a fire burned in the grate and the lamps were turned low. Brandy had been set out for her parents' return.

"Now that we're alone, I want to say to you, Dan Castle, that if you treat me the way you did tonight one more time, our engagement is off!"

"We're not even engaged yet, Louisa. And if we were, I'd think the engagement would be off if you rode home with Reuben," Dan answered quietly.

"You sound as if you want it to be off."

Dan knew there would be no easy way to get through

the next few minutes. "Louisa, do you think you and I are really suited to share the rest of our lives with each other?"

She blinked, and he wondered what consideration she had actually given to marriage. "Of course I do, or I wouldn't have consented to become engaged."

"Are you certain of that?"

"You don't want to become engaged," she said. The shock made her eyes go wide as he saw that the possibility that a man might not want to marry her was almost beyond reason. "Is that it? You have changed your mind?"

"Louisa, are you wildly in love with me? Can you go off and kiss Reuben and still say you're in love with me?"

He saw the moment when her shock changed to anger. She crossed the room and slapped him hard. "I hate you! No, I don't love you! Mama was right. You're common, and beneath me, and the engagement is off. I'll never marry you!"

He listened patiently to her tirade, knowing she was entitled to it. He hoped it would help her salvage her feelings and relieve him a fraction, just as her tryst with Reuben had relieved him. Dan didn't think she had loved him at all. It had been a wild physical attraction, perhaps something different and exciting and fun for her. He waited, watching her storm at him and clench her fists and stomp her foot, thinking that whatever lay ahead in his life, he had just had a narrow escape.

"Get out of this house, Dan Castle, and don't ever come back."

"All right, Louisa. I'm sorry for what happened between us."

Surprise flitted in her expression, and he saw she still didn't believe that he had lost interest in her. He started toward the door.

"Dan, who is she?"

He shook his head. Her face flushed, and her lips firmed. She picked up one of the brandy glasses and threw it. Dan caught it and set it down carefully.

"Think about Reuben and his kisses, and you won't be half as angry."

He left and closed the door, and he let out his breath. She followed him into the hall.

"I hate you!"

"If you do, you could not possibly have loved me a week ago," he replied, and went outside. As he turned into the street, he passed her parents returning home, and he was thankful he was out of the house and away. He drew his carriage to a halt.

"Mr. Shumacher, may I have a word with you for a moment?"

Charles Shumacher glanced at his wife, who nodded, and he climbed down. Dan jumped to the ground and walked away from the carriages, where he could talk. He knew Hortense would be listening, and could probably hear, but he wanted the appearance of trying to speak privately with Louisa's father.

"Sir, I'm sorry. I have great respect for you and like doing business with you. For a time I thought you'd be my father-in-law. Louisa just said she won't marry me. She doesn't want to become engaged."

"Louisa? Are you sure?"

"Yes, sir. I'm quite sure. She's unhappy with me at the moment, and she told me her wishes. I suspect Reuben Knelville may be the lucky fellow who has her heart."

"Oh, I see!" Shumacher said, his eyes round with surprise. "Well, this is a shock. Sorry, my boy, but a lady has to make up her mind."

"Sir, I'm sorry too, but it's better that these things are worked out now. I appreciate your kindness to me and that of your wife, and of course I'll always remember Louisa. She's one of the most beautiful women I've ever known."

"Yes, my daughter is beautiful. Well, sorry, son."

"If you'll give my regrets to Mrs. Shumacher and explain to her. I have an idea it won't come as a surprise to her."

"Yes, well, maybe the ladies have talked." They walked back to the carriages.

"Good night, Mr. Shumacher," Dan said politely, and shook hands with Charles. "Good night, Mrs. Shumacher," he said, tipping his hat to her. The men climbed into their carriages and drove their separate ways. Dan felt some degree of relief, but it was small, because he had known since returning to town that he wouldn't marry Louisa and that she would be out of his life right away. But the woman he loved could never be a part of his life, and that weighed like a boulder on his heart. He thought about his choices, leaving Denver, staying and watching Silas come home or claiming Mary.

He gazed toward town, where she was, and wondered how her foot was. He rode home and dismounted, thinking of how empty his house was, and imagining her in it. He lay in bed in the dark, remembering every moment in the mountain cabin with her, remembering clearly holding her and kissing her, thinking he had never known sweetness as he had with Mary. His thoughts shifted to the O'Malley brothers, and he thought about what Ta-ne-haddle had told him. He knew he had to talk to Brian. Michael was old enough to make his own decisions, but there was no point in the boys breaking Mary's heart and getting into trouble. And that's exactly what they were headed for if they didn't stop what they were doing.

19

On Monday of the next week, Mary dressed carefully, favoring her injured ankle. She had Brian bring the carriage to the door, telling him she had an errand to run. She left early, when few people would be awake. She was uncertain as to the best time of day to do the task, but supposed that this would draw the least attention from ladies in the town. She had long ago learned that the men in town were far nicer to her, and far more tolerant than the women.

When she drove past the bordellos along Holladay Street, her cheeks flamed simply from being in the area. She knew which bordello Dan had built for Dulcie, and it was easy to find. There wasn't another carriage or horse in sight when she stopped at a hitching post, and Mary let out a sign of relief, assuming there might not be a customer in the house. She stared straight ahead as she marched up the porch steps and raised the heavy knocker.

The door was opened by a maid, whose eyebrows arched.

"I'm Miss O'Malley, and I came to pay a call on Miss Hazelwood," she said, feeling her cheeks burn with embarrassment.

"Yes, ma'am. Just a minute, ma'am." The door closed and Mary's discomfort increased. She was frightened one of her dinner customers who patronized the house might appear.

Inside the house, Dulcie's jaw dropped. "Who?"

"A Miss O'Malley."

"Green frogs in Hades! And you left her on the porch?"

"Yes, Miss Dulcie. You want me to bring her inside?"

"Yes, get her off the porch. If any of the men run into her, they won't ever come back! Where's her carriage?"

"In front of the house."

"Tell Grizzly to get it around back now! Hurry, Arletta. I'll get Miss O'Malley off the porch myself."

"Yes, ma'am."

Dulcie raced down the hall and yanked open the door. "Miss O'Malley, come inside." Dulcie felt as if she were dealing with a child. Mary O'Malley's cheeks were pink, her eyes round, and she looked terrified. "Miss O'Malley, you shouldn't have come here."

"I need to talk to you. I want to thank you. Can we go somewhere to talk?"

"Ma'am, you really shouldn't stay. I appreciate your gratitude, but—"

"Can we sit in a parlor?"

Dulcie saw she wasn't going to be able to send Mary off without talking to her, so she led her down the hall to her room and closed the door. "Sit down."

"I know Dan hired Faucheux from here while we were away taking care of my brother. I want to thank you for helping. And I think you sent the food we took when we left Denver. You can't imagine how much I appreciate it."

For a moment her voice faltered, and Dulcie followed her gaze, turning slightly to glance behind her. One of Dan's shirts still hung on the wall on a hook. She saw the color deepen in Mary's cheeks, and a strained look came to her face. Suddenly Dulcie didn't want Mary hurt by Dan's past. She liked Mary O'Malley, and although she looked like a child, she was not. Mary was a woman, and a determined and considerate one, or she wouldn't be present in Dulcie's room.

"Thank you for coming to tell me," Dulcie said

gently. "That shirt has been here a long time. It hasn't been touched in months."

Mary's face turned a deeper red and she nodded. "I want you to take this to pay Faucheux and for the food we took." She held out an envelope, but Dulcie shook her head.

"The cook has been paid. I didn't pay him, so that's between you and Dan. There's no call to pay me twice. You'll have to pay Dan if you want to compensate someone."

"I'd like to show my appreciation to you. Dan may have paid you, but I benefited from it, and so did my brother."

"I'm glad. You pay him if you want, but I've been paid generously. As for the food I sent, I was trying to help. It was a gift."

"Thank you."

"Even though you shouldn't have," Dulcie said quietly, "your coming here to thank me is sufficient. You know most nice ladies in town won't even speak to me. They would never come to call. I appreciate this, but you shouldn't come again, Miss O'Malley. It could tarnish your own reputation if someone should see you."

To Dulcie's amazement, Mary laughed. "I don't think I have to worry about pleasing the society ladies, and the others won't give me trouble!"

Dulcie realized in a flash why Dan was so captivated by Mary. Not only was she quick and intelligent, but she was a warm, practical person. And when she smiled, she was very pretty.

"Have you ever had your hair done, sort of in curls and fancy?" Dulcie asked.

"No. I usually wear it braided, but I fell and have quite a bump, so for now, I'm just tying it behind my head."

"Are you sure Faucheux shouldn't come back for a day or two?"

Again Dulcie received a charming smile. "No, thank you! I didn't think I would ever get him out of my kitchen!"

Dulcie chuckled, knowing her temperamental French cook. "Faucheux is very possessive about his kitchen. Actually I think he liked working there more than here. You have customers who can brag about him and hire him. My customers can't tell their wives where they met him."

Mary laughed, and Dulcie warmed to her more, praying Dan had enough sense to follow his heart. "He can cook in both our places, you know. We keep unusual hours."

"I'll manage, thank you."

"If you'd like your hair done sometime, I'm good at it. I could slip over to your house and help you with it. If you go to a party or anything."

"Thank you, but I don't go to many parties."

Dulcie realized that with different clothes and a bit of work on her hair, Mary could be quite eye-catching. Dulcie had helped enough of the girls who worked for her to know how to enhance a woman's natural looks.

"Miss O'Malley—"

"Please, just call me Mary."

"I don't think I should. You mustn't come here again. It's bad for my business. If my customers should see you—"

"I'm sorry."

"Don't apologize. I'll always remember. And I want to give you another bit of advice. Marry the man you love. Whichever one he is. If it's Silas, then don't let Dan persuade you to do something you shouldn't. But if it's Dan, don't be bound by old promises. Silas Eustice's first love is gold. He was a fool to leave you like he did."

Mary nodded and stood up, her gaze going once again to Dan's shirt. Dulcie doubted if they would ever talk again, and she felt a wistful envy. "Dan needs a woman like you more than even he knows. I'll show you out. I had your carriage brought around to the back. If you go down this alley and the alley in the next block, then turn on the street, you'll get home without being spotted."

Mary nodded, and they walked to the back door,

where Dulcie had the carriage waiting. Mary looked at all the carriages and horses in the back, where there was a long stable and corral, and she was shocked as she guessed that the house must be full of customers. She turned to face Dulcie.

"Be good to him," Dulcie said, and Mary realized Dulcie loved Dan. Or had loved him. She reached out to squeeze Dulcie's hand before climbing into her carriage. She wondered if Dulcie had told the truth when she said that Dan's shirt hadn't been touched in months, or if Dan stopped to see her regularly. Dan had brought her to Denver with him and built the house for her. One thing Mary knew without a doubt, she had no intention of sharing the man she married with another woman.

Early on the first morning in May, Dan appeared at the boardinghouse. Mary came to the kitchen door, and the sparkle that flared in her eyes when she saw him made his breath catch in his throat. She wore a blue gingham dress, and her hair was simply tied behind her neck the way he liked it. She looked so marvelous to him, he wanted to hug her.

"Good morning, Dan. Come inside."

"How's your foot and head?"

"My foot is a little sore and my head has a knot."

"Where?"

"Right here. I can't braid my hair, so that's why it's down."

"Let me see the knot. I won't hurt you."

She tilted her head and pointed, and he saw the lump beneath her hair. Mary felt his hand slip over the back of her head in the faintest touch, but it was *his* touch, and it sent a ripple of pleasure through her. She looked up at him. "My ankle is wrapped in a bandage."

"Should you be walking on it?" he asked in a tone far deeper than before. He stood only inches from her now, and as she gazed into his eyes, she wanted to be in his arms.

"I'm all right," she answered perfunctorily, barely aware of the words they were saying.

"Did Doc Felton tell you to stay off your foot?"

She blinked and started to turn, but Dan caught her by the arm. Instantly she sucked in her breath, and a stricken look crossed his face.

"Mary," he whispered, and she swayed toward him, wanting him to hold her, feeling desire burn up through her.

He blinked and jammed his hands in his pockets. "Did he tell you to stay off your foot?"

"He might have," she answered, "But I have a boardinghouse to run."

"Dammit, where's that cook I hired?"

"I sent Faucheux back to his other job. I can't pay a cook."

"I can."

"There's no reason for you to pay!"

"That I want to is enough reason," he said, leaning toward her, anger and frustration building. "If you shouldn't be on your foot, and I want to hire a cook, that's the way it should be!"

"There's nothing you can do about it," she said airily. Excitement ran through her simply because he was here with her. She didn't care if they argued or if they talked, Dan was with her and the argument didn't really have any bite.

"Oh, yes there sure as hell is! I'm not one of your brothers you can browbeat, and I'm not your sweet little pa. You're staying off your foot and I'm sending for Faucheux. How many customers do you have now?"

"None, and don't you interfere with me, Dan. This is my kitchen."

"And in the next few minutes, your kitchen will have a different cook!" He left, slamming the door behind him. In twenty minutes he returned with the thin, dark-haired Frenchman. They walked in the back door without knocking. Mary was standing at the stove, one knee bent and resting on a chair, her injured foot behind her in the air while she stood on the other foot to cook.

She looked over her shoulder, her eyes widened, and she turned.

"Now, see here, Dan—"

"*Bonjour,*" Faucheux said, studying the contents of a kettle.

Dan scooped her up. "Just take over, Faucheux," he ordered, and carried Mary out of the kitchen.

"Where do you want to be, the parlor or your bedroom?"

"You are so . . . so . . ."

He looked into her eyes, and Mary felt all her anger slipping away. He stepped into the back parlor and kicked shut the door as she burst into laughter and wrapped her arms around his neck. "Thank you."

"It's high time someone took care of you!" he said, and then a pained expression came across his face and he set her down quickly on the sofa.

She kept her arms around his neck, holding him. "Dan, I've missed you," she said quietly.

He took her arms and extricated himself, his heart thudding. "I have to go now."

"To Louisa," she said stiffly. Mary watched him, hurting inside, wishing things were different. She knew she shouldn't have mentioned Louisa, but was unable to resist it.

He gazed at her solemnly and shook his head. "She doesn't want to marry me. We won't go out together again. That's over."

Mary stared at him, trying to comprehend the implications of what he had told her. "You're not in love with Louisa?" she asked, holding her breath as she waited for his answer.

"No, and I don't think I ever really was. I don't think I realized what love really is until . . . lately."

The words made her head spin, because there was only one possible reason for them.

"You caused her to break it off."

He shrugged, and she knew she was right. Her heart soared, because it could mean only one thing. She stood up and steadied herself, and his frown increased.

"Dammit, get off your foot."

She crossed the room to him. "I thought you loved her."

"No. I don't, and I really didn't," he said, his gaze raking over her features with a hunger that plainly revealed his feelings. Mary was astounded, because she had accepted that he loved Louisa, who was so beautiful, was everything he seemed to need and want. So now all that stood between them was Silas. She reached out to touch his chest. He drew a long, deep breath. "Mary . . ."

Dan felt as if all the demons in hell were warring within his heart. Mary's hand rested on his chest. She stood only inches away, and her joy was evident in shining eyes. He struggled with his impulses, and for an instant, he yielded, bending to brush her lips with his. The touch made him shake with need. With an effort he moved toward the door.

"Get off your foot, Mary. I'll come back at noon." He left in long strides, as if he were fleeing from something, and she stared after him, knowing now she would have to make a decision. Did she want to wait indefinitely for Silas, who might fall in love with someone else or might change his mind and never return? Or did she want Dan, who was fighting his feelings for her because of Silas? The answer seemed evident and settled, because she had never felt for Silas what she did for Dan. And she thought her answer about Silas would be the same as Dan had just given about Louisa—Mary hadn't realized what love really was until lately. She didn't love Silas. It was Dan who had her heart, and she knew this time it was forever.

Dan strode away angrily. He hadn't intended to do more than stop to talk to her brothers. Instead, he was tangled in an emotional upheaval with Mary. He had come too damned close to taking her in his arms and kissing her long and passionately. He had promised he would be back later today, but he should stay away. He wanted to talk to her brothers, but once he did, he should stop seeing Mary. She was Silas' woman, and he would not take her from a friend who had trusted him completely. "Silas, you fool, I told you I shouldn't take her out!" Someone turned to stare at him, and Dan realized he was talking aloud to himself.

His concentration at work was gone. His thoughts drifted constantly. He hit his hand with a hammer. He cut two fingers badly, he had to redo some work, and finally he told his men he would be gone for an hour and rode back to the O'Malley house to eat his noon meal.

When he entered the dining room, Mary was serving. She set a plate in front of Herschel Windham. Dan stopped to talk to him, moving around the room to speak to others he knew, and he followed Mary into the kitchen.

"Faucheux, can you serve as well as cook?"

"*Oui, M'sieu Castle,*" Faucheux answered eagerly, his black eyes sparkling.

"Then you do just that."

"Dan, that's absurd. My ankle is better," Mary said, backing away from him, a spoon in her hand.

He took the spoon, picked her up, and went out through the hall door to take her to the parlor again. "Mary, if Doc told you to stay off your foot, do what he says."

Her eyes sparkled, and Dan wanted to swear. "Am I going to have to hire two more people to work in the kitchen?"

"No!"

"Where's your coat?" he snapped.

"In the hall. Why?"

"I'm going to take you to my house for the day so you can't work."

"You can't do that!"

He strode down the hall and set her on her feet to yank down a sweater and hold it out. "Put this on, Mary. The wind is brisk."

He strode outside to his horse and swung her up into the saddle, mounting to ride behind her.

She laughed. "Are you going to lock me in? What's to keep me from coming right home?"

She sounded happy as a lark, and it made Dan's

anger soar, because his nerves were frayed. She was pressed against him, warm and soft. He wanted to kiss her the rest of the day, to hold her and love her. He had to constantly fight the urges that became stronger with each day that passed. And she wasn't helping. Her laughter and twinkling eyes made it twice as difficult to resist temptation.

"Will you stop wiggling?" He ground out the words, aware of her soft bottom pressed against him. He was acutely conscious of the reaction of his body to her, of his arousal that was swift and hard in response to her.

Her face had turned pink and she became still, momentarily subdued as they rode in silence. He carried her into his house and into his office. "There are books here. You can read and relax and stay off your foot." He set her down, but her arms stayed around his neck.

"Thank you, Dan. That's the nicest thing anyone has ever done for me," she said quietly, watching him, surprised to see his face flush. He tried to move away, and she tightened her arms.

"Dan," she whispered, gazing at him. She saw the battle that raged in him reflected in his expression. His eyes were filled with longing, yet a frown creased his brow. "Damn," he whispered, and bent his head to kiss her.

Mary thought she would faint with ecstasy as his lips came down on hers, opening her mouth to his while his arms went around her waist and pulled her against him. His arousal was hard, pressing against her, making her conscious of his desire. She clung to him, kissing him in return.

Suddenly he pulled away. "No, dammit! Mary, I'm Silas' friend. He's my best friend. I can't and I won't take his woman. I won't! I'll leave Denver first." He spun around to stare at her. "I won't betray that friendship."

"I don't want to marry Silas any more than you want to marry Louisa Shumacher."

"You feel that way only because Silas has been gone so long. If he came through the door now, you'd change. Silas is a fine man. He's good and intelligent.''

"And he's ignored me for years. I was a child when we met. He was the first man who paid attention to me, and I was pleased and drawn to him, but I couldn't share things with him that I can with you.''

"Oh, hell, you're older now. You can share them with Silas too. I was friends with him, Mary. He isn't flighty, or irresponsible, or dull. He's quick, and intelligent, and strong.''

"I can't help what I feel. Your feelings about Louisa changed.''

"Louisa is an exceptionally beautiful woman. I was dazzled by her, just as I've been dazzled before by beauty, but when I could look at her and see just another woman, I realized we didn't have anything in common. I wasn't the man for her. I couldn't care for her the way she'd want, pamper her and cater to her. She couldn't please me. I need—''

"What do you need, Dan?'' Mary asked with a solemn challenge in her words.

A painful expression crossed his features. "A woman I can share my life with. My love is not going to be given at the expense of a good man who trusted me to watch out for his woman. I'm going to work, Mary. Is there anything you need before I leave?''

"You'd put Silas before the woman you love?''

"I think you're misinterpreting your feelings because he's been gone so long. Absence goes against nature, and that's one mistake Silas has made, leaving you alone like this. But no one is absolutely perfect. He's a good man, and when he gets back, I know you'll love him. And he trusted me, Mary.''

He strode to the door and paused. "I'll be back at suppertime.'' He left quickly, slamming the front door.

Staring after him, she felt more strongly than ever about her choice. And today she was in Dan's house, and he would be back this afternoon.

She moved around the room slowly, studying the architectural drawings spread on the desk, looking at his books and at the boxes of books that hadn't been unpacked and placed on shelves. She bent down to pick up a few, looking around for a cloth. She went to the kitchen, found a rag, and returned to unpack the boxes and put the books on the shelves. When she became tired of that, she went upstairs, looking at the unfurnished rooms. Downstairs she prowled through the house, through the empty dining room, the kitchen that had pipes waiting for the day water would be piped into homes in Denver, and a fancy new iron stove. She was fascinated by every object in the house. Because they belonged to Dan, they became special and far more interesting to her. She discovered the brandy he liked, the books he liked, the idle drawings he had made, and she saw that he was a good craftsman.

She moved down the hall and found Dan's bedroom at the back corner. It was a spacious room with high, airy windows that let sunlight pour into the room. There was a fireplace, a big brass bed with marble-topped tables flanking it, and fancy lamps stood on both tables. A tintype stood on the high dresser, and she studied it, looking at a beautiful woman with pale hair who bore a faint resemblance to Dan, and a swarthy man who was dark-skinned and dark-eyed. She wondered how, if they were his parents, Dan came to have such blue eyes. There was another picture of a couple, and she knew instantly it was April, the sister he had talked about, and Noah, April's husband, who owned the fancy saloon in Albuquerque.

Mary lay down on the bed, her body tingling while she thought of Dan sleeping there, remembering his body pressed against hers. She napped and woke, finding it a novel experience to have nothing to do. She had always kept busy, and while it was unique and pleasant to be idle, her emotions were in such a turmoil that it was impossible to relax and enjoy the solitude. No matter how much she thought about Silas, she felt sure about her decision. It was Dan she loved, and she knew him well enough to know he meant what he said about leaving Denver. His loyalty to Silas was strong, and his guilt over loving her was equally strong, yet she wanted him to look beyond that, and she intended to see that he did.

Dan made so many mistakes at work that his anger increased as the afternoon passed. Working furiously at simple tasks, he knew he had to do something to get his mind off Mary.

"Mr. Castle?"

He turned to see Trent Waltham standing just inside the door. Dan dropped down off the ladder and strode across the half-finished room to shake hands with him. "Nice to see you."

"I've looked at the plans you drew and I know we should have an appointment to go over them, but I want to know how soon you could commence building."

"I've got this one to finish, and I just agreed to build a house for Edward Ringwood. You can be next, but it will be several months before I can start," he said, forgetting completely he had just been thinking about leaving Denver.

"I like the plans. When can we get together to go over them?"

Dan wanted to shout with glee. This was what he had hoped for. This house and the Ringwood house would draw other customers to his business. "Name your time."

"Next Tuesday morning at nine?"

"Yes, sir."

"I really like the plans."

"Good. I'll do the finest job I can."

"And that's pretty damned good, from what I've seen," Trent said, his gaze running over the room. "See you Tuesday." He shook hands with Dan and strode outside. Dan knew the last shred of his concentration was demolished for the day. He tried to slow his work, to give it his full attention, but constantly his mind wandered back to Mary, to Trent, to the house he would get to build. When quitting time came, Dan had his tools put away at the same time as his employees.

He swung into the saddle and started home, his thoughts jumping to Mary, making a mental condemnation of Silas for getting him into such a predicament. The closer he drew to his house, the faster his pulse raced. He approached it, knowing Mary was inside, and for just a moment he wished that he could come home every day with her waiting for him.

20

_____

"Mary?" Dan called when he entered the house.

"I'm in here," she said. While waiting for him, she had bathed and washed her hair, dressing again in the same gingham and tying her hair behind her head. Her heart beat swiftly when she heard his approaching footsteps.

He stepped through the kitchen doorway and stopped, his gaze wandering down to her toes and up swiftly. It was a blatant look that told her exactly how he felt and made her tingle in the wake of his glance.

"I can take you home now," he said in a husky voice.

"I cooked us some supper. You'll let me stay to eat it, won't you?"

He looked away as if caught in an enormous dilemma.

"Dan, it's only supper. Wash up and come sit down. I poured a hot bath for you in your room."

He looked at the table, the usually empty kitchen filled with tempting aromas, and he wanted to swear aloud. He had tried to make things better for her, and had succeeded in making them worse for himself. "Mary, you were supposed to stay off your foot. That's why I brought you here. Can't you stop working for a day?"

She laughed, happy he was home, determined to prove to him what she felt. "I haven't really worked, and I did what I wanted. Your water is getting cold."

He spun around and went to his room. The coverlet

on the bed had a slight wrinkle on it, and he guessed she had been on the bed, a thought which tormented him. He saw the wet cloth hanging at the side of the tub, and the damp floor boards, and he realized she had bathed this afternoon. He turned to stare at the door. "Dammit," he whispered, feeling torn by his mixed emotions. He stripped off his clothes and plunged into the tub, trying to soak and soothe his nerves. Instead, he found himself fighting images of Mary in the tub, in his bed, in his room, until he splashed out, dried, and dressed in clean clothes to go to the kitchen.

"How was the house this afternoon?" she asked when he appeared in the doorway. He leaned against the jamb and watched her move around the kitchen, relishing the scene, knowing he would never forget it.

"I cut myself. I hit my hand with the hammer." She turned to stare at him as he listed the calamities, and suddenly he saw her eyes sparkle with mischief and delight.

"It isn't amusing, Mary. I can't concentrate. And this isn't going to help."

"I'm not laughing because you hurt yourself. I'm laughing because you won't acknowledge what's happening, no matter how obvious it becomes. And because you're doing the same things I did. I walked off stairs I've been going up and down for years. I should know them blindfolded. At least I can acknowledge why I did that."

"Lord, something's burning." He saw smoke rising, and stepped past her to move a pan quickly.

She turned around and let the subject drop while she got food on the table. The beans had burned, but the rest of the dinner was fine, and Dan sat down to a table laden with delicious steaming potatoes, brown gravy, and thick slices of salted meat he had stored in his cellar. She had baked bread, and he shook his head as he stared across the table at her.

"You've worked all afternoon."

"No, I really didn't. I napped for a short time. I

had a bath and washed my hair. I looked at your house.''

As she talked, Dan thought about her napping and bathing and roaming through his house, being here alone all day, and his appetite vanished. He had been famished, and the food was delicious, but suddenly he ached to hold her. He hurt so badly he couldn't eat, and he couldn't think.

''Mary, I have to take you home,'' he said, and she stopped talking to look at him, a wide-eyed, solemn look coming to her face.

''Can't you eat the supper I cooked?''

''No. It doesn't look as if you've touched much of yours either.''

''I don't eat very much a lot of the time, but I know you do.''

He stood up and she stood up as quickly. She moved out from behind the table, coming closer. ''Dan, we're going to have to face what we feel,'' she said solemnly, and he could have groaned. She was lovely. Her hair, soft and shining, framed her face and was tied behind her neck the way he liked. His kitchen was warm and smelled inviting, and Mary was in it, but each minute with her made it more difficult for him to keep his control.

''I've told you how I feel, and I'm sticking by that. I won't betray a trust.''

''No matter how much it hurts someone else?''

He blinked, feeling as if he had been struck. ''You know I don't want to hurt you, but I don't think you have any idea what you're doing. I don't want to take advantage of Silas' absence. I think the minute he comes back to town, you'll find you love him.''

''Do you think I can't understand my own mind and heart?''

''I think you're too inexperienced to make the right judgment. And I can't betray Silas' trust. Our friendship went deep. When a man saves your life, you owe him a great deal.''

''You don't owe him a lifetime of misery. And that's what it will be for me. I love you.''

Dan stood quietly, trying to breathe, feeling as if he were being pulled apart by an invisible force that tore at him bit by bit. He hurt, and it took all his self-control to keep from reaching for her.

"Mary, I can't go back on my promises. If it helps any, you know I love you. And I'm going to take you home."

"If you do, Dan Castle, you may regret it forever."

Jamming his hat on his head, he yanked on his jacket and held her sweater.

"Dan."

He picked her up and carried her outside to swing her onto his saddle. Then he climbed up with her to head for town and the boardinghouse.

"Dan, please," she said, turning to press against his chest, to cling to him, winding her slender arms around his waist beneath his jacket.

Staring stormily ahead, he couldn't answer. He hurt too badly, and didn't trust himself to do the right thing if she kept on pleading with him. He was acutely aware of her arms locked around him, her breasts pressed against his chest. The ride to her house was interminable, but they were finally in front of the boardinghouse and he dismounted, setting her down. "Should I carry you inside?"

She looked up at him, and tears streaked her cheeks. "Good-bye, Dan," she said quietly, and moved away, her back to him. He watched her climb the stairs, and wheeled his horse around to ride back home to a house that was filled with her scent, her memories. He worked almost through the night before finally falling into bed.

He stood a block away from the boardinghouse, waiting. He saw Brian leave, moving with a jaunty stride. Dan turned the corner of the block, stepping back to wait. He knew Brian would come this way, headed toward the livery stable. He heard bootheels, and Brian came around the corner. Dan pushed away from a wall and stepped into his path.

"Dan. What are you doing?"

"I'm waiting for you. How's Michael?"

"He's better," Brian said cheerfully. "He's up help-ing Mary and getting stronger by the day. That Kiowa has the magic touch. Or Doc Felton. I don't think Mi-chael will have bad scars."

When Dan didn't move or say anything, Brian frowned. "Was there something you wanted?"

Dan moved his hand quickly, waving his palm in a gesture that was sign language for a warning. Brian's frown changed to a scowl, and he shot Dan a ques-tioning look.

"What the hell's that mean?"

"You know what it means. Now, I wouldn't give a damn if you ran with every thief from here to Califor-nia, but you have a sister I do give a damn about, and consequently I'm not going to let you hurt her. If you don't stop running rifles, I'll turn you over to the sher-iff."

"Dammit, the Kiowa talked! You can't tell me what to do, and what I do won't hurt Mary. She'll never know, unless you turn me in. That's a hell of a way to keep her from getting hurt."

"That's better than what will happen to you if you keep it up. What about the goods you're getting in exchange? Think no one is getting hurt?"

Brian's face flushed. "I'm warning you, Castle, you're sticking your nose into other people's affairs and you're liable to get hurt."

"No, Brian, that's what you don't understand. I'm not the one who is going to get hurt here."

"Are you threatening me?"

"I'm threatening you with bodily harm as well as arrest. I'll take care of you myself before I turn you over to the sheriff. When I think what you're doing and how it can hurt Mary, I could tear you apart. And Michael will wish he were back with the bear."

"Michael? You'd threaten Michael?"

"Yes."

"I thought you had some sense. Michael can smash you like an ant."

"He's going to have to. Find some honest endeavor. Mary didn't raise you to be a criminal."

"Look, I can take care of myself, and what I'm doing isn't that bad."

"The hell it isn't."

"You came from San Antonio, a city, not the frontier. It's a tough life here, and I don't want to live like Pa and Mary."

"Have you ever thought about helping Mary?"

"Sure, I help her. And Silas will come home a wealthy man and take care of her, but I have to take care of me!"

"You're going about it a damned poor way."

"Mind your own business, Castle, before you get hurt badly. And leave me the hell alone."

He started to shoulder his way past Dan, but Dan yanked him into the space between two buildings. It was early and the street was deserted, the buildings empty. The moment Dan yanked Brian, Brian's temper exploded. He swung his fist. Dan ducked, slamming into Brian, and both of them went down, rolling. Dan gave him a chop against the side of the neck. Brian slammed a fist into Dan, making him stagger, but he came right back with a swift punch that sent Brian stumbling.

Brian rushed up at him to strike him a blow on the jaw that made Dan reel. Dan threw his weight behind a punch and knocked Brian into the wall. Dan followed, raining blows on him until he knew Brian was barely conscious. He held him up, pulling out a knife, placing the point against his throat and pricking his skin.

Brian's eyes grew wide and he frowned. "Hey, Dan!"

"Listen to me!" Dan snapped. "I know what crime is. I'm wanted for murder. I've killed before. I'm a wanted man."

Brian focused on Dan, swiping at the blood on his cheek and mouth as he blinked. "Murder?"

"They can only hang me once. You're not to trade

rifles or do anything else illegal that can hurt your sister. Do you understand.''

"If you murder me, it'll hurt her.''

"I won't murder you. I'll turn you over to the sheriff. But don't come after me.''

"You're wanted for murder?''

"Where can I find Michael and talk to him?''

"He's working around the house. If I get Michael, we can hurt you, Castle,'' Brian said, but all conviction was gone from his voice.

"Yes, I suppose you can. But you'll get hurt in the process, and it won't stop the sheriff from learning about what you're doing. Remember, I'm not the only one who knows.''

Brian blinked. Dan released him so suddenly he fell. Dan wiped blood off his mouth and put away the knife.

"Why did you tell me you're wanted? I can turn you in.''

"Yes, you can. I don't think you will. Your brother would be dead if it weren't for me. And your sister wouldn't have fared so well up there in the mountains with your 'friends.' ''

Brian's face flushed, and he looked away. "Where are you wanted for murder? In Texas?''

Dan gave him a level look as he brushed off his pants and turned to walk away. His back prickled, because Brian O'Malley was tough. Dan had fought a dirty fight. They had become friends in the past months, and he had caught Brian by surprise. He knew both factors slowed Brian's reactions and dampened his anger.

Michael O'Malley would be another matter, because Dan could imagine Michael's strength, and he didn't know Michael at all.

As he approached the boardinghouse, he halted at the back to avoid seeing Mary. His nerves couldn't take the continual encounters. Each one became more difficult to handle, harder to control. He watched the house and finally he saw Michael emerge. Dan whistled to catch Michael's attention.

Michael looked up, saw Dan motioning to him, and

sauntered toward him. He was almost completely healed, with only a bandage around his temple and one around his wrist and forearm.

"Mr. Castle?"

"Yes, can you come back here where we can talk in private?"

"Sure." Michael's eyes were filled with curiosity. "You don't want Mary to see you?"

Without answering, Dan moved around to the back of the shed and leaned against the wall.

"What is it?" Michael asked politely, studying Dan. "Looks as if you've been in a fight."

"I have, with Brian."

"Did Brian give you trouble?"

"No, as a matter of fact, I gave Brian trouble. And I'm going to give you some too."

A twinkle came to Michael O'Malley's eyes, and Dan knew how sure Michael was of his own strength.

"I don't want to hurt you, Castle. You saved my life. We don't have any argument between us, but I'd whip you in a minute."

"I'm surprised you didn't whip the bear," Dan said dryly.

"He was a big one. My rifle jammed. What's the problem?"

"I happen to think a lot of your sister."

"I heard how you and Silas are such friends."

"Yeah. Well, it goes beyond my friendship for Silas. Mary is special."

Michael frowned and placed his hands on his hips. "Get to the point."

"I don't want her hurt. You owe me, Michael. And I can hurt Brian. While you're stronger than I am, there are things that make us equal."

"Such as what?" Michael snapped, his easygoing manner vanishing.

Dan drew a sawed-off Colt from his waist and pointed it at Michael.

"You wouldn't shoot me," Michael said with more amusement, a smile tugging at the corners of his mouth.

"I just told Brian. I'm already wanted for murder. And robbery, and theft. I've been on the wrong side of the law and I know how disastrous it can be."

Michael's amusement vanished, replaced by shock. His blue eyes filled with curiosity.

"I'm not going to sit by and let you two get hurt while in turn you hurt your sister. Mary deserves better, and it was a pleasure to give Brian the beating he deserved. I wish I could give you one, but your ribs are taped and you're in no shape to fight. I know about the rifles and the stolen goods."

"You'd fight me?"

"Yes, Michael, I'll fight you. Without the Colt."

"Come on," Michael said belligerently. "Come on, Castle. Put the pistol away. I don't care if my ribs are taped. I'm not afraid of you, and this shouldn't take any time at all."

"If I hurt you now when you're just recovering, Mary wouldn't ever forgive me. I'll fight you, but you have to get well first. In the meantime, you're to stop trading rifles to the Apache."

"How the hell did you know? Someone at camp talked?"

"No. It was something Brian did."

"Go to hell and mind your own business."

"I'll turn both of you in. I'm not the only person who knows, so if something happens to me, you won't be safe. You're running with damned poor company with the likes of Sorghum and Donner. Do you know what they would have done to your sister if they could have?"

"What are you talking about?"

"They tried to take her one night behind the cabin."

"You're lying."

"Ask Mary."

"I will. Dammit, I will. How badly did you hurt Brian?"

"Not as badly as I should have."

"When I leave Denver, you won't know what I'm doing. You can't be everywhere at once."

"No, but I can keep up with Brian, and if I find out

that you two are still at it, I'll go straight to the sheriff.''

''That's a hell of a way to keep Mary from getting hurt.''

''I wish your ribs weren't taped. Do you have any idea how much she loves you? You two are like children to her. And it'll be a pleasure to fight you, Michael, because you're the one who should be more responsible and know better. You're older than Brian. You're the one who should be looking out for his younger brother, not trying to get him into trouble.''

''Oh, to hell with that!'' Michael's face flushed. ''Dammit, we aren't hurting anyone.''

''You know better than that. When you get over being angry, we can talk. I'd be glad to have you work for me. I'm not offering because you're Mary's brother. I'm damned particular, and I only hire good carpenters. Mary showed me the furniture you made. You do good work. And for that matter, if you'll ask, you'll find out that your brother is doing a good job at the livery stable. I did ask. He's a competent carpenter. Not as good as you—you have a natural touch for it—but he can do a satisfactory job. I'd even put him on my payroll if he wants. You think about it. Now, get on back. I've got to go to work.''

''You're wanted for murder? Why would you tell me?''

''The same reason I told Brian. You should know what kind of man I am. And I know what it's like to be on the wrong side of the law. It's bad, Michael. It's hell to be hunted.''

Michael studied him as Dan moved away. Dan tucked the pistol in his waistband and turned his back to walk away. Once again, he tensed, expecting to be jumped. He knew if he hurt Michael at all, Mary would be in a rage. He also knew that Michael O'Malley could probably beat him badly.

He prayed he had done enough to make them stop what they were doing. He didn't want Mary hurt. He would do whatever he could to try to protect her, but he really couldn't control her brothers. If he could just get through to Michael and make him think about it, Michael might do the rest. But the O'Malley boys would have to want to change.

21

Louisa stormed back and forth in her room, furious with Dan. She kept thinking about Reuben, who was becoming more possessive and ardent as time passed. Tonight he had urged her to break off with Dan, telling her that he wanted her for his wife. Now she wished she had given him more encouragement. She rubbed her brow, trying to figure out how she could get back at Dan. She also wanted to see Reuben again. He was usually out of his office during the noon hour. If she passed by in her carriage at noontime, she might see him. Or she could just wait. Lately he had been dropping by at odd times in the evening and on weekends with the excuse he wanted to talk to her father, yet he had spent more of his time talking to her.

She mulled over what to do, and finally decided on a course of action. Midmorning the next day, she dressed in one of her new creations, a pink dimity. At twenty minutes before twelve, she left home in the carriage, telling her mother that she was going to call on Emily. She gave the driver instructions to go back and forth along the street where Reuben worked with his father. On the second time past, she saw Reuben come striding out. She called to Franklin to halt the carriage, and she waved at Reuben, who changed direction and came over to speak to her.

"Get in, Reuben," she said. He slid onto the seat beside her and ordered Franklin to go ahead and drive around town for a few minutes.

"I need to talk to you, Reuben. It's urgent."

"Ah, he said, his gray eyes lighting with curiosity. "You were waiting for me?"

"Yes." She lowered her voice and leaned close to speak into Reuben's ear. "Dan Castle has insisted I give him an answer, and Papa has agreed to announce our engagement this weekend. I have to tell him if I'll wed him."

Reuben turned to look at her. "You know I want you. I have so much to give you, and I can make you happy." He studied her, knowing Dan Castle was a wanted man, yet uncertain how Louisa might react to this information. Her parents would never allow such a marriage, but Louisa might find it appealing and exciting. Reuben didn't want to give the information to Louisa to use. He would find his own uses for it. "I want you, Louisa. Will you marry me instead?"

She gave him a flirtatious look that made him wish they were alone. She had teased and tormented him for years now, and he wanted her. She would make a good wife, and it was time he took one. And as long as he kept Louisa happy, she would be submissive and all he wanted in a woman.

"Louisa," he coaxed, stroking her throat.

"Yes, Reuben," she said. "Yes, I will."

He swept her to him to kiss her. For an instant she let him, her heart pounding. She was so thankful it was over and Reuben had asked for her hand. He would never know that Dan had lost interest in her. "Reuben," she said, moving away, "we'll be scandalized. Everyone can see us."

He laughed and squeezed her hand. "I don't want a long engagement, Louisa."

"Talk to Papa soon. I don't want Dan to talk to him first. Please."

"I'll stop at the bank this afternoon and see him. As well as I know your father, this should be a simple matter, except he'll want to know your wishes, Louisa. All he knows is you plan to marry Castle."

"Talk to him tomorrow. That way I can tell him tonight and give Dan an answer."

Reuben looked at her with burning desire that made

her pulse race eagerly. "Tomorrow night, Louisa. And only a few months after we announce our engagement, we'll have a wedding. I've waited long enough for you."

She no longer cared about Dan Castle. She wasn't sure she had ever cared. Reuben was exciting, handsome, and far more wealthy. She placed her hand on his thigh and drew her fingers higher, watching him inhale deeply.

"I'll make you happy, Louisa," he said, thinking he would have a dazzling ring made for her. She would love it, and it would be the talk of Denver. "I wish we were along now." He leaned close to whisper in her ear, "When you're mine, I'll put my hands and my mouth all over you," he whispered, his tongue flicking over her ear.

She gasped and pulled away, feeling her cheeks burn. "Reuben, you're scandalous!"

He laughed and called to Franklin to halt. "I'll ask Mama to have your family over tomorrow night so we can celebrate."

Delighted, she smiled at him, happy at the turn of events, and thinking that this may have been what she wanted all along.

Reuben watched her carriage move away. He knew he would have the most beautiful wife of any man in this part of the country. There were a few beautiful women around—Dulcie was one—but they weren't marriageable. And he anticipated taking Louisa's virginity, initiating her into the rites of love that he expected her to enjoy as much as he did. She enjoyed what she allowed him to do now! He was glad to think the time would soon approach when he could possess her. His smile faded when he thought of Dan Castle. It changed the picture somewhat, and he rubbed his jaw. Should he go ahead with his plans or not? Now Castle was no longer a threat. Someone who would seldom cross paths with them, and he didn't think Louisa gave a fig for the man. She hadn't acted as if she did. But Reuben could get rid of him forever, and that might make life easier. Reuben didn't want Castle

to look like a martyr or hero to Louisa. At least Louisa
hadn't become engaged to him. She would have been
publicly embarrassed when word got out about the
man.

Reuben decided to go ahead. Denver would be a
more pleasant place without Dan Castle.

That night Reuben leaned against the bar at the Nevada House. He spotted the men he wanted, and when
he caught their attention, he jerked his head in the
direction of the door. He had found them a week ago,
telling them to wait until he talked to them again. He
planned with care, wanting to make certain he was
going to achieve his purpose.

He stepped outside and palmed the derringer he carried. He didn't trust any of the ruffians that passed
through town.

Reuben watched the men come out of the saloon,
and he turned to step between two buildings where it
was dark and they could be alone.

" 'Evening, sir,'' one of them said.

"Do you still want to do what I asked?''

"Sure do. If there's a reward, we'll be happy to turn
in a murdering thief.''

"There's a big reward, and I'll also pay you, but I
want it done right.''

"We're good at it. We've earned plenty turning in
wanted men.''

"Very well. Here's you man.'' Reuben pulled out a
piece of paper and handed it to them. They unfolded
it to study the picture.

" 'Tigre Danby Castillo,' '' one of them read, and
looked up. "He dropped out of sight, and rumor had
it that he was killed out around the California border.''

"He's here, living in Denver. He goes under another
name, and he doesn't look like he did in that picture.
His hair is cut and he's a respected citizen, but he's
the same man. I want you to take him back to New
Mexico, where they'll hang him. I want you to cross
the border and go to the first large town. He has a
lawyer brother in San Antonio. Get it done fast, before

that brother can come defend him. Raton, Santa Fe, any town you can get to in a hurry. Do we have a deal?''

"You said you were going to pay a little extra."

"That's right, but I want to know if you're going to do as I ask.''

"Yes, sir.''

"And you're not to return to Denver. I don't want to hear any more about this. Is that clear?''

"Yes, sir. We won't be back.''

"Very well. Here's the money.'' Dan handed over a packet of bills and they took it, one of them counting swiftly.

"It's more than I originally said. I want the job done.''

"Don't give it another thought.''

"The sooner it's done, the better it will suit me. He plays poker at the Front Street Saloon most nights now. And if you wait until late in the night, he'll have more whiskey under his belt.''

"Yes, sir.''

Reuben waited until they realized he was finished. "Thank you, sir. Consider the task done.''

They left, and Reuben walked out behind them, crossing the street to his horse and mounting. He looked back once to see if they were gone. He smiled with satisfaction. Dan Castle would no longer be a part of Denver life, and that suited him fine. And by this time tomorrow night, he expected to be engaged to Louisa.

22

As May changed to June, Mary tried to run the boardinghouse, take care of Michael, and forget about Dan, but it was impossible. Thoughts of him affected everything she did. She burned food, something she had rarely done before, and now it occurred with increasing regularity because she simply couldn't remember to watch it. She set the kitchen on fire—a small fire that Brian and Michael extinguished swiftly. She misplaced things, forgot things, and lost her concentration in the middle of conversations. Finally Michael confronted her one day when they were alone in the parlor.

"Mary, for Lord's sake, what's the matter with you?"

"I'm fine, Michael."

"Fine, hell! You've never been like this before. Are you ailing?"

"No, really, I'm fine," she said, turning pink. Michael stared at her. She had been this way since they returned from camp. And he still hadn't decided what to do about Dan Castle. The man had saved his life. And Michael had asked Mary about Sorghum, and learned Dan had saved Mary from something terrible. Every time he thought about Sorghum, he grew more anxious to get back to camp. He would teach Sorghum to frighten his sister!

He owed Castle, yet the thought of acquiescing to Dan Castle, an outsider who had no business meddling in his affairs . . .

Michael's thoughts suddenly shifted. He looked at Mary and remembered Dan's anger. His fury had been directed at Michael and Brian because he wanted to shield Mary from hurt. The man would have to care a hell of a lot to threaten the O'Malleys.

"Mary, how well do you know Dan Castle?"

She blinked, and her face became a deeper shade of pink. Michael stared at her in amazement. "I've known him since he came back to Denver. Since last winter."

"He prospected with Silas."

"Yes, he did."

"Does he have a woman in his life?"

"No, I don't think so. He went out with Louisa Shumacher, but that's over," she said, dusting faster. "I'm going upstairs to change the beds."

"Mary. If I get in a fight with Castle, will you be angry with me if I hurt him?"

She turned to stare at him, and he had his answer before she spoke. He knew Mary's temper and he could see sparks starting to flash in her eyes. "Yes! What a thing to ask! You owe your life to him and so do I! He had his friend ride all the way from San Antonio without stopping to get to you, and you're better for it!"

"Oh, Mary, calm down! I won't hurt him, but he can be annoying."

"What's he done to you that's annoying?"

"He doesn't like the men I run with at the cabin and he threatened me if I go back."

"Dan did that?" she said, round-eyed. "Why would he interfere in your life?"

"He doesn't want me to associate with men like that. If something happens to me, he thinks it'll hurt you."

She snapped her mouth shut. "Dan threatened you? Oh, Michael, I'm so glad you didn't fight!"

"He wouldn't fight while I have broken ribs. He said you'd never forgive him if he hurt me," he said, studying her and thinking about his discovery.

She blinked several times. "Well, I didn't think I'd

see the day when I thought someone might hurt you badly, but if there is anyone that could, it would be Dan.''

"I'm not scared of him. I'm bigger than he is."

"Well, big doesn't always mean you'll win. That bear was bigger than you, from what you said. Now he's skinned.''

"I can whip Castle," Michael said, trying to see what reaction he would get.

"Michael O'Malley, you're not to try!"

"Have you heard from Silas?"

"No."

He leaned back, thinking about Dan. "I hear Castle is going to build houses for Trent Waltham and Edward Ringwood. That should set him up solidly with folks here.''

"Yes, isn't that marvelous!"

Michael wondered why he had been so blind to see what had happened right beneath his nose. Now that he realized what had caused such a change in Mary, it seemed as obvious as her red hair. He thought about what Dan had told him about his past and weighed it with the kind of man he seemed to be, the future he appeared to have. "Mary, has Dan ever told you anything about his past?''

She paused to stare at him. "Yes, he's told me. And he must have told you," she said, closing the parlor door.

"He's wanted for murder," Michael said.

"In New Mexico Territory. Why would he tell you, Michael?''

"I think he was trying to scare me. He threatened me because he doesn't want me to do anything to hurt you.''

"You won't," she said gently, her features softening. "You won't ever hurt me, Michael."

He turned angrily to stare out the window. "I'm no saint, Mary, and don't make me feel like I have to be one!''

She laughed. "I'm not asking you to be a saint." She crossed the room to hug him, and he turned to give her a squeeze. He looked into her eyes. "You love him very much, don't you?"

"Who?"

It was his turn to laugh. "Don't act so innocent and shocked. Why I haven't realized the truth before this is beyond me. Dan Castle."

Her smile vanished and worry filled her expression.

Suddenly he realized something was terribly wrong. "Surely it isn't because you promised to wait for Silas? That man hasn't written you or come home—"

"No, it isn't. I never loved Silas like I do Dan," she said quietly. She looked into Michael's eyes. "Dan promised Silas to take care of me. He says he won't betray Silas' trust. That he can't take Silas' woman while he's gone."

Michael studied her in silence, thinking that over. He realized he could understand. "Mary, it would be a low-down skunk who would woo a man's love while he's away from her."

"But do you know how long Silas has been away? He hasn't written me one letter. Not one, Michael! Am I to wait until I'm thirty or forty?"

"No, I understand how you feel. I agree with you. But at the same time, I can understand Dan's reaction. Men who are honorable, and trustworthy, and have a shred of conscience just won't do something like that."

"Even if it means the woman may be unhappy the rest of her life?"

He rubbed his forehead. "No wonder you set the kitchen on fire!"

"Oh, Michael! You're a fine help!"

"Sorry. You'll work it out. You always work everything out," he said cheerfully, standing up and patting her shoulder as he left.

Mary glared after him. "Men!" She moved around the room, dusting. Today she would see Doc Felton and perhaps get the wrapping off her ankle. It felt better, and she would be relieved. Her thoughts went from that to Dan. She hadn't seen him for days, and it hurt more with each passing day. She missed him terribly

and wondered if he missed her or if he had already
forgotten her.

She sat down on the chair to stare out the window.
Time was passing, and the man she loved was going
to do the honorable thing and refuse to see her or acknowledge that love. She cried now, when she had
spent a lifetime in bad situations without resorting to
tears. She stared at the trees, thinking of Dan and how
deeply she loved him. And he had to love her. Any
man who would threaten Michael to keep him from
hurting his sister had to love her deeply. Suddenly she
remembered the fight Brian had been in a while back.
He wouldn't say who it was with or why it happened,
and she never quizzed him too much about his activities. Could it have been with Dan, for the same reason
as he had threatened Michael? Why would he threaten
Brian, though? Brian didn't live in a mining camp with
ruffians. But he had disappeared for days at a time. He
could be riding out to see Michael, and both could be
doing something they shouldn't. Dan must have
learned about it some way when they were in the
mountains. The more she thought about it, the more
sense it made.

She ran her hand across her forehead. All the men
in her life worried her, each in his own way. Pa with
his drinking and inventions, Michael and Brian with
their wildness, Silas with his absence, Dan with his
stubbornness.

"Hi, Mary," Brian said from the doorway. "Michael and I—"

"I hate you all!" she snapped, standing up and hurrying past him to run to her room to slam the door.

Brian stared after her with his jaw hanging open
while Michael came the rest of the way down the stairs.

"What on earth happened to her? You'd think I
dropped a scorpion down her dress."

"You can't guess what's befallen our sister?" Michael asked with a grin.

"No. Do you know?"

"Yes, and if you had a little brain in that head of

yours, you'd know too. I should have guessed sooner.
Who's been threatening you if you hurt her?''

"Dan Castle. So what the hell does that have to do
with anything?''

"I forget your youth.''

Brian's eyes widened. "Mary's in love?'' he asked.

"Ah, maybe you're becoming a man of the world
after all. Yes. And he won't betray his trust to Silas
and take his woman while he's away.''

"Mary doesn't want to wait for Silas?''

"No. Would you want to wait years for someone?''

"Hell, no. She shouldn't.''

"And would you like a man who would marry his
best friend's woman while the friend was gone from
home?''

"No, but this is different. I mean, Silas has been
gone a long time. A hell of a long time. I told Mary
she should forget him. I don't think Castle ought to
honor his promises to Silas if he really loves her and
she loves him.''

"Oh, she loves him. Why do you think she fell down
the stairs and set the kitchen on fire?''

"Holy saints. It's that bad?''

"And why do you think he threatened us with our
lives and revealed his past?''

"Lord, he must love her something awful. I'm glad
you didn't kill him.''

"I'm glad too.''

"But what are we supposed to do? Do we stop or
risk seeing if his threats were idle?''

"We stop. Except I'm going back up there to get
Sorghum and Donner for what they tried to do to
Mary.''

"Michael, why should we stop? He didn't scare you,
did he?''

Michael looked at his younger brother, realizing
what jeopardy he had put him in and what kind of an
example he had set for him. It had seemed harmless
at first, but he had seen Sorghum and Donner take
captives and sell them, and he knew he had to get out.
He and Jethro had planned to move on anyway. Dan

had made him really think about it, though, and when
he learned the men had tried to attack Mary, it was
the final straw. "No, Brian, I'm not scared of Dan.
But he's right. We stop."

"Well, you may stop, but I—"

Michael yanked him up by the shirtfront. "You do
a damned good job at the livery. You're going to make
a good smithy, and Dan told me you're a good carpenter. I catch you doing anything illegal, you'll have
me to answer to before Castle! I'll whip your ass into
pudding."

Brian kicked Michael and doubled his fist to punch
him in the belly. Michael grunted from the blow that
sent pain shooting through his ribs. He doubled his
fists and slammed his right into Brian's jaw, and followed with a left, sending him crashing across the hall.
Brian hit the wall and slumped to the floor. Michael
stood over him, his fists clenched.

Mary came out of her room. "What was that noise?
Michael! Brian!" she screeched, and ran across the
hall to Brian. "You hit him! Holy saints, you hit your
brother!"

"Mary, believe me, if you knew why I hit him, you'd
hit him yourself."

She blinked and stared at Michael, remembering the
nights Brian had vanished, the discovery that Dan had
threatened them, and she clamped her mouth closed.
"I hope if I ever have children, they're all girls!"

He grinned. "You've always hoped that anyway."

She turned with her chin in the air and hurried back
to her room to slam the door. Brian groaned and Michael stood over him.

"You're a bastard," Brian muttered.

"If I am, you're one too." He reached down and
pulled Brian to his feet.

"Damn, you're strong. I think you broke my jaw."

"You couldn't talk if I had. I *know* you hit me in
my broken ribs."

"Serves you right."

"Come on. Let's get busy. I want to get the shed
repaired."

They walked out and Brian looked up at Michael. "So what are you going to do? Get a job here in Denver?"

"I'm thinking about what I want to do." They went to work, their quarrel forgotten.

By the end of the day, Michael told Brian he had an errand to run and left with the wagon. He stopped at the lumberyard to get some boards they still needed for the shed and back fence. He bought ammunition, a new hat, and he got directions to the house Dan was currently building. He slowed in the yard beside the house and jumped down as men were leaving to go home for the day. He quickened his stride, wondering if he had come too late.

"Where's Dan Castle?"

"Inside," one said, and Michael hurried toward the house, his gaze going over it and realizing what a good carpenter Dan was. He walked through the open front door, studying the carpentry. He found Dan working in the kitchen, sanding a cabinet.

"Hello."

Dan turned. "Oh. I heard someone and just thought it was one of my men." He shook hands with Michael.

"Nice house."

"Thanks."

"Go ahead and work. I can talk while you work."

Dan gave him a curious look and turned to sand again. Michael leaned back against the counter near him, watching him. "I've been thinking about what you said. You were right about Brian. I didn't set a good example.

"And I've been thinking about your job offer. I appreciate it, but there's too big a chance right now to make a real fortune to pass it up. I'm young and I want to look for gold and silver."

"I've done it and had enough success to do what I want with the gold, so I can understand. But a lot of men aren't lucky at it."

"I want to take the chance now, not look back years later and wish I had, or I'll always be chasing dreams like Pa. And first of all, I've got a score to settle with Sorghum.''

Dan wiped off his hands. "You can forget that.''

"You're going to protect the man? Donner too. After what they tried with Mary? She told me what you did. You can't stop me, so don't try.''

"I can stop you,'' Dan said dryly. "You can't kill dead men.''

Michael stared at him, his eyes widening. "You killed them?''

"I didn't say that, but I happen to know they're no longer with us.''

"That's why you sent Brian ahead with Mary and me in the wagon. You and the Kiowa—'' He grinned. "I'll be damned.'' To Dan's surprise, Michael grabbed his hand and shook it vigorously.

"Thanks, Dan. Lord, Sorghum was bad. Jethro and I were planning to pull out of there anyway. I'm going back to get Jethro. He's a good man. Thanks.''

Dan shrugged. "I was just defending myself, and fortunately Ta-ne-haddle can trail people without getting caught.''

"That's damned good. No loss to the world there. Brian doesn't even know it.''

"Neither does Mary,'' Dan added solemnly, "and that's the way I want it. There's no need to worry her.''

"Speaking of Mary, I want you to know, Brian and I both wish . . . Well . . .'' He shuffled his feet and paused, his face flushing. "I'm not one to meddle in another man's business, but that damned Silas hasn't done my sister any favors by staying away all this time. And if it matters to you, she sure as hell is in love.''

Dan turned to stare at him, and Michael blushed, waving his hand. "She'd kill me for telling, but hell, she walked off the stairs and got hurt because her mind was elsewhere. She's set the kitchen on fire, and she burns something nearly every day. And Mary is the best cook in the whole world. She's touchy, and frankly, I can understand how you feel, but I don't think she loves Silas one whit. I don't think your actions will help your friend. She'll never marry him now. And Brian and I, well, we understand why you respect your friendship for Silas, but we'll sure as hell respect you if you ignore it.''

''Thank you, Michael,'' Dan said solemnly, suspecting the speech had been as difficult for Michael as fighting the bear. ''I appreciate knowing that. I don't know what I'll do. Silas saved my life. Bounty hunters were taking me in and they planned to kill me. We mined together, and you get to know a man well when you're shut up in a cabin with him for over a year. We had scrapes and good times and he means a lot to me. I grew up the only child in my family, and in some ways Silas is the closest I've ever been to a man. He's closer to me than Luke, who is a blood brother, because I've spent more time with him. It's hard to go against that, and I know he's a good man. And if he comes back, he'll be the millionaire he said. He can give Mary more than I ever can.''

''Do you think my sister gives a damn about the money?''

''No. I know she doesn't, but I can't stop thinking about what he will do for her and how much she deserves it.''

''Well, it's between you two. I'm not one to meddle, but you have our approval. And I'll tell you, when I see him, I'm going to knock Silas into the Platte River from our front yard for what he's done to her. No woman should be expected to wait and wait. I haven't ever seen one before who would.''

He looked away to stare out the window, suddenly chuckling. ''She'd knock me clean into the river if she knew what all I've told you. Damn, is she in love! She went to the store yesterday and only bought half the things she meant to get, and when she got home and unhitched the wagon, she let Blackie go. I found him roaming down Arapaho, chewing up flowers.''

He chuckled, but Dan couldn't see any humor in what was happening to him or to Mary. He ached for her and he was sorry she was in such a daze, but so was he. ''Someday you'll understand, Michael,'' he said gruffly, and Michael looked as if he were biting back a smile.

"Mind if I look around?"

"No. Go right ahead."

While Dan worked, he heard Michael striding through the house. Finally he returned. "It's nice. When I make my fortune, you can build a house for me."

"Sure."

"I hear you've been at the Front Street Saloon winning at poker the past few nights."

"I've been lucky."

"I might see you tonight."

"Glad you came by, Michael."

"I owe you for what you did." They gazed at each other, and Dan realized he had won a friend in Michael O'Malley.

"I better get back. I promised Mary to bring home some things from the store."

He left, and Dan went back to work, making an effort to concentrate and succeeding in losing himself in his work until the evening. He was engrossed in finishing the cabinets, and he continued working until late, finally going home after midnight and stretching out across the bed for a few minutes. The next thing he knew it was dawn and time to go back to work. He was famished, and all he could think about was Mary serving delicious hot breakfasts.

He washed, shaved, and dressed in a clean shirt and pants, and in half an hour knocked on Mary's kitchen door. His heart felt as if it stopped and restarted at a racing pace as Mary came into view. Her hair was back in braids and she wore a blue gingham he had seen often, but she took his breath away.

"Dan?"

"Mary, I'm starved and sick of my own cooking, and there's no food at home."

She laughed and motioned him inside. "Want to eat with the diners or in the kitchen while I work?"

"In the kitchen," he said quickly, brushing her shoulder, unable to resist touching her.

Mary drew a deep breath as his fingers touched her shoulder and nape. He looked marvelous, and she was thankful he was there. She quickly fixed him a heaping plate of eggs and flapjacks, and she cleared a spot at the counter for him.

She was constantly busy and unable to stop for more than a minute or two at a time to talk to him, but he was happy to be near her as he devoured the plate of food. She gave him another plateful, and when he finally had to go, he caught her by the arm.

"Thanks. I think I'll live now."

She gazed up into his eyes. Her heart pounded when she saw the blatant longing there. "Dan, can't we talk?"

He clamped his lips together and gazed beyond her. "It won't change anything."

"You're just going to go on and let us both get hurt?"

"Mary, I have to do what's right. Thanks." He brushed her cheek with a kiss and left, striding away swiftly. She moved to the door to stare at him, aching and wishing he wouldn't be so stubborn about holding to his principles. "Damn Silas Eustice," she whispered. She went back to work, her mind only half on what she was doing in spite of repeated resolutions to give her full attention to running the boardinghouse. During the middle of the morning, she had come to a decision, and she penned a note, asking Faucheux to deliver it for her.

"*Sacre bleu!* Impossible! You want me to take this to Madame before lunch? The beans need—"

"I'll cook. You take the message for me and bring me an answer."

"Mademoiselle, I cannot take responsibility for my dinner if someone else touches the food!"

"I understand," she said happily. "*Au revoir,* Faucheux."

He threw up his hands and yanked off the apron, muttering to himself as he left. Mary watched him go, frightened a little at what she was doing, yet determined to make Dan realize that sometimes principle had to give way to other considerations. And she was frightened too of what Dulcie might think. Dan's shirt had been hanging in her room, and Mary didn't think it had gone untouched for months.

23

Dulcie stared at the note and swore under her breath. "Doesn't she realize she can put her own reputation in jeopardy?"

"And my beans are being ruined! You cannot meddle in beans and expect a masterpiece!"

"Faucheux, only a man more interested in beans than women could cook like you do. Go back to your beans, and tell Miss O'Malley I said yes."

"Oui, madame."

He strode out the door while Dulcie stood frowning, mulling over Mary's request. Finally she went to her room and began to gather her things, tugging on the bellpull for Arletta and telling her to have a carriage readied.

At a quarter to two, Mary stood on the back porch. She shelled peas, watching the lane. When she heard a horse, her hands became still. A carriage came around the corner of the house to the back and halted.

Dulcie climbed down, and Mary went forward to meet her. "Thank you for coming," she said, blushing. "I didn't know if you would want to."

Dulcie faced her. "I know you're the woman for Dan, whether he knows it or not. He won't ever be mine, and I'm realistic enough to face that fact. And there are other men in the world."

"Will you come inside?" Mary asked.

"I brought some things, if we're going to do your hair. I need curling irons and some ribbons and things I thought you might not have."

"My ma died when I was young, and I haven't ever done anything fancy to my hair. I appreciate your coming," she said, helping Dulcie with a bundle. Together they went to Mary's room and closed the door.

"Do your brothers know I'm here?"

"No, ma'am, no one does."

Dulcie laughed and placed her hands on her hips. "Miss O'Malley, don't call me 'ma'am.' It's 'Dulcie.' "

"And you call me 'Mary,' " she said unpinning her hair. "I want to look as pretty as I can."

"You have water ready?"

"Yes. I heated enough to fill a tub."

"Good, just get in, and we'll go to work."

Three hours later, Dulcie stood back to survey her handiwork. Mary's hair was cut short in front, with curls around her forehead and temples. The rest fell in a shimmering cascade that curled softly and naturally. When Dulcie tried to get Mary to allow her to paint her face, Mary refused politely, until Dulcie finally gave up and packed her things.

"I'll leave these curling irons. I have plenty of them."

"Dulcie, please let me pay you."

"No. I did it because I wanted to. I know how stubborn Dan can be, but I know he needs a good woman."

"I'm afraid he'll leave Denver or—" Mary bit off her words, but Dulcie knew full well what she was thinking. He would find another woman. He was not one to go long without one. "Thank you for coming. If I can do anything for you, I'll be glad to."

Dulcie laughed. "Honey, you have enough problems right now. Good-bye, Mary, and good luck."

"Good-bye." Mary followed her to the carriage and waved as Dulcie left.

She went inside to the kitchen. To her amazement, Faucheux turned to stare at her.

"Mam'selle, la, la! How beautiful you look!"

"Thank you, Faucheux. I won't be here to help today."

"Do not concern yourself. I will run the kitchen!"

"Thank you, Faucheux," she said, leaving the work to him and going out to hitch the wagon. As soon as she finished, she hurried to her room, her heart beating faster as she thought about what she was going to do. She had heard that Dan was playing poker at nights in a saloon, and she was afraid she would miss him and have to wait until the early hours of morning before he returned home, so she moved quickly. She changed clothes, pulling on a dress she had made and had worn only once so far. It was pale green muslin trimmed with tiny silk rosebuds and dark green silk ribbons. Her fingers shook with nervousness, and she prayed that Michael and Brian left home and didn't come in until late.

Finally she slipped out to get the wagon. She climbed up and moved out of the yard in the dark of night, her pulse pounding.

A dozen blocks away, Dan walked around his bedroom. He had washed and was dressing in plain denim pants and a cotton shirt to go play poker. He hadn't seen Mary for days now, but time couldn't erase her from his thoughts. He was relieved to have had the talk with Michael. He would have been happy to hire Michael, because he could use his help.

He heard a knock at the back door and frowned, moving through his house to open it. Mary stood in front of him, her hair softly framing her face, falling in a shimmering cascade. She looked more beautiful than ever.

His heart seemed to slam against his ribs as he stared at her as if she were an apparition.

"May I see you, Dan?"

He glanced beyond her at the wagon behind his house, the horse hitched to a post. "Come inside."

She entered and looked at him in uncertainty. He motioned her toward the parlor, and lit the lamps while she sat on the settee. She looked embarrassed, frightened, and uncertain as he moved around the room. Her cheeks were pink, and as he looked at her, he realized there was something different about her. She looked prettier than ever, and all he really wanted to do was kiss her.

"I'd like to talk to you," she said quietly, and suddenly his heart felt torn in two. He knew how shy she was where men were concerned, and how difficult it must have been for her to come to his house. If it were anyone else, her reputation would have been at risk, but Dan suspected everyone in town accepted Mary as being so prim and proper that a breath of scandal couldn't touch her.

He walked over to pull her to her feet. Her hands were like ice in his, and he looked down at her, feeling touched, fighting all the natural urges he felt. "You shouldn't be here," he said gently. "Michael would give me hell."

"Michael doesn't know. Now I want to talk to you," she said solemnly, and his hurt deepened. She sounded as if she had rehearsed for this moment.

"Mary, I appreciate your coming to talk, but we've talked," he explained gently.

"You've broken your engagement to Louisa Shumacher, so I take it you care for me," she said, as if he hadn't said a word to her.

He groaned. "You know it's more than care, but, Mary, this isn't right. I'm going to take you home."

"No, you're going to listen to me. I'm entitled to that from you."

"Honey, don't you know what this is doing to me? I'm trying to exercise some control, Mary. I'm trying to keep promises. If we get into another discussion—hell, if you stand here alone with me another ten minutes . . . You have to go home, honey."

"I'm not going until you tell me something. Do you love me?"

He drew a deep breath and felt as if he were drawing a knife into his lungs. "You know I love you!"

"You haven't ever told me." That was the one thing that had made her uncertain. She had to hear him say what he felt. She had to know without a doubt that it was only Silas holding him back. "Dan, for just a minute, forget Silas. I'm not a beautiful woman like Louisa or Dulcie—''

"Oh, damn," he said, and sounded so pained that she was shocked. He moved back a step and clenched his fists. His voice was a rasp. "You're the most beautiful woman I know. Absolutely, Mary. And you look more beautiful tonight than ever."

"Thank you," she said, suddenly swamped with uncertainty. She hadn't expected the reaction she got, and it shook her momentarily and deterred her from her plans. She took a deep breath.

Before she could speak, he said, "I want you to go. I can't carry you out to your wagon, but you shouldn't be here. I can't keep my control much longer. Mary, please. This is the hardest thing I've ever had to do. Please. Think of Silas."

"I do not love Silas Eustice," she said clearly, raising her chin. "I'll never love him. I will never marry him. We're not engaged. He said to wait for him, and I thought I loved him when he left, but that was years ago, Dan. Years! I've grown and changed in that time, and I can see that I never loved Silas the way I do you," she said simply.

Dan paced across the room, stoking the fire, turning coals and watching them burn and glow. He tried desperately to keep from rushing to Mary to haul her into his embrace. He faced her as she talked.

"If you love me, then we need to talk, because you'll take all my joy and happiness if you leave Denver. I won't find it with Silas. It's you, and it will always be you."

Her cheeks had become heated and her words slowed. She burned with embarrassment, making such declarations to him while he stood there staring at her.

"Mary, do you know what kind of man takes another man's woman? His best friend's woman?" He ground out the words and his face had paled.

Suddenly she felt more certain of what she was doing. "It would have to be the kind of man who is very deeply in love with a woman who loves him deeply in return. I am not Silas Eustice's woman," she said firmly, facing his fiery blue eyes. 'I was never his in any sense of the word. There's no ring on my finger, and he never possessed me. Nor did he have my heart. Dan, this is so hard. How long are you going to make me stand here and suffer and feel foolish?''

His control vanished, and all thoughts of Silas went along with it. He swore and closed the distance between them to wrap his arms around her and bend his head to kiss her. His mouth came down on hers so firmly she couldn't breathe, and she loved it. She shrugged her arms free to wrap them around his neck and cling to him as the kiss overcame her. She felt something wet and opened her eyes, leaning back to see that his cheeks were wet.

"Dan!"

He groaned and pulled her to him to kiss her again. She clung to him wildly, knowing in her heart that he loved her. This was her man and she was his woman, and sooner or later he would have to acknowledge it openly.

With his pulse roaring in his ears, Dan held her and kissed her. His control was gone, and he wasn't going to struggle to get it back, because Mary was the most precious person on earth, and for right now, he was going to do what she wanted. She had sworn she didn't love Silas, and he would wrestle with that later. At the moment he couldn't get enough of her—he wanted to kiss her senseless, to touch her and hold her. He wanted to tell her how much he loved her, but he couldn't talk. His throat was raw, his emotions equally raw.

He wound his fingers in her soft hair and kissed her, feeling her hips move against him. He swung her into his arms and sat down on the sofa, holding her on his lap while he kissed her, running his hand down over her high, small breasts. She gasped and moaned softly as he flicked his thumbs over the peaks of her breasts.

Mary felt his arousal press against her. Her senses spun in a tumbling jumble of emotions and sensations. Joy and desire burned like a flame while Dan stroked and kissed her, and stirred feelings she had never known.

He wanted her so badly, and reason couldn't be summoned back now, in the heat of passion. Mary was responsive and eager in his arms, so innocent, and he wanted her desperately. He kissed her, his hands going behind her to unfasten the buttons of her dress. Finally he pushed away her dress, and she wore only a simple cotton shift. Her eyes were enormous as he looked at her. "Dan, my knee is scarred from the childhood accident."

"Do you think that would bother me?" he asked so tenderly her heart swelled with love.

He stood up, his hands on her hips as she stood in front of him. She reached out to tug his shirt out of his pants and pull it over his head. He saw that her shyness and timidity were gone. Her hands played across his chest, and the look she gave him mirrored his scalding need.

He pulled away the chemise, dropping it on the floor, and stood back to look at her, his hands on her hips.

"Mary," he breathed softly, wanting her. He scooped her into his strong arms and carried her back to his bedroom to place her on his brass bed.

"I love you," she whispered, watching him. He finished undressing until he was as naked as she, and then he moved close to the bed to stroke her.

"I don't know anything about this, Dan," she said hesitantly, her cheeks flaming. "I never . . ."

"Shh," he whispered, coming down to pull her into his arms. "Let me show you what's good when a man and woman really love each other."

She stroked him, moving back to look at him. His body was golden, muscled, with a mat of golden curls across his chest. His hips were pale in contrast, his legs covered in short blond hair. While her heart pounded violently, she drew her fingers down his chest, over his flat belly, finally touching the most private part of him. She heard his deep intake of breath while she stroked and held him.

"Mary," he said with another groan, and moved

her hands. "Let me touch you," he whispered. He caressed her, and her eyes closed as his lips met hers. He kissed her passionately. Her senses were stormed as he continued to shower her with kisses, touching her, caressing her until she felt wild with need, a physical yearning she had never known before.

Finally he moved above her, nudging her legs apart with his knee, coming between her smooth thighs. Her heart pounded with joy because this was the love of her life. His gaze raked over her, and her blood thundered in her ears.

She touched him before he came down. His mouth covered hers, his arms holding her, and he thrust slowly into her softness. Mary held back a cry. She felt as if she would burst with him.

"Move your hips," he whispered. "Put your legs around me, Mary."

She did, and let out a small cry that was muffled by his kisses as his control vanished. His slender hips thrust swiftly. Suddenly pain was transformed to sensations that rocked her and made her gasp with need. Ecstasy tore at her, and she moved in a frenzy, wanting more, wanting Dan forever, finally crying out softly.

"Mary, love!" he ground out the words in her ear as he held her. "My Mary, my love," he said, and she tightened her arms around him, clinging to his strong body, yielding in the knowledge she was giving herself forever.

His weight finally came down on her, and he stroked and kissed her, trailing light kisses across her shoulder, her neck, her ear, until he rose to look into her eyes.

"I love you," he said solemnly.

"And I love you," she returned, stroking his cheek.

"I have to marry you now," he said.

"I think maybe you do," she answered. Wonder filled her at the thought that this marvel of a man loved her.

"Silas may try to kill me, Mary. I don't want to hurt him."

"I'll talk to Silas, but it wasn't right for us to have to refuse our love over a man who doesn't really love me. Dan, Silas loves gold."

"No. He talked by the hour about you. He loves you, Mary."

"I don't think he really does. Would you rather go away for years and find a fortune than see the woman you love?"

"No, but that's different. Your hair is different. It's beautiful."

"Thank you," she answered, having decided hours ago that she wasn't bringing Dulcie into the conversation. She ran her fingers through his hair and across his shoulder. "I'm so glad you love me. I don't know how you can. I'm not Louisa Shumacher, but I'm—"

"I'm thankful you're not Louisa Shumacher, and you're the most beautiful woman on earth."

She laughed and stroked his jaw, suddenly burying her face against his throat and crying. Dan held her tightly, stroking her, letting her cry because he understood what she felt. "Mary, I never really knew what love was. I was so captivated by women who were gorgeous that I didn't look beyond beauty for anything else."

She lay back, looking up at him, running her finger along his jaw while he talked. He moved beside her, propping his head on his hand and gazing into her eyes with a look that made happiness flood her. "I got to be friends with you, and I realized you were the most important person in the whole world to me. I like to share everything with you. I never talked to Louisa. I never talked to anyone else, for that matter." He paused and looked down at her. "Will you marry me?"

She wrapped her arms around him and kissed him wildly before finally pulling away. "Yes!"

He gazed at her somberly. "So now I have to face Silas."

"Dan, I don't love Silas."

"You would have if I hadn't come along."

"You don't know that for sure, and he may never come back."

"Oh, hell, Mary. He seemed so damned in love with you, and I know why he felt that way. You're one in a million. He wants to marry you. He's doing all that for you."

"Oh, no, he's not! He prospecting for himself!"

"Well, he still thinks you're the most special woman in the world, and I do too." Dan sat up in bed. Worry filled his voice, but Mary was wrapped in the love he had shown her in the past hour, and she wasn't worried about Silas. She ran her fingers along Dan's thigh, amazed that she had the freedom to do so. She delighted in touching him, feeling her cheeks grow warm as she looked at his naked body.

"Mary, you're not helping the problem."

"There isn't a problem. I'm in love with only one man, and that's that. I don't know much about what you want, except you said once you wanted a family like you grew up in. Do you want children?"

"Yes. Do you?" he asked, knowing her answer.

"I want them. Lots of them," she said, drawing her fingers along the inside of his thigh and watching the effect she was having.

"I can see I'm going to have to marry you soon," he said, catching her hands to hold them. He had intended to make her stop, because he was still worried about Silas, but when she raised her green eyes to meet his, he forgot Silas and the world.

Later Dan lay stretched beside Mary, stroking her, her hair spread over his chest. "Damnation!" he exclaimed, sitting up and nearly tumbling her from the bed. "I have to get you home. If Michael and Brian find you here, I'll be six feet under, with lilies growing over me!"

She giggled and flounced back on the bed. "No, darling. You'll be marching to Father Wertly's with two shotguns aimed at you."

Dan laughed, suddenly realizing he would have more fun with Mary as his wife than he had ever dreamed possible with Louisa or Melissa. "Mary, I've got to tell you something," he said.

"What's that?"

"Well, I like women. And I have had one in my life here in Denver, but I won't be seeing her again after this."

"Dulcie knows that," Mary said, stepping out of bed to gather her clothes.

Dan stared at her openmouthed. "How do you know Dulcie knows that?"

"I've been to see Dulcie, and she's been to see me."

Dan watched her move. She was slender, her skin pale, and her breasts high and small. Her fiery tresses spilled over her shoulders, and she took his breath away and rekindled his desire.

"Mary, come here," he said in a husky voice.

Mary paused to look at him, her gaze flicking down over him. Her cheeks turned pink as she slowly opened her hands and let her clothing fall back to the floor. As she crossed the room to him, he stepped out of bed to wrap his arms around her.

"You're beautiful."

"I'm not, but I will forever love to hear you say so."

"Yes, you are," he whispered. "You are absolutely the most beautiful woman I've ever known. You don't know what my heart does when I look at you," he said as she stood on tiptoe to place her lips on his.

Later she lay in his arms in bed. "If I don't go home, Michael and Brian will find out how late I've been here."

"Yes," he said in a distracted manner. "Mary, when did you go see Dulcie? And why?"

Mary smiled up at him. "Darling, let us have an understanding right now. We're finished discussing Dulcie. And I'm not generous where you and other women are concerned. You have to make a decision for all time, Dan."

"I already have." He bent down to kiss her. "Mary, we'll have to talk about a wedding date and whether we should wait to tell Silas first."

"I could be ancient before Silas returns. We aren't waiting for him."

"I think I just lost control of my life," he said, a twinkle in his eyes. "Oh, Mary, I can't believe my luck! Suppose he comes home a millionaire. Are you—"

"Don't ask me again if I'm sure," she said in a tone he had heard her use with Brian. "After tonight you should know."

"If we don't have to wait for Silas, I'd rather not wait long at all. I need you," he said solemnly, meaning it with all his heart. "I need you so badly, Mary."

"I want to take long enough to make a dress to be married in."

"And my family will come. I'll have to give them enough notice."

"Next month? In July?"

He nodded in agreement. "And then we'll go away for a little while. Oh, I've forgotten about my houses!"

"You finish the houses, and we'll be married."

"No," Dan said, knowing there was no turning back now. Houses could wait. "I'll talk to the men about their houses."

She stepped out of bed and he caught her, pulling her back down, his eyes twinkling. "Where's the scar from the time Michael shot you with the arrow?"

"Never mind!"

"Let me see," he said, trying to turn her over while she struggled with him.

She laughed and grabbed him around the neck. "You already know where the scar is!"

He grinned and kissed her, running his hand over her bottom and across the scar.

"You'll have a worse one from Michael if I don't go home. Come help with my buttons," she said, standing up.

He stood and kissed the nape of her neck, lingering, making tingles course through her until she turned to face him. "You're supposed to do the buttons. You know there'll be trouble if I don't get home."

"If I didn't want to keep your reputation intact and

the friendship of your brothers, I'd keep you here all night." He gazed down at her solemnly. "That's what I want, Mary. I want you alone with me, just the two of us, with no interruptions. I want to love you until you're on fire, make you laugh, make you happy."

"You will," she said softly, twisting around to kiss his hand as he fastened her buttons.

"I'd like to take you away somewhere for a wedding trip, where I can have you all to myself. Mary, when we come back, you'll have to give up the boarding-house. I can hire someone to run it if you want to keep it going so your Pa will have a place, or we can bring him to live with us."

"I'd rather keep the place going for now. What will I do all day, Dan? I can keep it going."

"No. It's time you had some fun. You're not running the boardinghouse any longer. Do what you want."

"Dan, I don't know the ladies in society."

"You'll make nice friends. There are new families coming to town all the time, and you have friends here you've known a long time. Now, as much as I hate to, I have to take you home." He scooped her up in his arms and held her, both of them laughing. "I'd rather take you right back to bed." He tightened his arms and kissed her, holding her close against him while she clung to him with joy.

She put her head against his shoulder. "I'd rather go right back to bed."

He groaned. "Mary, don't put temptation in my way again!"

"When have I put temptation in your way?"

"You know damned well what you had in mind when you came to see me." Her face flamed, and he grinned, his brows arching. "That was exactly what you planned, wasn't it? Admit it!"

She buried her head against his neck. "I just wanted you to face what we felt, and I wanted to make sure you really love me."

"And you wanted me to take you to bed," he

teased, feeling as if he could shout with joy and jump in the air.

"Yes," he heard her say softly, her breath fanning against his neck. She raised her head and looked him straight in the eye. "Yes, I guess I did."

"You guess?"

"You're teasing."

He laughed and kissed her again. "How I hate to take you home." He swung her up in the wagon, saddled his horse and secured it to the back of the wagon so it would follow them, then climbed up to take the reins from Mary.

At the boardinghouse, Dan sat in the back parlor talking to her until after two in the morning. "I should go, Mary. I suppose Brian is all right, since he's out with Michael."

She shrugged. "I don't worry about him so much with Michael here. They're together."

Dan locked his fingers in hers as they walked to the back door. He turned her to face him. "Thank you for coming to talk to me," he said softly.

She nodded. "I decided I should follow what I feel in my heart."

He tightened his arms around her waist, his head coming down as he kissed her hard and long. Mary's blood pounded, and she clung to him, letting him know as much as possible how badly she needed him, how much she wanted his kisses.

Finally desire made him hard and aroused. Mary pushed away. "We should stop, Dan. The boys could come along . . ."

"Yeah."

"Come for breakfast."

"I will, Mary." He bent down to kiss her ear, whispering, "You're beautiful."

"How foolish and wonderful you are," she whispered in return.

Dan winked and mounted swiftly, knowing he had to go in a hurry. But he felt wound up like a spring, and knew sleep wouldn't come tonight. He headed toward the saloons, deciding to while away another hour at poker.

He dismounted and strode into the Red Rooster unaware of the man outside who stood up and waved his arm. Down the block, another figure moved away from the front of a saloon and waved in return.

In a few minutes both men were standing at the bar of the Red Rooster.

24

A man entered the saloon and glanced around, then finally threaded his way to Dan, who studied his cards. The man waited until the hands were played, and while Dan was raking in his winnings, tapped him on the shoulder.

Dan took the cheroot from his mouth and looked up at Grizzly.

"Miss Dulcie said to give you this." He thrust a folded paper into Dan's hand and strode to the door.

Dan unfolded it to read Dulcie's cramped writing: "Dan. Word has it from a customer passing through Denver that Silas found gold—more than a million."

Dan crumpled the note and jammed it into his pocket. He continued with the game for another hour, then finally gathered his winnings and left. His mind shifted to Dulcie's note. Silas would come home now. Dan hoped he would come before the wedding. He thought about Mary and ached to be with her. Over a month. A hell of a long time. It seemed he had been waiting half his life for a woman, but this one would finally be well worth the wait. And she wouldn't keep him at such a distance while she waited. He adored her. Dan was so lost in thoughts about Mary that he didn't hear the two men following him until each one clasped him by the arm tightly, one thrusting a pistol in his side.

"Just keep walking. We have a wagon up ahead."

"What the hell?" Dan said, going cold all over,

knowing before they answered him what had happened.

"Tigre Castillo, we're taking you back to New Mexico Territory, where you're going to hang and we're going to collect our reward."

Dan's mind raced. He had been so wrapped up in euphoria over Mary, he had let down his guard completely. He didn't wear a weapon; he could feel the pistol jammed in his side, and both men had tight grips on his arms. They approached another row of saloons whose sloping roofs came out over the boardwalk. They'd have to angle out to the street to walk three abreast, and as they did so, they passed the first post that ran from the roof to the boardwalk.

Suddenly Dan yanked forward, slamming one of the men into the post and twisting away from the other. The gun fired, and he felt a burning sensation across his middle, but he knew it was merely a graze. He locked his fists together and slammed them into the man with the pistol, knocking him to his knees.

The other one hit Dan, and both went down, rolling in the street. Dan slugged him and knocked him back, then sprang to his feet. He spun around as the other hit him over the head with the butt of the pistol.

Dan sagged to the ground, and the man hit him again. He fell face-forward, dimly conscious of the pain. Hands picked him up roughly, both men getting a tight grip on him again. "You try anything else like that and we'll shoot you right here and you'll never stand trial," one of them hissed.

They began to walk, half-dragging Dan between them. "I told you we should have brought the wagon closer."

"Shut up!"

A momentary longing for Mary tore at Dan. He finally had found a woman he adored, and she loved him in return. Now he would lose her, though, and at the moment that loomed more terrifying than the prospect of hanging. His head spun as he was half-supported by the men who moved him along quickly.

Across the street, four men burst from a saloon.

They were singing an Irish song, the tenor carrying the melody, and Dan turned his head to look their way.

"Hey, Dan!" came a drunken call.

"Get rid of them or they get hurt!" one of the men holding Dan snapped under his breath.

"Do you want them shot? You say the wrong thing, and I'll oblige."

Dan watched as the O'Malley boys left their friends and staggered toward him.

"Dan, how's poker?" Michael asked, swaying in front of him.

"Fine, boys."

"Want to have a drink?" Brian asked. "Who're your friends?"

"My friends. Remember, Brian, how we met? Well, I met these two tonight, and we're friends just like you and I were when we met. Instant friends."

"Hey, you have blood on your cheek," Michael said dully in words thickened by liquor.

"I fell down and these gentlemen are helping me home. Like you did, Brian. Just exactly like you and I did the night we met. These gentlemen want to see my house. I may build one for them. Good night," he said as they walked on past the O'Malleys.

Michael and Brian went on down the street. "Where shall we go next?"

"We can go to the California House or a beer garden or the Lazy Dog."

"I didn't know you were friends right off, the first night you met Dan."

"Weren't. Nearly killed each other. Mary—" He stopped and looked up at Michael, who looked at him.

"You nearly killed each other?"

"Well, it was a fight." They both looked back at Dan, who went around a corner with the two men. They stood staring after him in silence. "He said it was just like when we met," Brian repeated.

Both of them were silent a moment. "Bounty hunters," Michael said, his voice sobering. "Try to be quiet. Let's go."

They ran back in long strides, slowing where they

had seen Dan turn the corner, and Michael leaned around. Two men were tying up Dan, and then they tossed him into the back of a wagon. Michael yanked on Brian. "Let's go."

"Hey!" Michael began to sing, and Brian fell in beside him, both weaving and bellowing. "Hey, friends, have you seen where Dan Castle went?" Michael called, narrowing the distance between them.

"He went back that way!"

"Do you know which saloon? We need to pay him."

"Look at the Lazy Dog."

"Get away from the wagon."

Brian was singing, walking around to one side, while Michael moved closer to the man on the other. "Mister, you want to know what we won tonight?" He swayed and laughed and slapped his knees and jingled money in his pockets. "You want to see? We won thousands! Hit the mother lode tonight! Hit it right there in the Missouri House! Couldn't believe my luck."

"You won thousands?" the driver asked, interest flaring in his voice as he lowered the reins.

"You don't believe me?"

"Maybe not. You want to show me?"

"Yeah, look here." Michael tossed a fistful of coins in the air. As the man looked up, Michael yelled and grabbed him, yanking him down. A gun blasted the air and Michael hit the man's hand against the wagon, doubling his fist and slamming it into the man's jaw. His head snapped around and he sank to the ground without moving.

"Brian?"

"I'm okay. Can't say the same for the other fellow. What about Dan?"

Both of them climbed into the wagon to look down at Dan tied and gagged.

"Hey, look at old Dan. Now, this lends itself to possibilities," Brian said. "I mean, he has whipped my tail badly a few times in the past."

"Shut up and cut him loose. He's not in the mood for fun." Brian slashed the rope that held Dan, and they pulled him to his feet while Brian neatly cut away the gag.

"Thanks, boys. I hoped you'd get my message."

"Bounty hunters?"

"Yes. Now, what do we do with them?"

"I'd say we wake 'em up and tell them how it isn't healthy to stay in Denver," Michael answered. "You go home, Dan. Brian and I will take care of this task. We'll convince them. You won't have to watch over your shoulder for them, I promise you."

"Don't get yourselves in trouble over it," Dan said gruffly. He clamped both of them on the shoulder. "Thank you. I was going to wait until tomorrow to do this, but tomorrows have a way of changing on you. I need to find Paddy. Have you boys seen him?"

"He's home in bed."

"Is that right? Well, I have to pay a visit to your father."

"Anything special?" Michael asked, tilting his head to one side.

Dan grinned, worries falling away for a moment. "Yeah, something special. I want to ask for your sister's hand."

"Son of a bitch. You'll be family!" Brian said.

"That's right. Let me ask Paddy before you tell him, okay?"

"Sure. That's good news, Dan," Michael said, pumping his hand.

Brian offered his hand. "I'm glad. I'm damned glad."

They climbed down, and Dan wondered if the two bounty hunters were alive, but he decided to leave them alone and let the O'Malleys handle the problem.

Michael picked up his coins. "Men like that can't resist money. Go on home, Dan. They won't bother you again, I promise."

"Don't get yourselves in trouble."

Dan left, his happiness now clouded with more than one worry. He went back for his horse, mounting up to ride home, wondering how the bounty hunters had found him. They had known exactly who he was, and he hadn't noticed anyone trailing after him during the past days. He mulled it over and thought about Silas. Dan hoped he came before the wedding. Nothing was really going to make it easy to tell Silas.

The next morning, along with Faucheux, Dan went to Mary's early, when he knew she would be alone in the kitchen. When she came to the door, he motioned Faucheux to go ahead.

"Bonjour, mademoiselle," he said. "I'm happy for you!" He raised her hand to his lips to brush her knuckles with a kiss. With a sigh he hurried past her into the kitchen.

While Mary arched her brows in question at Dan, he swept her up in his arms to kiss her, crushing her to him.

Mary held him, her heart pounding with joy. He set her on her feet. "I brought my carriage and I brought Faucheux. Dulcie hired a new cook, and Faucheux is going to take over here," Dan said, untying her apron and taking a spoon out of her hand, "and you're going for a carriage ride with me. Grizzly is driving us."

"That's why he's so happy!" she exclaimed in a whisper, rolling her eyes in Faucheux's direction. "He's getting my kitchen all to himself."

With a grin Dan took her hand and they hurried to his carriage. As Grizzly started down the street, Dan pulled down the leather flaps, giving Mary and him complete privacy. In seconds she sat on his lap while he kissed her passionately. Then she pushed away a fraction. "Are you sure Grizzly won't stop?"

"Absolutely," Dan said, watching her. "When we get married, I wish you'd leave your hair down."

"You can have whatever you want," she drawled languorously, closing her eyes and leaning close. He kissed her, and in minutes his hand slipped beneath her skirts, caressing her thigh, stirring longings that were new, more intense than any she had known before their night of lovemaking. She loved him with all her being, and wanted him badly. She envisioned Dan's golden body, remembering ecstasy, wanting him. She trailed her hand over him, working the buttons loose on his denim pants to free him from restraint.

She touched him, and he groaned, closing his eyes to kiss her. In minutes he pulled her over him, settling her down as they moved together wildly. Rapture burst in her. Both gasped and cried out. She leaned against him, spent, perspiration beading her brow while she turned to give him a mischievous look.

"Damn, you're a lusty wench!" he said with amazement, stroking her bare legs, kissing her long and hard. She moved away from him and straightened her clothing while he tucked his shirt in and buttoned his pants. "I won't be fit to get out of this carriage."

"Are you complaining?"

Pausing, he pulled her beside him, his fingers biting into her flesh, he held her so tightly. "No, I'm not complaining. I'm thinking I have a woman who is even more exciting than I ever dreamed."

Her eyes sparkled at his words, and Dan pulled her to him to kiss her.

After a moment he leaned back. "Mary—"

"I know that tone. It means trouble."

"Yes. I heard a rumor that Silas hit it big."

She studied him and thought it over. "Then he'll be coming home."

"Thinking he'll marry you."

"That's all settled, Dan. I want you to promise me you'll let me be there when you tell him."

"I may not be able to keep that promise. He might not give me a chance."

"I should talk to him and you should talk to him."

Dan nodded. "There's something else."

She felt as if a cold wind had assailed her, because she could see from the worried expression on his face that it was serious.

"What is it?"

"Last night I was jumped by bounty hunters. Fortunately, your brothers freed me and ran them out of town."

"Oh, Dan," she said, giving his hand a squeeze. The look in his eyes frightened her.

"I want to go back and give myself up and stand trial."

"No!" Terror such as she had never known gripped her. She had grown up on a frontier and she knew the unfairness of some of the rulings, the rough and violent justice meted out. "You don't have to, and they could hang you! No!"

"Now, listen," he said gently, extracting her arms from around his neck. "I don't want to go through life with this hanging over me. I have a brother who is a fine lawyer. My father is established in the community now, and the Craddocks, the family who wanted to hang me and who caused all the trouble, aren't as powerful now. I think I can be vindicated and I want to try."

She couldn't keep back a sudden gush of tears. She had gone through hundreds of calamities, yet she couldn't cope with Dan's news without crying. It shamed her, but she was terrified by what he wanted to do. "No! Please! I couldn't bear to lose you. I couldn't bear it!"

"Shh." His arms tightened and he held her close against him. "Look, if we have children, would you want something like last night to happen? Next time, your brothers might not be around to save me. If they hadn't come along, I'd be on my way to New Mexico to stand trial without Luke and without your knowing what had happened to me. The reward is for me dead or alive, Mary. They might have shot me as soon as we were out of town."

She wouldn't answer, burying her head against him, clinging to him tightly.

"Honey, I have to go back," he said gently. "I just have to."

She knew he was right when she faced the situation logically, but in her heart she didn't want him to give himself up. She raised her head, framing his face with her hands. "You have to let me go with you. We'll do it after we're married. We can wait that long. I want that, Dan."

He nodded. "If you're sure that's the way you want it."

"I'm sure." She felt tears coming again and buried her face against his chest. "I love you. You can't imagine how much I love you!"

He held her tightly. "I promise you, Luke will get me off."

"If he doesn't, Michael and I will get you out of jail if we have to turn outlaw to do it!"

He laughed, wiping away her tears with his thumbs. "I believe you, Mary Katherine. I believe you without the slightest doubt!"

He pulled her to him to kiss her until they felt the carriage halt. "Our ride is over," he said in a husky voice, gazing at her with a scalding look. "I told Grizzly what time we had to be back. Hon, I don't think I can come in for breakfast right now. I'll go home and be back shortly."

She laughed, looking down at his denim trousers which bore signs of their lovemaking. Her eyes sparkled, and he squeezed her. "It was fun."

She climbed out and hurried inside and he rode back home. When Dan returned to the O'Malleys' he was astride his horse. He dismounted and knocked at the front door. When Mary opened it, she moved into his open arms to hug him.

"Where's Paddy?"

"He's in the parlor. I told him you wanted to see him."

"Run along and leave us alone," Dan said, giving her a hug. He rapped on the open door. "Good morning, sir."

" 'Morning, Dan. Come in." Paddy was whittling, and Dan watched him work, the short stubby fingers holding the knife with certainty.

Dan closed the door so they wouldn't be interrupted by the boys. "Sir, I want to talk to you about a serious matter."

"Talk away, my boy."

Dan wanted Paddy's full attention, but saw he wasn't

going to get it yet. "I'd like to marry your daughter. I love Mary and I'll take good care of her."

Paddy stared at Dan. "You want to marry her? Does Mary want this?"

"Yes, sir. You can talk to her. I wanted to wait until Silas returns, but she said she doesn't love Silas and she never will."

"I declare." Paddy put down the figure he was whittling. "My boy, you have my permission, and we'll just drink to the occasion." Paddy crossed the room to pump Dan's hand vigorously and clasp him on the shoulder. "I'll get the family and we'll celebrate. Glad to count you one of us. Yes, sir. Know you'll make my little girl happy."

"I intend to try," Dan said, breaking out in a grin. He recalled the afternoon he had asked for Louisa's hand and the stiff and cool reception he had received. Paddy went to the door and whistled. In minutes Michael and Brian came down the stairs.

Paddy poured four glasses of whiskey. "Boys, we have cause to celebrate. Our family is going to get larger. Dan wants to wed Mary."

They shook hands as if they were hearing the news for the first time, and they all drank to the occasion. "We need to tell Faucheux!" Brian said, disappearing into the hall in spite of Dan's assurance that the Frenchman already knew. In seconds the two returned and Paddy poured another round of whiskey for more toasts. Each proposed a toast, until Mary heard their voices and came across the hall. She paused in the doorway. "Pa! It's before breakfast!"

"We're having a toast, Mary, love," he said happily while Dan crossed the room to her. When she looked into his eyes, her consternation vanished.

He draped his arm around her, and she smiled up at him. She felt a bond with him that separated her from everyone else in the world and tied her to Dan. She felt as if he were part of her all the time, her heart one with his. She couldn't bear to think about going to New Mexico, but she knew he was right. And for now she wouldn't think about it.

She drank a toast with them, and shooed Dan and the boys to the dining room for breakfast, leaving Paddy to his carving while Faucheux hurried back to the kitchen.

Dan kissed Mary good-bye and left for work, deciding to stop at the bank on his way. He strode into the lobby. Charles Shumacher stood only a few feet from the door talking to Reuben, whose back was to Dan.

"Good morning," Charles said. Reuben turned, and when he saw Dan, all color drained from his face. As his hand went beneath his coat, Dan instantly realized he was carrying a weapon and that he felt threatened. And Dan knew who had given the information to the bounty hunters. Rage flooded him that Reuben would go to such lengths, but as swiftly as the anger had come, it vanished. Dan shook hands with both men. "Good morning."

"I suppose you'll hear it soon enough," Charles Shumacher said. "Reuben and Louisa are engaged."

"Congratulations," Dan said. "I'm sure you'll be happy."

"Thank you," Reuben said stiffly, studying Dan.

"I came to deposit some money, Mr. Shumacher," Dan said, moving on past them. He deposited his winnings from several nights' poker games and left. Outside he heard his name called, and turned to see Reuben following him.

"I suppose you're angry over Louisa."

"No. I said congratulations and I meant it."

Reuben looked puzzled, staring at Dan intently.

"And don't send someone after me again," Dan said softly. "Next time, you might regret it badly." He strode away without looking back.

Each day seemed to pass in a flurry of activity. As they watched the arrival of the first train into Denver, Dan squeezed Mary's waist, and eagerness filled him, because he knew this meant a boom for the town. Mary was busy getting things ready for the wedding, sewing her dress. Dan worked diligently to get as much built as possible before the wedding. And he had something else he needed to do. He stopped to see Mary one Thursday morning in the last week of June. After breakfast, when he told her good-bye, he kissed her long and hard. As he straightened up, he became solemn. "Honey, I know what we said, and after this one time, it won't ever come up again, but I want to see Dulcie sometime today. I have to get some things from her, and I owe it to her to say good-bye."

"I know."

"Mary," Dan said, bending his knees so he would be on her level, "this is the last time I'll go there, and I won't touch her."

She smiled and touched his cheek. "I trust you, Dan. That's part of love."

He kissed her long and passionately, his hand splayed in the small of her back as he held her pressed to him. When he stopped, his breathing was ragged and his voice husky. "I swear there will never be another woman to interest me. I couldn't conjure up any interest if I tried. Because I did try, Mary, with Dulcie and Louisa when we came back from the mountains, and I just couldn't . . . They might as well have been posts."

She laughed and hugged him, so happy she thought she might burst with joy. "Oh, Dan! That's absurd, but I'm so glad!"

She squeezed his waist and he swung her around for a last long kiss. He finally went to work, deciding to go to Dulcie's about noon, when she was the least busy. He bent over a cabinet, smiling as he worked.

Mary hummed, cleaning up Paddy's wood shavings in the parlor. She dusted the room, going over tables that were already polished and free of dust, her thoughts on Dan constantly. She stood near the front windows, pausing to watch an elegant carriage halt in front, and she wondered who could be coming to the boardinghouse in such a fine vehicle.

She stared with curiosity as a man opened the door and stepped down, striding up toward the house, packages in his hands. He was dressed in an elegant gray suit, a beaver hat perched jauntily on his head, and her heart seemed to stop beating as she looked at his pale skin and white hair. Handsome, dashing in appearance, the man strode up the front steps and knocked at the door.

Mary's heart thudded. Silas was home.

She went to the door, gazing through the oval beveled glass at him. He must have made his million, because he looked as if what he was wearing cost a fortune.

She opened the door and faced him.

"Mary," he said, stepping inside and setting boxes on the floor, turning to take her in his arms. "I'm back, love, and I did just what I said I'd do, and more! A whole-lot more, Mary. I'm a millionaire several times over and I've come home to you!"

25

Silas laughed and squeezed her and leaned down to kiss her. Mary turned her head and pushed against him, twisting away out of his grasp. ''Silas! You'd send a person into shock!''

''Mary, I'm home! Come here.''

''This is a surprise. You should have let me know you were coming.'' she said, studying him, thinking that even if Dan hadn't come into her life, she couldn't rush into Silas' arms now. He was a complete stranger. He looked taller, more filled out, and incredibly successful. And flamboyant, so different from the Silas who had told her good-bye and to wait for him.

''That's a fancy carriage,'' she said, realizing he hadn't come straight home to her. He had been to some city to acquire such elegant clothes and the expensive carriage.

''It's a brand-new Hamilton coach I bought in St. Louis. I had it delivered here on the train. I can't believe Denver has a railroad now!''

''You were in St. Louis?''

''Yes. I couldn't come home to you looking as if I'd just crawled out of a mine shaft!'' He laughed. ''Don't look as if you can't believe it's me. I told you I'd come back to you.''

''Four years ago,'' she said, her thoughts running over the fact he had gone from prospecting out west to St. Louis. He had passed Denver. ''Actually four and a half years ago now.''

''I know it was a long time and I didn't write, but I

brought things to make up for it. "Here." He thrust boxes into her hands.

"Come into the parlor," she said, wondering if Silas had considered her feelings at all. "We need to talk."

He followed her, glancing around, moving about the room to touch things. "Mary, I thought you'd have all this fixed up better. I sent money."

"I wouldn't use it."

He frowned. "You wouldn't take it? Did Dan give it to you?"

"Yes. He said it's in the bank in my name. I tore the papers up and threw them at him."

"Why? You were angry because I didn't write," Silas said, answering his own question. He had tossed his hat aside, and moved to stand only a few yards from her, a puzzled frown on his face. He was handsome and he would draw attention everywhere he went, and she suspected he was pleased to do so. The carriage would make everyone in town take notice. And she had a feeling that it was going to prove more difficult than she had expected to convince Silas of her decision.

"That was part of why I didn't take the money. It wasn't mine to use, and I'd rather have had you come home than send money. Money wasn't that important."

"I don't know how you can say that. This place needs attention. I'm glad to see you did do some repairs. It has new walls all along this side."

"Yes. We had to do that, and I used my own money. Pa had an accident and blew a hole in the wall," she said, feeling as if she were talking to a stranger.

"Paddy is the same as ever," he said impatiently.

"No, not quite. He's stopped inventing so much of the time and he's into carving more."

"I'm sorry, Mary, that it took me so long," Silas said. "I'll make it all up to you, the years, the silence." He picked up a stack of boxes and held them out to her. "Open your presents."

"Not yet, Silas. Sit down and let me talk to you. Where did you make your strike?"

"In California. And it was a big one." He stared at her with a frown, and she saw he was beginning to comprehend that things had changed.

She looked at the large ring on his finger, the gold pocket watch and chain draped across his satin vest, the soft woolen coat and trousers and polished boots. "You got exactly what you wanted," she said quietly.

"Yes. We can do as we please, live where we want. I want to take you to a big city. I always thought I'd want to come back to Denver, but now I've seen other cities. As fancy as Denver is, I don't want to stay on the frontier. I want to go east."

"Silas, you were gone too long. You left me alone. I didn't hear from you, I didn't know whether you were dead or alive until Dan came to Denver."

"I promised you I'd come back."

"People can't always keep their promises, and you know it. I didn't hear anything. I didn't know if I'd have to wait one year or twenty years." She took a deep breath. "And I really wasn't in love with you—while you were gone, I found that out."

He frowned. "What are you talking about? I've dreamed of you. I've—"

"Silas, you've dreamed of a woman who was part memory, part imagination. We weren't wildly in love when you left. You love gold a lot more than you love me. I didn't know what love was when you left. You were good and kind and fun and handsome, but it wasn't love."

"What are you saying?"

"I didn't wait for you."

"Lord! You're married?" he asked, standing in agitation.

"No. But I'm in love and I expect to marry him."

"It's just because I was gone. I love you now, and I loved you when I left Denver."

"No, you didn't and you don't. You couldn't have left me like that and never written or come back or anything. It's over, Silas. I love someone else."

"Give me a chance," he urged, crossing the room to take her hand. "You have to give me a chance."

"I know what I want," she said, raising her chin, "just as you always knew exactly what you wanted. And you went after it."

"I want a chance to win you back."

"It's far too late. I'm deeply in love, and it's forever."

He swore and stared at her. "I've dreamed about you all these years. I've wanted you and been true to you."

"Silas, you were true to yourself and your wishes. I'm sorry. You could have taken me with you—you know I would have gone."

"A man can't prospect with a woman hanging on his coattails," he said stiffly.

"I'm sorry."

"I'm not going to give up so easily."

"I'm getting married and I'm very much in love with him."

"Who's the man?"

She wondered how long it would take him to ask. This was the moment she had dreaded the most. "He fought this as hard as anyone can. I finally won him over to see that I wouldn't wait and it wouldn't matter when you came back."

Silas scowled, his eyes narrowing. Anger surfaced in his eyes, changing to rage. "Who is it?"

"You have to listen to reason. He didn't want to marry me because of you. He tried to resist what he felt and what I wanted."

"It's Dan."

"Yes, it is."

Silas swore, his voice so filled with rage that suddenly she realized how little she knew him. He had always been gentle and easygoing with her, but the man in front of her now was far from that. He spun around. "Where is he?"

"Silas, don't harm him," she said, becoming deeply alarmed. She had seen enough fights in Denver to know when she faced a man on the verge of violence. ''Silas, please! I could never forgive you.''

''Where does Dan work? I'll find him if you don't tell me.''

''Promise me you won't do anything rash. Promise me!''

He swore and stormed out of the house to his carriage. Mary flew out the back, racing to the carriage house. She took her horse and climbed on bareback to ride astride, urging it across the back of the lot to the next street. Dan was working a few blacks away from the boardinghouse in a newer, fancier part of town, and now the distance seemed vast.

There had been no mistaking the rage in Silas' eyes. Her heart thudded with fear. Silas had changed, and she was terrified of what he might do to Dan. And Dan would be caught by surprise. She urged Blackie faster.

Dan opened his mail as he rode down the street. He had a letter from Hattie, and his gaze skimmed it swiftly. She was answering his letter, and they were coming a week early for the wedding. He reread the letter, smiling, thankful again she had gone home with Javier. And he would get to see them both for the wedding! He let out a whoop of joy, remembered he was riding down Larimer, and looked around sheepishly, but no one seemed to be paying him any attention. He turned to head toward Holladay and rode around to the back of Dulcie's, turning the reins over to a stablehand.

Dan strode down the shadowed hallway, going to Dulcie's room. Her door was open and she was brushing her hair.

He tapped on the door, and she gazed at him in the mirror, turning around to face him. She wore a green gingham dress and her hair was loose, falling over her shoulders. He didn't feel a flicker of sexual interest in her, regarding her only as an old friend.

'' 'Afternoon, Dulcie.'' He looked around the room

but didn't see any of the things he had left with her. He closed the door. "Are you busy?"

"No. Come in, Dan. You've become a stranger." She sat down, crossing her legs, the gown falling open to reveal black stockings on her long, shapely legs. He sat down on the edge of a chair.

"I came to get my things and to say good-bye."

"I wondered how long it would take. I've bundled up your things for you. They're all ready to go. I'm not much of one for good-byes. One thing, Dan, I'm glad you stopped waiting for Silas or feeling guilt you shouldn't have felt. And I'm glad it's Miss O'Malley instead of Miss Shumacher."

"I'm glad too, Dulcie." His gaze swept over her. "We had some good times."

She crossed the room to him and he rose to his feet. "Your things are in the armoire, wrapped up in your shirt. Are you in a hurry?" she asked in a sultry tone, running her hands over his chest. "We could have one last good-bye."

Dan gazed down at her and realized how deeply in love with Mary he was. He couldn't resist Dulcie when he had thought he would marry Louisa, but now he didn't want to love anyone except Mary. And he couldn't bear to betray her trust. He stepped back, taking Dulcie's hands in his, his voice as gentle as possible, because he felt a fondness for her. Their memories were good.

"Dulcie, I really love her. I can't do anything that might hurt her. I couldn't live with myself."

"Well, well! So you finally lost your heart to a woman! I never thought I'd see the day. You're lucky, Dan, that she loves you back. That she didn't want to marry Silas."

"Dulcie, if you don't think I know how lucky I am— I thank heaven every day, and all through the day!"

"Go get your things." She heard a commotion in the hall, but someone else could see about it. Whatever it was, it didn't involve her, and she didn't want to lose the last minutes with Dan.

"I had a pistol here, Dulcie," he said.

"It's tied up in your shirt. The hammer's on the empty, so it's safe."

Standing in the corner across the room from her, Dan grinned, staring at her with the bundle of his belongings in his hands. "Dulcie, thanks for the memories. They were damned good."

"If it were anyone else except Mary O'Malley, I'd try to keep you for an hour. You two deserve each other Dan. It's high time she had someone to look after her, and she'll be good for you."

"You're a good woman, Dulcie."

"Oh, hell! I'm not so good. I just know when I'm defeated. Think I can have a good-bye kiss?"

He laughed, moving toward her. The door burst open and a man stepped into the room, a pistol in his hand.

It took only a glance at his white hair and pale face and eyes, and Dan knew that Silas had already talked to Mary.

"You son of a bitch! You took my woman while I was gone!"

"Silas, are you going to give me a chance to explain?"

"Shut up!"

"Silas, Mary O'Malley made up her own mind," Dulcie said. "I know Dan fought—"

"You bastard!" Silas cut across Dulcie's words without glancing at her. "I trusted you. Trust! I brought you a present of gold ingots. Well, the hell with that, you sneaky, lying son of a bitch."

Dan's mind raced. His pistol was tied in the bundle of clothing. Silas' pistol was aimed at Dan's heart, and Dan knew how well Silas could shoot. He tried to work his fingers into the clothing, but Dulcie had it tied tightly together. He grasped the butt of the pistol, but he couldn't pull it free.

"We'll see how much she loves you when you're dead! I trusted you all these years!"

There was another commotion in the hall, and Mary burst into the room, screaming at Silas.

His eyes narrowed as he squeezed the trigger.

26

As Silas aimed, Dulcie lunged at him, knocking his arm higher. The blast was deafening.

Dan slammed against the wall aware of a burning pain, hearing Mary scream again. Soon the sounds faded, becoming dim and disappearing into black oblivion.

Mary raced to Dan, seeing the spreading crimson spurt of blood. She felt his pulse and turned around to Dulcie. "Send someone to get Doc Felton!" She saw the butt of Dan's pistol in the bundle of clothes and yanked it up, turning to confront Silas.

"If you really loved me, you would never have done that. He was willing to step aside and watch me marry you because he thought it was what I wanted. That's love, Silas! Now go, before I shoot. They don't hang women."

"Mary . . ."

"Go!"

Having given orders to Grizzly to get the doctor, Dulcie took Silas' arm and steered him out of the room, leading him down the hall. He seemed in a daze, letting her take him where she wanted. They entered a bedroom, and a woman dressed only in a lacy chemise looked up. "Tille, let us have your room."

"All these years, I trusted him," Silas said.

"Silas, you left her. You didn't send a letter or come back or anything. And it was for years! Dan tried to fight what he felt. And you may hang now, and then what good will your gold do?"

"Hang?"

"You just shot Dan."

Silas buried his face in his hands. "Damn. I've planned everything, where we'll live, what I'll do, the children we'll have. I bought her a ring."

"You stay right here. I'll be back." Dulcie went back to her room as Doc Felton came down the hall.

"Where is he? Who was shot?"

'Dan Castle. He's in my room, right there." She followed him inside.

Mary knelt over him, pressing his shirt to the wound to stanch the flow of blood. She looked up as Doc Felton knelt on the other side of Dan.

"Good girl. Take away the cloth now. Wash your hands, and you can help me."

Dulcie took Mary's arm. "Come down to the kitchen and we'll get some hot water."

In minutes they were back and Mary knelt beside Dan. "How is he?"

The bullet went clean through and nothing vital is torn. Good thing the man was a damned lousy shot."

"He wasn't. Dulcie hit his arm."

Doc Felton glanced at her and continued working in silence, giving her directions.

"He'll live?"

"Yes, he'll live, Miss O'Malley." He raised his head. "Dulcie, can we put him in a bed?"

"Can he be moved to the boardinghouse?" Mary asked quickly.

Doc Felton looked down at Dan. "Do it tomorrow, maybe. Not now."

"He can stay in my bed," Dulcie said. "I'll get Grizzly to help you move him."

A man filled the doorway, and Dulcie paused to face Sheriff Borden. "Someone sent for me. Said there had been a shooting and a man was killed."

"He's not dead," Doc Felton said, standing up and rolling down his sleeves. "Come help me move him to the bed."

"Who did it?"

Everyone was silent, and the sheriff looked around

the room. "Come on, Dulcie, who did it? I'm going
to find out, and you don't need trouble. And you don't
want him to come back and finish the job."

"Silas Eustice," Mary said.

"He's in a room across the hall," Dulcie added.

Sheriff Borden and Doc Felton moved Dan to the
bed. He looked pale as snow, and blood was smeared
all over his clothing and on his jaw and chest. A fresh
white bandage was tightly wrapped around the wound.
"Dulcie, get me some more hot water. Miss O'Malley, you can clean him up now."

"Now, where's Eustice?" Sheriff Borden asked
again.

"Come with me." Dulcie left, and Doc Felton put
away his instruments. "I'll leave something to relieve
the pain. If any unusual bleeding occurs, come get
me."

He closed the door, and it was quiet. Mary took
Dan's hand in hers, leaning down to press her cheek
against his hand. In a few minutes the door opened
and Mary looked up to see Dulcie. She closed the door
behind her, moving quietly across the room to stand
on the other side of the bed. "Sheriff Borden arrested
Silas."

"Doc Felton said Dan would be all right."

"It's against the law to shoot someone. Besides, let
Silas cool off a little before he's set loose again. It'll
give him time to get used to the changes. You can stay
here with Dan. I can stay in another room."

"Thank you," Mary said, accepting at once, because she didn't want to leave Dan's side.

"Grizzly can come help nurse him. You may need
a man until he gets up and going."

"I can call Grizzly if I need him, thanks. Is there
someone who can get word to my house that I won't
be back? And to my brothers. Michael might look for
me."

"I'll see to it, honey. You just take good care of
Dan."

"Thank you, Dulcie."

Dulcie laughed. "I guess my hair-fixing job did the trick, huh?"

"Yes." Mary blushed and smiled.

Dulcie chuckled as she moved around the room. She paused to look at Mary. "He just came to get his things."

"He told me he was going to."

"He's all yours, honey. He can't even see other women."

Mary looked at Dan, her heart full of love, hating that he was hurt, but so thankful he would live. She ran her fingers over his knuckles, thinking about Silas. "I'll go talk to Silas again. He's going to have to see that I don't love him."

"I think he's going to have a lot of women who'll be happy to take your place. He looks like a king."

"He said he did well."

It was hours later when Dan stirred. He groaned and turned his head, his eyes opening to focus on Mary. He frowned and groaned. "How bad is it?"

"You'll be all right. Doc Felton gave me something to relieve your pain. I'll get some water."

"The hell with that. I don't want to lie here unconscious. Help me sit up."

"I don't think you should."

"Get around on this side, Mary, and help me."

"I think you should lie still."

He gave her a look that made her get up and move around to the other side of the bed. She had to crawl up on the bed to reach him.

"I'm still at Dulcie's."

"Yes, she said I can stay with you tonight. Doc Felton didn't think you should be moved until tomorrow. Dan—"

He wrapped his good arm around her. "Now, help me."

She knew enough about men to know when to argue and when to oblige, so she helped him. He groaned, and she bit her lip.

"There," he said with satisfaction, sitting up straight. "Jesus, that hurts!"

"Well, it wouldn't if you'd lie still."

He turned his head, his arm tightening around her, and he kissed her, stopping her words. It was a hard, passionate kiss that finally made her forget his injury for a few seconds. When he released her, he looked into her eyes. "I was so damned scared he was going to do me in and I wouldn't get to marry you."

"You've got to be still. How can you think about kisses when you're hurt?"

He kissed her again until she responded and her heart beat in flurries. When he released her, he studied her. "That makes me feel better."

"I think I'm in for some interesting years," she said in a breathless voice that finally softened his features.

"Mary, I was afraid we'd lost everything."

"I tried to tell him. He's been to St. Louis, Dan. He made his discovery in California. He took time to go to St. Louis to get his fancy clothes and a new carriage. That's not a man wildly in love."

"Sure as hell not. I'd have come home covered in dirt from the damned mine if it meant getting back to you!"

"I know it. Now, you have to let me prop you up against the pillows. You should lie still."

"Did Doc say I had to?"

"No, because I don't think it occurred to him that you wouldn't. He left something to keep you quiet and out of pain."

"I'd rather hurt like hell and be conscious. Where's Silas? And where's my pistol? I want it within reach."

"Sheriff Borden arrested Silas."

"Oh, damn!"

"Dulcie said it will give him time to think things over and adjust to the changes."

"I'd still like my pistol close at hand."

She climbed off the bed as carefully as possible without jiggling him.

"Dammit, I hate to be trussed up like a Christmas turkey! I'd like to do what I want with you," he said in a husky voice, watching her cross the room. Shivers of pleasure ran through Mary as she turned back to see the burning passion in his gaze.

She blushed and laughed. "Dan, you're supposed to be weak, and hurt, and thinking about other things."

"I'm weak and I hurt like hell."

"That's all the more reason then you should—"

"Should what?"

She placed the pistol on the table beside the bed. "If you're getting this feisty, I want you moved to the boardinghouse and out of this bedroom," she said firmly.

He opened his mouth as if to argue, then snapped it shut and nodded. "Get a wagon and your brothers. I can get home to my house and you can take care of me. If I go to the boardinghouse, you'll cook and clean and nurse and work like three people."

"My brothers might not let me stay at your house."

"Sure they will if they think I might not survive. Besides, Michael owes it to me."

Mary left the room to find Dulcie. She was suddenly assailed by shyness. She was unaccustomed to a bordello and was afraid to knock on doors, but she knew the way to the kitchen and, to her relief, found Dulcie standing beside the cook.

"Dan wants to go home. He said to find my brothers."

"I'll do that. Want to take him something to eat?" Without waiting for an answer, Dulcie took down a plate and filled it with potatoes and chicken. "Here. If I know Dan, he'll eat every bite."

Mary carried the plate back to Dan. He ate and then leaned back against the pillows, his face pale and a grim set to his mouth.

"Dan, take something for the pain," she said as she took the plate and set it on a table.

"I will when I get home. Right now, I want to be able to move."

"Stubborn, stubborn."

He opened one eye and grinned at her. "Come here, Mary."

His words stirred another ripple of pleasure in her,

because his voice and gaze told her what he wanted. "Dan, can't you remember you've just been shot? I think you're delirious."

"Indeed, I am," he said in a husky voice. "Come closer." She tried to avoid jiggling the bed, but saw him wince as she moved. "This is absurd. You should be quiet."

"This is the best medicine in the world," he said before he kissed her.

The door opened and Mary turned around, blushing until she felt on fire as Dulcie came in. "Your brothers are here."

Mary scooted off the bed and went to the door to meet them.

"How is he?" Michael asked, stepping into the room with Brian behind him. "We brought the wagon."

Dan lay back against the pillows, his eyes closed. "Doc Felton said he'll be all right. Dulcie ruined the shot because she hit Silas's hand," Mary answered.

"Silas?"

"I thought you knew."

Michael looked at Brian.

"He's been arrested," Mary added hastily. "Now, don't you two do anything to him. He's in jail and Dan will live."

"Did he shoot to kill?"

"What matters is, he didn't kill him. Dan wants to be moved to his house, and I'm going to take care of him."

To her surprise, both brothers nodded. "Doc say it was okay to move him?"

Dan groaned, and Mary walked to the bed. "Did you bring the wagon?"

"Yes," Michael answered. "And a board. If we can lift him to this board, we can carry him out on it and place him in the wagon."

Michael laid the board on the bed beside Dan, and Brian shook out a blanket to cover it.

"Dan," Mary said in a louder tone, knowing that

Dan was conscious and fully aware of what was happening. He groaned and opened his eyes.

"Sorry," Michael said.

"Don't do anything to Silas, boys," Dan said. "Promise me you won't."

They looked at each other, and Michael nodded with obvious reluctance.

"Brian?" Dan said into the silence.

"I won't hurt him unless it's self-defense."

"Thanks," Dan mumbled.

"Ready to move?"

"Mary, you go out and wait."

"I will not."

"Oh, hell. All right. I'm ready."

They moved him and he groaned, Mary watching as his fist clenched and his knuckles turned white. His face became ashen, and suddenly he relaxed.

"He fainted," Mary said.

"We can move him better if he has," Michael said. "I'm surprised Doc said he could be moved. Let's go, Brian. Easy, now."

Mary gathered up Dan's pistol and clothing, pausing once as she faced Dulcie. "Thank you."

"Take care of him," Dulcie said, and turned away quickly. Mary hurried outside to climb into the wagon beside Dan. He didn't regain consciousness until he was home in bed. She watched his wound continually to see if the jolting had started it bleeding, but so far the bandage was as white as it had been when Doc Felton finished.

"Michael said he would come back to help you around. Now," she said, pouring liquid into a spoon, "you got moved to your house just as you wanted. You are taking this, just as I want."

"Aw, Mary, come on."

"You're home, and it will be good for you to sleep. I know you hurt. Open your mouth."

He did, and swallowed the medicine. In a short time he was sleeping peacefully. Michael came late in the afternoon and helped Dan up while Mary went to the kitchen to cook. After he had eaten, she made him

take another dose of medicine, and in a short time his
eyes closed.

"Mary, I'm going to sleep. Come lie down beside
me."

She moved close to him and he put his good arm
around her, groaning with pain when he moved. "Dan,
you should lie still."

"Shh. Everything's fine now."

She lay against him, knowing that in minutes he
would be sleeping quietly, thankful he was all right.
She spent the time thinking about the wedding dress
she was making. Finally she slept, moving out of Dan's
embrace because she thought he would sleep better.
She put his arm down at his side, then scooted close
against him to sleep.

He was better the next day, sitting up when she came
in with his breakfast, his feet on the floor. "Doc Felton will be by today. He'll go into shock."

"He likes a healthy, cooperative patient."

"How would you know?"

"He told me when he was riding out to take care of
Michael. He said Michael would be a good patient.
And he was."

"He hasn't had one the likes of you."

Dan laughed. "The move didn't hurt me, and don't
tell me you wouldn't rather be here than there."

"You're right," she said happily.

In the middle of the morning, Doc Felton came and
declared the patient was doing fine. Dan had been up
and had eaten breakfast, and as soon as the doctor left,
he went back to sleep. Mary tiptoed out and went down
to hitch his horse to the carriage. First she went home
to change clothes and see that things were running
smoothly. Then she gathered up some of her things,
put on her blue bonnet, and drove to the jail.

They let her into Silas' cell to talk to him alone. He
looked ridiculous sitting in jail in all his fine clothes.
He had shed his coat and rolled up his sleeves, his
vest hung open, and his hair fell across his forehead.
He raked it back with his fingers and stood up when

she entered the cell. In spite of his rumpled appearance and the jail, he was a strikingly handsome man who looked as if he had found a million in gold.

"Dan will be all right."

Silas looked away from her, a muscle in his jaw working. "Silas, I want you to listen to me. I don't think it would have mattered if I had never known Dan. It was just too long a time."

"I could have won you back."

"Perhaps, but I love Dan in a way I've never loved before. And he fought it as hard as a man can fight anything. He didn't court me or try to talk me into forgetting you. The only time he took me out was when we first met because he had promised you he would."

"God, that was stupid!" He finally faced her. "All right, Mary. I believe you. It was a shock. All those years I've lived with dreams of you, dreams of what we would do together."

"Silas, you've dreamed of what you wanted to do. You have no idea what I'd like."

He blinked. "I think I could have made you happy with my plans." He rubbed his jaw, gazing beyond her. "I guess I should have done things differently, but I can't look back with regrets now. I've been luckier than most."

"I don't want you to hate Dan."

"I can't ever feel friendly toward him. I won't try to shoot him again. Thank God he's alive. I don't want to hang now and never be able to use the fortune I found." He smiled with a cynical look in his eye. "You'd give up being the wife of an enormously wealthy man to marry Castle?"

"Yes."

He shrugged. "Sheriff!" he called. "I think we might as well say good-bye," he said coldly, and she didn't think he would ever understand.

She nodded and left when the sheriff opened the door. Behind him stood Dulcie, dressed in a blue faille dress with a trim hat perched on her head.

"You're a busy man, Mr. Eustice," Sheriff Borden

said with a note of envy. "Miss Dulcie wants to see you."

"Come in, Dulcie."

Mary nodded to Dulcie as she passed.

Dan was sitting up on the side of the bed when Mary came into the room.

"I thought maybe you'd left me for good."

"No."

He stood up.

"Should you get out of bed?"

"I want to see what I can do. Come help me."

She put down her packages and moved to his side. He pulled her to his good side, winced as his grip tightened around her, and leaned down to kiss her. She was afraid she would hurt him, and stood with her arms at her sides, then tentatively put her arm around his waist.

Finally she moved away. "Dan, you'd better stop. I brought your mail."

He sat down in a rocking chair, easing himself back carefully. She sat on the floor beside him, sewing tiny pearls on a strip of material for her dress while Dan read his mail aloud. She felt his hands in her hair, constantly running it through his fingers, and she leaned back against his legs, wanting to touch him.

"I've finally heard from all of them. Hattie and Javier will arrive a week before the wedding. Catalina wrote that along with Ta-ne-haddle and his family, she and Luke and the children will be here five days before. Here's April's letter, and they're planning to come with Luke and his family. Tomorrow I want you to help me dress. I'm going to see Silas. I want Sheriff Borden to set him free. I won't press charges and I won't testify."

She nodded, agreeing with him.

Six days later he could move around with ease, and she moved back home in spite of Dan trying to cajole her into staying longer. He let her go, knowing Mary deserved to be courted even the short time that was left before their wedding. He took her out at night, and came to call during the day. Work on the Waltham house slowed because of Dan's injury, but because of the wedding, Michael delayed his plans to leave Denver and went to work for Dan so the house could be finished on schedule.

As the wedding approached, Dan and Mary both became so busy they could see little of each other. She was sewing and tending to last-minute details about the boardinghouse, while Dan was putting in every hour possible on his work so he could take time off afterward.

And then the wedding was only a week away. It was a hot Saturday in July, the sun shining brightly, trees and lawns green and flowers in bloom. Hattie and Javier were waiting for Dan when he came home from work. He saw the carriage in the yard and ran up the front steps into the house. Hattie stood in the kitchen at the sink, getting supper ready, and Javier was seated at the table reading a newspaper.

It had been so long since Dan had seen his mother. He crossed the room in long strides to hug her tightly, his wound having healed enough that he didn't have to favor it.

"Ma, you're as beautiful as ever!"

"Oh, Dan, I'm so happy for you." She leaned back. "I can't wait to meet her."

"Mary's special. You'll like her." He turned to hug Javier. "Pa, God I'm glad you're here!" he exclaimed, his gaze sweeping over Javier, who had filled out somewhat since the last time Dan had seen him. He looked better, far happier than before.

"We're glad to be here. And we're so happy for you, Dan. When do we get to meet her?"

"Tonight. I asked her for supper, because I thought you would get here in time."

"Go wash up and get her so we can meet her," Hattie said.

"Sure, Ma," he answered, needing no urging. An hour later he returned with Mary. Hattie hugged her, and Javier gravely acknowledged the introduction.

Mary was always thankful later for that quiet evening to get to know them. She was astounded at Hattie's beauty, seeing where Dan got his handsome looks. In another day the rest of his family came, and Mary was lost in a bewildering group of relatives that she tried to sort out.

"Dan, the women in your family are gorgeous!" she said that night as she stood alone with him in back of the boardinghouse after a party with all their relatives.

"That they are, and we'll have another gorgeous one in two days."

"I don't look like them. My word, Catalina is striking and April is so beautiful, it's difficult to keep from staring. Lottie is beautiful. Even if she isn't a blood relative, she might as well be. Your mother is exceptionally pretty."

He kissed her throat and ear. "None of them are half as beautiful as you, Mary," he said solemnly.

Happy and secure in his love, she hugged him. "You're blind, Dan Castle, but I'm glad!"

After a few minutes she pushed him away. "I should go inside."

He wrapped his arm around her waist to walk her to the door. "Honey, I heard today that Silas left town."

"I'm not surprised. He didn't want to settle in Denver. He told me he wanted to go back east. He wants a big city."

"He took Dulcie with him."

"Dulcie?"

"I heard he married her."

Mary thought about his news. "If they married, I wish them happiness."

"Dulcie could make him happy."

"I hope I don't hear a forlorn note in your voice."

He hauled her around to kiss her passionately, bending over her until she had to cling to him. Finally he swung her up and released her. "Does that tell you how forlorn I feel?"

"Sometimes you make me almost faint!"

"I don't want you to faint," he said dryly.

* * *

When Dan went back home he sat up late talking to his family. The children were already asleep, and in a short time Hattie and Javier went to bed. Then the wives left, so Dan sat with Ta-ne-haddle, Noah, and Luke. Ta-ne-haddle and Noah finally said good night, and when Luke stood up, Dan spoke to him. "Luke, wait a minute."

Luke sat back down, stretching out his long legs, unbuttoning his shirt and pushing it open.

"I had trouble with bounty hunters a short time ago."

"Oh, hell, I thought maybe that had ended forever."

"There's a man here in town who knows my identity. There are wanted posters at the jail."

Luke's green eyes met his. "And?"

"I want to go back and stand trial, try to clear my name. I don't want to go through life with this hanging over me. I'd like your help."

Luke thought about it, sitting in silence, and Dan waited. "What does Mary say about it?"

"She agreed when I pointed out that we wouldn't want it to come up later, when we have children."

"It's a risk, Dan. They could hang you."

"I know, but you're a good lawyer."

"I don't know if I'd want to risk it," Luke said thoughtfully. "Sentiment can change in a day. I can understand why you want to have it done with, but I can't urge you to go back. I wouldn't."

Dan sighed, staring at the hearth. "I'll give it some more thought, but after the last time . . . I was just lucky Mary's brothers came along. Those two would have killed me and taken my body back for the reward. I hate living with that hanging over me. And if we have children and it happened later . . ."

"I understand completely, but the more time that passes, the less likely it is to happen. Unless you have someone who really hates you here in Denver."

Dan shrugged. "I have enemies. Silas for one, and also another man, Reuben Knelville. The problems between us have diminished. I took out the woman he plans to marry. They'll be married in another two months. I don't think I'll ever bother him again, but I don't know. Will you be available, say, in three or four months?''

"I'll be available whenever you want. Give it some thought, though. I think the risks are bad.''

The day of the wedding came, a Saturday morning at Mary's church. Dressed in ice-blue taffeta with white lace and white silk ribbons, Mary went down the aisle on Paddy's arm, barely glancing at the rows of Dan's family, her brothers, and friends watching. All she could see was Dan in his handsome new black suit. They repeated their vows and Dan kissed her briefly with a tight hug. Then they went back to the boardinghouse for a reception.

Finally Mary and Dan left for the new depot to take the train. It was Mary's first time on a train, but that excitement was overridden by the excitement of her wedding. The family and guests had piled into buggies and wagons to ride to the depot to see them off. Michael and Brian set off firecrackers, sending one of the horses into a run, but they soon had it back under control.

Kissing Hattie good-bye, Dan picked up his bride to carry her aboard the train, and they waved at everyone. Dan had rented a private car and ordered champagne, and when the train pulled away, they sat at the open window waving to everyone until they were out of town on their way to a hotel in Cheyenne. As Denver slid past and out of sight, Dan turned Mary to face him. ''You look beautiful,'' he said, removing her veil to lay it aside. He pulled pins out of her hair, and long locks fell over her shoulders while he leaned forward to kiss her. ''I want to take forever, love,'' he whispered, as more locks came down, the pins discarded on the floor. He framed her face with his hands. ''I'll do everything in my power to make you happy,'' he said in a husky voice. He leaned forward again to brush her lips.

His mouth was warm, tantalizing, and Mary felt love and desire fan through her with a white-hot blaze. She adored him and longed to have him love her the rest of the day and all night long. His mouth settled more firmly, his tongue playing over hers, demanding a response she gave eagerly. He stood up, balancing with the gentle sway of the train, and shed his coat, the dark cravat, and his fine linen shirt. She drew a deep breath, reaching for him, seeing his arousal strain against the soft woolen pants. He sat down beside her, taking her in his strong arms. Her hands played over his shoulders while he reached behind her to unfasten the long row of tiny buttons down her back.

He kissed her with tenderness that changed to passion, and finally he leaned away, peeling off her dress. Taffeta rustled as he pushed it down around her waist. She felt her cheeks warm beneath his blatant perusal. Her lacy chemise hid little from his view, and he bent his head to kiss her through the material.

Dan stood up again, bracing his leg against the seat and pulling Mary up. The dress slipped down and he lifted her out of it, carrying her to the bed. Sunlight from the open windows spilled over her, making her auburn hair look like flames as it spread over the pillows. He pushed away her chemise, drawing it down and dropping it aside, pulling down her underdrawers and discarding them. He felt as if he would burst with need as he stood and looked at her while he unbuckled his belt.

Mary watched him through half-closed eyes, thinking he was handsome beyond belief and she could never tire of looking at him. His body was corded with muscles, the fresh scar on his shoulder still red, old scars white on his dark skin. His hips were narrow, his stomach rippled with muscle, his arousal throbbing and ready, yet he stretched out beside her to pull her against his long length and wrap his arms around her and kiss her. He pushed her back and knelt over her to shower her with kisses, moving down her body, his hands caressing her slender legs.

"Dan, please," she whispered, moving so he was between her thighs. He gazed at her with a burning hunger that made her heart pound wildly. "Please," she said, reaching for him, and he came down to possess her, thrusting slowly into her softness. She thought she would faint from the sensations that assailed her. She wrapped her legs around him, moving with him, clinging to him while he whispered endearments.

He said her name hoarsely, and she rose to meet him while passion burst in release. She cried out in ecstasy, her eyes squeezed shut as she held him, feeling his heart pounding with hers, feeling a union that was more than physical.

Passion ebbed, and Dan's weight came down on her. She held him close, relishing the feel of his strong body pressing so hard against hers. She traced her finger along his smooth-shaven jaw, thinking it had been the perfect wedding day, a promise for a glowing future.

They stayed shut in their train car in seclusion all the way to Cheyenne. They dressed to go to the hotel, and as soon as they were in their suite, Dan undressed her, his hands moving with haste, dropping clothes as he led her toward the bed.

"Dan, I barely saw the train and I didn't see any of the towns we passed. I haven't seen Cheyenne, and I haven't seen the hotel, and I'm starving right now."

"The hotel is sending up food, love. I fed you on the train, but I can't help it if you wouldn't eat."

She giggled. "How could I eat, sitting naked on your lap?"

He grinned, drawing his finger down her bare hip. "So you want to get out of bed and go somewhere?"

"No!" She sat up, her red hair cascading over her pale shoulders as she looked down at him. He put his hands behind his head, gazing at her openly. Her voice was breathless as she tangled her fingers in the soft curls on his chest. "No. I don't want to go anywhere. I was simply making an observation. We could have stayed home."

"No, we couldn't have. Michael would have had a crisis, or one of my houses would have needed some attention, or Brian would need you, or Paddy would blow up the boardinghouse. No, I want you without interruptions or interference.''

"Dan, is there any chance you might change your mind about going back to New Mexico Territory?''

He sobered instantly and reached out to wind his hand in her hair. "Yes. If you don't want me to go back, I won't.''

She looked down, running her fingers over him. "I couldn't bear it if they found you guilty. On the other hand, I understand why you want to go.''

"We don't have to worry about it now. Mary, Reuben Knelville knows who I am.''

"How do you know?''

"A hunch, but I'd bet everything I'm right.''

"Everything?" she asked, unable to keep her mind on problems or people or anything except Dan. Instantly worry left his expression as his gaze raked over her and his fingers drifted across her bare breasts.

"No, not *everything,"* he said, letting his hand drift down across her, moving between her legs.

She gasped and closed her eyes as he kissed her.

They came home two weeks later. Michael had made them a table for their dining room as his wedding present, and they knew he was still working on the chairs. In Cheyenne they had ordered two new chairs for the parlor and a rocking chair for their bedroom. They settled into a routine, and Dan stopped work promptly at half-past five every afternoon, hurrying home to her.

He waited for a month, and then one night as they lay in bed, he tightened his arm around her. "Mary, I've thought about it constantly. I want to go back to New Mexico and I've written Luke. I go in October. He'll meet me at the border and go with me.''

"I want to go.''

"No.''

She sat up and gazed down at him in the moonlight. "You have to let me,'' she said quietly.

Dan heard the determination in her voice and knew he had married a strong woman. Mary would be a comfort. He nodded. "I don't think it's wise, and I'd like to protect you, but if you want—"

"Thank you," she said in satisfaction, lying back down beside him. She stared into the dark, thinking about Dan on trial for murder, and suddenly she was afraid. She turned to him to wrap her arms around him and cling to him tightly.

He felt her tears on his bare chest. "Hey! Mary, honey, if you cry, I won't go."

"Yes, you should go. You have to win, Dan. You just have to!"

Mary went out the next morning, hunting down Michael. "Michael, I need to talk to you alone. I didn't want Dan to know I was coming."

Michael scowled and turned to stare at her. He stood beside the horses, feeding them. "Isn't he good to you?"

She laughed, for a moment forgetting the problem. "Of course. He's wonderful!" She sobered, dreading what lay ahead. "He's going to give himself up in New Mexico Territory and stand trial."

"Why?"

"Because it will always hang over him. If you and Brian hadn't come along that night, he would have been killed." She carefully explained, and finally Michael nodded.

"I guess I understand why, but damned if I'd want to go back."

"That's what I want to talk to you about. If they find him guilty and they try to hang him, I want someone to get him out of jail and safely away."

Michael stared at her. She faced him squarely. "I know it would mean putting yourself in jeopardy, so if you want to say no, I'll understand. There are others I can ask. Brian is too young, but Dan has a brother, and a brother-in-law, and Ta-ne-haddle."

"Forget them, Mary. I'll go and I'll do it, but Brian isn't too young. We can do better together."

She bit her lip. "If something happened to either one of you, I don't think I could live."

He grinned. "We'll be okay. And don't you worry. We'll get him out."

"Michael, don't sound so happy over it."

"Leave it to us and forget it. When does he go?"

"We go—"

"You're going?"

"Yes, and you can't keep me from it, Michael. Dan has already agreed."

"All right. When?"

"In two weeks," she said woodenly, the future suddenly becoming a giant unknown. Her gaze ran over her brother's solid shoulders and chest and she felt a little better. "Michael, Dan may have to shoot his way out. He's been practicing again, and he's a good shot. He doesn't know I've asked you to do this."

Michael grinned. "I heard about his shooting in camp from Jethro when he came through here. And I've seen Dan shoot. I know he can. Better than anyone else I've seen."

"He says his brother Luke is as quick."

"Don't worry, Mary. I promise we won't let him hang," he said, but she knew Michael was young and an optimist, and he couldn't keep such a promise with certainty. She went back home, dreading each day and clinging to Dan and loving him at night with desperation, praying that Luke Danby was as good a lawyer as Dan claimed he was.

27

Catalina paced the floor of the bedroom, waving a letter in the air. "You have to stop him! *Madre de Dios!*"

"He's a grown man, Catalina. I can't stop him."

"If you won't defend him, he won't do this!"

"How can I refuse to defend my brother?"

She threw up her hands and whirled around to put
her chin on her hand, her elbow resting on the chiffonier. Smiling, Luke crossed the room to face her.
"He's doing what he wants, so calm down."

"He just got married. He will hurt his sweet little
wife. She's a baby."

"No, she's not," Luke said gently. "She's as strong
as you are, and probably as feisty. He told me a little
about her. Mary has run a boardinghouse for years."

"That's cooking and cleaning."

"And she's taken care of a tipsy father and raised
two younger brothers."

"Hmpf. He will break her heart! And what if you
can't get him off? It will divide the family again!"

"I'll do my best."

If I had just married you, I would not want you
turning yourself in for a trial where you might hang!"

"Honey, it's something he's tired of living with. And
he's afraid someone may kill him one day. There's a
reward whether he's dead or alive, which makes shooting him in the back mighty tempting. Would you want
to live with that? Or explain that to your sons?"

"Luke, I'm frightened for him. We never see him

much, but he's so much like Hattie, and I know he's good. He's part of the same blood as you.''

"You have a soft heart," he said, hugging her. She clung to him, her head against his chest.

"I wouldn't be able to stand it if I were Mary."

"You've stood a lot of things."

"I want to go with you."

"Catalina, trials like that can get people stirred up and angry. And it's in an area that's very remote. It won't be in a city. It'll be a little adobe jail surrounded by the local people."

"I want to go. Mary will need a woman with her."

"Hattie will probably be there."

"I want to go," she persisted. "It will look better if he has family there. It will make him look like a better character."

"That's true. Why do I win courtroom battles and lose in the bedroom?"

She wiggled her hips against him and held him tightly around the waist.

Luke laughed. "That's why?"

She slid her hand over his thighs. "I think the boys should go with us."

"Dammit, no! They don't belong in a courtroom."

"They can go with us the first day. It will look better if he has a lot of family."

Her hands moved over him, sliding along his legs, and he shook his head. "What an unfair, cheating way to win an argument!"

"And you like it, Luke Danby. You know you do. Tell me to stop if you don't."

"You're going to get what you've asked for," he said in a husky voice, bending down to kiss her and wrap his arms around her.

Later he lay in bed, staring into the darkness, mulling over what she had wanted. It would look better for Dan if some family members were present. He didn't want the boys in it, yet Jeff and Knox were growing, and Luke had taken both the older boys to trials before. He looked down at Catalina, who lay in the crook of his arm, and smoothed her black hair away from her face. He was thankful he didn't have to face the trouble Dan did. And coming so soon after his marriage would make it doubly bad, but Luke suspected Mary wasn't the child Catalina thought she was, and he hoped she would be there at her husband's side.

As Dan packed the night before they were to leave, Mary stepped in front of him. "I've waited until the last minute to tell you something, because I don't want you to argue about it."

He grinned at her. "And what's that?"

"My family is going with us."

His smile vanished. "Aw, Mary, no! I don't want them involved."

"They're already involved, and if they didn't go, I don't think I would ever speak to them again! But I didn't threaten them. They said they'd go. Pa and Michael and Brian."

"Look, if something happens to them, I'd never forgive myself."

"Shh. I don't want to hear that. They're going. They'll be here to go with us when we leave in the morning. They have their wagon."

He crushed her to him, wanting to hold her and never let go. He dreaded going back. It brought back too many bad memories, and he could still remember being in jail and how he had hated it. And he was afraid of hanging. Bending his head to kiss her, he knew they both felt desperate to keep what they had found. He picked Mary up to carry her to bed, prolonging their lovemaking, trying to stop time while he held her in his arms.

They met Luke at the New Mexico Territory border. He rode forward to meet them, standing in the stirrups, shaking hands with the men, giving Mary a quick hug, and moving around to Dan's side of the wagon. "I left Catalina and the boys in town."

"Catalina and the boys came?"

"Yes. I think it's good. It was her idea. The whole family is there. Hattie and Javier are waiting at the hotel. April and Noah are there. Ta-ne-haddle said he didn't think a Kiowa would weigh things in your favor since there's so much trouble right now, but he's in town with Lottie and Dawn.''

Dan felt his throat tighten as emotion gripped him, and for a moment he couldn't answer Luke. He nodded. Luke clasped him on the shoulder. ''Here we go.''

He turned to lead the way, and Mary leaned close to Dan to hug him. ''See, they all came because they love you,'' she said. ''They won't hang someone who has all these good people with him.''

He squeezed her tightly to him. ''One thing, I have the best wife and family a man can have.''

They rode into a sleepy little town, settled years earlier, called Santa Rosita. Adobe houses lined the roads, and cacti grew among the dirt. Chickens ran across the road, and a goat ambled slowly past, a bell jingling around its neck. People sat in shadowed doorways and watched them until they reached a small one-story adobe building that said ''HOTEL Y CANTINA.''

They dismounted and went inside. ''Let's unpack, get settled, and then you and I'll go over to the sheriff,'' Luke suggested. ''I've already checked. The judge will be here tomorrow or the next day. That's why I picked today for us to arrive. I've heard about this judge, and if it's the one we're supposed to have, he's fair.''

Dan nodded, hoping the Craddocks weren't as powerful now.

They paid and got a key to a room, then went down a wide hall. Luke knocked on a door, and it opened on a roomful of people. Dan and Mary entered to find the rest of his family and Ta-ne-haddle and Lottie, and while everyone hugged and greeted each other, for a short time Dan could forget the grim purpose that had brought the family together. An hour later he and Mary stood in the tiny sparsely furnished room they had rented, and he kissed her long and hard.

Her heart pounded with fear for him and she clung to his hard body. ''Whatever happens, my brothers will get you away from here!''

He held her away. "Dammit, you have to promise me you won't ride with them if they try to get me out of jail. Promise me, Mary, or I'll tell Luke to lock you up."

"You don't have to do that. I'll leave it to the men . . . but I *would* be willing."

He gave her a crooked grin that made a knot come in her throat as he crushed her in his arms for a final hug.

"It'll be over soon," he said. He unbuckled his gunbelt and took Mary's arm. "Come down the hall and stay with my folks."

He left Mary at the door where Luke waited. Then Dan walked away with Luke, without looking back at her. Grimly the two men crossed the wide, dusty road. Dogs barked and two boys ran across the road. Dan and Luke entered the jail. Just inside the door was the sheriff's desk. Dan stepped up to it and unfolded a wanted poster. "I'm Tigre Danby Castillo."

"Related to Javier?" the man said, standing, his dark eyes friendly as he offered his hand.

"Yes, I'm his son," Dan said as he shook hands. "This is my brother, Luke Danby. I want to turn myself in. Luke is my attorney."

The sheriff stared at them, blinked, and looked down at the paper. He looked up at Dan. "Wanted for murder?" he said, sitting down to study the poster.

"Yes, sir. For murdering Fred Craddock."

"That was years ago. You're Javier's boy. I've heard about you. Heard you were killed out west. I'm Gilberto Padilla."

"I was told Judge Farnsworth will be here tomorrow or the next day, so we can have a trial right away," Luke said.

"You're giving yourself up?" the sheriff asked.

"Yes, sir."

"Where you folks staying?"

"At the hotel," Luke answered. "As a matter of fact, if possible, Sheriff, since my client has voluntarily come in and given himself up to stand trial, can he just stay at the hotel tonight? His parents are here."

"Javier is at the hotel?"

"Yes."

Dan couldn't believe what Luke had just asked, but he kept his features impassive.

"Yes, you may stay at the hotel. And tell your father I'll come say hello. My brother worked for him for a time. I don't like the Craddocks."

"Thanks, Sheriff," Luke said cheerfully.

"Thank you," Dan said, shaking hands again with Sheriff Padilla.

"Judge Farnsworth gets here tomorrow. We'll have court right here in this room. Get yourself over here about eight in the morning. The Craddocks will be here. They know everything that happens."

"Thank you, sir," Dan said.

"You're wanted for murder. I don't remember the details of the case."

"You'll hear about it in court," Luke said, taking Dan by the arm to get him out of the sheriff's presence. They walked back across the road, Luke's spurs jingling with his long steps.

"Damn, if the rest is as easy as that—"

"It won't be. I can promise you," Luke said grimly. "You tangled with men who are powerful in this little bit of the territory. Word will go around like wildfire now. First of all, we have to keep watch that Craddock's boys don't ride in to finish the job they started years ago."

"You think they'd try to come to the hotel and take me after all these years?"

"How easily are these things forgotten? You've gone other places, done other things, but they've been sitting right here, and your pa won his battle with them."

"How will they even know to come in and testify against me? Who's going to prosecute?"

"Dan, this won't be like a city trial. Hell, last time, they didn't give you a trial at all before they tried to string you up. We're damned lucky a federal judge is coming through here to listen to this. There may not be anyone to testify against you. There won't be a prosecutor. I'll stand up and plead your case. If word gets out, someone will testify against you. The judge will decide, and it's over. You're still on a frontier, where justice is primitive and law is often determined by a Colt.''

When they returned to the hotel, the men agreed to watch for trouble, and the family cooked in a shady expanse behind the hotel. They had brought food, and soon enticing aromas wafted into the air. Dan felt reprieved to have one more night with Mary instead of spending it in a cell, as he had expected. They told the others good night early in the evening and shut themselves in their room. He held her tightly in his arms, unable to sleep after their lovemaking, knowing she wasn't asleep either, both of them clinging together.

In the morning, in the early light of day, Dan heard a rap on the door. Mary was dressed, braiding her hair, when Dan went to the door to see a grim-faced Luke. "You want to see your opposition. Go to the window.''

All three of them crossed to the narrow windows that looked out to the east. A string of riders was coming down the street, eight abreast.

"Holy saints,'' Mary whispered, sliding her arm around Dan's waist.

"It occurred to us—Ta-ne-haddle brought word of them riding into town—that if we win today, they may try to gun you down before you go. I don't think they'd do it in front of the judge, so it'll come on the way home.''

"Dammit! The whole family is here. Get them out of here.''

"I agree,'' Luke said over Mary's protest. "After the trial, Mary's father can go with the women and children. They can all ride southwest toward Albuquerque. These men will expect you to go back north. There are eight of them, six of us.''

"A gunfight?'' Mary sounded stricken.

"It's better than being shot in the back,'' Luke said grimly. "We have to be ready for it. If it doesn't come in a day's ride, I don't think it will. We can drop back, and Mary's brothers and Paddy can bring her back to you.''

''What about them leaving before the trial?''

''No. You should have family here.''

Dan nodded as he watched the riders pass. ''What's to keep them from gunning me down right now?''

''We're ready for that. It's time to go. The judge is in town. He came in half an hour ago.''

The family waited in the lobby, the women dressed in stylish clothes, the men in suits with broad-brimmed hats. They crossed the street and filed into the small room where planks had been laid across cottonwood stumps for seats. The small jail was crowded. The Craddock men already filled seats to the left of the center aisle, and Dan's family filled the seats to the right, nearest to the door. Spectators took any empty space and crowded around the back of the room.

Mary felt as if she had turned to ice. Dan and Luke sat at a table to the left of the judge. The sheriff was at the front. People crowded in to watch, and the morning air warmed with the crowd. Sheriff Padilla called the court to order and Judge Farnsworth sat down behind the desk.

The first to testify was Paul Craddock, a tall, heavy-set man in a broad-brimmed hat. He came forward, spurs jingling. He told how Dan had killed one of his men and escaped when they tried to hang him.

Luke was next, his deep voice eloquent in the small room as he told Dan's side and then asked to swear Dan in as a witness. Mary glanced to her left at the men who filled two rows. They wore pistols and looked grim and strong, and she feared them more than the judge.

''You tried to defend yourself?'' Luke asked Dan after he had told his version.

''Yes, sir.''

''And you almost had your throat slit by one of the men?''

''Yes, sir.''

''Show us the scar.''

With a jingle of spurs Paul Craddock stood up. "He could have the scar from anything!"

"Sit down, Craddock," Judge Farnsworth snapped, and the man sat down.

Dan pulled down his shirt to show the faint white line. "And you were not given a trial before a judge or jury at the time?"

"No, sir."

"That's all. One more witness, Judge. Will Dr. José García come forward."

A man standing in the doorway moved forward. His hair was gray and he was stoop-shouldered as he walked to the front and was sworn in by the sheriff.

"Have you seen this man before, Doctor?"

"Yes."

"Will you tell the judge when and where?"

They listened as the physician told about tending Dan's wound. Dan had been brought to him by two men the night of the incident.

"Thank you," Luke said, dismissing him. Luke gave his summary in front of the judge, pointing out Dan's lawful life in Colorado, his family, his voluntary return.

"Now, look, Judge—"

"Craddock, you get up and interrupt again, and I'll fine you. Sit down."

Luke finished and sat down beside Dan.

Judge Farnsworth studied notes he had made, shuffled papers, and finally looked up. "After hearing testimony in this case, I declare Tigre Danby Castillo not guilty of murder." He banged his gavel. "Now we'll get to the bank- and train-robbery charges. Mr. Danby, what have you to say for your client?"

"Judge, I protest!" Paul Craddock shouted, standing up. One of his men yelled, and another stood up.

"Craddock, you're fined. Sheriff, put this man down for contempt of court. Five dollars." He banged the gavel again. "Mr. Danby?"

Once again Luke stood and gave a long plea about circumstances, Dan's youth, that he had reformed and voluntarily turned himself in. Luke swept out his arm and pointed to the family, extolling Dan's character, and finally he sat down.

"Any arguments?"

"Yes, he's a thieving, lying—"

"Sit down. I didn't ask for opinions."

There was silence in the room and Judge Farnsworth banged his gavel. "Tigre Danby Castillo, I hereby find you not guilty. Case dismissed."

"No!" Craddock thundered, jumping to his feet to fire at Dan with pistols in both hands.

Noah came up in a crouch, his colts blasting while women screamed. Glass shattered as shots hit the windows.

People dropped to the floor. Mary pushed Aaron down, covering him. In seconds there was silence. Noah stood with his pistols aimed at Craddock's men. Javier also held a pistol pointed at the men, and Michael aimed at them as well as Brian. "Drop your weapons," Luke ordered. "Doc, look at the judge first."

"I'm all right. Padilla was hit. Two of Craddock's men are down."

Dan's gaze swept the room, which reeked of gunpowder, and he felt faint with relief when he saw the family was all right. The windows behind him were smashed. He noticed a red stain on Luke's coat sleeve.

"Doc!" Rage filled him and he wished he had a pistol. He looked at the man who had caused the trouble. White-haired and broad-shouldered, Paul Craddock stood with his hands in the air. Two of his men lay still on the floor, and another clutched a bloody leg.

"Doc, get over here as soon as you finish with the sheriff," Dan called.

Judge Farnsworth stood up. "You're under arrest, Craddock. You and your men, every damned one of you. One of you boys with a pistol, herd 'em into a cell. Drop your weapons first. Slow and easy."

Dan wiped his forehead, feeling a wet stickiness, and realized he had been cut by glass from the windows. He helped Luke remove his coat, and Catalina ran to him.

"I'm all right."

She talked in rapid Spanish in an undertone, peeling back the sleeve of his shirt.

"They're locked up, Judge," Noah said, tossing the keys in front of Farnsworth.

"How's Padilla?"

Dr. García stood up. "He'll be fine. Some of you come carry him to the saloon. Put him on the bar. I can work on him there. It isn't bad. If he comes around, give him some whiskey." He walked over to Luke to look at his arm. "Not bad. Lucky it wasn't a few inches to the right."

"I know that," Luke said, looking at Catalina and pulling her to his side. "See, it's not bad."

"Wow, Pa, that was something!" Jeff exclaimed, scooting close to Luke. "Did you see Uncle Noah?"

"Pa's bleeding, Knox!"

"I saw," Luke answered, "and I'll thank him in just a minute."

Catalina glowered at Luke while Dr. García cleaned and bandaged the wound. Luke looked down at her. "I'm all right, Catalina."

She let out a long breath and moved closer to him, lacing her fingers in his. "It frightens me when you are in such danger."

"He's going to be fine," García assured her.

April was sitting on the bench when Noah finally put away his pistols and joined her. "Sorry if I startled you."

"Noah, that was frightening, and Luke was hit!"

"Luke's okay. I heard the doc say so, honey. And it could have been far worse if I hadn't done something."

"I know. She leaned against him. "Noah, I couldn't bear anything to happen now."

"Are we going to tell everyone our news or not?"

"I told Ma and Catalina last night, so I guess we can tell everyone."

"Good."

Javier stepped to his side to clasp him on the shoulder. "I owe you much, Noah. Thank you. You may have saved my son's life, as well as the lives of others.''

"I just happened to see Craddock go for his six-shooter. I had some help from all of you.''

Javier nodded and went to Luke to thank him. Outside, a crowd had gathered, staring with curiosity at the jail. Finally the Danbys and O'Malleys filed out into the sunshine to congratulate Dan and Luke.

Dan hugged Mary. "I'm free, honey. I'm not a wanted man.''

She was still shaken by what had happened so quickly. "Dan, let's go home,'' she pleaded, and he held her tightly and nodded.

It was another two hours before they had told everyone good-bye and loaded up for the ride back to Denver. Noah and April had wanted them to come to Albuquerque, but they needed to get home, so they promised they would come later in the year. And while everyone was together, Noah announced that they were expecting another child.

Dan and Mary spent almost half an hour in farewell hugs before parting, Mary, Dan, and her family heading north, the others heading south. They reached Denver the next night, telling the O'Malley men good-bye and turning toward their home. He unhitched the wagon while Mary drew a hot bath. She hummed as she bathed, hearing bootheels in the hall and looking up to see Dan in the doorway. He was dusty from the ride, his clothes rumpled, a gunbelt slung low on his hips as he paused in the doorway. His golden hair was tangled from the wind, but he looked marvelous to her and she felt refreshed and happy, because on the trail back to Denver she had made a discovery.

"You do look good!'' he drawled, pulling his shirt over his head and tossing it down.

He poured a brandy and drank it. "I'm glad to be home. I'm thankful to be a free man. And we're finally going to have our own little celebration.''

"Are we, now?''

She had her hair pulled up and tied on top of her

head with a blue ribbon. Water filled the tub up to her breasts. Her flesh was glistening, and she looked beautiful. Dan felt desire kindle and burn. He took a long drink of brandy and set down the glass, wanting to take Mary to bed now.

"I'm dusty, Mary," he said, unbuckling his belt and pulling off his boots. He undressed swiftly, taking the bottle of brandy and climbing into the tub with her.

"Dan!"

"This is the advantage of such a big tub. Takes longer to empty and fill, but it sure as hell is fun while you're in it!"

She laughed as he moved her over him and she faced him. He poured a little brandy between her breasts and leaned forward to lick it off. "Oh, hon, I'm glad to be home and I'm so damned glad to be free."

"I'm happy about that too, but there's something else that I think is even better."

"There's not much better than being free and in a tub with you when you're bare."

"Oh, yes, there is."

He squeezed out a cloth and ran it over her, relishing her soft curves, thinking he wanted to love her all night long. She leaned forward to kiss him, tasting brandy, feeling his warm solid body. His arousal pressed against her belly as she leaned forward to slide her arms around him.

"What's making you so happy, then?" he asked, taking another long drink of brandy and setting the bottle on the floor beside the tub.

She trailed kisses from his ear to his mouth. He tightened his arms around her, kissing her hard, then pulled away. "All right, there's something you know that I don't. What is it? Something about my family or yours? Something you learned on the trip?"

"Both," she said smugly, leaning away from him with her hands on his shoulders. "It's about our family, and I realized it on the trip. We're going to have a baby."

Dan stared at her in amazement, and Mary's heart beat with joy. "You're sure?"

"Absolutely."

"Oh, Mary!" He crushed her to him, turning her to kiss her long and hard.

She clung to him, relishing his strong arms around her, his long hard body, thinking of the new life they had started and the promise their future held.

About the Author

Sara Orwig is a native Oklahoman who has had many novels published in more than a dozen languages. She is married to the man she met at Oklahoma State University and is the mother of three children. Except for a few unforgettable years as an English teacher, she has been writing full-time. An avid reader, Sara Orwig loves history, acrylic painting, swimming, and traveling with her husband.